SPECIAL MESSAGE TO READERS

THE ULVERSCROFT FOUNDATION
(registered UK charity number 264873)
was established in 1972 to provide funds for research, diagnosis and treatment of eye diseases. Examples of major projects funded by the Ulverscroft Foundation are:-

- The Children's Eye Unit at Moorfields Eye Hospital, London
- The Ulverscroft Children's Eye Unit at Great Ormond Street Hospital for Sick Children
- Funding research into eye diseases and treatment at the Department of Ophthalmology, University of Leicester
- The Ulverscroft Vision Research Group, Institute of Child Health
- Twin operating theatres at the Western Ophthalmic Hospital, London
- The Chair of Ophthalmology at the Royal Australian College of Ophthalmologists

You can help further the work of the Foundation by making a donation or leaving a legacy. Every contribution is gratefully received. If you would like to help support the Foundation or require further information, please contact:

THE ULVERSCROFT FOUNDATION
The Green, Bradgate Road, Anstey
Leicester LE7 7FU, England
Tel: (0116) 236 4325

website: www.foundation.ulverscroft.com

Alexandra Burt was born in a baroque town in the East Hesse Highlands of Germany. Mere days after her college graduation, she boarded a plane to the U.S and worked as a freelance translator. Determined to acknowledge the voice in the back of her head prompting her to break into literary translation, she eventually decided to tell her own stories. After three years of writing classes her short fiction appeared in online magazines and literary reviews. She is also a member of Sisters In Crime, a nationwide network of women crime writers. Alexandra currently lives in central Texas with her husband, her daughter, and two Labradors. She is an outspoken animal welfare supporter, and a proud vegan. One day she wants to live in a farmhouse and offer rescue dogs a comfy couch to live out their lives. *Little Girl Gone* is her first novel.

Youcan discover more about the author at www.alexandraburt.com

LITTLE GIRL GONE

After a near-fatal car accident, Estelle Paradise wakes up in hospital with a fragmented memory. Soon a terrifying reality sets in: her daughter Mia is missing. Days earlier, Estelle discovered Mia's empty crib in their Brooklyn apartment. Her diapers, her clothes, her bottles — all were gone. Frustrated and unable to explain the disappearance, Estelle begins a desperate search. But when the lack of evidence casts doubt on her story, she becomes the number one suspect in the eyes of the police and the media. As hope of reuniting with her daughter becomes all she has left, Estelle will do anything to find answers. What has she done to her baby? And what has someone else done to her?

ALEXANDRA BURT

LITTLE GIRL GONE

Complete and Unabridged

CHARNWOOD
Leicester

First published in Great Britain in 2015 by
Avon
a division of HarperCollins*Publishers*
London

First Charnwood Edition
published 2017
by arrangement with
HarperCollins*Publishers*
London

A catalogue record for this book is available
from the British Library.

ISBN 978–1–4448–3207–5

Published by
F. A. Thorpe (Publishing)
Anstey, Leicestershire

Set by Words & Graphics Ltd.
Anstey, Leicestershire
Printed and bound in Great Britain by
T. J. International Ltd., Padstow, Cornwall

This book is printed on acid-free paper

Acknowledgements

Publishing a book takes a village and here is mine. Eternal gratitude to my agent, Laura Longrigg; Helen Huthwaite and the entire AVON team, especially those who work behind the curtain — Oli Malcolm, Victoria Jackson, Sabah Khan, Jo Marino and Jade Craddock. You all rock.

Equal thanks go out to all my fellow writers and early readers who accompanied me on my journey: too many to name and the only appropriate words to express my appreciation: Thank you from the bottom of my heart.

At its core this book is about mothers and therefore it is only fair that I thank my mother who shared her beloved books and short life with me; and to my daughter, who is my biggest inspiration.

Last, but not least, thanks to my husband. You gave me the proverbial room of my own and the money so I could write this book. You are my rock.

For all mothers, especially mine.
For all daughters, especially mine.

Part one

'I can't explain myself, I'm afraid, Sir,
because I'm not myself, you see.'

Lewis Carroll,
Alice in Wonderland

MISSING: 7-MONTH-OLD INFANT DISAPPEARS FROM CRIB

Brooklyn, NY — **The New York City Police Department is asking for the public's help in locating 7-month-old Mia Connor.**

The parents and the NYPD are pleading to the public for any assistance in the investigation and are asking residents in the North Dandry neighborhood in Brooklyn to come forward if they witnessed any suspicious behavior on the night and early morning of the 26th.

Mia Connor was last seen by her mother Estelle Paradise (27) around midnight when she laid her down to sleep. The mother discovered the child was missing when she woke up the next morning. The father was out of town when the infant disappeared.

'It's very frustrating,' said Eric Rodriguez, spokesperson for NYPD, when he appeared briefly at a news conference on Friday. 'We're hoping somebody will come forward and give us the information allowing us to locate the child.'

Immediately call the TIPS hotline at 1-888-267-4880 if you have any information about the infant's whereabouts. All calls are strictly confidential.

1

'Mrs Paradise?'

A voice sounds out of nowhere. My thoughts are sluggish, as if I'm running under water. I try and try but I'm not getting anywhere.

'Not stable. Eighty over sixty. And falling.'

Oh God, I'm still alive.

I move my legs, they respond, barely, but they respond. Light prowls its way into my eyes. I hear dogs barking, high-pitched. They pant, their tags clatter.

'You've been in a car accident.'

My face is numb, my thoughts vague, like dusty boxes in obscure and dark attic spaces. I know immediately something is amiss.

'Oh my God, look at her head.'

A siren sounds, it stutters for a second, then turns into a steady torment.

I want to tell them . . . I open my mouth, my lips begin to form the words, but the burning sensation in my head becomes unbearable. My chest is on fire, and ringing in my left ear numbs the entire side of my face.

Let me die, I want to tell them. But the only sound I hear is of crude hands tearing fragile fabric.

'Step back. Clear.'

My body explodes, jerks upward.

This isn't part of the plan.

★　★　★

When I come to, my vision is blurred and hazy. I make out a woman in baby-blue scrubs, a nurse, slipping a plastic tube over my head and immediately two prongs hiss cold air into my nostrils.

She pumps a lever and the bed yanks upward, then another lever triggers a motor raising the headboard until my upper body is resting almost vertically.

My world becomes clearer. The nurse's hair is in a ponytail and the pockets of her cardigan sag. I watch her dispose of tubing and wrappers and the closing of the trashcan's metal lid sounds final, evoking a feeling I can't quite place, a vague sense of loss, like a pickpocket making off with my loose change, disappearing into the crowd that is my strange memory.

A male voice sounds out of nowhere.

'I need to place a central line.'

The overly gentle voice belongs to a man in a white coat. He talks to me as if I'm a child in need of comfort.

'Just relax, you won't feel a thing.'

Relax and I won't feel a thing? Easy for him to say. I feel lost somehow, as if I'm in the middle of a blizzard, unable to decide which direction to turn. I lift my arms and pain shoots from my shoulder into my neck. I tell myself not to do that again anytime soon.

The white coat wipes the back of my hand with an alcohol wipe. It leaves an icy trail and pulls me further from my lulled state. I watch the doctor insert a long needle into my vein. A forgotten cotton wipe rests in the folds of the cotton waffle weave blanket, in its center a bright red bloody mark, like a scarlet letter.

There's a spark of memory, it ignites but then fizzles, like a wet match. I refuse to be pulled away, I follow the crimson, attach myself to the memory that started out like a creak on the stairs, but then the monsters appear.

First I remember the darkness.

Then I remember the blood.

My baby. Oh God, Mia.

⋆　⋆　⋆

The blood lingers. There's flashes of crimson exploding like lightning in the sky, one moment they're illuminating everything around me, the next they are gone, bathing my world in darkness. Then the bloody images fade and vanish, leaving a black jittering line on the screen.

Squeaking rubber soles on linoleum circle me and I feel a pat on my shoulder.

This isn't real. A random vision, just a vision. It doesn't mean anything.

A nurse gently squeezes my shoulder and I open my eyes.

'Mrs Paradise,' the nurse's voice is soft, almost apologetic, 'I'm sorry, but I have orders to wake you every couple of hours.'

'Blood,' I say, and squint my eyes, attempting to force the image to return to me. 'I don't understand where all this blood's coming from.' Was that my voice? It can't be mine, it sounds nothing like me.

7

'Blood? What blood?' The nurse looks at my immaculately taped central line. 'Are you bleeding?'

I turn towards the window. It's dark outside. The entire room appears in the window's reflection, like an imprint, a not-quite-true copy of reality.

'Oh God,' I say and my high-pitched voice sounds like a screeching microphone. 'Where's my daughter?'

She just cocks her head and then busies herself straightening the blanket. 'Let me get the doctor for you,' she says and leaves the room.

2

Voices enter my room like a slow drift of clouds, merging with the scent of pancakes, syrup, toast, and coffee, making my stomach churn. I feel a hand on my arm.

'Mrs Paradise? I'm Dr Baker.'

I judge only his age — he is young — as if my brain does not allow me to appraise him further. Have I met him before? I don't know. Everything about me, my body and my senses, is faulty. When did I become so forgetful, so scatter-brained?

He wears a white coat with his name stitched on the pocket: *Dr Jeremy Baker*. He retrieves a pen from his coat and shines a light into my eyes. There's an explosion so painful I clench my eyelids shut. I turn my head away from him, reach up and feel the left side of my head. Now I understand why the world around me is muffled; my entire head is bandaged.

'You're at County Medical. An ambulance brought you to the emergency room about . . . ' He pauses and looks at his wristwatch. I wonder why the time matters. Is he counting the hours, does he want to be exact? ' . . . on the fifth, three days ago.'

Three days? And I don't remember a single minute.

Ask him, go ahead, ask him. 'Where's my daughter?'

'You were in a car accident. You have a head injury and you've been in a medically induced coma.'

Accident? I don't remember any accident. He didn't answer my question. He talks to me as if I'm incapable of comprehending more elaborate sentences.

'They found you in your car in a ravine. You have a concussion, fractured ribs, and multiple contusions around your lower extremities. You also had a critical head injury when they brought you in. Your brain was swollen, which was the reason for the induced coma.'

I don't remember any accident. What about Jack? Yes, Mia's with Jack. She must be. One more time. 'Was my daughter in the car with me?'

'You were alone,' he says.

'She's with Jack? Mia's with my husband?'

'Everything's going to be okay.'

The blood was just a vision, it wasn't real. She's with Jack, she's safe. Thank God. *Everything's going to be okay*, he said.

'We're not sure of any brain damage at this point, but now that you've regained consciousness we'll be able to perform all the necessary tests to figure out what's going on.' He motions the nurse who has been standing next to him. 'You lost a lot of blood and we had to administer fluids to stabilize you. The swelling will go down in a few days but in the meantime we need to make sure you keep your lungs clear of fluids.'

He picks up a contraption and holds it up in front of me. 'This is a spirometer. Basically you

10

keep the red ball suspended as long as you can. The nurse will give you detailed instructions. Every two hours, please.' His last comment is directed towards the nurse.

The gurgling in my chest is uncomfortable and I try not to cough. The pain in my left side must be the fractured ribs. I wonder how I'll be able to stay awake for two hours or wake up every two hours or use this contraption for two hours, or whatever he just said.

'Before I forget . . . ' Dr Baker looks down at me. He is quiet for a while and I wonder if I missed a question. Then he lowers his voice. 'Two detectives were here to talk to you. I won't allow any questioning until we've done a few more tests.' He nods to the nurse and walks towards the door, then turns around and offers one more trifle of news. 'Your husband will be here soon. In the meantime can we call anyone for you? Family? A friend? Anybody?'

I shake my head 'no' and immediately regret it. A mallet pounds against my skull from the inside. My head is a giant swollen bulb and the throbbing in my ear manages to distract me from my aching ribs.

My lids have a life of their own. I'm nodding off but I have so many questions. I take a deep breath as if I'm preparing to jump off a diving board. It takes everything I have to sound out the words.

'Where did this accident happen?'

Why does he look at me puzzled? Am I missing more than I'm aware of?

'I'm sorry, but I can't tell you much about the

accident,' he says. He sounds subdued, as if he's forcing himself to be composed in order to calm me. 'All we know is that your car was found upstate at the bottom of a ravine.' Pause. 'You have a lot of injuries. Some are from the accident. Can you remember what happened?'

I reflect on his words, really think them over. Accident. Nothing. Not a thing. There's a large black hole where my memory used to be.

'I can't remember anything,' I say.

His brows furrow. 'You mean . . . the accident?'

The accident. He talks about *the* accident as if I remember. I want to tell him to X-ray my head, and that he'll find a dark shadow within my skull where my memory used to be.

I'm getting the hang of this; concentrate, think of the question and repeat it in your head, take a deep breath, then speak.

'You don't understand. I don't remember *the* accident and I don't remember anything *before* the accident.'

'Do you remember wanting to harm yourself?'

'Harm myself?'

I would remember that, wouldn't I? What is he talking about? I'm getting frustrated. We're going in circles. It's difficult to stay awake.

'Either that or you were shot.'

Was I shot or did I harm myself? What kind of questions is he asking me?

I turn my head as far to the left as possible, catching a glimpse of an outstretched leg of a police officer sitting by the door, out in the hallway. Hardly normal procedure. I wonder

12

what that's all about.

Dr Baker looks over his shoulder and then faces me again. He steps closer and lowers his voice. 'You don't remember.' He states it matter-of-factly, no longer a question, but a realization.

'I don't know what I don't know,' I say. That's kind of funny, when I think about it. I giggle and his brows furrow.

Then he tells me about my voice. How it is 'monotone' and that I have 'a reduction in range and intensity of emotions,' and that my reactions are 'flat and blunted.'

I don't understand what he's telling me. Should I smile more, be more cheerful? I want to ask him but then I hear a word that puts it all to rest.

'Amnesia,' he says. 'We're not sure about the cause yet. Retrograde, maybe post-traumatic. Maybe even trauma-related.'

When you hear *amnesia* from a man in a white coat it's serious. Final. *I forgot*, sounds casual, *oh, I'm forgetful*.

I have amnesia, I'm not forgetful after all. Is he going to ask me what year it is? Who the President is? If I remember my birthdate? That's what they do in movies. I don't have to rack my brain, I know the answers. But why don't I remember the accident? What else did I forget?

'Retrograde means you don't recall events that happened *just before* the onset of the memory loss. Post-traumatic is a cognitive impairment, and memory loss can stretch back hours or days, sometimes even longer. Eventually you'll recall the distant past but you may never recover what

13

happened just prior to your accident. Amnesia can't be diagnosed with an X-ray, like a broken bone. We've done an MRI test and a CAT scan. Both tests came back inconclusive. Basically there's no definitive proof of brain damage, but absence of proof is not proof of absence. There could be microscopic damages and the MRI and the CAT scan are just not sophisticated enough to detect those. Nerve fiber damage doesn't show up on either test.'

I remain silent, not sure if I should ask anything else, not sure if I even understood him at all. All I grasp is that he can't tell me anything definitive, so what's the point?

'There's the possibility that you suffer from dissociative amnesia. Trauma would cause you to block out certain information associated with the event. There's no test for that either. You'd have to see a psychiatrist or a psychologist. But we're getting ahead of ourselves. The neurologist will order some more tests. Like I said, time will tell.'

I take a deep breath. The medical facts he's relaying to me are one thing, but I just can't shake the feeling that there's something he is not telling me.

'They found me where again?'

'In a ravine, in Dover, upstate. You were transferred here from Dover Medical Center.'

Dover? Dover. Nothing. I'm blank.

'I've never been to Dover.'

'That's where they found you, you just don't remember. It's part of the memory loss.' He slips the pen back in his coat pocket. 'You were lucky,' he adds. He holds up his index finger and

14

thumb, indicating the extent of the luck I had. 'The bullet was this far from doing serious harm. There is extensive damage to your ear but I want you to remember that you were really lucky. Remember that.'

Remember that. How funny. My hand moves up to my ear, almost like a reflex. 'You said there's damage to my ear. What happened to it?'

He pauses ever so slightly. 'Gone. Completely gone. The area was infected and we had to make a decision.' He watches me intently. 'It could have been worse, like I said, you were lucky.'

'That's some luck,' I say but when I think about my ear I don't really care.

'There's reconstructive surgery.'

'What's there now, I mean, is there a hole?'

'There's a small opening draining fluids, other than that, there's a flap of skin stretched over the wound.'

An opening that drains fluids. I'm oddly untouched by the fact that a flap of skin is stretched over a hole in my head where my ear used to be. I have amnesia. I forgot to lock my car. I lost my umbrella. My ear is gone. It's all the same; insignificant.

'And you call that lucky?'

'You're alive, that's what counts.'

There's that buzzing sound again and then his voice goes from loud to muffled, as if someone's turned a volume dial.

'What about my ear?'

He looks at me, puzzled.

'I remember you told me it was gone.' *Completely gone*, were the words he used. 'I

15

mean my hearing, what about my hearing? Everything sounds muffled.'

'We did an electrophysiological hearing test while you were unconscious.' He grabs my file from the nightstand and opens it. He flips through the pages. 'You've lost some audio capacity, but nothing major. We'll order more tests, depending on the next CAT scan, we just have to wait it out.'

'My ear, did that happen during the accident?'

'They recovered a gun in the car. They are not sure how the injury came about, if someone shot you or you shot yourself. Hopefully you'll remember soon.'

Bullet. Was I shot or did I shoot myself? That explains the police officer sitting outside my door and I wonder if he's guarding me or if he's guarding someone from me. This talk of bullets and guns and ravines, my missing ear. I'm blank, completely blank. Except . . .

'I remembered something.'

The words come spilling out and take on a life of their own.

'I need to know if what I see . . . I . . . I think I remember bits and pieces, but it's not like a memory, it's more like fragments.' It's like flipping through a photo album not knowing if it's mine or someone else's life. *Blood. So much blood.*

'It's a Humpty Dumpty kind of a situation, maybe you just can't put it back together. You may not be able to remember minute by minute, but you'll be able to generally connect the dots at some point.'

16

All the king's horses and all the king's men. Wild horses. I make a decision. The blood was just an illusion. A figment.

'I'm very tired,' I say and feel relieved.

'Let the nurse know if there's anybody you want us to call. Don't forget the spirometer — every two hours . . . '

He points at something behind me. 'Behind you is a PCA pump. It delivers small amounts of pain medication. If you need more,' he puts a small box with a red button in my hand, 'just push the red button and you'll get one additional dose of morphine. The safety feature only allows for a maximum amount during a certain timed interval. Any questions?'

I have learned my lesson from earlier and barely shake my head.

I watch him leave the room and immediately a nurse enters and I try to concentrate on her explaining the yellow contraption to me. I'm supposed to breathe into the tubing until a ball moves up, and I have to breathe continuously to try to keep the ball suspended as long as possible. Because there's fluid in my lungs.

I have amnesia. My ear is gone. I feel . . . I feel as if I'm not connecting like I should. I should yell and scream, raise bloody hell, but Dr Baker's explanations of my lack of emotions, 'blunted affect' he called it, seems logical. Logic I can handle, it's the emotions that remain elusive.

There's something they're not telling me. Maybe because they don't subject injured people — especially those who've been shot, who lost an ear, who were *that close* — to any additional bad news. That must be it. Maybe the police will tell me, or Jack, once he gets here. They already told me I've been robbed of hours of my life, how much worse can it get?

I hold the spirometer in my right hand. I blow into the tube and allow my mind to go blank while I watch the red ball go up. It lingers for whatever amount of time I manage to keep it suspended. I pinch my eyes shut to will the ball to maintain its suspension. Suddenly bits and pieces of images come into focus — the empty crib, the missing bottles — as if they are captured on the back of my eyelids. My mind explodes. It disintegrates, breaks into tiny particles.

Mia isn't with Jack. She's gone.

The realization occurs so abruptly and is so powerful that the wires connected to my chest seem to tremble and the machines behind me pick up on it. The beeps speed up like the hooves of a horse, walking, then trotting, then breaking into a full-blown gallop. Mia's disappearance is a fact, yet it is disconnected from whatever consequences it entails, there's a part I can't connect with. An empty crib. Missing clothes, her missing bottles and diapers, everything was gone. I looked for her and couldn't find her. I went to the police and then there's a dark hole.

Like a jigsaw puzzle I study the pieces, connect them, tear them apart and start all over again. I remember going to the police precinct but after that it gets blurry — hazy, like a childhood memory. My mind plays a game of 'Chinese whispers,' thoughts relaying messages,

18

then retelling them skewed. Easily misinterpreted, embellished, unreliable.

Every time I watch the spirometer ball move upwards, more images form: a bathroom stall, a mop, a stairwell, pigeons, the smell of fresh paint. Then a picture fades in, as if someone has turned up a light dimmer: fragments of celestial bodies; a sun, a moon, and stars. So many stars.

Why was I in Dover? Where is my daughter and why is no one talking about her?

As I lie in the hospital bed, I am aware of time passing, a fleeting glimpse of light outside, day turning into night, and back into day. I long for ... a tidbit of my childhood, a morsel of memory, of how my mother cared for me when I was sick, in bed with the flu or some childhood disease, like measles or chickenpox. But then I recall having been a robust child, a child that was hardy and resistant to viruses, to strep throats and pink eyes.

I don't know what to tell Jack once he shows up. They told him Mia is missing and he will question me. Jack will return from Chicago, he will ask questions, many questions. He will want to know about the day Mia disappeared. About the morning I found her crib empty. Amnesia is just another shortcoming of a long list of my other countless inadequacies. Shortfall after shortfall.

I must be insane, for the only explanation I can come up with is of my daughter and my ear, together in the same place. And above them, floating suspended like a mobile, the sun, the moon, and the stars. Bright as bright can be,

19

surrounded by darkness. A chaotic universe illuminated by heavenly bodies.

I rest my hands on my lap. My body stills, comes to a halt. I was in an accident. I was shot or tried to harm myself. My ear is gone. There's a hole that's draining fluids.

I don't care about any of that. Mia's gone. I can't even bear the thought of her. I want the pain to stop yet her image remains. I raise my finger to push the red PCA button, longing for the lulled state the medicine provides. I hesitate, then I put the box down. I have to think, start somewhere. The empty crib. The dots. I have to connect the dots.

3

After Mia was born I relived her birth every single night; her first gasp triggered by the cold birthing room, that gasp turning into a deep breath, then a desperate cry escaping her lips, her attempt to negotiate the inevitable transition between my womb and the outside world.

And every morning I realized that her actual cries reached me deep in my dreams and I woke up feeling like a million tiny bombs exploded inside my head. Then my muscle memory kicked in. *Wake up, get up, feed her, change her, bathe her, rock her, hold her. Feeding and changing and bathing and rocking and holding.*

I had stopped keeping track of time, the date or even the days of the week. I was unaware of whatever events might be gripping the rest of the world and I hadn't picked up a book or a magazine in months. My life was reduced to a process of consolidating motor tasks into memory, loop-like days and repetitive responsibilities performed without any conscious effort.

As I rose from the couch, the world spun and then stilled. I listened for the echoes of Mia's colicky morning cries, by then seven months after her birth, hundredfold replicas of her initial primal moment that visited me in my dreams. Lately her cries had been reaching me time delayed, distorted almost, as if communicating a certain distance between us.

21

That morning, I listened, yet the house remained silent. A sense of normality enveloped me, an image of a round-cheeked child pressed against the mattress manifested itself, an elfin body heavy with peaceful sleep. I had been waiting for this moment when Mia would wake up and not begin to scream before she even opened her eyes. Maybe today was the day, the end of her colic, the end of her constant crying?

I debated rolling over, going back to sleep, but something irked me. Shouldn't there be cooing, babbling strung-together sounds? Usually by this time, Mia was attempting to pull herself up by the bars of the crib, her eyes rimmed with tears and rage.

Barefoot down the hallway I went and paused by her door, still ajar. I had forgotten to take my watch off the night prior and the band had left an imprint as if I had been tied up all night. It was just before nine and I'd been asleep for an unprecedented continuous six hours.

Mia's door was cracked just as I had left it hours ago. Opening it wide enough to pass through, I entered the room. Something jabbed at me, made my heart stumble.

The Tinker Bell mobile overhead, unbalanced and lopsided, somehow imperfect, and disturbed. The room, barely lit by the sunlight spilling through the window, soundless. Her crib in front of the window. Silent and abandoned. Not so much as an imprint of her body on the sheets.

Pyrotechnics went off in my brain. I was trapped in the Twilight Zone, something that *cannot* be, I'm clearly looking at it. How can she be gone? My molars pulsated as I inspected the windows and rattled the cast-iron bars. I searched the entire apartment, rechecked every window twice. Not a trace of her.

I ran to the front door. The locks were intact, the metal still scratched, the paint still chipped, signs of my clumsy attempt to install a deadbolt. All locks were engaged and everything was where and how it was supposed to be. Except Mia.

There was no proof that anyone had been here — no footprints on the floor, no items left behind — nothing was disturbed, yet this peculiar energy hovered around me. The apartment seemed physically undisturbed, but felt ransacked at the same time.

I realized the contradiction of the moment: Mia was gone, yet there was no evidence, no clue, that someone had taken her. No shards on the floor, no gaping doors, no curtains blowing in the breeze of a window left ajar. No haphazardly bunched-up sheet, no pacifier, no toy discarded on the floor.

9-1-1.

I ran to the kitchen, took the receiver off the wall mount, and stopped dead in my tracks. The dish rack was empty. No bottle, no collar, no nipple. No formula can, no measuring cup.

I rushed to the trash. Surely her soiled diapers must still be in there. The can was empty, even the plastic liner was gone.

I ripped open the fridge. All the prefilled formula bottles I had prepared the night before were gone.

23

Back in her room, the shelves of the changing table, usually stacked with diapers and blankets, were empty. The closet door was wide open, not a hanger dangling, not a shoe left on the closet floor.

I pulled the dresser drawers open. All her clothes were gone. Every single drawer of the dresser empty. Not a button or a tag tucked in a corner. The basket on top of the dresser, where I kept the diapers and the ointment, was empty. Nothing but empty pieces of furniture.

I checked every inch of her room, every drawer, every corner of her closet. My heart dropped into my intestines. Not only was Mia gone, but so was every trace of her.

* * *

The 70th Precinct on Lawrence Avenue in Brooklyn was a five-minute walk from North Dandry. As I passed through the building's glass doors, the front desk clerk lifted his index finger, pointed at the earpiece, indicating he was talking on the phone.

A janitor pushed a neon yellow bucket and a scraggly mop across the floor. He wore blue overalls and clear booties over his white sneakers. I watched him as he wheeled the bucket across the linoleum, mopping in circular motions, dipping the mop in the wringer and squeezing out the water.

I studied my reflection in the glass door and saw a woman rocking back and forth with the movement of the mop, cotton strings slithering

24

over the floor, *wipe, dip, wring, wipe, dip, wring*.

Standing there, it was just me and the sound of my beating heart. I had rehearsed this moment countless times. What I was going to say, which words I was going to use — missing implied a moment of inattention, kidnapped was all wrong because I didn't see anyone snatch her — *I can't find my daughter* the perfect choice of words.

Footsteps jerked me back into reality. Behind me, simultaneously a door opened and a phone rang. A detective in slacks and a light-blue shirt, his tie tucked into his waistband, walked up to the counter. He was holding a short, skinny man by his tattooed upper arm. The man was almost catatonic. The detective gave him a shove to move him along, making the man's chest hit the edge of the counter. The man had a crooked smile on his face and seemed indifferent, as if he had been through this too many times to care.

'Get an officer to take him to booking,' the detective said to the clerk. 'I don't want to see his face again until he's sobered up.'

'I need to speak to someone.' My voice was loud, so loud it made the clerk look up from the phone. 'Please, I need help.'

'Just a minute,' the detective said. 'I'll be with you as soon as I can.' He was too far away for me to make out his name on the tag clipped to his shirt pocket. He seemed young, maybe too young. *Will he understand me, is he a father, has he worked with missing children before? I wonder if I should ask for a more experienced detective.*

'I need to talk to someone,' I repeated, even louder than before.

He stepped closer, reluctantly. 'How can I help you?'

Words sped through my mind, then images of locks emerged, doors secured with bolts, hasps and locksets.

HELP, I screamed in my mind. I opened my mouth but no words emerged. I swallowed hard, the gulp in my throat echoed through the silent precinct hallways. I wanted to confess to whatever it was I had done, *must have done*, for no one disappears through locked doors or walls, especially not a baby.

Nausea overcame me. I welcomed the strangled retching, wanted to let go of the words, the confession of what I must have done. I refused to fight the heaviness in my throat. Saliva collected in my mouth and instinctively I pinched my nose to keep the vomit from ejecting through my nostrils.

He stepped backward, as if I was a contagious leper. 'There's a bathroom right over there.' The detective pointed towards a door less than ten feet away.

The bathroom was vacant. I knelt in the stall and on all fours I convulsed with spasms. Ripples shook my body, my cold skin was covered in a layer of sweat. As I studied my reflection in the mirror, I rummaged through my mind for an explanation, never lifting my gaze off the stranger that stared back at me. I felt fury for the woman in the mirror, a woman with unwashed hair, her eyes sunken in and sad, the woman who had replaced the real me. I willed myself to leave the bathroom and to do what I had come here for; ask for help to find Mia.

Back in the hallway, the detective was waiting for me. 'Ma'am?' He seemed impatient, as if dealing with someone who had no real police business after all.

I didn't know what to tell the detective anymore. Had someone walked through brick walls, had some ill-fated Houdini act occurred while I was sleeping? When a magician pulls an endless scarf out of a hat, everybody knows it's a simple trick, but this was real. And I didn't know if I was a victim or if I was guilty. A crime had been committed. But what kind of crime?

I don't know where my daughter is.

An all-encompassing statement, implicating everything possible but not implying anything specific. No fault, no crime, no blame. Just a fact.

I don't know where my daughter is.

I couldn't fathom a single logical way of explaining how Mia had disappeared.

Say it, I kept telling myself, *say it. JUST SAY IT*. I pushed myself to speak but the woman I had become didn't comply. There was nothing anyone could do for her.

No one can help me. No one can help me. No one can help me.

Like an oath, I repeated it three times, hoping the reiteration would conjure up some sort of sense and logic.

As I looked past the detective, down the hallway, the tattooed man from earlier darted for the front door. The detective's eyes followed him and then he ran after him. The tattooed man, unsteady on his feet, had reached the glass door by the time the detective got a hold of him.

I focused on the floor and the tiny specks in the blue linoleum. I felt my knees weakening, I had to keep moving, keep the blood circulating through my body.

No one can help me.

I exited the precinct and kept on walking. I felt numb inside, anesthetized, yet somehow purged, ready to accept the facts. The numbness dissolved long enough to allow the gravity of what I must have done to sink in. As I passed a store window, out of the corner of my eye I saw a woman studying her hands as if she hadn't seen them in a long time.

In that brief yet gruesome moment of clarity I realized those hands might just be the hands of a monster.

4

Jack arrives and he's all business; his suit, his posture, his demeanor. The thing that strikes me is how in control he is. I used to crave his attention, his company. But not only am I disgusted by him, I can't even conceive of ever having had feelings for him.

My hands shake at first, then my whole body trembles. Whether with fear or anger I don't know. I fix my gaze on his anxious face. He whispers, yet his words pierce through me.

'I came straight from the airport. I can't even wrap my mind around this. What the hell happened?'

His comment feels familiar. Not the words, but the feeling it evokes. I've been belittled so many times. So many faux pas committed by me — little ones first, then major ones.

'Someone took her, Jack.'

'What do you mean someone took her? Where were you?' He slides his briefcase across the nightstand sending a plastic cup tumbling over the edge and to the ground. 'What the hell is going on?'

'Jack, I — '

He swipes his hand through the air as if to dismiss me when I open my mouth. 'Who loses a baby, Estelle? Who? Tell me who loses a baby?'

I press my lips together.

'I leave for a couple of weeks and you get in an

29

accident in . . . Dover? That's hours from here! What were you doing there?'

I don't dare make eye contact with him.

'Why did you take her to Dover?'

The beeping and buzzing of machines behind me is the only sound in the room. 'I didn't, Jack, that's the thing, I don't know why I was even there.'

'I was questioned by the police — no, wait — questioned isn't the right word . . . ' His face twitches, then he steps closer. He lifts his index finger as if to scold me like a child. 'I was *interrogated*. I was detained at the airport, taken to the police station and interrogated like a common criminal. Just what did you tell them?'

'I didn't tell them anything. I haven't even spoken to police — '

'*I* was questioned by police.'

'They always question the parents first, you know that.'

'I was treated like a suspect. I've never been so humiliated in my life. Once my boss gets wind of this . . . ' He doesn't finish the sentence. 'Where is she? Tell me where she is?'

'She's missing, Jack!' I'm alarmed by the distance in his eyes. I want to cry but that would only make him angrier. All this time with Jack has paid off. I've learned to hold back my tears.

'I know she's missing, they're searching for her. I want to know how it happened, tell me everything. I talked to the police and the doctors, but I want to hear it from you.'

I start with how I found the empty crib. How it was a Sunday and none of the workers were in

30

the house, it was empty and quiet. Lieberman was out of town, like every weekend. How nothing made sense. How I went to the police and left without saying anything. Jack doesn't say, 'It's going to be okay' or 'we'll sort it out.' He just says, 'Go on.'

When I'm done, he shakes his head. 'I should've never left town. Never. You fooled me. You told me you were okay and I believed you. Did you leave her somewhere? Tell me where you left her.'

Jack's got it all figured out, like always. In his world you put one foot in front of the other and you're sure to arrive anywhere you want to be.

'Jack — '

'You promised me, *promised me*, you were okay, and now look at what you've done.'

'I'm sorry, Jack. I'm so sorry.' I don't know what I'm sorry for but it seems like the proper thing to say.

'Sorry isn't going to cut it. My daughter is gone. *Gone*. Did that sink in yet?'

'I wish I knew what happened. All I know is she was gone when I woke up.'

'You don't know where you left her?'

'No, I didn't leave her *anywhere*. I don't know where she is.'

'Did you leave her with a sitter? Did you leave her at an overnight daycare? Maybe — '

'No, no, there was no sitter. No daycare.'

'I should've known something was going to happen. I never should've . . . ' He doesn't finish the sentence.

Remember, a change of scenery would do me

31

good, you said. It would be like starting over, you said. I believed you, Jack. I thought I could leave the other woman, the one who had taken over my life, I could leave her behind. But she followed me.

'None of this makes any sense.' Suddenly his face relaxes. 'You've been acting strangely ever since you had Mia. Either I worked too much or I slept too late. Nothing was ever right. I'm starting to think this was your plan all along.'

'My plan? What plan?'

'Yeah, you land a lawyer, get married, have a baby, divorce him, and get alimony and child support. *That* plan.'

'You're the jackpot and I'm the gold digger? We're broke, remember? You took this job in Chicago because we are broke.'

'I'm just trying to understand what happened. I've done nothing but support you. What happened to you, Estelle? Did you wake up one day and just say to yourself, *fuck Jack, fuck Mia, fuck everything?* Just like that? I've done everything you wanted me to do, given you everything you've ever wanted. Now it's time to do something for me.'

I just look at him.

'Tell me the truth. We can still fix this.'

'I was in an accident. I have amnesia. I don't know what happened.' My voice is monotone, like a robot, repeating a prerecorded statement.

'Let's assume you really don't remember, let's entertain that for a minute, then explain to me how you don't call me. Explain that to me. I'm her father, how do you not call me? Was this another one of your crazy moments?'

'My crazy moments?'

'One of those moments when you go off the deep end. When you can't hold the baby, when you can't stop crying, when you follow me to my office, when you go through my stuff, when you can't pick up the phone, can't dial 9-1-1! One of those moments. Do I need to go on?'

Everything in his world is either black or white. The scary thing is that I have to agree with him, I wasn't good for anything. I tried to be a good mother, I tried to do what mothers do. I wish I could make him understand how hard I tried.

'Everything okay in here?' We turn towards the door where a nurse stands, holding an empty tray.

'Sorry,' Jack says and I nod in agreement. 'We'll keep it down. Everything's all right.'

Jack doesn't like to be told how loud he can speak. He lowers his voice but the look in his eyes makes up for his contained rage.

'There's a cop sitting outside. Do you get how serious this is?'

I nod.

'Any idea why he's here?' He doesn't wait for my answer and lowers his voice to a whisper. 'It's not for your protection.'

'What are you saying?' I ask and can't keep my voice from shaking.

'You need a criminal defense lawyer.'

I cringe at the word *criminal*.

'Jack, I'm not a criminal. I don't remember what happened. I'm beside myself!' Is it possible for a nonexistent ear to throb? I know my outbursts only reiterate the fact that, in his eyes, I've lost my mind. I know I must look like a deer right before the bumper makes contact.

'I woke up and she was gone. Everything was gone. That's *all* I remember.'

'Something must have happened. Did she cry and you got upset? Did you do something to her?'

I try to sit up but the pain in my ribs is excruciating.

'Look at me.' Jack steps closer and he grabs my chin, turning my head towards him. 'Look me in the eyes and tell me what happened.'

'Do you think I'd hurt our daughter?'

The candor of my question startles him. His eyes widen, but immediately he catches himself and lowers his voice to a whisper. 'I'm not saying you hurt her, all I'm saying is that I blame you for what happened.'

Jack opens his briefcase. 'One more thing,' he adds.

There is always one more thing with Jack.

'I'm not sure if you're getting this, but there's a possibility you'll spend the rest of your life behind bars or strapped to a gurney. Now is the time to grasp the severity of your situation.' He pinches his lips into a straight line and adds, 'I've talked to the doctors at length and if I can convince the DA, I'll get you into a clinic with a doctor who specializes in memory recovery. I don't see any other way, all I want to do is find my daughter.'

I stare at him, and then I lower my eyes.

34

'Where's this clinic?' I ask.

'Here in New York. The doctor, some foreigner from the Middle East, specializes in trauma-related memory loss.' His shoulders relax but even his expensive suit can't hide the fact that suddenly he looks like a deflated balloon. 'I need you to sign a voluntary admission to a psychiatric facility for an unspecified length of time.'

'I don't belong in a psych ward.' I attempt to organize my thoughts into separate, manageable portions. It barely seems possible. *Memory recovery.* I imagine wires hooked up to my brain, truth serums, and my retinas relaying images to computer screens. *A psychiatric facility. Unspecified amount of time.* I'm agreeing to go to a loony bin and I won't be able to check out.

Jack cocks his head and raises his brows as if he has caught a kid in a lie.

'In your eyes I'm just this crazy lunatic, right? Why don't you just say it? You think I'm crazy, don't you?'

'Not crazy in a certifiable sense, not crazy as in failing a psych exam, but I believe that you need help and that this clinic might just be your only chance. And most of all, it's Mia's only chance.'

His voice is soft now, almost seductive. 'I don't think you have any other choice. This is it.'

Jack has spoken, there's no alternative. He's right, this is Mia's only chance and so I force my legs off the side of the bed. My rubbery socks search for the sticky linoleum floor. I feel suspended, unable to find the ground. I sign my name in shaky letters and the second the pen

35

rests, I feel an overwhelming urge to take it in my fist and scratch out my signature until the paper is torn to shreds.

Jack grabs the pen and pulls it from between my fingers and checks his watch.

'That doctor will help me remember and we'll find Mia. We'll find out what happened, right, Jack?'

He closes his briefcase and leaves the room before I can even get my feet on the ground.

5

One year, I told myself, take one year and figure out what you want. The concept of 'wanting' was a very vague one and after spending a larger part of the self-imposed deadline in bars, flirting with men who meant nothing to me, I was waiting for some sort of a sign, some sort of higher intervention one might refer to as palm reader stuff. I'd walk down 57th Street and tell myself the next billboard that catches my eye, the next car graphic, tote bag, or flier blowing my way was going to be the answer.

At the time, I worked at a health insurance call center where I met a woman who, at first glance, seemed out of place. Delilah, middle-aged, short and heavy set, was covered in tattoos she hid amazingly well under white oversized blouses and cardigans. She was far removed from the twenty-somethings filling up the cubicles around her. Every time she pushed back her cardigan sleeves, a gesture signaling a difficult customer, a tattoo on her forearm emerged: 'Dead Men Tell No Tales.'

'You keep looking at my tattoo,' she said and muted her headset in the cubicle next to mine.

'Quite the message,' I replied.

'Kind of a funny story,' she said.

She told me she'd been a prison guard for 25 years and with every passing year her people skills took a turn for the worse. Her husband left her and none of her children were speaking to her. As a matter of self-preservation she decided to spend the rest of her working career in customer service.

'Forces me to work on myself every day,' she added and switched to a noncommittal voice accepting the next call in the queue.

The concept intrigued me and I wondered about my own character shortcomings. If I had to challenge a part of myself, what part would that be? At the end of my shift I came to the conclusion that I did not like people very much, never sought lasting friendships, and distrust of humanity was an issue I ought to tackle. That day, I quit my job at the call center and decided to become a waitress.

Two days later I found a job as a hostess at 'La Luna,' a bar and grill in Manhattan, mostly frequented by judges, DAs, defense lawyers, prosecutors, and armies of executives working in the surrounding buildings. La Luna's neighborhood on Lexington and 50th was a hodgepodge of restaurants and bars, office buildings, law offices, and an occasional Starbucks to break up the monotony.

I saw Jack standing in line, waiting to be seated. He wasn't stunningly attractive or anything unusual that caught my eye, but still I couldn't wait for him to get to the front of the line. I liked the way he looked into my eyes and weighed his words before he spoke.

'Jack Connor,' he said and straightened his tie. He was expecting a party of two to join him and demanded the best table in the house.

'Important meeting,' he added and followed me to a table at the far end of the restaurant.

When we reached it, he looked around and pointed towards a table by the front window.

'I think I'd prefer that one.'

That's how I met Jack. Me challenging myself, him telling me what I offered him wasn't good enough. Later Jack read my name off the tag on my blouse, his voice a soft baritone.

'Estelle Paradise.'

Over the years, I had heard many jokes regarding my name and I was prepared for one then. Too often, high-powered lawyers saw me as easy prey or a cheap thrill on a Friday afternoon.

Jack was lanky and wholesome, but the dark circles under his eyes spoke of long hours and work beyond his physical capacity. I realized that his left eyebrow was noticeably raised and had a much more pronounced curve, as if the world was under his constant scrutiny.

'You keep looking at my eye,' he said.

'I don't mean to, I'm sorry.' I blushed and turned away. There was something slightly off about his face and his facial expression seemed to be in a constant state of disapproval.

'Hypertropia,' he said and wiggled his brows. 'It's a muscle imbalance, the visual axis of one eye is higher than the other. It's hereditary. I wore glasses when I was younger but short of surgery one eye will always be slightly higher.'

We parted and I forgot about him until the very next day when he dropped by for a drink. He sat at the bar and watched me as I walked the floor.

'You know what you should do?' Jack asked that day.

'What's that?' I held a stack of menus between us like a shield.

'Check to see the progression of the tables instead of just marking the occupied tables at your station.'

'And why would I do that?'

He looked at me, puzzled. 'To see if the tables are on dessert or if they've paid their checks. It expedites the operation.'

'I'll keep that in mind,' I said and laughed, trying not to focus on his eye again.

'Would you go out on a date with me?' Jack's voice shook slightly, enough to be noticeable if you paid close attention.

'We're not allowed to go on dates with patrons,' I lied and brushed invisible crumbs off my blouse. No one cared who we dated, the waitress and hostess turnaround was staggering. Looking back, was I playing hard to get? I guess deep down I didn't want him to give up.

His eyes remained on my chest, and then he got up and downed his drink. 'If I stop coming will you go out with me then?'

'Don't hold your breath,' I said and smiled at him.

A month later, we went on our first date. I wore my best dress, black, sleeveless, while he wore khakis and a blue unbuttoned shirt. A movie and then dinner, during which we both had too much to drink. In my tipsy stupor I must have told him about my rent being late because he offered to pay for the next month.

40

'Come on,' he said, 'let me do something for you.'

That line got to me. Any other night the comment wouldn't have, I was used to getting by and had always been able to muddle through, but money was tight, I was struggling to keep up with my student loan payments, and I was stuck in a hostess position because all the waitress slots, popular due to the high tips, were filled.

That night, Jack's shirt smelled of starch and I wondered how his lips would feel on mine. My mouth on his mouth. A taste of his lips, of what life could be if I let him do something for me. I had yet to increase my love for humankind in general and wondered at Delilah's story setting me on this unexpected path.

Our second date, during which I expected reality to set in and expose how different we really were, Jack sealed the deal for me. On our way to the restaurant we walked down Lexington, and as the temperature dropped, he put his coat around my shoulders. The itchy wool and the smooth lining was every cliché of every romantic movie I had ever seen. The guy who put his coat around the girl's shoulders is the good guy. Good guys give you their coat, bad guys take your clothes off.

After dinner I told him about my dating rules. 'Thirty days. No making out, no sex.' It was more or less a joke but Jack — unshakable, undeterred Jack — didn't flinch.

'I've got my own rule. It's more like one hundred and eighty days, but okay. I accept,' he

41

said and added, 'So, we're officially on probation?'

'Speaking of probation, whose side are you on?' I asked while we passed the Met Life building. 'Career wise,' I added and moved my body closer to his as we walked hand in hand. 'I've always wondered how lawyers figure out if they should become a defense lawyer or a prosecutor. Seems like two sides of the law to me.'

'You just pick a side,' he said and furrowed his brow as if my question made no sense at all.

When I asked him what he wanted to do years from now, he said, 'I like being a defense lawyer but I'm leaning more towards Assistant DA. From there, District DA, then judge.'

'And then you'll run for public office like mayor or something?' I joked.

'Mayor?' He paused. 'Probably not. I don't do well with crowds and public speaking. Supreme Court maybe. They submit their rulings in writing. Seems like the perfect fit.'

I didn't know what to make of his comment — his choice of career seemed odd to me — but maybe there was a difference between speaking in front of crowds and arguing a case in court. All in all his arrogance was harmless and refreshing.

'Defenders probably see the good in everyone,' I said. 'Prosecutors expect everyone to be a criminal. Don't you have to take a stand in your heart?'

'My heart? That's a very emotional way of looking at the world.'

'Tell me about growing up,' I said, wanting to change the subject.

Jack named his childhood experiences like a grocery list. 'New Jersey, public schools, wrestling team, single mom.' He paused slightly, then continued. 'An only child, sort of. My mother was a state employee at the NY city library. We struggled, to say the least. My mother was a saint, she never even raised her voice at me.'

'You were *sort of* an only child?'

Jack then told me how his father, Earl, had left his mother when he was still in diapers. Earl, a big rig driver who spent a majority of the year on the road, met another woman, a beauty salon owner named Elsa. He gave up his trucker job, something he had refused Jack's mom for years, and started driving a city bus instead. He didn't disappear from Jack's life, no, he did something much worse.

'I ran into my father in school, in front of the Principal's office. I hadn't seen him in years, couldn't even remember the last time he spoke to me. For some odd reason that only a ten-year-old can comprehend, I felt he had come for me. Just when I was about to bury myself into his arms, I heard the Principal's voice over the loudspeaker. *George Connor, please come to the front office.* That was the day I learned of my half-brother George. And that we lived close enough to go to school together. Five blocks to be exact.'

I didn't know what to say. When I asked him about his mom, he let out a breath that sounded

43

like a groan. 'In a way, she killed herself,' he said and I could tell it was an emotional subject for him. 'She started working three jobs trying to send me to private school after the incident with my brother. She wasn't feeling well for a long time and when she finally went to the doctor it was too late. She had ignored all the signs for too long and was diagnosed with colon cancer. She had surgery but they just stitched her back up, there was nothing they could do. Eventually the cancer spread to her brain and her liver.'

I thought about my own family and how my mother didn't seem to feel any guilt pursuing her photography career. I remembered all the nights without dinner on the table and the door to the darkroom locked. Many years after my parents died in a car accident, I still couldn't make up my mind if I should feel cheated out of her attention or happy for her to have had a career of her own.

That night, we broke the 30-days-no-sex rule and made love for the first time. It was a chaotic mess of fidgeting with the condom wrapper and not knowing where to put our legs. When I woke up the next morning, Jack was sitting in bed, furiously writing in a notebook.

'Are you writing me a poem?' I asked jokingly.

'A speech,' he said. Jack had been selected to deliver the keynote speech for an annual function sponsored by the New York City Bar Association for over eight hundred law students. For the next two weeks he outlined the speech, then revised it, just to start all over again. The night of the event I watched him deliver the speech. He spoke with confidence, made eye contact, and told anecdotes and jokes. There wasn't even a hint of anxiety in his voice or his demeanor and later I found out that speaking in front of crowds wasn't his problem at all.

On our way to the event room, Jack excused himself, drops of perspiration emerging from his hairline. People were asking for him, wanting to meet the bright young attorney who had delivered such an inspiring and confident speech. I waited in front of the bathroom, checked the coatroom and behind the stage, but Jack had all but disappeared. His cell went to voicemail and I finally decided to hail a cab and go home. I found him vomiting behind a portaloo in a construction zone in the parking lot.

Jack was covered in sweat and mumbled something about an upset stomach. 'Go in and let my boss know I have a stomach virus,' he said in one uninterrupted breath and then continued to dry heave. I always doubted the explanation and wondered if it wasn't about speaking in public but having to mingle with people afterwards that did him in.

'A slight bout of anxiety. Not a big deal, I'm working on it,' he confessed later. 'I prefer a courtroom to a cocktail party. Can we drop it now?'

Jack was unpredictable in many ways. He was confident on one hand, yet socially inept on the other. I observed a temper when things went out of control but Jack's attitude was covert to anyone who didn't know him. As moody as he was, he didn't take kindly to people who exhibited the same characteristics; if I seemed grumpy, he assumed I was mad with him — no other explanation occurred to him. There were battles I chose not to fight, and I learned early on which ones those were.

* * *

A few months later, I told Jack I might be pregnant. There was an unsure smile and a long silence as we waited for the test results. I watched him pace around the room while the minutes passed slowly; there was so much sincerity in him and it felt as if we'd known each other forever. By the time the faint pink line appeared in the result window, reality started to set in. Before I fully comprehended what just happened, happiness spread across his face. I remember thinking he's the person I want to love forever.

'Let's get married,' he said.

'Don't do this because of what your father did, Jack,' I said and wished I hadn't said it out loud. Jack's face seemed to melt, his eyes turned big, wounded almost. He recovered quickly and smiled at me.

'What my father did is irrelevant. I don't allow other people's shortcomings to affect my life decisions. You have to remove yourself from that. But . . . ' his voice became gentle and he held my face and kissed me, 'my child won't be raised by another man.'

Like shells on a beach I collected my feelings;

there was excitement and joy — I loved Jack, of that I was sure — and trepidation. Apprehension that we were making the right decision, that I was about to become the most important person in someone's life, and then there was sheer confusion. I had never asked myself if I wanted to be a mother. Becoming Jack's wife wasn't that far of a stretch but motherhood seemed almost alien. My mind attempted to make a switch from pregnancy to baby, from *I'm pregnant* to *I'm going to be a mother*, and everything about that seemed to leave me raw, like sunburned skin, and the fact that I felt inadequate, even at that moment, would emerge again and again in the months that followed.

We went to the courthouse and married in front of the Justice of the Peace. No white stretch limousine, no heaving of the bridal bouquet into a group of shrieking bridesmaids, no rice, no festivities, no honeymoon. No father-in-law telling Jack to take good care of his daughter. No family to toast the bride and groom. Jack wasn't big on celebrations and it was all the same to me. I decided to keep my maiden name and Jack didn't put up a fight. Later I thought about it and realized maybe it was my way of holding on to my family that I had lost a long time ago? I didn't dwell on it.

The courthouse clerk took a photo of us, the only one we have of our wedding day. We didn't ask, the clerk basically insisted.

Later, months later, as I flipped through our only photo album, it occurred to me that there were so few pictures of us they were almost not

47

worth organizing. A picture of us in front of a Christmas tree at Jack's law firm, our smiles bright, Jack's bowtie and starched shirt immaculate, my hair slightly ruffled, my eyes somewhat cast with the effects of too many martinis. We won a trip to the Bahamas that day, but Jack donated the tickets to a charity because he couldn't take any time off. One on New Year's Eve, table decorations of upturned black top hats, confetti in our hair. The only memory of that night's the hangover I had the next day.

In our wedding picture Jack wore a black suit and a dark blue tie. I was in a cotton dress, white, versatile, appropriate for many occasions. The pregnancy wasn't showing yet, my stomach was still flat. In the picture, Jack's got his arm around my shoulder, allowing me to lean into him. Behind us on the wall, a blueprint of the original courthouse layout, the light colored lines on the blue background reminiscent of prints on my father's study wall. In the left corner of the photo, even though I tried to crop it out later, the hallway courthouse bench, Jack's briefcase photobombing us from the edge of the photograph.

We always meant to find a special frame for the wedding photo, but it was to remain in its original frame. Plain black wood. We never really thought about it anymore.

* * *

On the day of the 20 weeks scan, we were ushered into a small examination room. I

48

glanced at the screen mounted above the keyboard.

'Hi, I'm Debra.' A woman in a spotless pink uniform entered. 'Before we get started,' she said and vigorously pushed buttons on the keyboard, 'would you like to know the sex of your baby?'

The sex of our baby. I looked down at myself, anxiously scanning the small bump protruding from my abdomen. So far I was hardly showing and the fact that there was a human inside of me, however small, seemed inconceivable, let alone the fact that it was a boy or a girl.

'Yes, we'd like to know,' Jack said.

The truth was that I hadn't decided if I wanted to know the sex and the fact that he answered for me made me furious. Furious that he was speaking on my behalf. But I knew that if I was to question him later, he'd just come up with an example of what I had said to make him believe that I wanted to know, that it was a good idea, that we had agreed, and knowing the sex was the right thing to do.

The nurse looked at me and I nodded and managed a smile. She got up and turned off the lights. The room was warm and intimate and the dark allowed me to blink away the tears that had formed in my eyes.

'I apologize, this is going to be cold,' Debra said as she squeezed gel on my belly so cold that it made me shiver. Jack reached for my hand and together we stared at what looked like a triangular slice on a pitch-black background.

'Here we go,' Debra said and put the head of the wand on my abdomen. 'That's the spine,' she said and pushed harder to get a better picture.

My baby's spine, tiny little bones in a perfect line, was a beautiful string of pearls. My throat closed up and tears gathered in my eyes. Debra pushed another button and the image went fuzzy. I blinked quickly so I wouldn't miss anything.

The nurse adjusted the wand and a face came into being. It seemed spooky at first, like a skull mask, but it was the most beautiful face I had ever seen. The lips seemed to pucker, the chin was slightly recessed. What I had known for a while was now visible on a screen; a human being floating inches below my skin.

I heard the nurse's voice from far away, pointing out all the major organs. *Larynx is fine, cross section of the brain, kidneys, liver, lungs, heart.*

When she said *heart*, Jack squeezed my hand. Hard.

Much to Jack's dismay, I had not only read compulsively on fetal development, I was also obsessing about anything hereditary. Fascinated by a story of a doctor who performed fetal heart surgery on a woman with an ectopic pregnancy, I had found an article that described the intact and fully transparent embryonic sac. And there was the image of a tiny human, no larger than an inch, swimming in amniotic fluid, its head bowed and legs flexed upward.

I religiously followed Dr Bowers' advice, took my daily vitamins, got a lot of sleep, didn't lift anything heavy, but the part about her being in my potentially faulty body was something that pushed me over the edge. I assumed I was unlucky somehow — I had lost my family, had had no luck with relationships in general, romantic or otherwise, I'd bought a used car once and its engine went up in flames two weeks later, neither college nor jobs had ever resulted in a career — so there was some sort of tragic tie to everything I did. My marriage to Jack was different; Jack was his own person — and for all accounts, everything he'd ever touched he'd turned into gold — but this pregnancy was *all* up to me. This fetus inside of me relied on my body, but what about those things beyond my control? Would *I* be able to pull this off without a hitch?

I wasn't even in my second trimester then, and I knew every congenital heart disease by name, *aortic valve stenosis, ventricular septal defect, anomalous pulmonary venous return*, and had asked for extensive testing to be done but my obstetrician had declined.

'There is no reason whatsoever to suspect your baby has any kind of hereditary coronary malformation or defect.' Dr Bowers had taken off his glasses and looked at me as if I was a child asking for a trip to Disneyland. 'Both you and your husband are healthy and it's just not justifiable,' the doctor had said.

Even before Dr Bowers had declined to do any more tests, Jack had long refused to accompany me to any appointments, had even gone so far as to forbid me to see another specialist. Jack also refused to engage in such conversations and so I tried to silence the worry in my head, kept it in a safe place along with the anxiousness and the

51

panic. I didn't want to go there then, when we had just seen our baby's face on the monitor.

The nurse had just told us everything was fine, the ultrasound was perfect, but I was so anxious that suddenly the baby started doing somersaults inside of me. I wanted to tell Jack about my fears, about my attempts to do everything possible to make sure this baby was going to be healthy.

'A perfectly healthy baby, did you hear that?' Jack said and stroked my cheek.

'And now the sex of the baby,' the nurse said and dug deep into my abdomen, 'if the baby is willing to give up the information, that is. Girl parts look like three lines, boy parts, well, pretty much like you expect them to look. Unfortunately baby's legs are pulled up and we can't see anything.'

'I see it, right there, it's a girl.' I pointed at the lines I thought were the unmistakable signs of a vulva.

'Don't get carried away, you'll be in for a rude awakening if you interpret it yourself,' Jack said and furrowed his brow. His hand tightened around my hand as if he was trying to squash my enthusiasm.

The nurse smiled at him. I understood, it was hard not to smile at Jack. All that boyish charm, a father-to-be, eyes blazing, making even her feel special sharing this moment with us, as if nothing mattered more than that Jack was engaged and reassuring.

'A girl,' I said.

'She's right, you might as well buy all pink,'

Debra's voice reached me from afar. 'I'll print that profile shot for you.'

A flurry of images popped into my head: bows and dresses, tea sets and dollhouses, braids and ponytails and nail polish. All my worries had magically disappeared, like footsteps in the sand erased by a single ocean wave, one minute there, then gone.

★ ★ ★

After 32 hours of labor, 'normal for a first-time mom' according to Dr Bowers, I was exhausted and had almost forgotten why I was even there. All I wanted was for the pain to stop and to close my eyes. After four hours of unsuccessful pushing, Dr Bowers ordered a caesarean section.

When Mia finally came into the world, she was purple and limp. The doctor suctioned her throat and, after what seemed like an eternity, put her on my chest. Wrapped in a flannel blanket, she rested in my arms, and we looked at each other. Even though I had prepared for childbirth, had done Lamaze and infant care and CPR classes, had watched countless births on TV, natural and caesarean, and imagined it a hundred times, this moment still took me by surprise. She was so beautiful and fragile and I felt an overwhelming sense of trepidation, as if I might break her.

The fact that she was healthy was the biggest miracle to me. Had I really pulled this off? Had I been able to make bones from my bones, flesh from my flesh, a healthy and perfect baby? She looked the part but the whole ten fingers, ten toes thing didn't make a lot of sense to me. What about her heart, her brain, her lungs? How could I ever be sure she was all right? So much room for error, so much at stake.

I asked the nurse for the Apgar score and she looked at me, puzzled. 'You have a beautiful baby, she's perfect in every way, everything is fine.'

What does she know? What I held in my arms was the product of cell division and multiplication, a process that had begun at a furious rate only minutes after conception. Cells had travelled down the fallopian tube to the uterus. By the end of the first week, a single cell had transformed into millions and into a body big enough to be seen without a microscope. Cells had formed muscles, the circulatory system, the skeleton, the kidneys and the reproductive organs, the nervous system, senses and skin. And the heart had begun beating after three weeks. And now she was here and I was unable to go back and make right what had potentially gone wrong. Rogue cells, unlucky DNA, how could I ever rest assured?

But then I looked into Mia's eyes, steel gray and unable to focus, seemingly out of line and slightly crossed, the puffiness of her eyelids making it almost impossible for her to open them wide. And I knew then that she needed me and that I was put on this earth to protect her and for a short moment in time I didn't worry about her heart.

6

The very next day, after Jack's arrived back in town, I'm cleared to be interviewed. The smell of breakfast and coffee still lingers in the air when I hear a forceful knock on the door. By the time I open my eyes, two men in suits have entered the room and introduce themselves as Detective Walter Daniel and Detective Sydney Cameron. Detective Daniel is a large middle-aged man. His bulky body renders him soft, especially around his eyes. He takes out a small notepad with a flip cover and stands beside my bed ready to take notes.

I start with the day I moved to North Dandry and Jack went to Chicago. I tell them about the locks I had installed, which causes Detective Daniel to nod approvingly.

When I finish my story with leaving the police precinct, Detective Daniel motions to the younger detective whose name I can no longer remember. The younger detective, very short with feminine hands, gets up and leaves the room. Detective Daniel pulls up a chair and sits next to my bed.

My head is pounding and I feel like I'm hooked up to a bag of caffeine. I'm trying to remember, and at the same time I'm trying not to say too much. I've been watching his face closely and as my story has progressed, his demeanor has changed. First he stopped smiling.

His brows intermittently rose, then furrowed. Then his face went blank.

When I catch myself rambling, I slow down. I must consider carefully what I'm going to say next. When I tell him I don't know where my daughter is, he continues to take notes but doesn't act with any sense of urgency. Eventually he just sits and looks at me. Looks at me like you'd look at a child telling a tale of monsters under the bed. And I realize he doesn't believe me. Then it hits me like a brick; there's no Amber Alert, no press conference, no urgent phone calls, no commands given to uniformed officers. That's what's supposed to happen.

Is it that I haven't displayed any sense of urgency myself in the past? They must know that my injuries and all that medication made me feel as if I was in a fog. My thoughts are clearer now. I can't think of a more serious word than kidnapped and so *kidnapped* is the word I use.

He doesn't believe me. I *must* make him believe me. 'I locked the doors! No one could've come in — I'm sure of that. I know I should've ... but I wasn't ... I never left the door unlocked! I checked every night.'

'They're looking for your daughter as we speak.' He closes the cover of his notepad and slides the pen in his suit pocket. He lifts himself off the chair, sighs heavily, and pinches his lips as his kneecaps make a cracking sound. 'We don't understand your reasoning, Mrs Paradise. Why didn't you get help immediately?'

The headache that started behind my eyes has moved to the back of my head. It's paralyzing, and the odor of disinfectant is overwhelming. There it is again. The image approaches like a set of oncoming headlights, blinding and painful, and I'm unable to look away. The blood. The memory just won't quit. Mesmerized by the vision of crimson patches the shape of tiny feet, soaked into the sheet, I close my eyes and take a deep breath.

'Please, somebody must have seen something. I can't remember anything but I know I've never been in Dover. I'm bad at reading maps, I wouldn't know how to get there. I don't think I'd just drive up there for no reason. It's all very confusing.'

'Maybe you just drove and you decided to stop there. It may not have been your destination. Just a place to stop.'

'Stop for what?'

He ignores my question. 'We'll need a photograph of your daughter.'

'Hundreds. I have hundreds of pictures of her. At my house. They are in a black camera bag, on memory cards.'

'We found those.' He pauses ever so slightly, then continues. 'We need a recent portrait, you know, with her face. A likeness of her that people can recognize.'

I must think about this carefully. 'The flash startled her and I haven't taken any photographs, not lately. She's been so fussy, I didn't want her to . . . ' I must be vigilant. Speak slowly. I must make sense. I must convince him. 'I don't have any recent photos of her. She's only seven months old. The doctors said, they told me she

'. . . she . . . she's a colicky baby. The doctors told us there was nothing wrong with her. Just a colic. It was going to pass any day.'

'How old did you say she is?'

'Seven months.'

'Babies are colicky at that age. I have three kids. I can't say I took care of them, but my youngest was colicky. They usually grow out of that pretty quickly.' His brows are raised. So are his suspicions. 'Did you take her to a doctor?'

Pacifier, warm baths, soft blankets. Burp the baby. Hold the baby. Rock the baby. Walk the baby, drive with the baby. Soothe the baby.

'They did a couple of tests for reflux disorders. She gained weight, never had a fever. He said she was fine and to wait it out.' They also told me if I ever felt that I couldn't cope, to go to the nearest emergency room, but I don't mention that part to the detective.

'All right,' he says and scribbles something in his notepad. 'How about DNA — a brush maybe? Or a bottle she drank out of? Or a handprint or a footprint? You know, those kits you buy at a department store, where you use clay and take an impression of a foot or a hand?'

I shake my head.

'A hair brush? A toothbrush? You know those little plastic things you attach to a finger and brush their teeth?'

I shake my head.

'A diaper? There must be a dirty diaper somewhere?'

Again I shake my head. 'It all disappeared.' I say it so softly that I don't know if he heard me.

'It disappeared,' he repeats as if I just told him the day of the week.

Why isn't he alarmed?

'Yes, everything disappeared, her clothes, her bottles. All of it, everything's gone. Her closet was empty, her diapers were missing, her formula, her bottles. Everything.'

'We are aware of that fact.' He sits up straight and crosses his arms in front of his chest. 'So, someone took her and that person also took her things?' He puts his notebook away as if the ramblings of a madwoman are no longer significant enough to be written in his precious pad. 'That's a very odd crime. If the doors were locked all night and were still locked the morning you found the empty crib, there must be another explanation. I have to be honest with you, that doesn't make sense at all.'

My story not making any sense is a cruel statement. 'I know how it sounds, but that's all I can tell you.'

Daniel's face relaxes, he leans forward. 'I can only find her if I know where to look.' He pauses and then adds, 'Where should I look for her?' His voice is gentle as if he is trying to convince a child to tell the truth.

'What are you trying to say? That I know where she is?'

'You knew she was gone and you didn't ask for help.'

He's right. I don't know how to respond to that.

'If you know where she is you have to tell me,' he continues. 'She's so little, helpless, she is cold, hungry. She's all alone out there.'

I wonder where his *out there* is. I pinch my lips to keep the tears in check. I don't want to cry in front of him. When I cried in front of Jack it made everything worse.

'Did you ever feel you were capable of hurting your baby?'

Was I capable of hurting her? I shake my head for I dare not speak out loud.

'Did she cry a lot?' he asks.

There they are, the images emerge as if the detective hit a button and they splatter against the wall like photographs from a slide projector: Clenched fists, legs pulled up to the stomach, a baby's tearless rage directed towards me. My love for her powerless, incapable of easing her pain.

'She was a colicky baby, you know, very fussy . . . but I would never hurt her. She was my life.'

Something in his eyes twitches, then he nods as if I said something he expected to hear.

He abruptly turns around and leaves the room, as if everything I just told him is beyond what makes sense.

Then I realize I spoke of Mia in the past tense.

NO NEW DETAILS RELEASED OF 7-MONTH-OLD MISSING FROM CRIB

Brooklyn, NY — After a frantic search for the infant missing from her crib in Brooklyn on early Sunday, October 1st, no new details have been released.

According to Eric Rodriguez, spokesperson for NYPD, police have no idea how a kidnapper may have gained entry to the home. 'At this moment we have no suspect description. We have no vehicle plates to trigger an Amber Alert. There are no eyewitnesses and the entire surrounding area has been searched by officers, including a K9 unit,' Rodriguez said. 'We are following several leads but we know nothing for sure yet.'

'Many child abductions involve parents or parental abductions, but we have both the parents here. So that puts us on a higher state of alert,' Detective Robert Wilczek said.

A source told CTAB TV that the child's disappearance was especially concerning given the fact that the mother didn't report the abduction immediately.

Police are urging anyone with information to call the TIPS hotline at 1-888-267-4880.

7

Mia Paradise Connor and I were released from the hospital five days after the delivery. Jack went back to work, took over the night feedings on the weekends, and I slept, ate and showered whenever possible.

I was in awe of what I had created. I stared at Mia, her plump cheeks, her little bird mouth twitching in her sleep. I bathed her and padded her dry, gently rubbing lavender lotion all over her. By then she was far from the puffy-eyed, bowlegged newborn. Her curvy legs had straightened, her cone-shaped skull had rounded out, and her flaky skin was now pink and spongy.

I loved how she studied my face, trying to memorize it, as if I was all the comfort and love she needed. She'd wake up in my arms, open her eyes, and frantically search for my likeness, immediately settling down when she recognized me.

Mia's cries were distinct, one seemed to complain about a minor discomfort, like a sock too tight, a jacket too warm. There was the tired cry, fussy, drawn out, telling me she was ready to take a nap. Then there was a more relentless cry that seemed to signal hunger. Nothing a bottle couldn't fix. And then, at about three months old, another cry emerged. An abrupt cry, a cry that seemed to signal pain, as if stuck with a needle, a cry that made my heart pound in my chest, tuning out everything else. All that remained was her wailing and my pounding heart. And she suddenly shunned containment, something that had calmed her before, and protested every time I swaddled her. It seemed as if there were wires inside of her every time I wrapped her in a blanket; fists clenched, back arched, muscles tensed, limbs stiffened.

Need to make a fussy baby feel safe? How about the age-old tradition of mimicking the condition in the mother's womb? All you need is a blanket and a clever folding technique.

Her abrupt cry was not a mere request, but an urgent demand to fix whatever bothered her. Mia put more energy into her demands, cried more loudly, fed more voraciously, and protested more forcefully. If I didn't respond to her needs immediately, she'd fall apart, come undone.

She seemed to feel deeply, and therefore she reacted with fierce power when her needs were being ignored. I went into overdrive to respond immediately and I became obsessive in trying to prevent her from getting upset. She extracted every bit of energy from me, and I willingly complied, but still, she wanted more.

I gave her all I had, yet something had gone amiss, had gone awry. I was somehow removed from the person who had entered the hospital and emerged with a baby in her arms, as if I had left one person behind and had returned home another. I woke up just as tired as I had gone to sleep and blamed it on not getting enough rest. Every waking hour was a never-ending stretch of time with the volume turned up. Chunks of sleep

64

broken up into pieces that left me exhausted. Every day posed a new nightmare; not waking up when Mia is in distress. Jack too busy to help on the weekend. The pediatrician administering the wrong vaccine. I will feed her too often or not enough. Even though I went on with my life, took care of Mia, sang to her, gave her a bath, something felt horribly wrong. What had happened to the euphoric love I initially felt? Why wasn't I happier? Who was this woman living inside of me?

Every morning when I woke up, before reality closed in on me, after a peaceful second or two, a dank layer of sadness wrapped itself around me. I felt as if I was playing a role and never was that more apparent than when I met other moms at the park. They seemed more cheerful, happier and content to be mothers than I ever was or ever could be. And even so, I could have adopted their story as mine, could have pretended to be one of them. I decided to accept my lack of enthusiasm as a personal character flaw, and make up for it in other ways.

★　★　★

One day during breastfeeding, Mia dozed off and unlatched. She had long unlocked her lips, but her tongue still made clicking sounds. I reached for my camera, snapped images of blue veins running across her eyelids, too small for even a thread to fit inside of them. There was a larger vein by her temple, like a widening channel of a river nearing the sea, its currents

65

waiting to be met by the tides.

My camera, small enough to operate with one hand, turned into my new obsession. I photographed Mia from every possible angle, perspectives of feet, toes tucked under, spread apart, soft tiny nails, bending easily, and elfin hands grasping small objects. My lips seemed to sink into her, her limbs were malleable and soft, yet the core of her body remained inaccessible to me. I attempted to capture the part of our relationship that remained inadequate, and though our bodies connected — ears folded like rose petals moving up and down as she drank from my breast, pink lips curling around the nipple — we remained strangers.

I took close-ups of breast milk running down her cheek, towards her ear, as if the amount of milk had just fallen short of reaching its intended destination. I took shots of my engorged breasts, drops of nourishment trailing from my cracked and sore nipples.

The camera flash irritated her, sent her into a frenzy, up a notch from her usual agitated state. She cried and wouldn't stop, as if my attempts to capture her likeness repulsed her somehow. I rocked her, allowed her head to rest on my chest. Nothing consoled her, not my songs, my gentle voice, not my nipple, nothing. She cried every single day and nothing I ever did soothed her.

I sang to her, *Sleep, baby, sleep, your father tends the sheep, your mother shakes the dreamland tree, and from it fall sweet dreams for thee, Sleep, baby, sleep.*

In what twisted universe is a mother incapable

of consoling her own child? How it must feel to live in this tiny helpless body with such obvious discomfort and your mother just looks on, incapable of easing the suffering, inept to give you what you need. It was undeniably my fault. My way of making up for my shortcoming as a less than mediocre mother was by going from doctor to doctor and the same diagnosis was thrown at me as if I ought to know what to do with it: *Colic. Otherwise healthy. Cause unknown. No obvious reason.*

While her constant state of crying seemed acceptable, Jack became increasingly worried about the bills and out-of-network doctors; 'Colic,' he said. 'They all told you the same thing. A lot of babies are colicky. It'll be gone before we know it.'

Jack's objections were logical to say the least; after all he seemed so natural, capable of bouncing her on his knee as he studied case files, putting her to sleep within minutes, never a single sound of fury directed towards him. But his logic fell on deaf ears.

'I want to take her to another hospital. Maybe there are some more tests they can do? If I can't get a referral, we'll have to pay out of pocket.'

I saw pity in his eyes but at the mention of money Jack stiffened. Ever so slightly, but I saw it. The way his spine straightened, his eyes narrowed. I was afraid to mention that my credit cards were maxed out.

'Give it another month or two,' he added on his way out the door, 'she'll be fine.'

I nodded, even more exhausted than I had

been minutes earlier, as if that were even possible. Two months, that was 60 days and 60 nights.

'You know you're nuts, don't you?' Jack said and slammed the door shut.

★ ★ ★

One morning, a Saturday, too early to get up and too late to fall back asleep, I reached beside me and found Jack's side of the bed abandoned.

I heard a voice that almost made me panic, a high-pitched babble voice unknown to me. I got up and went to Mia's room. There was Jack, holding Mia, a five-month-old grouchy bundle of anxieties with fingers moving around like an orchestra conductor, under her armpits.

'Why won't you sleep?' Jack said.

Then he switched over to a whiney, high-pitched voice. *I don't want to. I want to be awake so I can look around.*

'How come you can talk?' Jack pretended to be confused.

I can do anything, daddy. Jack, mimicking a conversation, impersonating Mia, switching from his regular tone to a squeaky voice.

'Why won't you settle down, little girl? Something on your mind?' Jack's facial expression was sheer concern.

Mia's arms were flailing, her legs kicking. *Nothing wrong with me, daddy.*

'I know there's nothing wrong with you. You've been fed, you've been changed, you've been burped. No need to be fussy.' Jack then rocked her gently in the cradle of his arm, the crook of his elbow a perfect fit. 'There you go, princess, that's better isn't it?'

Much better, daddy.

'Just relax, go back to sleep. Mommy doesn't like it when you cry so much.'

★ ★ ★

I'd go one, sometimes two days without closing my eyes. When I did sleep, I crashed. Hard and deep. And I always woke up with a start. I went from comatose to alert, as if someone had grabbed my shoulder and shaken me awake.

Life was a blur, the bottles, the diapers, the crying. Zombie-like, I shopped for baby clothes, loaded the cart, walked the aisles, and bought multiples of everything: booties, outfits, socks. I purchased everything that promised relief from her crying; rosemary-scented satchels, calming lotion, and alarm clocks with waterfall recordings, white noise boxes, and a bear with recorded womb sounds. Regardless of how much I purchased, I never felt as if I could give her what she needed. I could buy entire stores and yet my attempts didn't amount to anything. Because deep down inside I was a fake.

One day, with another collection of bags in hand, I went home. Jack was in his office, talking on the phone, holding Mia in his arms. She looked peaceful and calm, her face relaxed, her lips loose. The moment I reached for her, her face tensed, her lips curled downward as if to say *how dare you approach me*. I immediately let go of her as if my fingers had touched hot stone.

'Every time I pick her up, she cries. She hates me. What am I doing wrong? It's me, Jack, it's all me. I'm the one who is to blame. You are everything to her while I might as well be her nanny.'

'How do you come up with that kind of stuff?'

'But she cries when I hold her. I must be doing something wrong.'

'You're not doing anything wrong. Relax, she's just a baby,' Jack said.

I told Jack that I constantly worried; of someone hurting her, her suffocating on a pillow or blanket, choking on something. Jack told me to stop imagining the worst.

'Don't overthink everything,' he said, 'and don't be so tense all the time,' as if taking it in strides was going to make it better. In his world, everything was fine. In his world, children didn't die of SIDS, didn't choke on marbles, didn't succumb to high fevers, didn't suffocate on their vomit. Didn't have mysterious illnesses that went undiagnosed until it was too late.

There was this animal inside of me, created while she was in my womb, born on the same day Mia was born. At first, it had quivered ever so slightly, then it stirred, agitated at times, but I was able to pacify it by keeping watch. Lately it scrambled and thrashed and I was powerless. I went there. I went there all the time and then I stayed there. The thought of impending doom loomed over me, tethered like a wild animal with a rope, making it impossible for me to get away. And nothing could convince me otherwise. I didn't want to hold her because as long as she was in Jack's arms she was his responsibility, as if I could pass my duty like a baton on to him. On his watch, she'd be fine.

That day in his office, Jack handed Mia to me, one hand under her head, the other supporting her legs, her body wrapped tightly in the blanket.

'I have to go to work, I'll be back in a few hours.' He presented the bundle as if she was an offering.

Suddenly images of a sacrificial goat slaughtered on a mossy stone altar flashed across my mind. I could almost feel the sticky blood between my fingers. I saw a radiant light the size of a baby's pupil glowing beneath the soft spot on her head. There was a demon trapped beneath that spot, a demon that made her reject me, made her cry and wail every time I touched her. If I could get to that spot, create a tiny hole, the demon could escape, and we could both find peace.

I remained still, didn't reach for Mia. Jack looked at me, bewildered. His lips curled into a half-smile as he tried to gain control. I grabbed the scissors from the pencil holder and left his office.

In the hallway powder room, as the scissors rested on the edge of the sink, I pumped antibacterial foam into my palms. I studied my reflection in the mirror and tried to come up with some sort of courage to tell him about the darkness and the shadows that had become my life. A life reduced to a small pinhole, depicting the entire world misshapen and distorted.

71

Through this tiny hole, I saw blood, I saw the cold stone of an altar, covered with sharp instruments, jagged and spiky and able to drill their way through soft fontanel tissue. A sharp instrument, like a pair of scissors, resting on the edge of the sink.

The nursery was fecund with smells: powder, oil, lotion, chamomile and rosemary, and dirty diapers. Jack had scolded me many times not to let them pile up.

The mobile above her crib — a colorful array of butterflies, June bugs, blossoms, and Tinker Bell at its center — moved gently in the breeze of the ceiling fan. The blinds were drawn, the curtains closed. The rocker sat silently next to her crib, covered in white linen, its footstool soiled with black shoe polish streaks from Jack's shoes.

I emptied the shopping bags, one by one, placed every item in baskets on the white shelf, convinced that as long as I kept her room in order, I could also keep the chaos at bay. I took out the clothes, and reached for the scissors to cut off the tags.

The cold metal rested in my hand. Before I even cut off a single tag, Jack walked in, Mia in his arms. She was quiet and her eyes scanned aimlessly about. Then she focused on the ceiling fan. Jack placed Mia's body against my chest, and kissed her on the forehead.

'I have to go to work, I'm already running late.'

I needed him to stay home, but I didn't know how to ask for it, didn't even know what exactly

I needed from him. Was I supposed to admit defeat? Acknowledging I was a fake as a mother was no longer a concern of mine. This was beyond me, I had nothing left inside of me to give.

Jack gently brushed Mia's cheek with the back of his index finger. Her lips opened and the pacifier popped out of her mouth as if giving way to the pressure inside of her. Her lips searched for its comfort and came up empty. Her face contorted.

The front door slammed shut. Jack was gone and so was Mia's composure.

I held her inches away from my body as if distance between us could soothe her; take the edge off her discontent with my presence. She broke out in a wail, its volume increasing with every passing second. I turned to place her on the changing table when my eyes caught a glimpse of a shiny silver object. The light and the turning blades of the fan created ghostly shadows that prompted me to pick up the scissors and cradle them in my palm. Her body seemed to be vibrating, her crimson face determined to ignore the need to fill her lungs with air.

I willed myself to ignore the scissors, but they seemed to pulsate as if they had a life of their own. I pinched my eyes shut, yet the scissors floated up and towards me, first only inches, and then farther up, turning their sharp points towards Mia's skull, determined to release the glowing demon underneath its connective tissue.

I gently placed Mia in her crib. As I pulled my

hands up from under her body, I prayed that she would survive. Despite me.

That day, I knew I was capable of anything; capable of silencing her cries. That's when I knew her life was at stake. And I screamed and for the first time the volume of my screams topped hers.

★ ★ ★

Jack's 'few hours' that day turned into a full twelve-hour work day. I did the only thing I knew how to do; remain on autopilot all day. As I pressed my forehead against the window that night, waiting for his return, I tried to recall for how long he had been avoiding my company. Jack was becoming more and more detached, icy even, barely talking to me. Working late was no longer an exception but a rule and his distance added more insecurities to my already frazzled thoughts. He never answered his cell, hardly ever returned my calls at all. There were files he closed when I entered the room, the phone he tucked in his pocket when it rang and he had been shunning all physical contact. When was the last time he had hugged or kissed me, and for how long had he been secretive?

I watched Jack exiting a sleek black town car. When he walked through the front door his eyes were two seas of silent reproach.

'Sorry, I'm late,' he said meaning *if you had picked up the dry cleaning, I'd have been on time. And with all the time you have, why isn't dinner ready and why is the house still a mess?*

'Took me forever to get a cab,' he added.

His briefcase was already open, his BlackBerry in his hand.

'A cab?' Hadn't I just seen him exiting a town car?

We stared at each other for a moment, then I lowered my eyes. I knew I had changed physically, I could see it in Jack's eyes every time he looked at me. I weighed about as much as I did in high school, maybe even less. My facial features seemed to have corroded and I had aged a decade in the past two months. Before Mia, I had a haircut every couple of months. I used to go to the gym, yoga, Pilates, you name it. Now, I never seemed to have any energy anymore.

'You said you'd be back in a couple of hours.'

'What the hell, really?' Jack said. 'Can you tell me what you want from me? I just want to understand because I can't see how making money is not the right thing.'

I tried to work out what to say. How could I explain when my head felt so cluttered and fragile? For a fraction of a second he looked like a little boy about to listen to a parent preach, and I saw how afraid he was that I was going to say something else, would question him further, something neither one of us had the energy for. Even if there was another woman, I didn't have the energy to even entertain the thought for long periods of time. What else could it be? I wanted to ask him why he'd tell me he took a cab when he got out of a town car, and if he was having an affair, but I wasn't sure I really cared. His distance paled in comparison to whatever crazy I

75

had living inside of me.

Hey, honey, welcome home! Guess what, there's a demon trapped inside of our daughter's head and with every passing minute it's getting harder to resist the temptation of jamming a sharp object into her fontanel.

'She cried all day, Jack. I don't know what to do anymore.'

It's because of the demon.

'Did you take her out?'

You haven't left the house in days.

'All she does is cry. Why would I take her out?'

The demon is making her cry. If I can get to the demon, everything will be okay.

'Well, what *did* you do?'

I didn't answer.

Help me Jack, help me. I'm afraid of hurting her.

'She doesn't cry all the time, Estelle. She's not crying right now, is she? She cries sometimes, all babies do, that's how they communicate.' He plopped on the couch and opened his briefcase. 'I have work to do, let's talk later, okay?' Jack absentmindedly jabbed chopsticks at Chinese leftovers while hacking away on his BlackBerry.

'It's okay,' I said more to myself than Jack. I stared out the window, my reflection nothing but a distorted body in a sea of darkness.

Jack's mood tended to improve the sleepier he became. Later, in bed, he caught me staring at the ceiling. He asked, his voice now soft and gentle, what I was thinking about.

'Dark, horrible thoughts,' I answered but kept my voice light and cheerful. 'Demons. Blood.

Murder. That kind of stuff.'

He brushed my words off with a half-hearted smile. 'Well then . . . as long as it's nothing serious. You can always get a sitter a couple of times a week. I'll help out as much as I can.'

Which means what? You hold her while I get a bottle?

'Sure,' I said. Our conversations had turned into a distorted reality we both liked to believe in. There was nothing he could do for me.

'Well, then let's not dwell on it.'

'Yeah, let's not,' I said and felt a cold fist tightening around my heart.

'I'm sorry about earlier, how was your day?' Jack said, flipped over and pulled the blanket over his shoulders.

'Just the usual.'

Let me see. I haven't slept longer than one hour continuously for the past five months. I use wet wipes more often than I shower. The thought of tomorrow being just like today makes me want to jump off a bridge. Any moment I'll hit rock-bottom which I imagine to be similar to the bottom of a dark well. Murky ankle-deep water, toad cadavers floating atop the slimy water's surface, spider webs full of dried-up cocooned bugs and beetles. And that's before I light a match and look closely.

Jack's breathing was slow and steady. I didn't have to look at him to know that he was asleep.

But it really didn't matter because even if he was awake, he couldn't bear half of what I had living inside of me.

8

The very next night — Jack again phoned me telling me he'd be late — I parked in front of his office building and kept an eye on the front desk behind the glass doors. Was Jack hiding something? A thought had grown, slowly at first and I was reluctant to listen to it, but lately the voice had become louder. I wanted to see for myself, after all, had I not asked for it? Was I not incapable as a mother and just as incapable as his wife? I couldn't blame him, looking in the rearview mirror seeing myself, couldn't blame him at all. Even I didn't recognize the woman staring back at me, pale and haggard.

I sat in my car, watched the traffic lights change and cars float by, and I waited until the security guard made his rounds. I took the elevator up to the fifth floor and found all the offices dark, except Jack's.

I couldn't make sense of the contorted voices drifting towards me through Jack's office door, and so I imagined what hands were doing, where tongues slithered like snakes, what pieces of clothing were draped over office chairs or bunched around ankles like turtlenecks, what the room smelled like. As I listened to the voices and the laughter, I observed myself in the glass door panel, and I was dumbfounded by the woman I had become. No longer a woman, really, but a crone, in baggy clothes and stringy hair with a chilly triumphant cackle. I knew I was helpless, for the crone's powers were infinite.

Seconds after I began pounding the door with my fists, Jack ripped open the door, looked at me, with surprise at first, then his eyes turned into rage. I didn't speak, just turned and ran. I reached my car, shaking, unable to think, but I managed to drive home. When I pulled into the driveway, I was surprised I had made it there.

Aashi, the sitter, was asleep on the couch in Mia's room. A medical student from India, chronically sleep-deprived yet easy-going and patient with Mia's colicky behavior, she smelled of cardamom and anise and her upper lip appeared darker than the rest of her face.

My hand still hovered over her shoulder when she opened her eyes.

'Ms Paradise, she didn't wake up at all. I fed her around ten, and she fell back asleep right away,' she whispered and brushed a blanket of black hair from her face, her colorful bangles dancing on her wrist.

'She must have been really tired,' I said. 'We spent all day at the park, all that fresh air . . . ' What sounded like a pleasant outing had been nothing more but a screaming baby in a stroller until she fell asleep out of sheer exhaustion.

I looked over at Mia, picture perfect in her crib, her face angelic and placid while earlier she had thrashed her hands towards my face, her mouth a gaping wound.

Aashi left and I wandered around the house, unable to settle. I found myself in front of Jack's office. I didn't want to snoop; the trip to his office earlier, now nothing more than a moment of lunacy — but Jack was going to demand an explanation and I had nothing to give him. Nothing but a sea of irrationality. He was going to ask questions, he'd want to know what had possessed me to do what I had done. I needed a logical reason, proof of his infidelity, proof that he couldn't be trusted any longer. I had to find a picture, a letter, a photograph, anything that would justify my outburst.

I stood in the doorway, taking in the shelves and filing cabinets. I had no idea what I was even looking for. Jack had started paying all the bills after Mia was born, handled all the paperwork, and I was glad he did. There wasn't another chore I could manage, especially not anything that involved deadlines. But maybe his taking over the finances was just a way of increasing control over the woman who had floundered. It was ironic that the differences that brought us together — Jack's sense of purpose, and his attraction to my carefree attitude towards life and, as he saw it, unpredictability — were the very things that were also driving us apart. That and the fact that I was an absolute failure as a mother.

The floorboards creaked as I entered the office and a familiar aroma of leather greeted me. Like an observer I stood beside myself, watched a woman scan fake paneling between rows of books, push at conspicuous spots. I observed her as she looked around, expecting an antique oil painting to fall off the wall, an envelope yellowed by age dropping to the ground, containing some

80

clandestine content. The woman pulled open the desk drawers. Her fingers slipped, almost snapping her nails off, as she tried to open a locked drawer. I watched her run her fingertips alongside the bottom of the desk's surface. She pushed here and there, looked under the keyboard and mouse pad and in the desk organizer. Reality greeted her harshly: no hidden drawers, no secret compartments, just a piece of contemporary office furniture. The woman jerked back into reality when the phone rang.

I backed away from the desk. The chair fell to the floor. *Thud.* The phone continuously nagged to be picked up.

Ring.

Ring.

Its pesky urgency was followed by a faint gurgle of an infant echoing through the house. The baby monitor on Jack's desk with its light display indicated the volume of Mia's cries. Six out of ten. Then the lights alternated from the middle scale of the digital display all the way to the top. The phone went silent and so did the baby monitor. I looked at the clock on the wall. It was midnight.

The phone rang again, slicing the air with urgency. I wiped the tears that were running down my neck, trailing inside my sweater.

Once again, the gurgling baby monitor turned into a whimper, the whimper into a howl and then into a full-blown bellow. The lights remained at the very top of the display window, until one last gurgle drifted off into the distance. Then there was silence. I left the study and went

81

through the bedroom into Jack's walk-in closet. A masterpiece of built-in shelves constructed of maple wood and hardware of brushed steel, next to mine, separated by a wall, both accessible by individual doors. Jack's dress shirts, arranged by color, immaculately pressed, aligned on one wall, his shoes along the other. I looked up at the top row of storage shelves, reachable only with the attached rolling ladder.

Reluctantly I passed Jack's full-length mirror in which he checked his designer suits, belts, and shoes every morning, afraid of the woman I'd encounter. I stepped closer and she stared back at me. I tried to force a winsome smile, yet her opaque eyes seemed empty, like doll's eyes. Not one of those pretty dolls with an elaborate dress and curly hair, no, less than that, really more like a rag doll with crooked button eyes. I was unable to lift my gaze off her for she was familiar, a grotesque twin, a chilling replica of myself. When did the woman in the mirror become so powerful, so potent that I allowed her to make off with my prized possessions? My composure, my sanity, my joy, and the part of me that was a mother. The figure in the mirror was a stranger, one who looked at me with anger.

White noise on full blast. A voice escaped the subdued grain of the maple shelves, and unlike mine, it made sense.

The box, it said. *Where is the box?*

The box that didn't fit with the rest of the items in the closet?

Yes, that one.

The box that was old and torn, which I

82

noticed every time I hung up his clean clothes, he moved from the overhead storage one week to a lower shelf the next?

Yes, the old yellowed photo box with reinforced metal holes, rectangular and flat, larger than a shoebox.

Am I supposed to look for it and open it?

Yes, look for it. Then open it.

I pulled the ladder to the far corner of the shelf, its metal balls sliding along the tracks, humming like a swarm of hornets. I kicked off my shoes, and climbed up.

There it was. A quite unremarkable and ordinary cardboard box. I managed to climb down the ladder without dropping it, sat it on the floor and knelt next to it.

The box was cumbersome to open; the lid had to be lifted on both ends simultaneously. I recognized the castle logo in the lower right-hand corner: Rosenfeld, Manhattan — one of the largest wedding gown stores in New York, maybe even the country.

I parted the tissue paper. Photos with scalloped edges, tinged yellow by time, depicting people unknown to me. A little boy in a blue coat, a woman standing next to him, leaning on him, her arm around his shoulders.

A property deed. Jack had mentioned that he had flipped properties while in Law School but I didn't know he owned a house. A deed for a brownstone on North Dandry in Brooklyn.

Before I could make sense of the deed, I came across a black pouch, heavy in my hand. I felt the shape of a gun through the velvety fabric. I removed the revolver from the pouch and cradled it in my hand. It seemed old-fashioned, but I really knew next to nothing about guns. I pointed it away from me and randomly pushed the cylinder and it swung to the right. It was empty.

Below the black pouch was a concealed handgun license card, laminated, with Jack's information. I never knew Jack owned a gun, let alone a license to carry, but it seemed logical for a lawyer to have one. Tucked in the corner was a full box with bullets. The gun I could stomach, lawyers owning guns is not unheard of, what was hard to believe was the fact that it had been there all along and I never knew.

I took a few bullets and cradled them in the palm of my hand. They were cold and made a gentle clinking sound when they touched. I stood up and filled up the chamber and engaged the cylinder.

I froze when I heard the ticking of a wristwatch. A crinkly plastic sound of a diaper demanded my attention. A whiff of baby powder and the stench of deceit, a combination that had the power to silently command me.

I looked up. There was Jack, standing in the closet, Mia in his arms, squirming, arching her back. There I was, gun in hand. Just in the nick of time I hid it behind my back, slowly backing into his dress shirts.

He stared at me, his eyes blank. I kicked the box and it slid under his dress shirts, the Berber carpet allowing it to glide like a ghost to a clandestine hiding place. I needn't have worried,

84

Jack was focused on the usual.

'Didn't you hear her cry?' Icicles around his every word. Again, I wasn't vigilant enough. Again, I failed to be the mother I should have been.

There were words Jack never said, words Jack never used, yet I had heard him say them over and over again — *flawed, unfit. A bad mother, a bad wife.* I had no business being there. I had no business being at his office earlier, in his closet, his house, his life. I had no business being the mother of his child.

'What's this?' I said holding up the deed in front of him. 'All you ever talk about is money. How we can't afford this, and how we have to save more. You are making us out to be broke. It's always about money.' I was surprised by the strength of my voice. Everything was wrong. Jack, Mia, the ticking clock, the gun, the photographs, the property deed. 'How come we are struggling when you own a brownstone, Jack? Explain that to me? What's the place worth, a million?'

'Own? I don't own anything. The property is heavily mortgaged. I wanted to flip it within a few months but there were problems with the permits. I've been carrying two mortgages. Come on now, tell me you understand real estate? The moment I'm one payment short the bank takes everything.'

'Were you ever going to tell me?'

'I was in over my head, okay? Is that what you want me to say? I didn't know what I was doing? There, are you happy now?'

His posture wilted, he looked like a little boy;

small, softened, less confident.

'Jack — '

'I'm not rich, Estelle. Not by any means. And I never said we were broke. I never used that word. All I said was we should be frugal with money. And that . . . ' he pointed at the papers in my hand, 'is nothing more than a property deed to a brownstone in shambles with a huge mortgage on it. I took a risk and it didn't pay off. Are you happy now?'

I stared at him, suddenly realizing that I knew next to nothing about him. Buying and selling houses was one thing, but taking on such a risky and expensive project, one that by his own admission failed miserably, when he didn't even own a toolbox?

'I'm working on it. The permits have come in, they are in the process of completing the renovations. It's not a big deal. It's just an investment property. You make it seem like it's such a betrayal on my part. What did you want me to do? Tell you I'm behind on a mortgage I can't afford? Worry you even more? You're doing a great job at that already.'

'I'm your wife, I think I ought to know about our finances.'

'There wasn't any trouble until you started with your obsessions, all those doctor visits while you were pregnant, and all those tests you insisted on, all those specialists you consulted, over nothing. Do you have any idea how much I had to pay for those tests and doctor visits that you went to without any referral? It cost me a fortune.'

'Everything is always about money for you. I'm trying to get help for our daughter.'

'She doesn't need help. She doesn't need another test, another doctor. She needs you to be her mother. So don't make this about me. You are the one who — '

'The one who spent all your money on needless tests.'

'I didn't say that. But I'm the one paying those medical bills.' He raised his voice louder now, I could feel him dropping the façade. 'We have perfectly adequate health insurance. But you insisted on all those specialists. And I get it, you know I get it. You were worried. But you didn't stop there either, did you? Even after Mia was born, you continued . . . '

I could tell he was looking for words, looking to put a name on my madness. Am I even mad? Was there such a thing as a little bit crazy? A lick of mad? I worried about Mia. I still do. Every waking minute.

'You've been feeding that dragon ever since, haven't you?'

I chuckle. Nice analogy.

Feeding the dragon? But what about our daughter? I knew what he was going to say. But what kind —

'You started taking a perfectly healthy baby from doctor to doctor. And that's not normal.'

Normal? What kind of mother would I be, Jack, if I didn't try to help my child? What kind of mother would I be?

'There's something wrong with her. She cries too much. Don't you get that?' My accusation

87

seemed to trigger additional resentment on his part, and, as always, Mia's excessive crying was just a figment of my imagination.

'There's nothing wrong with her, *nothing*. The fact that you can't handle a baby doesn't mean there's something wrong with *her*. You've been taking Mia from doctor to doctor and they all tell you the same thing. A colic, she'll grow out of it. You can't continue to insist on all these tests that make no sense. I've been allowing you to do this for the longest time but I need you to stop this madness.'

Jack stared at me for a long time. Then he took a step back. His voice was calm but his neck was covered in blotches.

'I don't know what to do but I can't allow you to go on like this.'

Jack's mind was not prepared to wrap itself around such an unwelcome emotion; *he didn't know what to do*. He had been trying to put me back together but now he realized he was finally out of options. You shatter into a couple of pieces, Jack can put you back together again. But when I shattered, the pieces were too many to count. It wasn't even a matter of how many, but how much. Like sand. Uncountable.

His decision to get married because I was pregnant had backfired on him. Not only was I not keeping up my end of the bargain, but at the same time I kept him from fulfilling his. There was work to be done, lots of work. An infinite workload of case files, preparing witnesses, and interviews. And even though he was exhausted, I knew that the pressures of his job felt perversely comfortable to him compared to what awaited him at home every night. I threw my head back and burst into an overly animated gesture of joy.

'This whole marriage was a mistake. Come on, Jack, this is your way out.'

Jack walked towards me as if to grab me. 'Just listen to yourself . . . you're irrational. You follow me to work, you come to my office, embarrass me? That's not rational. I don't know what's going on, but you need help.'

I just stared at him as I watched him pause just long enough to shake his head.

Then his voice turned to ice. 'I find you here, in my closet, while Mia is screaming her head off. Does that strike you as rational?'

Mia stirred, her little hands reaching for something invisible, sounds of distress escaping her lips. Jack's eyes were darting left and right. When he finally spoke, his voice was down to a whisper.

'You're irrational and I no longer trust you with my daughter. This stops tonight.' He kept switching Mia from one arm to the other while she was growing visibly upset. Tears started to well up in her eyes and short of a bottle nothing was going to calm her down. 'Estelle, this can't go on any longer. Why can't you just — '

'Just what? Be normal? Is that what you want me to be? Normal?'

He stood there, didn't say a word. A normal woman was all he wanted. And I was everything but. *Cha ching, you lose, Jack.*

'You need to get help,' he said. 'I'm taking tomorrow off and we'll go see somebody. You need professional help.'

I stood there, waiting until he left the closet, cautious not to turn my back on him. I went to the kitchen and, while the bottle warmed in the microwave, I slid the gun into the back of the junk drawer.

I fed Mia, put her in her crib, and went into the study where Jack was perched over a case file. He looked as if nothing had happened at all. When he saw me, his demeanor changed. He looked agitated.

I sat in a chair in front of his desk and crossed my legs. I managed a smile and hoped my face didn't seem too contorted. I wanted to appease him, to seem as rational as possible.

'There's something we need to talk about,' Jack said.

I took in a deep breath, then I exhaled. 'This is when you're going to tell me about your girlfriend, the one from your office earlier?'

'There's no girlfriend. I . . . I wanted to tell you when the moment was right, but hell, no moment is right lately.' He paused for a second. 'The woman at my office was Victoria Little-field.'

The name sounded familiar but I couldn't quite place it.

'She's from the DA's office and we were discussing a position.' He got up, stepped closer and lowered his voice to a whisper. 'Until you barged in like a maniac that is. I can't even blame her that she didn't offer me the job once she found out I have a lunatic for a wife. This job is all I ever wanted. Ten years from now I could be DA. But that doesn't matter anymore now, does it?'

His eyes communicated what he didn't say out loud. That the way I acted earlier was the wrecking ball that tore a gaping hole into the walls of our already fragile marriage. And his career. Jack wasn't an adulterer, affairs are messy and unpredictable, no, Jack wanted to become DA and I had busted yet another dream of his; no happy family, no career.

'You've no idea what I've been going through,' he said. 'Sometimes I drive an hour out of my way just to get gas. That hour in the car, by myself, is the closest I've come to normality in months.'

I held back the tears. He was a trapped man. A man trapped by a woman who didn't measure up.

'I know you do more, you have more responsibility with Mia, but I get up in the middle of the night and feed her and I still go to work the next day. And it's not like I'm just shuffling paperwork. I can't come home every time you call. I've been working my entire career for this job and you . . . ' He paused, deflated. 'It stops tonight. Tomorrow you're going to see a doctor.'

★ ★ ★

When I arrived at the clinic, I was late. Jack was waiting by the door, looking impeccable in his suit, dark gray, Hugo Boss — his favorite — stylish and simple, he wore it, as usual, with a

91

white shirt and a gray tie.

When he spotted me, he looked tired. And irritated. I could tell by the way he raised an eyebrow as I walked up. His forehead was deeply wrinkled, furrows I hadn't noticed before.

'Sorry I'm late.' I raised my face and he lightly brushed his lips across my cheek. I felt guilty. After all, Jack's time was precious.

Jack was all business during our appointment. His lint-free suit, his starched shirt, all signs that he'd made a success of his life. He told the doctor how I was obsessing over 'minute details' and how I didn't want to 'accept colic as a diagnosis' and how he'd been able to 'hold things together' all by himself.

I watched him steal a glance at me while he spoke, probably wondering how we arrived at this implausible moment when all he'd ever done was 'provide and support.' He was the perfect husband and father yet here I was, frazzled and sunken in.

At the end of our appointment I realized the doctor wasn't a psychiatrist or therapist, just a family practitioner. Because specialists cost money, and Dr Wells is capable of prescribing an antidepressant.

Dr Wells took one look at me, got out his prescription pad and scribbled on it. 'If nothing's happening we'll just adjust the dosage.' Then he told me to come back after a month so I could tell him all about the improvement. 'Once the baby sleeps through the night, life will be different. Some new mothers need adjusting. Give it some time.'

You poor sap, a bit of time and a good night's sleep is what I need?

'Right,' I said, smiled, and cradled my purse. It was heavy. Inside was Jack's gun, vibrating joyously.

★ ★ ★

On our way home, in the car, Jack seemed appeased. In his world you solved a problem by coming up with a remedy and the fact that the bottle of pills in my purse would make everything okay was just the way he knew the world to be. An orange bottle with three refills and his life was back to normal.

'Tell me you're going to be okay.' His voice was soft, fragile almost.

He sounded caring but I knew Jack, he never remained concerned for long. He was pragmatic to a fault and this was all alien to him.

'Please take the medication and just get on with it.'

'It?' That's more like him. *Just get on with it.*

'Life, get on with life. Take the baby out, meet other moms in parks, I don't know, whatever moms do.'

I was tired of him selling me his logic like a snake oil salesman offering a cure for ulcers. It was laughable. Mingle with other moms and a pill a day will take my sorrows away.

'It's not complicated if you really think about it.' He put his arm around me, pulling me towards him. 'You overanalyze everything, that's what your problem is. It's not about being perfect. It's about changing a diaper, warming up a bottle.'

His embrace felt staged. I looked out the car window, focusing on a tree almost as tall as the building behind it. I wondered if the roots of a tree were really as deep as a tree was high. It seemed impossible almost, a secret part of the city, invisible to its inhabitants. Once you knew it was there, it seemed terrifying.

★ ★ ★

The pills gave me strange dreams. I hardly slept at all and I was so tired I couldn't care less about anything else but pretending to be okay. When I told Jack I wanted to stop the medication, he frowned.

'But they make my hair fall out,' I complained.

He glanced at my hairline. *Are you sure?* his eyes seemed to say as if I was attempting to fit a round shape in a square hole.

'Those are not side effects according to this,' Jack said and flipped over the medication flier. 'Dry mouth, skin rash, nausea, vomiting, and shallow breathing. Hair loss is not one of them. Maybe you should take some vitamins.'

'What about numb hands and feet?'

'Go to a gym, one that has childcare. Maybe you're not moving enough.'

What about the fact that I'm just pretending to be okay? I wanted to ask. *What about being a con? Is that a side effect?*

★ ★ ★

Other than that I just cared less. Cared less about not caring, my body in the grasp of nausea and dizziness from the pills. Mia and I muddled through. There were days I felt better followed by days that were worse. Everything seemed lulled and life had lost its edge. Mia grew and gained weight, yet the crying never stopped.

Jack seemed to be in a better mood and I continued the medication. About a month or so later, Jack came home early from work. He was cheery and handed me a box of Chinese takeout.

'Your favorite,' he said.

'I think you've been doing a lot better,' he said. 'Don't you think so?' he asked, but didn't wait for my response. He spoke of money and our credit, and that the high mortgage payments of the brownstone weren't going away anytime soon. And no one really knew how long it'd take to find a buyer with the market the way it was. He couldn't be in that amount of debt and have a possible foreclosure hanging over his head and expect to get a DA job. But that he'd come up with a plan.

'A plan,' I said, 'what kind of plan?'

'We've run out of options. I had to make a decision.' His words flew by, hardly reached me. 'Here's the deal,' he said, 'the economy is in a shambles, huge salaries for associates at big law firms are no longer, but there's money to be made in foreign exchange deals, equity and debt. There's a company in Chicago.'

'We're moving?' I asked.

'Kind of. The brownstone is part of my plan. Renters won't put up with the noise of the construction. With the money I make in Chicago we can pay the mortgage, finish the renovations and in a year at the most we'll be able to either sell it or rent it out.'

There was so much energy in his voice. Plans were his thing. The coordinated and organized formation of solutions. I had also been part of the plan once, before I changed. Now it was all about getting out of debt and everything else would just fall into place. I had my pills and I was getting on with it. He looked at me with his eyes blazing as if he'd just solved all our problems. He was smart, I knew that, I loved that about him, but he was also shrewd. Driven. He was hardwired to get what he wanted, and whatever Jack wanted, Jack was going to get.

'I've accepted a job with Walter Ashcroft, a legal staffing firm in Chicago,' he said. 'I'll be moving to Chicago. And I've arranged for you to stay in the brownstone in Brooklyn.'

* * *

Jack wasn't a bad man. I was neither seeing him with rose-colored glasses nor was I overly critical. We used to be gentle with each other. We both had good intentions. We had hope, no, more than hope, faith even. Tender moments when unpacking groceries, putting up the Christmas tree, spending a Sunday afternoon on a blanket in the park. And now he was moving me into a brownstone in Brooklyn, one that was, according to him, under renovation but quite habitable. I needed him to be there but I didn't

96

know how to ask for that.

Two months later I was in my car on the way to North Dandry while Jack was at the airport waiting for his flight to Chicago.

'I can't say I like it but I don't see any other way right now,' he said when I called him from the car on my way to the brownstone. 'The project manager is living in the upper apartment while he's supervising the construction on the other two units. His name is Lieberman. If you need anything and I'm not available, call him. You won't have to lift a finger. The movers will unload and unpack. It'll be the easiest move you've ever made.'

'I don't need anyone to check up on me, Jack.'

'I'm just saying if you need anything, call him. I'll be gone for three weeks, four tops, after that I'll come home for a weekend. I told you that last week, remember?'

Was he trying to tell me that I was senile?

'I'll fly home as often as possible, I promise, depending on the workload.'

I heard muffled voices and the sound of him switching his cell from one ear to the other, then a metal detector alerting and a voice telling someone to step aside. I imagined Jack, his arms raised, the handheld metal detector following the contours of his body.

'I'm at the gate. Take your meds, okay?'

'Sure.' I knew Jack had been counting the pills and only stopped after I had phoned in the refills. The truth was I could no longer remember how it felt to be normal and I wanted to believe that I would get better, eventually. It

97

could take weeks or months, the doctor had told me, and I didn't see any alternative. And so I appeased everybody and told myself any day now it would all be better.

I swerved to the right and hit the curb. It took me only a few seconds and the car was back under control.

'Bye, I'll call you, okay?'

I didn't answer, hung up the phone and threw it on the passenger seat. I had always been a careful and defensive driver, I didn't even recognize myself anymore. I was acting like a lunatic. If I looked in the rearview mirror and saw a foil beanie on my head, I wouldn't be surprised.

I spotted the North Dandry sign and pulled up to the curb. I killed the engine and looked at the brownstone. In the back Mia's contorted body was hanging over the side of the seat, her head turned at an odd angle. She had fallen asleep. And I had failed to buckle her seatbelt.

NEW DETAILS RELEASED: MOTHER OF ABDUCTED INFANT WAS FOUND UPSTATE ONE WEEK AFTER THE DISAPPEARANCE

Brooklyn, NY — Police have released new details in the abduction of 7-month-old Mia Connor. According to an unnamed source, the mother, Estelle Paradise, was found in a ravine near Dover, NY, about three hours from NYC. She was found days after the actual disappearance of the infant. Estelle Paradise had critical injuries to her head and her torso and was treated for hypothermia and other serious accident-related injuries.

A man walking his dogs made the discovery. 'They just took off,' he said about the two Chocolate Labradors, 'like hounds from hell. There was no holding them back. Usually I whistle and they come, but they ran down the ravine. I thought I'd lost them, then I heard the barking.'

The ravine locals refer to as 'Echo Ravine' makes an 80-foot drop to the riverbed below.

Officials said it took six hours to remove the injured mother from the site due to the steepness of the embankment. The Dover Fire Department assisted with the rescue.

The mother was first taken to a Dover hospital and later transported to a hospital in New York City. She has been spending the past week in County Medical and her condition has been revised from serious to fair. No official source has commented on her exact injuries.

No further information regarding the abduction of Mia Connor has been released.

9

'Detectives.' Dr Baker nods at them on his way out. 'Thirty minutes tops. If her vitals make somersaults I'll put my foot down.'

The detectives wait until Dr Baker has left the room.

I recognize one of the detectives but not the other. Just yesterday they had questioned me and it seems like they should be spending their time looking for Mia. I have nothing more to add but the detectives regard me like an insect under a microscope. I can't read their faces, they are all but blank.

'My name is Detective Wilczek. I'm with the Special Victims Unit and I'll be heading the investigation. You remember Detective Daniel?' Wilczek is in his forties, buzz cut, thin and wiry. His nails are bitten to the quick. He points at the middle-aged rotund man. 'We appreciate you talking to us, Mrs Paradise,' he says and pulls out a notebook.

Dr Baker has removed the morphine pump and I try to ignore the pain behind my left eye.

'I'd like to go over everything again, if you don't mind. I understand you must be getting tired of repeating the same thing over and over but I prefer to hear it from you.'

Traces of morphine linger in my system and I long for the warmth that went through my entire body at the push of a button, making me feel weightless. Everything was surreal then but now my body is heavy. My heart sinks. They would lead with the fact that she's safe if they had found her and so I resist the urge to ask them.

I walk them through it, my routine during that first month since I had moved into the brownstone, Jack's job in Chicago, the days leading up to her disappearance, the morning I found her crib empty. While Wilczek takes notes, he never interrupts me. When he doesn't take notes he twists the narrow wedding band on his right hand with his thumb.

'Tell me about the locks. Why did you have those locks installed?'

'Just to be safe.'

'Did you feel threatened in any way? Did anyone make a threat towards you?'

'No, nothing like that. I was basically living there by myself most of the time, it was just a precaution.'

'Nothing odd happened in the days before your daughter disappeared?'

'Not that I can think of.' I want to tell them that I have already answered all these questions but given the fact that one of them is from another department, I decide to go along with the questioning.

'Who had access to the apartment?'

I think about it for a while. 'Jack. The movers. The man who installed the locks.' Suddenly my pulse quickens. 'The guy who installed the locks . . . he was odd, he looked at me the entire time.' I'm grasping at straws but for all it's worth, they haven't asked me about him yet.

'We dusted the entire apartment for prints. The ones on the door are from the gentleman who installed the locks. We checked out his alibi and he's been eliminated. He takes care of his elderly parents. There are a few from your husband, mainly on the furniture. Some other prints on the furniture checked out as prints from the movers.' Wilczek's voice turns composed, almost kind. 'Were there any strange phone calls? Anyone watching you? Anything out of the ordinary? Even something insignificant to you might be a very important fact.'

Once, there was an imprint in my bed, the sheets crumpled, as if a supernatural visitor had taken the liberty of living here in my absence. Then one day I came home and the mirror appeared crooked. Was I imagining it, was my view of the world skewed somehow? My first thought was; there's someone here. But the house was empty. So I dismissed it. The next time it was the coffee table, haphazardly pushed aside. There were visible dents in the rug, as if my mother's ghost, annoyed by my lack of furniture placement, had come to rearrange my table properly. Remembering the crooked mirror, I dismissed it, as if I was accepting my warped and disturbed home, completely letting go of all logic.

'Nothing out of the ordinary,' I say.

And then: 'Tell me again why you didn't call 9-1-1?'

'I had the phone in my hand, dialing the number, and then I saw that her bottles were gone. Her clothes, everything. I didn't understand what had happened.'

'So you did what?'

'I looked for her, everywhere. In my car. In alleys, around the neighborhood, everywhere. I asked a homeless woman on the corner if she'd seen anything. I even looked in Dumpsters.' I catch myself but it's too late. The word *Dumpster* echoes in my mind. It just didn't sound right. *I looked for my daughter in Dumpsters.* Why did I even say that?

'You went up and down the street you say; did you ask for help?' Wilczek's voice remains calm.

I shake my head.

'How about the people working construction in the house?'

'It was a Sunday, everybody was gone.'

'How about your neighbor? There was one other person living in the building, right? Did you ask him for help?'

'He visits his sister on the weekends. He leaves on Friday afternoons. I called him a few times but I couldn't even leave a message.'

'What did you think happened to your daughter?'

Focus on his question. 'I didn't have any idea.'

'Did you call your husband?'

'No.' I lower my head and wonder where I'd be right now if I had called Jack right away. Jack would have called the police, he would have rushed home, and he would have known what to do, because Jack always knows what to do. Not calling him was just another one of my blunders. 'He had just left and started his new job. He was under a lot of pressure. I knew it would be hard for him to call every day and he was due to come

104

home in a week or two for a few days.'

Wilczek leans forward, adjusting his tie. 'Why didn't you ask him for help? He's a lawyer, he's got resources and connections other parents of abducted children only dream of.'

'I . . . no . . . I was confused. I thought many things.'

'Did he call you at all since he'd left New York?'

'Yes, we talked. Not at length, no, just how are you, how's the baby, everything okay, how's the house coming along, that sort of thing.'

'Tell us why you bleached your entire house.'

I bleached my house? Oh, yeah, that. I remember the bleach. The acid burning in my nose and eyes, struggling to breathe as if someone had his hands around my lungs, squeezing them, my wheezing and coughing. When I returned to North Dandry, after I left the precinct, a stench hit me, a fusion of coffee grounds and dead air behind windows that had gone unopened for days, maybe even weeks. And then I saw the filth; the grimy drain and the moldy ring around the faucet. I went to work among buckets, rags and steel wool, when one toothbrush wore down, I got another from the bathroom drawer. I dipped the bristles in bleach and scoured the grout between the floor tiles, ran ice cubes through the disposal. I moved from room to room, removing objects from shelves, mopping, wiping, scouring. As my hands started to burn and my cuticles all but dissolved, I realized that this sense of mission was designed to make something right, something that I wasn't sure I had wronged to begin with.

I cleaned with bleach, yes I did. Detective Wilczek wants to know why, and who could blame him, I know what he is insinuating. All I remember is that I didn't want to leave a mess behind, but I don't know why. And I recall that by the time I was done, the sun had gone down twice and come up once.

I look out the window as if to find the answer in the distance. The detective waits for me to answer but I have no logical explanation for him and so I remain quiet. He seems oddly content with my silence and just moves on as if he didn't expect a coherent answer to begin with.

'I need you to explain why you left the precinct without reporting the disappearance. Picking up the phone and then not reporting her missing after you realize her things have disappeared is one thing. But then you decide you need to talk to the police after all. You walk to the station but you don't ask for help. You must understand that this doesn't make sense. There's no intruder, no break-in. Just a missing baby and a mother who can't remember anything.'

'Dr Baker told you I have amnesia, right?'

'We are aware.' Wilczek scoots his chair closer, his eyes appear soft. 'But children don't just disappear out of locked apartments. They don't disappear without a trace. Are you telling me that someone walked through walls and made away with a closet full of clothes and a dozen baby bottles? Boxes of diapers? And all that while you were sleeping?'

I have to agree with him. It sounds like a melodramatic soap opera.

'You missed Mia's doctor's appointment,' Wilczek continues. 'Some sort of scheduled vaccination. You've been to all previous appointments, but not that one. Why didn't you go?'

'I forgot.' I didn't go to her scheduled vaccination appointment? I would never just miss a vaccination, there must have been a reason. Something irks me but I can't put my finger on it.

'The daycare said you never returned with her shot records.'

'The daycare needed the complete shot records to enroll her and since I missed the vaccination appointment, there was no reason to go back. And it wasn't childcare, really, just a couple of hours here and there.'

'Did you reschedule the appointment?'

'I was going to but then she . . . ' I pinch my lips shut. I need to be alone, I need to think this through, everything's unclear, too vague to put in words.

'She what?'

'She disappeared.'

Wilczek lowers his head and studies his notebook.

'Tell me about the homeless woman.'

'There was a homeless woman on the corner, I'd seen her before, and I thought if she'd been there all night, she might have . . . ' It dawns on me that if he knows about her, he's undoubtedly spoken to her. 'You talked to her? What did she tell you?'

I watch his eyes fly over the notes in his little

book. 'I don't want to go by what other people tell me when I can hear it from you.'

'She was confused. She had a dog with her. That's all I remember.'

'Tell me about the car seat,' Wilczek says.

I hear a peeping sound behind me, speeding up. Then it hits me: I left a car seat on the curb and I gave the homeless woman my suitcase. I shake my head in disbelief. My heart is beating in my throat. How stupid and how random. Why did I do that?

'I don't know what to tell you.' I try to sound calm but I can feel the tears gathering behind my eyes. My heart is beating fast and my head is shaking from side to side. Anxiety tremors, according to Dr Baker. 'The accident caused me to forget what happened the days before. My memory only goes so far.'

'So there's something you're not telling me?'

'That's what I'm trying to explain to you. I don't know what I'm not telling you. I can't possibly know what I don't know.' I want to be cooperative, want to help, and so I curl my lips into something like a supportive smile and even though I catch myself, it's too late. He must have seen me smile because he pinches his lips shut.

'Time's up.' Dr Baker pokes his head in the room and shuts down the interview. When the door closes behind him, Wilczek gets up to leave.

'Did you find any blood?' The words escape before I can rein them back in. *Careful. Be more careful.*

'Blood? What kind of blood?' Det. Wilczek's facial expression is blank.

108

Are there different kinds of blood? Blood is blood. *Don't say that.*

'I'm just wondering if there was *any* blood.'

'We're waiting on forensics,' he says, 'but like I said, all that bleach . . . Call me if you can think of anything else. We'll talk again soon.'

I nod and close my eyes.

Minutes later, I stand up, unsteady at first, then I get the hang of it. I slide my feet more than lift them off the ground which makes walking easier. I reach for the doorknob. I can't resist the urge and peek out the door down the hallway and wonder what would happen if I just started walking. My guard leans forward ever so slightly when he detects movement.

A baby's wail travels down the hallway, straight through the open door, aiming directly into my auditory cortex, hitting it like an arrow piercing a bull's eye.

I slam the door shut. I lean against it as if I'm attempting to keep the acoustic waves at bay. I run my fingers through my hair, upwards, and hold my head, gently at first, then I pull my hair as hard as I can. My scalp starts to pulsate but the pain drowns out the baby's wails. If I could cut off my other ear to deafen the wails, I would.

Mia is gone and I'm the suspect.

And as I sit on the floor in my hospital room, a uniformed leg ever present by my door, and I pull my hair to dull the baby's cries from down the hall, I see myself not so much for what I am, but for what I'm not.

There's a word for my behavior; 'blunted affect,' a lack of emotional reactivity, a sign of trauma, brain injury. I'm not a tearful mother whose eyes are red and swollen, begging the kidnapper to return her child. I wish Dr Baker was here right now to see what this crying baby is doing to me. I'm not a pleading mother. Instead I say things that I find suspicious myself, I smile when I have no reason for happiness. I ask questions when clearly I don't remember. I can only imagine what the detectives are thinking right about now.

I've seen distraught mothers on TV, mothers who clutch their kid's beloved stuffed animal, mothers who promise they'll never stop looking. The fathers behind them, arms wrapped around them, families in support of them, wiping tears, trying to hold in their emotions. I've seen mothers on front pages, eyes glazed over, the Valium doing its job of delaying the pain for at least a few hours. The agony in the parents' eyes is painful for the onlookers, even translates through television sets — it is unrestrained, unedited, and raw.

And then there are the monsters. Monsters lying about the disappearance of their children, tearful pleas to phantom carjackers, Munchausen Syndrome lunatics running into emergency rooms, cradling dead or near-dead babies. Newborns stuffed in trash receptacles after being born in Walmart bathrooms. With their umbilical cords still attached. Not mere tragedies like forgetting a baby in the car, but intentional, deliberated, maybe even premeditated harm done to a helpless child. In which category do I fit?

Jack's words 'we can still fix this' echo in my

mind. Did I do something that needs fixing? I remember how I nervously carried her in my arms walking down steep stairwells, the pull of scissors and sharp objects, the way they seemed to beckon me, and how the cord of the lamp by her crib made me nervous. Sharp edges and blunt corners, heights atop stairs seemed tempting.

I have a suspicion. I won't tell anyone, but I whisper it to myself.

10

The day Jack left for Chicago I met the property manager in front of the brownstone on North Dandry. Jack had hired Yolanda Drake to oversee the renovations of the brownstone. She started talking the moment I got out of the car.

'Sometimes properties are . . . ' Yolanda paused and searched her mind for the right word, 'cursed,' she finally said and lifted her index finger.

'Cursed? Isn't that a bit over the top?' I narrowed my eyes in disbelief and gently straightened Mia's head, so as not to wake her. I couldn't believe that I had forgotten to strap her in.

'No, cursed is the right word. The contractor ran out of money, the subcontractors quit, workers stole materials from the jobsite, and no one got the appropriate permits. You name it, it went wrong with 517. I've never had a property that had so many problems. The contractors have been ordered to fulfill the contracts but they have to be supervised. No one is very happy at this moment, especially your husband. The property should have sold or rented months ago.'

I tried to look enthusiastic about the gossip she was so willingly sharing with me and nodded in agreement.

'Nothing like a disgruntled contractor forced to fulfill a contract, let me tell you. The insurance company paid for the claims but everybody is getting impatient. Brilliant idea to have someone on site at all times to make sure everything goes smoothly. David Lieberman's quite proficient and he keeps the workers in line. Lieberman reports to me, I report to your husband.'

Suddenly a sound startled me. It started off as a murmur, then turned into a loud crash, making me flinch. A cloud of dust emerged from a huge green metal container connected to a bright yellow construction chute in front of 517. Within seconds we were covered in a cloud of construction dust.

'Is there a provisional date of completion?' That's what Jack had called it. A provisional date of completion, meaning the moment when renters wouldn't be bothered by the noise any longer. I wondered how Jack thought my living here in the meantime would even remotely be a good idea.

'We're playing it by ear. Contractors are never on time.'

'My husband told me it was a matter of a couple of months.'

Yolanda Drake shifted her considerable weight from one foot to the other and raised her eyebrows. 'Anything is possible, I guess,' she said and handed me the key. 'It's all yours,' she added, wiped her hand on her pencil skirt, and walked away.

My eyes followed her until she disappeared around the corner. The key to 517 felt warm to the touch. I glanced back at the car. Mia was

113

peacefully asleep in the car seat, calmed by the humming engine from the ride over here.

I switched on the baby monitors and left one on the passenger seat and tucked the second one safely away in my purse. The temperature was a comfortable sixty degrees, the sky overcast. The tinted windows hardly allowed any visibility into the car's interior. I told myself that I wasn't even going to close the front door, and she'll be fine for a few minutes.

Apartment A1 was located on the first floor. I calculated I could get to the car in less than thirty seconds if Mia started to cry. I was reluctant to wake her, knowing it would result in another crying fit, making me think how hard it must be on her to respond to life with such violent protest. Every nap was hope on my part, hope that she'd wake up and be calmer, more content.

I manually locked the car so the remote locking sound didn't startle her and walked up the steps to the front door. It opened before I could fully insert the key. In front of me stood a man in steel-toed boots covered in wood shavings like coconut flakes on a cake. He stood on the threshold, the rim of the yellow hard hat shielding his eyes. He lifted his head and his eyes skimmed over me. He continued down the steps and turned to the left. I followed him with my eyes, down the sidewalk and up the block. His stride was wide, his torso upright.

I entered the building. I stood still just long enough to take in the scent of fresh paint and a faint odor of disinfectant. 'A1' in cursive, gold letters on the door straight ahead. To the left was a large opening taped shut with heavy duty tarp to keep the dust and debris out.

A hair-raising shriek made me reach for the baby monitor. The green display sat idle, a faint sound of white noise in the background. Then a whining sound turned into a throaty grind. I shut the monitor off, then back on. Nothing but white noise. When I inserted the key into the lock and pushed open the door, I realized the sound was coming from behind a tarp: carpenters sawing wood, framing walls or working on the hardwood floors.

The two thousand square feet apartment floors were solid cherry wood, native to upstate New York. The distance from the front to the back was an impressive forty feet. The hallway led through two parlor doors into the living room, which took up the entire back of the building. There were two rooms on the left; the kitchen and the dining room, eventually leading into the parlor. There were three rooms on the right; the first one the bathroom, the other two bedrooms.

My footsteps echoed through the rooms and the light flooding through the windows was harsh and uncomfortable. The walls were bleak, painted in an abrasive white. I inspected the doors and windows. A double cylinder deadbolt on the front door, a type of auxiliary lock that required a key to project or retract the deadbolt from either side. There was also a mortise lock, usually found in older buildings, making any attempt to break in practically impossible.

115

Suddenly the monitor unleashed violent static and then went silent again. I manually switched over to the second channel. Again, nothing but white noise. I switched back to the initial channel and heard a man's voice. Before I reached the car, baby monitor in hand, the monitor changed to a gentle buzz, then to a protest and finally an eruption. Mia's stuttering gasps interrupted by attempts to fill her lungs with air.

I dug into my purse for the car key and when I looked up, the man with the steel-toed boots I'd seen earlier stared at me. His eyes went from the car — echoing with screams — back to me, to the monitor in my hand. My cell phone rang and the moving company confirmed the address. When I turned back around, he had left.

★   ★   ★

A week later, I stood by the window, parted the curtain with my hands, and looked out into the fall night. It was almost dark and the streets were deserted except for a few people taking their dogs for a last pit stop before they'd curl up on couches or on the kitchen floor. Leaves tumbled about like discarded paper, following their destinies into storm drains, iron window grates, and curbside puddles.

I pulled the curtain, layered it midway where the panels met, and shut out the dark. Night falling on New York City was not my favorite time of day. The outside noises — the traffic, the hurried voices, and the screaming children in the

116

school courtyard across the street — never completely stopped but slowed down like a clock that needed winding.

With Jack being gone, initially, I felt more relaxed. It became apparent that not having him around, I demanded less of myself with every passing day. I skipped the shower in the morning and didn't feel guilty wearing the same clothes day after day. The first few days I stepped into my sweatpants still bunched up on the floor and pulled a random shirt out of a pile of clothes. After the first week I didn't even bother changing my clothes at all. I didn't worry about going to the market and I lived off crackers, oatmeal, and stale bagels. I did however wash Mia's clothes religiously, folded her bibs and socks and shirts, and dressed her every day.

A voice inside myself chastised me, telling me that still Mia wasn't sleeping through the night, still she was crying more than she should have, and it wore on me more and more. I didn't allow her to soothe herself to sleep like the doctor suggested, instead I rushed into her room and held her in my arms, squirming and arching her back. Her cries echoed through the house and I wondered how much longer I'd be able to hold on. Jack called frequently but our conversations were short; my pretending to be okay and Jack promising to come home for a weekend soon. I wondered how I'd ever manage to get the house in order and stock up the fridge. I mostly dozed off during inopportune times just to be awakened by Mia's cries. As the days bled into each other, I felt caught in a vicious and

117

never-ending cycle of sheer exhaustion and angry baby monitor displays running amok.

That day I jerked up from a half-sleep state, a buzz echoing in my head. I listened but it was quiet. I shut my eyes again. Three more buzzes sounded and I realized it must be the doorbell. I peeked through the hole but all I could make out was a shadowy outline of a man.

'Yes?' I said through the closed door.

'Mrs Paradise?'

'Yes?'

'David Lieberman.'

At first, the name meant nothing to me, and then I remembered Jack and the property manager mentioning the name of the upstairs tenant who was overseeing the renovations. I had a feeling he wasn't going to go away unless I talked to him.

'Just a minute,' I said, ignoring Mia wailing in her crib. I opened the door, chain still engaged, and looked at him through the gap.

'How's the pressure?' His voice was like silt, something you felt the need to wipe clean afterwards. Lieberman checked his hands and proceeded to clean the fingernails of one hand with the nails of the other.

'What?' I wanted to tell him to go to hell but he'd probably tell Jack and Jack would call, expecting me to scold myself for being rude.

'The pressure. The water pressure.'

'I'm sorry?'

'The water pressure.' He emphasized every syllable, as if I was either incapable of understanding English or partially deaf.

118

'What about it?' I tried to sound engaged and friendly because, according to Jack, Lieberman was here to help.

He cocked his head. 'Someone's crying in there,' he said.

'What can I do for you?' I said ignoring his comment. Mia was barely whining by then.

'If you pick her up she'll stop crying. I've been listening to her all day.' He gave me a stare. 'Not that the walls are particularly thin in this building, but noise travels.'

'What about the water pressure?' I tried to keep my face expressionless.

'Have you taken a shower lately?' he asked and looked me up and down through the crack in the door: my greasy hair, my wrinkled shirt, and the pants I'd been wearing for a week. 'There's a problem with the plumbing, they're working on the pipes.'

'I hadn't noticed.'

'She isn't going to stop crying until you pick her up.' His neck craned to see what was going on behind me.

I started to think that my expressionless face might be a mistake. 'Let me call you after I check, okay?'

I closed the door and on my way to the nursery, I avoided looking at myself in the mirror. I went past Mia's room, to my own and slammed the door shut to escape the noise. What seemed only minutes later, the buzzer went off again. This time I opened the door and stood in the doorway. I had all but forgotten about the plumbing and the water pressure.

'The pressure seems fine,' I lied, 'but I can't tell a difference, to be honest with you.'

'Would you mind if I checked?'

I didn't say anything.

'I met your husband a couple of times.' He hesitated ever so slightly, then added, 'He asked me to check on you.'

'I don't need to be checked on.'

'Maybe that came out wrong. He wants me to help you if you have any issues. Plumbing, electric, whatever you need, just tell me. I'm either next door or upstairs. Except on the weekends, I'm never here on the weekends. I visit my sister upstate. But during the week, Monday morning until Friday afternoon, I'm all yours.' He smiled at me, then cocked his head. 'You didn't call me about the water pressure and I realized you didn't have my number.' He stepped closer and handed me a piece of paper. I got a whiff of sawdust and oil.

'I'm not sure what my husband told you, but the moving company gave me a list of plumbers and electricians.'

Lieberman nodded. 'Do you have any idea how long it takes to get a plumber to show up? You have more important things to worry about,' he said and raised his eyebrows.

Mia was fussing in the background, something I hadn't noticed at all. 'Right,' I said and grabbed the door.

'I'm around nail guns and saws all day, it can get pretty loud and the ringing in the ears sometimes takes hours to go away,' he said and tapped his right ear with his hand. He smiled

120

without showing teeth and took his New York Yankees hat off. 'I go home at the end of the day and then I hear the baby cry through the ceiling. That's all I'm saying.'

He looked even younger with his hat off.

'I'll check and I'll call you. Promise.'

'Okay then. If I don't hear from you I'll just come back,' he said and laughed.

I offered him a smile that was friendly without being encouraging. Before I shut the door, I heard the tarp move and for a second the construction noise increased. Then the tarp closed and all was quiet again.

★　★　★

A couple of blocks from North Dandry, A Child's Play offered childcare services by the hour.

'Here's a copy of our policies. The by-the-hour group drop-off times are flexible. The other groups adhere to a curriculum and you have to talk to the individual caregiver regarding the drop-off times.' A middle-aged woman in ice cream cone littered scrubs handed me a stack of papers from behind the counter and led me on a tour through the facility.

Behind a two-way glass wall two staffers in pink scrubs sat in padded gliders, each one rocking a baby in her arms.

'Her immunization record must be up-to-date,' she said and pushed her glasses back to the bridge of her nose. 'There's a list of shot records required by law in your paperwork. Take it to the

121

pediatrician and have them look it over. It's pretty standard.'

We passed the window of the toddler room where about two dozen children, in groups of three or four, were lying on the floor curling their bodies into the shape of each letter of the alphabet.

A woman in purple scrubs joined us. After she introduced herself as the director, she glanced down at Mia thrashing her arms and legs. 'Anything out of the ordinary we need to know?' she asked while Mia was catching her breath between two wails.

'She's just a bit fussy today,' I said and struggled to pop the pacifier back in Mia's mouth.

'Don't forget her shot record, we can't enroll her unless the paperwork is complete,' the lady in purple reminded me. I signed the required paperwork and handed her a check for the application fee.

After I left the daycare, I thought about things that seemed to be out of place lately: a formula bottle I thought I had left on the counter was now in the fridge, baby clothes I had left draped over the crib ended up in the hamper, windows left ajar, and dirty diapers I'd left around the house wound up in the trash. It was probably my imagination, it wasn't as if Jack was catching a flight from Chicago to New York, secretly checking in on me, moving things around. 'Mommy brain' they call it, I kept telling myself, assuming that the part of my brain that used to be involved in planning and foresight was taken over by the baby's schedule. It was probably the unfamiliar surroundings but I didn't need another worry.

Mia was asleep in her stroller when I entered a hardware store just a couple of blocks from North Dandry. The sales clerk at Taylor Hardware, Security & Lock wore an apron with the name 'Larry' stitched in cursive across the pocket, almost illegible in all capital letters and a slightly more complicated name would have been impossible to decipher. Larry climbed ladders and pulled boxes from the very top shelves while I listened patiently to his explanations, taking a mental note of possible lock choices, all the while looking into Larry's watery eyes stuck behind his enormous glasses.

'What kind of locks you have now?' he asked and pushed his glasses up on the bridge of his nose, leaving fingerprints on the lenses.

'A latch set with a key hole on the outside and a thumb-turn on the inside. There's also a chain door guard.' Mia started to stir in the stroller and I knew it was only a matter of minutes until she'd break out in a full-blown howl.

'Sounds pretty secure to me. Are you looking for additional security? Like a deadbolt or something?'

'There's no such thing as too much security,' I said.

Mia started to fuss and her hands began to flail. Larry's eyes were huge behind the lenses as he raised his voice to top Mia's crying. My embracing her was the most uncomfortable state of being for Mia and so I just rocked the stroller back and forth. I hoped I'd make it through the lock purchase without Larry giving me any advice on how to console a screaming baby.

'How about an old-fashioned alarm system sounding like sirens and hell rolled all into one?' he said. 'The security company will dispatch a car within minutes. We've got a special going on, twenty percent off and free installation.'

'I don't want to alert anyone, I just want to be able to lock my doors and keep them that way.' I kept rolling the stroller back and forth, trying to stop Mia's crying.

'I'm not sure if additional locks — '

'Just tell me what else you have that I can install myself.' I checked my watch. Larry took the gesture as impatience on my part and started pulling cardboard boxes and metal parts off the shelf behind him.

'And I need tools,' I added. 'Like a screwdriver and a handheld drill.'

'She's got a set of lungs on her.' He looked down at Mia whose face had turned red, her mouth a gaping well of fury.

'Just give me what I asked for. Don't forget the tools.'

He wasn't offended by my rudeness. 'Are you sure you can manage? I'll talk to the boss and maybe we can throw in a free installation. You live in the neighborhood?'

'Close enough,' I said and checked my watch again.

'I'll install the locks myself if you're interested.' He stepped closer and when I reached for the boxes, he didn't let go immediately. 'Seriously, I will. Like I said, it's free of charge.'

After he rang me up at the register, I left the store, knowing his eyes were following me as I walked by the glass storefront. I had seen the disappointment on his face when I paid in cash. I knew he wanted to look at my credit card and remember my name, even look me up later. Or ask for my driver's license to find out my address.

Back home, I went to work on the locks but realized quickly that I was in way over my head. I couldn't even hold the drill steady nor could I identify the exact spot where the screws were supposed to go.

Two hours later the metal door to my apartment was scratched and dented. I studied the parts I had bought at the hardware store. I read the back of the boxes until the words no longer made sense. The bolt throw seemed too long and I couldn't find the steel insert. One of the locks contained a free-turning cylinder but the screws were too short to reach the wood studding beyond the doorframe. I was frustrated, sweaty and discouraged, my knuckles were bruised.

The hardware store address and phone number were printed on the top of the receipt and I hoped Larry's offer for a free installation was still good. I called the hardware store and asked for him. I heard paperwork being shuffled, and the bell above the door jangling. Eventually Larry came to the phone. I explained who I was and what I'd bought and asked if the

125

free-installation offer was still valid.

'Yeah, about that,' Larry said and I heard the sound of the register open and shut. 'I was wondering how those locks worked out for you. I can come by after work and take a look. What's your address again?'

'517 North Dandry, apartment 1A. There's a lot of construction going on and I was going to ask one of the workers, but . . . anyway . . . I don't want to disturb them.'

'Like I said, it'll be after hours. It's just something we do out of courtesy for our customers.'

We agreed on a time and hung up. If Larry got the job done quickly, neither Lieberman nor Jack would ever find out that I had locks installed. After I hung up the phone with Larry, a faint whine crept towards me from Mia's room. There was no shower in my near future but at least the installation of the locks seemed certain.

After I fed and changed Mia, I stood with her in my arms looking out the window facing the street. The windows still had their original cast-iron bars and unless someone took a metal saw to them, they seemed very sturdy and safe.

Larry appeared and his tool belt fit snuggly around his waist, his belly hanging over the tools. He laid out all the locks carefully on the foyer tile.

'Locks have personality, you know,' he said.

'Well, they weren't speaking to me,' I said and passed Mia from one hip to the other.

She let out a sudden screech that prompted Larry to drop the electric drill. It left a jagged crack in the ceramic tile.

'Darn it,' Larry said and inspected the damage. 'Little one scared me. I'll replace that for you free of charge.'

I didn't care for him to come back. 'Don't worry about the tile. I'll have that fixed. There's lots of tiles stacked in the hallway.'

Whatever I hadn't managed to do a couple of hours earlier took him all of twenty minutes.

'Anything else I can do for you?' Larry asked and took his time returning tools into his red Craftsman box. 'While I'm here. I'm handy with a lot of stuff.' He winked at me and with the back of his hand wiped the sweat off his forehead. 'If you don't mind, call my boss and tell him about my work. It's almost Christmas which means bonus time.'

I promised I would and that I'd call him if I needed anything else and shut the door quickly. It was dented, the paint scratched, but I thought that I had all the locks I needed to keep us safe and I wouldn't have to second-guess my mental state every time something seemed out of place.

That night, as Mia rested in my arms exhausted after a day without a nap, she began to nod off as her eyelids continued to flutter. Her hands and limbs were flexed even though she seemed to be sleeping and just as I bent over to gently place her in her crib, she awoke and began to cry. We repeated the ritual three times before she finally relaxed into a deep sleep.

Later that night, after I walked across the room to the fireplace and poked the logs until the flames grew into a joyous blaze, I sat in front of the fireplace, yoga-style, and raised my palms until the heat of the flames became unbearable. I looked around the sparsely decorated room, which consisted of a couch, a chair, and an old table.

Jack's architect had decided to convert the brownstone into four separate units in order to take advantage of the rising real estate values. One unit was occupied by Lieberman and another by me. The two units next door were still under construction. I envisioned how this building must have been a century ago. Opulence lingered just beneath the coat of wear and tear. Single living rooms replaced double parlors, kitchens became smaller but more efficient, and entry foyers disappeared completely. The parlor doors had lost their shine and the marble mantels had long been replaced. The ceiling plasterwork was still intact but showed patches here and there. All interior doors and wood moldings showed deterioration and fatigue, but the charm was in just that: the beauty of imperfection. I wondered how every little scratch or scrape had gotten there. The rooms were spacious, their ceilings an imposing fourteen feet. The sleek mahogany doors were the most distinct feature of the apartment.

The ceiling work of the house was machine-made, rather than handmade, and of papier-mâché or stucco, rather than plaster. The combination of luxury, faded glory, and ornate shabbiness gave the apartment a kind of magical charm. Since the first story's floor plan was the exact mirror image of the second floor, four identical apartments had been created by using the former grand entrance as the hallway and separating two units by a simple wall.

Mrs Drake had explained the legal ramifications in our initial meeting, her yapping Pomeranian nestled in the crease of her fleshy arms. I hadn't understood most of it, but found out that the completion of the two unfinished apartments was behind schedule due to a lawsuit that Jack had filed against the contractor. The settlement, now concluded, would allow for new contractors to be hired to complete the left part of the building.

The blaze in the fireplace had eased and the shadows flickering across the walls were subtle, almost comforting. The rainbow-colored craze of flames was exhausting itself into a tamed orange glow.

* * *

The next morning — four empty bottles on the couch proof of the number of night feedings — I took two aspirin for my headache. I waited for the buzzing in my head to ease, for my thoughts to stop spinning.

The buzzer sent Mia into a frenzy. I went to her room, picked her up, and to my surprise she settled down the second the bottle hit her lips. Through the peephole I saw a shadow passing by the door.

Later, after Mia had gone back to sleep, just as I was pulling her door shut, the doorbell buzzed again. This time I just yanked the door open. It was David Lieberman. He bowed his head and took off his hat.

'I need to measure the pressure. Looks like we have to flush the pipes.'

'I thought it was all taken care of,' I said and added, 'Kitchen or bathroom?'

'Kitchen. The pipe connections in this building are a maze.'

'So just turn on the water and check for what?'

'May I?' Lieberman put his hand on the door. Then he paused. 'What happened here?' he asked, gently stroking the door's surface with his fingertips, the tips caressing every groove and dent.

'I had some locks installed.'

'You had some locks installed.' Lieberman seemed puzzled, rubbing the chipped paint. 'Low pressure is just inconvenient but high pressure can do a lot of damage,' he said and held up some sort of gauge device.

Mia was fussing in her crib. I could hear her getting more impatient, the intervals between her protests getting shorter, her objections louder and more urgent by the minute.

'I don't have much time,' I said but I opened the door and stepped aside. He went straight to the kitchen and screwed the gauge to the faucet. I mumbled an apology and went to Mia's room to change her diaper.

I put her on the changing table, leaned over her, gently cooing, hoping she'd cooperate. The toy I handed her flew to the ground. Mia was delighted to be free of the diaper, stretching her limbs, enjoying how her legs moved without a wad of diaper between them. She was all joy and play until it was time to put on a clean diaper. I distracted her as much as possible, but her body tensed and her legs stiffened to the point that it was tedious to pull the diaper through her legs to fasten the tabs. When I was finally done, I found Lieberman still under the kitchen sink.

'Shouldn't a plumber take a look at this?' I distinctly remembered that he said he was just supervising the contractors. He stood by the sink and turned on the faucet. It barely trickled and the pipes emitted a humming noise, then the walls around us seemed to vibrate and I felt a tremor under my feet.

'I'm going to have to turn the water main off.' He pointed at Mia in my arms. 'You'll have to use bottled water in the meantime.'

'How long is this going to take?' He hadn't even laid out his tools yet and I wondered what he'd been doing the entire time I had changed the diaper and dressed Mia. I felt a tinge of impatience.

'I'll take care of the pipes,' he said and grabbed a wrench off the counter. 'You just go and get some water.' He pointed at my purse on the counter.

I wasn't in the mood to get dressed and run to the store, but I was happy to get away from the noise of groaning pipes and having to deal with Lieberman in general. I went into Mia's room and held out my arms. Her face was blotched and her little mouth stretched wide. She reciprocated, settled down in my arms but then shook her head with a jarring motion from side to side. Instead of holding on to me, her arms grasped at the air, her shrill cries interrupted by her gasping for air.

I put her in her stroller and grabbed my purse, hoping she'd settle down as we walked.

As I passed by my usual market, Mia was still crying and I decided to continue further down the block to the next corner market. Minutes later it started to sprinkle and I covered the stroller with a blanket. Mia had fallen asleep when I entered the market. The clerk was framed by porn magazines in plastic pouches and probably had a shotgun stashed close by.

I grabbed a gallon of water and made my way to the counter. Setting the water down, I reached in my purse. There was no wallet. I rummaged senselessly through the compartments filled with tissues and receipts as the clerk looked at me sideways. I mumbled an apology and quickly left.

When I returned to North Dandry, Lieberman had gone. I checked the entire apartment for my wallet and found it sitting on the kitchen counter under a stack of mail and papers. Next to it sat a one-gallon jug of water. I shook my head, scolding myself for being so scatterbrained.

I opened the fridge door. I felt a sinking feeling of despair as I stared at an array of bottles with baby formula.

Between the wallet, the water, and the formula, I realized that at some point I had to admit to myself that the word *forgetful* was no longer accurate. Brain on fire was more like it. I didn't even attempt to construct an elaborate rationalization as to why I couldn't remember

132

what I had done mere hours ago.

A nagging voice in the back of my mind whispered *what are you going to misplace next?*

TIMELINE OF
MIA CONNOR ABDUCTION

Brooklyn, N.Y. — **The case of 7-month-old Mia Connor is gripping the nation. Nothing short of a tragedy, the facts of Mia Connor's disappearance seem to be pointing in a disturbing direction. In the days before the disappearance, Mia's mother, Estelle Paradise, had locks and bolts installed by a local hardware store. According to a store clerk from Taylor Security & Lock, she wanted to 'keep people out.' He described her as 'preoccupied, a bit on the edge.' He continued, 'And she never tended to the baby. She was crying the entire time.'**

On September 30th, Estelle Paradise (27) is seen on surveillance tapes attempting to purchase a gallon of water. After searching through her purse, Ms Paradise storms out of the convenience store, leaving the water behind. According to to the clerk the stroller was covered with a blanket.

On October 1st Estelle Paradise finds her

daughter's crib empty. She doesn't notify the authorities.

Ms Paradise, according to surveillance tapes, enters the 72nd Police Precinct in Brooklyn that same day. She is seen vomiting in the precinct hallway, then leaves without talking to the detective who remembers her as 'disheveled and worn-out.'

Estelle Paradise is found on October 4th at the bottom of a ravine in Dover, N.Y. with life-threatening injuries. Among other items, a gun was found in the car.

She is transferred to County General in Brooklyn on October 5th. Upon her arrival she is listed in serious condition. The next day her husband, and father of baby Mia, Jack Connor (38), arrives at the hospital. According to an unnamed source, an arraignment can be anticipated within two weeks, depending on the mother's recuperation. Her condition is now listed as fair.

No new developments have come to light in this case and the whereabouts of 7-month-old Mia Connor remain a mystery.

Part two

'Begin at the beginning,' the King said,
very gravely, 'and go on till you come
to the end: then stop.'

Lewis Carroll,
Alice in Wonderland

BREAKING NEWS:

NO ARRAIGNMENT IMMINENT FOR ESTELLE PARADISE, MOTHER OF MISSING 7-MONTH-OLD MIA CONNOR

Brooklyn, NY — **According to the DA, at this time no formal charges will be brought against Estelle Paradise, mother of missing infant Mia Connor.**

On Monday morning the courthouse was abuzz with anticipation of the appearance of Estelle Paradise for a possible arraignment. Legal sources anticipated that in the absence of a body, charges ranging from second-degree murder to aggravated manslaughter were most likely.

In a staggering turn of events, DA Barrymore came out to brief the awaiting media who had gathered hours before. He read out a very short statement. 'Estelle Paradise is at an undisclosed location awaiting psychiatric care. No formal charges will be filed at this point. This is an ongoing investigation and we cannot comment any further. I will not be taking any questions.'

When DA Barrymore walked away from the microphone, the media broke out in a frenzy. Phone calls to the DA's office from multiple news outlets have not been returned.

11

As we cross into Queens, I catch a glimpse of Creedmoor Psychiatric Facility sitting silently on a hill overlooking the East River. Jack's subdued, almost as if he's in a trance. We ride in silence until he jerks the steering wheel to the right and almost sends my stomach over the edge. I dig my heels into the floor mats because there's only one thing Jack hates more than a woman's tears, and that's vomit on his charcoal Corinthian leather seats. The car slides as if suspended on a bed of marbles and comes to an abrupt halt. Jack turns the key and silently we sit on a bed of gravel.

I watch him as he hides his face behind his cupped hands. When he starts shaking his head, I hear sobs and I know Jack's crying. He finally looks up and I'm amazed. Jack cries in style, silently, tears shaped like precious pearls rolling down his cheeks.

I take deep breaths to calm my stomach, at the same time I try to figure out what's going on with Jack. I remain removed from his pain, maybe because I've been alone with mine for so long that I just can't seem to comfort him. I stare at the tears emerging from behind his hands and random facts pop into my head — that happy tears emerge from the right eye, the first tear from the left eye signals pain, and I don't remember if that's true or a myth — but either way, he doesn't look right. Suddenly he's slouched over, his shoulders are bobbing and his hands are rubbing his eyes. Jack's composure resurfaces and his outburst is over just as quickly as it began.

When he finally speaks, his voice is so low I can hardly understand him.

'My entire life I knew how to deal with other people's problems and then this happens and I'm just fucking lost.'

He goes on to tell me how he hasn't been sleeping, how he's just muddling through and how all of this is swallowing him up and how I'm not the woman he married — *that* woman was dependable and capable — and how he's been wondering if *that* woman will ever come back and how it doesn't really matter because nothing will ever be the same. And how he is torn — he never says just what he is torn about — and how he just can't wonder about the truth day in and day out and that living like this isn't a life at all, and that there's nothing heroic about fighting all the time, and that he's no longer got the strength for both of us and now all he's got left is the love for his daughter. And that she is so small and fragile and never did anything to harm anyone, and everything is just a mess and he can't cope any longer but he will do everything in his power to bring her home.

And then: 'I don't know what it is you did or didn't do, Estelle, I just can't wrap my mind around it and that's why I have to step back.'

Stepping back. I can't fathom what stepping back entails, but I feel something taking hold, something sinister and rather final, but I'm behind with my thoughts and I'm not sure what's going on, and therefore I just sit and listen and look at him hoping my facial expression is sympathetic and attentive.

'I've defended people — guilty people, innocent people, people I didn't know if they were guilty or not, because everyone has the right to counsel and a defense and that's what being a lawyer is all about, that's what this entire legal system is all about. But this is nothing like that at all, this is personal, this is my daughter.'

His emotional quandary is the love for his daughter — and I give him that, he's got his priorities straight — but I wish he would just say it, just say *I don't know if you're guilty or not*. That's what it all comes down to.

And then he goes on about how he didn't do anything to deserve this, all he ever did was protect her and care for her and provide for her and he needs to concentrate on what's important, and he can't do that when he's around me. He continues and I space out, not on purpose, it's just something that happens, and once I jerk back into reality I'm not sure if I missed anything important. He uses words like *doubt* and *responsibility* — they roll off his tongue — and *apprehension* and *contempt* and my mind shrieks, yet I can't interpret any of the words buzzing around in my head, can't get them in the right order to make sense of them. I try to focus, come up with a coherent statement, anything that reassures him that I'm worthy of his trust. We share this space, the air, this moment, yet we couldn't be farther apart. I want

143

to scream at him that all *I* ever wanted was to protect her, and that *I'm* no different than he is, that *I* don't deserve this either, and for fuck's sake, what does *stepping back* even mean?

And for a split second I have a moment of clarity and I understand that he's failed me, that he's to blame for this, that he didn't live up to his responsibilities, that I at least tried while he just . . . just gave up on me. That Mia wasn't safe because I wasn't well and that he abandoned me and therefore he abandoned both of us a long time ago.

But I don't tell him any of this because we've talked too much about how I feel, and I know he's done illuminating my pain. It's all about him now and why he's come to the conclusion to . . . what was it again? To *step back*.

'I'm sorry,' he says and his voice cracks. 'I can't think about what happened to my daughter and love you at the same time.'

I look at myself in the exterior side view mirror. He's right, as always, Jack is right, there's no telling what I did. I can't be trusted. I want to come up with some sort of consolation for him, I want to tell him that I understand and that he's right, and that he needs to concentrate on finding our daughter, I want to say something coherent, something supportive, and I think I can get there, I trust myself enough that I can console him.

'Sometimes I imagine her dead,' I say and stare straight ahead. I hear my own voice, so small and meek, and I know I have failed him yet again.

★ ★ ★

Later, at the Creedmoor intake office, the nurse bends over to pick up my suitcase. I turn and realize Jack's left without my noticing, not so much as a last word. I feel myself unraveling like a ball of yarn but I manage to hold on. I wonder how many failures Jack's had in his life and I can't think of a single one, except me. He cannot connect with failure, it's that simple. And I decide to abandon hope and just let it be. Jack's left me and we have to cope, apart from each other. It feels familiar, I know what it means when someone is gone, comes up missing, stolen, kidnapped, whatever. Whatever.

Someone asks me to sign paperwork but my hands shake so badly that the pen slips right out of them. It lands softly on the marble floor, bouncing a couple of times, and then it comes to rest. I stare at the floor. The cream marble tile background is in stark contrast to the bold brown veining. There is an oval within the grain of the marble, the size and shape of an egg maybe. As I reach for the pen, I hear a small sob, almost gentle, that erupts and makes its way out of my very own throat. I drop to my knees, unable to take my eyes off the shape of a baby's bloody footprint embedded in the shiny floor. I try to wipe it away but I can't.

I don't remember much after. I later hear that I screamed, that I scratched my face, my nails digging deep, leaving bloody trails, like an infant who has no control over her hands. They stab a needle in my arm and then I just sit in an office

145

and stare at the clock above the door. That's when I remember the photograph in my father's study, the Riverside Church, built the same year as Creedmoor. I imagine how Riverside ascended brick by brick, Lego-like, towards the heavens while Creedmoor's magnificent castle-like building, wrought of brick and stone, slithered its way across the meadows on a magnificent estate here at the Upper New York Bay. Creedmoor is my life now and I suddenly panic. I can't turn around, walk away. No more choices. I'm here for Mia. Consequences beyond her don't concern me. When I take the first step towards my room I can almost feel my bones shift.

★ ★ ★

One hour later, I sit on a leather couch opposite a large glass window. From the couch, I can see the smokestacks of an old factory assembled of bricks the color of coagulated blood.

I swear that one of the stacks — the one located slightly off to the left — is leaning, like the Tower of Pisa. Even though it does not draw any tourists — no one takes family photographs in front of it, and no one sips coffee in a nearby café — it is my favorite smokestack.

The crooked stack seems like an intruder in a landscape of otherwise right angles and man-made harmony. Its wretchedness is familiar to me and I imagine myself extending a hand through the window, up the hill, tilting the warped stack back to its precise vertical

146

existence. I want to make everything all right for the stack; I want to save it from its troubled life, want to deliver it from its outcast status among the other stacks pointing straight into the sky.

A man enters the office and introduces himself as Dr Solska Ari. He is of Pakistani descent and a balding man in his fifties with rosy cheeks and perfectly capped teeth, impeccably groomed, smelling of starch and shoe polish. His glasses sit low on the bridge of his nose. It's not until we shake hands that I realize he's a man of average height yet he has the aura of a giant.

Our first session is filled with small talk and educational memory lessons. He doesn't take notes, but runs a digital recorder.

'Let me tell you about my first case as a psychiatrist,' he says and stares off into the distance. 'A woman ate an egg and suddenly, out of the blue, her memory was erased. I couldn't get what happened to her out of my mind. What caused her memory to not function properly?

'Short of brain damage, nothing is lost, the brain doesn't forget. Your memories are tucked away in drawers, and sometimes those drawers are locked. Locked by emotional distress, stress hormones. Historically, people who suffered from amnesia were believed to not want to remember. Brain researchers who are hung up on the hardware portion of the brain believe they can't remember. I'm somewhere in between; I believe it's a combination of both.'

As I listen, I realize that his most striking characteristic is his placid nature. Tireless in patience and attention, he's a reverse gravedigger of some sort, unearthing what is underground. I want to believe he can help me find my daughter, I want to one day look back on this moment and remember him as the man who gave me back my memory, my child, my life.

At the end of the session, he asks me what went through my mind when I was told I had amnesia.

'Confusion,' I say, 'a lot of confusion. The implications were endless.'

'I understand your daughter's life is potentially at stake. Time is of the essence and I need you to understand that there's a lot of work ahead of us,' he says and adds, 'and I have to ask you for your trust.'

I raise my eyebrows. Trust. Just trust me and everything is going to be all right, is that what he's asking me? Is it as simple and as uncomplicated as that?

'On one hand I need you to trust me that everything you say is safe with me,' Dr Ari continues. 'There is the physician–patient privilege. It's a legal concept and it protects all communications between you and me. The police are aware of that. Nothing you say here can be used against you in court.'

'You said *on one hand*.'

'The other hand is a bit more complicated.' He looks down as if he's studying my file. 'The circumstances of your case put me in a peculiar place. I call it the ultimate psychiatrist's dilemma but I have to ask you to waive the physician — patient privilege.'

'I don't understand.' Anything I say can and

will be used against me.

'I am asking you to agree to the fact that I alone will make the determination as to when we disclose our findings to the police. And what we disclose.'

'I don't care what happens to me,' I say.

'I care for the both of us.'

'How much time do we have?'

'I'd like to say we have *until* but that would be a lie. It's not a matter of a deadline as in a date. It's more about us making progress. It could be a week, it could be a month or more.'

'I see. But what if . . . ' What is it I'm not asking? What if I don't remember? What if the memory of the blood is all there is? What if . . . I don't dare finish the thought.

'I don't want you to think about the police and the investigation at all. I am in contact with the detective in charge and I will keep him informed with what I deem necessary. Your worries would only interfere with our work,' Dr Ari says and leans back in his chair as if the subject is no longer open for discussion. 'Let me handle the police,' he adds.

'Did the egg lady ever remember? It couldn't have been about the egg, right?' I ask and offer an ironic smile.

'Of course it wasn't,' he says and adjusts his impeccably knotted tie. 'Nothing is that simple and it was never about the egg. I'll make you a deal; we find out what happened to your daughter and I tell you all about the lady who ate the egg.'

* * *

The next day, at the beginning of our second session, Dr Ari asks me about the most peaceful place I can imagine. 'Like a refuge, a hiding place, where you feel safe.'

'I'm not sure . . . ' I say and look at him, puzzled.

'Have you ever paid attention to your breathing when you feel relaxed?'

His question seems silly to me. 'Can't say I have,' I answer and wonder if imagining myself on a beach is what he's looking for.

'In the middle of a very stressful situation we usually wish for a safe place,' he says. 'Have you ever wished to be somewhere else during such a moment?'

Every day I want to be somewhere else, I think but don't say anything.

'Imagine a safe place. Give it a try.'

I know what he wants to hear and immediately I come up with several options: 'A beach, a park bench, beside a waterfall, something like that?'

'No good,' he says and bounces a pen on his desk, 'those are no good.'

'I don't know,' I say, 'you asked. That's what I came up with. Why's it no good?'

'Stereotypes, nothing but stereotypes. Like wanting to travel around the world. Who wants to travel and never belong? Always on the move. That's just something people say. No one really means that. I want you to think about this.' He pauses and throws the pen on the desk. 'You've never been to a safe place then.'

I shrug my shoulders.

His eyes light up. 'How about getting there? Think of a mode of transportation that takes you to a safe and peaceful place. You don't need to know the specific place, let's imagine your journey there. Nothing you anticipated, something that just happened, a voyage of sorts. Let me give you an example.' He takes off his glasses and leans back in his chair. 'Long time ago, in a country far from here, as a young boy, I used to spend the weekends at my grandmother's house. I remember her bed being high above the ground, I seemed to sleep almost up in the clouds. Of course, I was young and short and *Daadi*'s bed was just high, but it seemed high up in the clouds to me. I had a lot of nightmares as a young boy but whenever I slept at *Daadi*'s house, I didn't wake up at night, there were no monsters. Her bed was magic, in a kid sort of way, but magic nevertheless.'

'I thought you said a mode of transportation. I don't get it.'

'It transported me to my good dreams. I don't remember the dreams anymore, but I had a lot of them in that bed. It seemed nothing on earth could touch me there, nothing could hold me back. And every morning I woke up to the smell of *nashta*. And she was singing while preparing it.' His eyes turn glassy, as if he's far away. But just as quickly he snaps out of it, furrows his brows, and his eyes demand my own little memory of childhood peace.

'Your peaceful place is your grandmother's bed, I get it. Unfortunately I can't compete with

151

that,' I say. 'No grandma and no *nashta* in my past.' I think about his story and try to remember all the places I've been as a child. But all I remember is getting sick in cars, on boats, even in buses.

'I love to ride elevators.' I'm surprised when I hear the words coming out of my mouth. Then I realize it's actually true, there's something about the humming, the feeling in my stomach, the door opening and closing.

Dr Ari's eyebrows relax, he looks pleased. 'An elevator it is. Describe your favorite elevator. Then enter.'

I close my eyes and imagine feeling the gravity and the rotation of the earth. It's as easy as imagining the warmth of the sun on my skin. 'Two shiny panels meet in the middle, silver panels. The doors slide open and I get in.'

Dr Ari's voice is soothing. 'It's comfortable and spacious. The lights are low, it's almost dark. You can go anywhere you want to go. No one controls the elevator but you. Walk in, turn around and face the panel by the side of the door. The panel is rectangular. The buttons are round, lit, and embedded in the panel. They start at number ten and go all the way to number one.'

I imagine the door closing. I push a button. The doors close silently. I'm safe and contained in this dark box. As the elevator descends, I have a moving sensation in my stomach, then the forces balance themselves, and right before the elevator stops, the force lessens and, again, I experience a floating feeling.

'Perfect,' Dr Ari says and smiles. 'I want this elevator to be a place of peace and control. Anytime you feel anxious, I want you to step in and go to a lower floor. The further down you go, the more relaxed you'll become.'

'And what's it for? The exercise, I mean?'

'When humans get stressed or experience fear, our bodies exhibit something that is called the fight-or-flight response. When facing a threat our bodies respond with very distinct signs: a change in blood pressure, breathing, heart rate, temperature, muscle tension, just to name a few.'

'Right,' I say and imagine saber-toothed tigers pursuing a zebra.

'Our body is basically getting ready to fight or run away,' Dr Ari continues. 'I want you to face your fears, and force your body into a 'relaxation response.' Once you manage to relax, over time, you will develop a heightened state of awareness. That's what we're after, being aware.'

'Sounds easy enough,' I say.

'Not quite. Combating primal responses requires practice. A trained nurse will instruct you later on today.'

The more I think about this concept, the less I can imagine any possible scenario that is positive for the zebra. 'That means while I'm trying to remember, I won't be afraid and I won't run. I'll tell my body to relax and be alert.' Fighting makes no sense when confronted with a saber-toothed tiger and I don't think a zebra can outrun a tiger. And yet staying put seems like certain death to me.

'That's the plan. You won't avoid, and you

153

won't struggle against it.'

'*It* being . . . ?'

'The past.'

'Right,' I say but I can't help thinking of a tiger sinking its teeth into my neck.

★ ★ ★

On the morning of our third session, a damp blanket of fog has spread over the East River and the familiar smokestacks in the distance have all but disappeared behind its dense layer. I am mesmerized by the fog wrapping itself around every building and every tree, eradicating what once was into something that's not. It hangs heavy over the hills, suffocating everything in its wake.

First I hear Dr Ari's voice coming from afar, and then I comprehend the words. 'Tell me about Mia.' His voice is low, yet urgent.

I wanted truth serums and potent pills, forcing my memories to the surface. I expected to be hypnotized, I imagined a chemical manipulation of my mind. But after two sessions with Dr Ari I've figured out that I am all there is. Just me, my clouded mind, and Dr Ari urging me on.

'Tell you about Mia?' I repeat his question to buy some time. I focus on the vague and ghostly smokestacks outside the window, looming a safe distance from this office within the thick cloud of water droplets. I wish the layers of skin that he is trying to peel away were just as safe from him as that old decrepit factory in the distance.

I don't know what happened to my daughter

Mia. I opened drawers, old shoeboxes, and unlocked doors that led to storage spaces under stairs. I climbed into Dumpsters, looked under beds. I searched for her. A daughter is not something one misplaces like a set of keys or a take-out menu. What I know for sure is that one morning I woke up and she had vanished as if she had been swallowed by a hole in the universe. Not so much as an impression of her tiny body left on the sheet-covered mattress. Someone took her without picking the locks or prying the hinges off the doorjambs. She's left a silence behind, a silence so loud it keeps me awake at night.

On a good day, after I've been able to sleep three continuous hours, I imagine her with a nice couple in Arizona, tucked away in loving arms. When I imagine this scene long enough, it feels almost real. On a bad day I see her mutilated and lifeless under a mountain of dirt and pine-needled soil, next to acorn caps and deer droppings somewhere in the woods of upstate New York. The worst days are the ones when I can feel a sticky substance between my fingers and I wonder if I'm the one to blame.

But good days and bad days are not conducive to the truth. What I need is a clear day. A day so clear and pristine, so sparkling and new, that I dare to explore what happened to Mia.

For now, I have to take solace in imagining the abandoned factory with the crooked stack. I envision homeless people sleeping on top of cardboard, junkies passed out in dark corners under colorful graffiti — their very own

155

billboards on the edge of human society. Old, battered shoes, their counterparts lost forever, with all the missing socks we never seem to find. I can hear feet kicking cheap plastic gin bottles. They take off into the dark like shooting stars, hit the walls and bounce back just to end up again in the middle of the long shadowy halls with their windows nailed shut decades ago.

After self-inflicted prodding, digging, turning over stones that resisted turning like boulders in front of caves, somewhere between mandatory journaling and lights-out, I am ready. I will hunt her last images; I will try to catch the coattails of the truth and hang on to them, even if they pull me straight into hell.

My eyes focus on Dr Ari's hands. We have both been waiting for this moment. He wants to solve the mystery not even New York's top cops have been able to crack. His legendary status for restoring the forgetful is at stake. As for myself, if I can't come up with a logical explanation, I will face life in prison. I am lucky in a way — for there is something resembling luck in my position — New York abolished the death penalty years ago. I can always plead insanity, for what mother in her right mind kills her infant daughter? And if I didn't kill her, what woman in her right mind does not know where her daughter is? Either way, my end of the stick is shitty.

'Tell you about Mia?' I can hear my own voice as if it was prerecorded. It sounds nothing like me. It's more than that; I feel as if I'm not inside my own body. 'Where do you want me to start?'

156

Dr Ari's Adam's apple is bobbing as he swallows. He pushes the chair off his desk and rolls back a couple of feet. He glances at the digital recorder to make sure it is on.

'Start wherever you want.'

Tell him about Mia? I'm trying to make a connection; I'm reaching for a marker, longing to connect the dots. I look down and avoid his eyes. I fold my hands in my lap.

'I remember . . . ' I hear my own voice trembling. I feel shaky, my stomach muscles are tight. I am trying to sit straight, keep my composure. I choose my words wisely, for they have the power to set my world on fire.

My thoughts remain unstructured and unorganized, like half-truths concealed as memories. It's hard to talk about her. Because there's all that blood. It just *won't* go away. Sometimes, for a little while, I indulge, I remain in the moment, just because I need to. It doesn't mean I will talk about it. But I hope that one day soon I'll take aim at the memory. One bullet, one shot, and it'll be done. But I have to be honest, candor has never been my thing. Why not just tell him? It is in every corner of my mind but there are other things, too. Things we should talk about first.

'Go on,' he says.

I know, I *know*, I'd go to the ends of the earth to protect Mia and keep her safe but please don't ask to see what's really inside of me. There is a part of myself I keep in a steel cage. It's the part that doesn't want to know what I'm capable of. It's almost as if I built brick walls so strong they keep me from touching the vulnerable part of me, the part that doesn't even care if I take another breath. The part of me that believes I did what I'm accused of.

12

During the day, thousands of coal-black crows spread out over the Creedmoor estate, but in the afternoons they flock together in smaller groups to gather in their communal roost once dusk nears. Their calls create a tremendous noise level, then suddenly they settle down and remain quiet during the night.

I watch them work in pairs, construct nests with dead branches, pick at their own feet when frustrated, play with acorn caps and sticks. The view of the building from above, a bird expanding its wings like a giant chief crow, might be the reason they gather here.

I discover a nest in the tree in front of my window. I watch a pigeon-like bird lay the first egg. She leaves the nest immediately after and I worry about the egg and what will become of it. The next day she lays another egg, just to abandon both of them. My anxiety heightens with every passing hour, but on the third day she returns and starts incubating the eggs and from then on out she hardly leaves the nest.

Creedmoor is a dinosaur in its own right. It was built in the 1920s, its cutting-edge psychiatric technology mocks the history trapped in its walls after decades of chemically induced seizures and lobotomies. Even electroshock therapy is back in the medical community's good graces; renamed electroconvulsive therapy and

159

performed under anesthesia without adversely affecting treatment effectiveness.

Creedmoor's legacy of long-forgotten architecture claims to have sheltered the likes of Sylvia Plath, Edie Sedgwick, and Ed Gein who gained notoriety in the fifties after authorities discovered he had exhumed corpses from local graveyards and constructed keepsakes from their body parts.

The 'Kirkbride-style' building is a leftover from the early twentieth century, a relic building style considered an ideal sanctuary for the mentally insane. Kirkbride buildings segregate the patients according to gender and severity of symptoms: male patients in one wing, female patients in the other, each wing subdivided with more severe cases on the lower floors while the better-behaved patients are confined to the upper floors.

Not everyone considers Creedmoor the relic it is. I hear investors once had big plans for the building. A conversion into condominiums was imminent, but the project was shut down since the layout was not suited for individual residences. Its corridors were too long, and its rooms too small.

My room, at least for the time being, is my own; I don't have a roommate. My bed frame is made of strong metal pipes, and the linens are soft, worn bare from years of laundering in scalding water.

The breakfast bell sounds at seven on weekdays, on Saturdays and Sundays at eight, and the patients descend to the cafeteria at the end of the hallway on the main level. We all have pre-assigned tables. The table next to mine is the gathering place for a flock of anorexic women. Their condition is obvious; instead of eating, they merely rearrange their food, pick over their plates like seagulls over a garbage heap. Their fingers seem dipped in blue ink and their hair is thin and downy like an infant's, while enamel erosion has claimed their teeth.

My only company during meals is a middle-aged woman, Marge Ruiz. Marge is placid and looks twenty years younger than she is. Her story is similar to mine, I guess one can say; we're both guilty of not speaking up when we were supposed to. Almost as if missing a deadline has sent both of us to the loony bin. Marge decided to keep the death of her mother a secret until the smell alerted the neighbors. She never told her husband or her children about her mother's death; she continued to visit her corpse for months, bringing fresh eggs, milk, and bread. I conjure up this vision of a fridge full of egg cartons, loaves of bread, one stacked on top of the other. It seems amusing, one of those crazy and insane stories, but then I catch myself; I straighten my back and shake the implications away. I'm nothing like her, that's what I tell myself.

Marge's family visits her every weekend. They invade the visitors' garden, lounge in lawn chairs on the covered terrace. Marge has five children and twice as many grandchildren. Her family's consolation prize for Marge is a weekly white paper box filled with sugar-topped croissants

161

— Cuenos de Azucar.

While Marge is surrounded by her family, I spend my time on a lawn chair under a big oak tree in the garden behind the main building. Jack's in Chicago, being updated frequently on my progress, I'm sure. Legal staffing, billable hours, work expenses and legal outsourcing are his thing; lost memories and therapy sessions and visions of blood, not so much. The memory of how he left me standing in the Creedmoor lobby with my suitcase in hand is nothing I dwell on. I practice the elevator technique obsessively and eventually I feel myself calming down the moment I imagine elevator doors opening.

I carry my journal with me; I write down every word and every image that pops into my head. Images that defy interpretation, I attempt to draw. After a few days pass, I neither recognize the drawings nor am I sure that I even drew them.

Dr Ari had handed me the journal during our first session.

'As many details as possible,' he had said, 'even if it seems trivial. It may turn out to be significant in the long run. Write down thoughts, images, even your dreams. The patterns and recurring themes speak volumes about what's attempting to resurface. Everything is important. Everything.'

I draw random squares in my journal. Four corners, then I go over the outline again and again until the lines fill the entire square. Those are the black boxes that contain the past. By writing and drawing in my journal, I try to force my hands to materialize a thought, to force that black box open. I descend into a state of relaxation and I allow my thoughts to wander, without borders and restraints. I see images, yet I don't know their meaning. The sun, moon, and stars are ever-present heavenly bodies; they never change.

Sometimes, when I sit under the oak in the visitors' garden, I catch a glimpse, a flash of an image. I know it's there, right below the surface. The image floats by me like a cloud, a duplicate of a thought I once had — I'm not sure what else to call it — during which I catch the distorted image of some sort of replica, a copy of a copy if you will, and I try to latch on to it like a fish to hooked bait. A theme emerges. Fruit. An abundance of fruit. Baskets overflowing; fruit, ripe and fragrant, bursting open. I want to be the fruit, want to will the fruit to deny its breaking point. Their insides luscious, their skins bouncing back as I poke at them. Eventually they burst open and I try to force the fruit — with some sort of mind control — to withstand.

Dr Ari is somewhat of a legend at Creedmoor. Countless framed official documents grace his office walls: undergraduate degree, medical school, residency, and finally Creedmoor's President and Psychiatrist in Chief. I wonder if he has a wife, a family. There are no photographs, no children's arts-and-crafts projects on his desk. No hint of his private life.

He speaks at length about the brain and it being 'the most complex object in the universe' and he seems to have an affection for the philosophy of his profession. 'We can only operate with the data we are consciously aware of. Everything's there, just covered in a layer of dust. Gaining access to what lies beneath is what it's all about.'

I like to think of him as a magician unearthing skeletons and bringing them back to life. He smiled when I told him and said, 'Thank you. It's not quite as glamorous as excavating vessels from antiquity, but I envy your point of view. Most skeletons refuse to be uncovered. Makes for hard work.'

He told me he specializes in RMT — Recovered Memory Therapy. That RMT sometimes, 'depending on the case,' includes psychotherapy methods like hypnosis, even sedative-hypnotic drugs, age regression, and guided visualization. And that RMT is not considered formal psychotherapy, nor is it used in mainstream psychiatry.

I assume that he stumbled upon the crime-solving part at some point in his career. There's the egg woman and there's Marge, one of his other patients, 'may or may not have killed her mother,' according to Oliver, one of the orderlies. Maybe my case will be another cornerstone of Dr Ari's already legendary status.

★ ★ ★

During the second week, Dr Ari talks a lot about how memory serves us. 'Memory is nothing more than a concept that explains the process of

164

remembering. Imagine you are trying to locate a parked car in a crowded parking lot. You were present at the act of parking the car, yet you're unable to recall its exact location. Your subconscious mind knows its precise position and RMT will allow you to go back to the moment you parked the car.'

More than anything, I'm surprised the DA allowed this experiment. But neither the state of New York, the DA, or the Medical Board of Psychiatry has anything to lose. It seems like they've agreed to ignore scientific integrity and allow junk science to give it a whirl. I am well aware that Dr Ari is operating on the fringes of science and my constant jokes about RMT standing for 'Rogue Medical Tests' have made him smile but haven't cracked his shell of professionalism.

On Tuesday, I arrive early for our session and, when I reach his office, the door is ajar. I enter unprompted and uninvited. I'm immediately aware of his disapproving demeanor. The digital recorder, usually on top of his desk, is still tucked away in a drawer. His white coat is still unbuttoned. I have walked in without his permission, and I have not only breached regulations, but also etiquette and, more importantly, his rules.

I did so because I am afraid. Last Friday, after I described to him the day my daughter Mia disappeared, he alluded to a new direction in our approach to my therapy. His eyes seemed restless that day, and I have a feeling that today we'll dig deeper, we'll do more than just gently brush

165

away the sand from a shard of an ancient vase. Today we might lift the entire vase out of its sandy grave and, like archeologists, we will proceed with caution, so as not to break the object into a million pieces.

I sit across from Dr Ari, who, as a matter of retaliation, ignores me for quite some time. I don't apologize for my impulsive entry; he is not the kind of man who expects an apology. Eventually we exchange a few banalities and he distractedly flips the pages of my journal. I have a feeling something that I'm not prepared for is about to happen. He seems to be rushing along today, his whole demeanor reeks of urgency. The official charge by the DA's office is less than two months away. He does not want me to be a nut he failed to crack. I wonder what he has left, what else he has tucked away in his pocket. Is there a magic trick that will clear the clouds in my head?

His voice jerks me out of my thoughts.

'Do you remember the conversations we had regarding forgetting and the reasons why we forget?'

During my research hours I read up on memory and how our brain copes with the loss of it. I actually find the entire memory business fascinating. I'm also trying to show off, I want him to know that I'm committed, even after our sessions end.

'I recall the decay theory and the interference theory. Memory retrieval — let's assume that the memories made it all the way into long-term memory — fails because the memories have

166

decayed over time or have been subjected to interference.'

'Your memory loss is quite peculiar. There's no physical evidence of brain damage and therefore I cannot say with certainty why you don't remember. If and when we're able to retrieve your memories, we will figure out the reason why. Not before then. There is no pill I can give you, no blood test or MRI that will tell us what causes you not to recollect the past. But there's something we can do.'

I know he's lying. He can administer sedative-hypnotic drugs to uncover the past stuck in my head, unwilling to budge. He wants the truth to come out organically, unrestricted, because someone might not believe him if he administers drugs. Who would be able to separate the wheat from the chaff, the truth from drug-induced visions?

'It's time for a trip to 517 North Dandry.'

I feel as if he's tossed a brick my way, its heaviness substantial. I want to cradle the memory of the brownstone but its walls seem impenetrable. North Dandry is where Mia disappeared.

My heart rate picks up and my head pounds. My mouth is dry and I'm covered in sweat. My thoughts race, culminating in one predominant message: *I can't go back there.* I try to remind myself of how inevitable this pain is. I force my breathing to slow, the image of the elevator an ever-present symbol of composure.

Dr Ari is watching me like a hawk. 'You seem to be feeling better. Why don't we — '

167

'I can't do this.' I fear my voice will start trembling, but I manage to keep it stable.

'Revisiting the place where it all happened will allow you to recreate memories,' he says. 'There's no need to get upset. Just let me explain what we're going to do.'

The place where it all happened. Hearing it out loud makes it real. We are going back to the scene of the crime.

'Memory retrieval is much more likely when we test in the same physical context in which the memory we're trying to uncover originally occurred. The application to recreate the past when it comes to trauma-related amnesia is frowned upon, yet the concept itself is nothing new. We will make an attempt to recreate the same emotion you felt when the memory was born.'

Memories are born. Do they die, too?

'You call it 'retrieval,' 'physical context,' and 'recreation,' ' I say and gesture quotation marks every time I use one of the phrases with which he disguises what is really going on. 'You want me to stand in her room, look at her crib?'

I'm not sure if I can do what he's asking me to do. The thought of going back to where Mia disappeared fills me with terror. Terror so deep it reaches around my heart like a fist, determined to destroy me. A concept pops into my head, an article I read in one of the medical journals scattered about the many waiting rooms at Creedmoor. Takotsubo. Stress-induced cardio-myopathy. Broken-heart syndrome. Takotsubo are Japanese octopus traps that resemble the

168

shape of the heart in an angiogram. I almost expect the sound of shattering glass and for my heart to explode into pieces.

As if Dr Ari can read my mind, he gets up, walks around his desk, and stands in front of me, half-sitting, half-leaning on his desk. He crosses his arms.

'Nothing bad will happen to you. Those memories are potent and powerful, but your daughter's life is at stake, Estelle. We need to try; *you* need to try.' His voice is urgent now and so are his eyes.

I want to be cooperative and I want to find the truth, like him. But what I want most of all is not having a breaking point. Like the fruit in my dreams I try not to break open.

The crib.

The locks.

The empty closet.

'How about guided visualization? Can't I just pretend I'm there? Isn't that the same? Maybe we can try that and then . . . '

He shakes his head and I know I've lost the battle.

'Believe me when I say, in the end, you will be okay. And if you are not okay, we are not at the end. Just trust me. Remember I asked for your trust?'

We are beyond guided visualization. We are beyond chatting and are all about doing. There's nothing else to say. No sage will emerge and offer me an ancient remedy. No shaman will throw the bones and predict the future; no crystal ball will tell us the truth. I alone hold the truth, but something inside me refuses to give in. I deny the truth's power, its thrall dark and potent. If I give myself to this process, give my mind and my body, I will find the truth. What if I'm responsible for her death? What if I'm not? What if she's still alive? If I tilt towards truth and believe in its light, can I illuminate the world around me? Illuminate so we can see the truth? I'm willing to walk on a wire but at the same time I fear I'll plunge into an abyss.

'Do you believe in hell?' I ask.

'Hell in a religious sense?'

'No, hell on earth,' I say.

He thinks about it for a while. His eyes wander, then he looks at me. 'I'm Muslim,' he says. 'We believe that hell is guarded by *Maalik*, the leader of the angels. He tells the wicked that they must remain in hell forever because they abhorred the truth when the truth was brought to them.'

'*Maalik.*' I repeat the name, testing its power over me. Nothing. I feel cold inside.

'According to my faith, once the truth is brought to you, don't deny it. Then you have nothing to worry about,' he says.

I am not familiar with Islam or any other faith, I barely know how to pray the Rosary. I haven't been to confession since my first communion. Having faith in the truth is easier said than done, even electroshock therapy seems like a walk in the park compared to his lofty philosophical ideals. His words echo, determined to reach me. *Allow the truth to be brought to you and don't deny it*, is what he said. And I won't have anything to worry about. He must know the truth can be many things and imagining the possibilities makes me shiver.

'And you believe that?' I ask, hoping for some additional words of comfort.

'I believe that, I do. I also believe that we were meant to sit here, like this. And that you will see this through.'

'Going back is like paying with a pound of flesh then?' The moment I say it the reference strikes me as familiar, something more than just an allusion to Shakespeare. My hand moves up to my ear, or rather where my ear used to be.

'When?' I ask, and hope for weeks.

'Soon. We still have a lot to talk about before we go, but you'll be ready. That's a promise.'

'I guess,' I say, and don't mean it.

He looks at his watch. 'Tomorrow we'll continue.'

Continue. Go on. Marge had asked me the other day how I go on. I didn't answer her, for I don't think I'm going on at all. I feel incomplete, as if someone made off with part of my body, leaving me an empty, tormented vessel. A vessel forever open-topped, never again capable of holding it all in. Every pain, every feeling magnified a thousand times. I have to find a way to go on, a way of living with this pain.

There's a knowledge that has manifested itself without my consent, and that knowledge is hard to swallow. I seem to have acquired it like a wooden nickel, by sleight of hand from some evil power. I will never be able to call it the past and bathe in some sunny, brighter future. The past is

171

all there is for me, it's what my life's made out of. Just that, and nothing else.

I used to sing to Mia. I would clear my throat and she would focus on my eyes, and then smile. The first note always made her cock her head.

Sleep baby sleep.

She'd babble along as if attempting to sing with me.

Your father tends the sheep.

There was a frown, a wrinkled forehead.

Your mother shakes the dreamland tree.

Her eyes never left my face, her eyes blinked, ever so fleeting.

And from it fall sweet dreams for thee.

The sing-song tone and exaggerated pitch prompted her to screech.

Sleep, baby, sleep. Sleep, baby, sleep.

Remembering those fleeting moments leaves me with a heavy feeling. Unlike a cut or a bruise it's invisible to outsiders and the fact that I caused the pain myself brings even more agony. With every ounce of my being I wish I had the courage to fling myself off a building or walk into the depths of an ocean, to take a gun and place the cool metal against my temple, pulling the trigger, shooting away what I feel. I realize that this pain will never cease. Like a shore pounded by waves, the force is perpetual and our cord will never be severed. North Dandry is the scariest place I can imagine but there's no alternative. And so I resign myself.

'Tomorrow you'll tell me about your family.'

13

Someone had shoved a lump of clay into my hand. Even now, so many years later, as I sit in Dr Ari's office, I fight the urge to look down at my hand. I don't think I ever threw that lump away. I have forgotten about it at times, but been reminded frequently, like a pebble in a shoe, its presence rendering me unable to move. I'm struck by the intensity of my feelings, even after all these years.

Tell me about your family. Such a simple request, yet such a complicated web. The weight of my family's history is not a matter of heaviness; it is almost weightless, like a ghost.

My mother had delivered a healthy baby girl: Marcia Paradise. I was eleven; my brother Anthony almost eighteen. It was a weekday, and we had stayed home from school. Mom and Dad finally called and said they were on their way home. The previous night I had gone through my bookshelf and closet and selected toys and books for my new sister.

The doorbell rang, but instead of my parents, two police officers and a lady in a beige coat stood on our front stoop. They were matter-of-fact: my parents had been in an accident on their way home from the hospital — pile-up he said and I didn't know what that meant but didn't ask — and did Anthony want to call anybody?

Within hours Aunt Nell, our only relative and

Mom's sister, arrived from New Jersey. She made the living room couch her home, her crimson-rimmed eyes were puffy and she had a habit of shredding Kleenexes. She was taller and heavier than Mom, but they had the same chestnut hair, and nearly identical profiles. Nell's hair was shorter and she seemed like a less refined and polished version of Mom.

The next morning I opened the newspaper and stared at the picture of the accident. There was an aerial photo taken by a news helicopter, cars piled up like an accordion — hood-bumper-hood-bumper — like endless road kill on a gray strip artificially painted onto an otherwise green landscape. The roads seemed like a concrete maze of asphalt and steel bridges, some looping above, some ducking under. It was hard to believe that somewhere in there were my parents and my baby sister.

I went into my father's study and retrieved the round magnifying glass he used when studying his antique map collection. My hand shook as it hovered over the newspaper. The harder I tried to make out our white Suburban, the more the pixels began to dance in front of my eyes. It was impossible to see what was left of my family and I wondered if anyone took a photograph of the baby before she died.

'We have to talk about what we're going to do,' Aunt Nell said the day before the funeral. She sipped her coffee, frowned, and added two more cubes of sugar. 'A lot of things are going to change but I want you to know that . . . ' she cleared her throat and eyed the coffee in her cup, 'the sooner we make those hard decisions, the better.'

I stared at the rings the cup had made on the poplar table, hoping they'd come out with the Old English oil Mom kept under the sink.

'Anthony and I talked earlier and we thought it'd be best if you come to Jersey with me, Stella.'

'To live?' I asked.

'Right,' said Aunt Nell.

'For how long?' I asked.

'That's the thing,' Aunt Nell said. 'After we go to Jersey, you won't be coming back.'

I looked around. 'What about the house? All our stuff?'

'Selling the house seems like the best thing to do.' Aunt Nell pushed her cup towards the middle of the table, making the rings worse. 'We'll sell the house with everything in it.'

Jersey. I thought of the friends I didn't have there and the park that was too far to walk to by myself. I suddenly felt a panic I couldn't describe. I looked over at Anthony who had lowered his head.

Aunt Nell emitted a constant odor of stale smoke and always carried a pack of Virginia Slims in her hand. At that moment I imagined her falling asleep with a slim white cigarette in the living room, burning down the entire house.

'*Waisenkind*,' I said and traced the coffee rings on the table with my eyes.

'What?'

'*Waisenkind*. It's a German word, it means orphan. We read about it in school. Children packed their suitcases the night before they were shipped off to the concentration camps. That's what they wrote on the suitcases. With chalk. *Waisenkind*. An orphaned child. I want to pack my own orphan suitcase.'

'I know this is very difficult for you and your brother, for all of us, but we shouldn't be so dramatic about everything. An orphan suitcase? That's just macabre.' Nell shook her head in disgust.

'What can I keep? What about my books and my furniture?'

'My place is small. Just the essentials. A small bag. We'll manage.' Aunt Nell smiled and nodded the way grown-ups do when they don't mean what they say.

'What about Mom's cameras? And Dad's stuff?' The darkroom was filled with photographs and equipment, my father's study lined with books and trunks full of maps.

'It will be donated,' Aunt Nell said and fidgeted with her hands.

I imagined strangers going through my mother's photographs and my father's maps being sold at some antique sale. I looked around the house. The surfaces were dusty as if the cold ashes from the fireplace had draped the house in a layer of soot. I wanted to take the layer and wrap it around me, the first layer to hide my sadness, the subsequent layers to form a coat that would protect me, so no one could touch me on the inside. Just pretend, I said to myself, pretend you're okay.

Aunt Nell got up and put the cup in the sink.

The rings on the table had widened and had soaked into the wood. I doubted they would ever come out.

That night I climbed into the attic and pulled the smallest suitcase I could find from a shelf of dusty boxes. I packed my father's maps, my mother's photographs, a white baby outfit and a pair of baby shoes, the newspaper with the article of the car pile-up, and Anthony's science fair award.

Days later, when I opened the suitcase in New Jersey, it was full of clothes. When I asked Nell what she had done with the items I put in it, she just shook her head.

'Hanging on to the past is just not very helpful in this situation.'

When I started crying she said, 'This is as hard on me as it is on you. Please don't make a scene.'

* * *

'Every morning I would wake up wondering if it was all a dream. It wasn't like I tried to convince myself they were alive, but I had to get used to them being gone, over and over again, and every morning, during the first few seconds after I opened my eyes, it felt as if they were still alive.' Every morning they died all over again, every morning I started out with hope and within seconds, hope died.

I pause and look around Dr Ari's office, a large rectangular space. A door behind his desk leads to what I assume is his private bathroom. I am aware that I picked the beginning of the story, but why the clay in my hand and the funeral? I hadn't thought of my parents in years, the last time probably in high school, when I stopped searching for my mother's face in a crowd, when my heart no longer skipped a beat when I saw a white Suburban.

'Dr Ari, why am I talking about this? There're no family secrets hidden away in the attic, no bodies buried in the backyard. Why are people always mesmerized with their childhoods?' I keep pulling on my shirt sleeves, they almost reach my fingertips. 'I don't have a single recollection of my childhood before the age of ten. Am I *supposed* to remember anything that far back? It seems like there is this point, there's nothing before and everything after. I'm not sure I'm making sense, I guess what I'm trying to understand is if there's a reason why I don't remember my early childhood.'

'Not remembering doesn't mean your child-hood was bad but not having bad memories doesn't mean that it was good, either.' He seems proud of the comment but confusion must be written all over my face. He crosses his legs and shifts in his chair as if to get comfortable, ready for an extended monologue. 'The first years are all about attachment. The kind of adult you are is the most reliable indicator of a positive or negative childhood, more reliable than any memory or the lack thereof.' Dr Ari looks at me as if this is supposed to explain something.

I am perplexed. 'Given why I'm here, that means what?'

'Thinking about your mother, what is the most — '

'Let's get real, let's just call it what it is. I'm here trying to remember if I had anything to do with the disappearance of my daughter. And I'm being kind, I could ask the real question, the one everybody's wanting an answer to.' I can feel myself getting upset, my heart is beating hard against my chest and I feel the urge to get up and move around.

'So you don't want to talk about your mother?'

'No, no, you're getting it all wrong. It's not that I don't want to talk about her. My senses don't remember her, not her scent, the touch of her hand, her presence, how it felt being around her. Just facts is what I recall. She was always busy, slightly distant maybe, but what does that mean? What's the conclusion I should draw from that? What does that say about me?'

'Like I said, it means nothing at this point,' he says.

'What if I . . . ' I stop, I don't know where to go from here.

'Being distant is not hereditary, it's not a genetic mutation, if that's what you're wondering,' Dr Ari says.

'Maybe not in a hereditary way but how about a pattern? Is that possible?'

'We can't draw any conclusions from that. Let me give you an example: The child of a drug addict will deal with the addiction — one way of coping would be to keep the drugs a secret. Which leads to keeping more secrets. Think of

179

the behavior of children more like an attempt to cope with their parents' shortcomings.'

'What a shame my mother is not around to answer any questions.' I try not to sound sarcastic but I can't help it.

'In my line of work we usually don't confront parents until it is too late. Makes for a one-sided conversation, doesn't it?'

'That's why so many people see shrinks.'

Dr Ari squeezes his lips shut until they disappear and his mouth looks like a slash made by a knife. He begins to tap his leg, then scoots to the front of his chair and leans forward.

'Don't think of me as a shrink. Think of me as, as . . . ' he is scanning his mind for the right word, and then his face lights up, 'your midwife, in a way. Think of me as your midwife. I'm here to assist you to birth the past. Neither compassion nor friendship will help you complete the process. You'll ignore me, beg me to make it stop, most certainly you will hate me at some point. Eventually, when you cradle the truth in your arms, you'll realize that I was on your side all along.'

You're on my side then, I want to ask him, but I don't. As I think about his words, I realize that the only thing I can ask for is someone to be on my side. That very moment, I decide to trust him and that I will allow him to take me places I would rather not go if I want to find my daughter. Or find out what happened to her. Or find out what I have done to her.

'You seem tense,' Dr Ari says, looking at my hands.

I'm a miner, I descend deeper into the mineshaft and all I have to do is bring gemstones up into the light. If memories are gems, I will continue on, leaving it to Dr Ari to separate fools' gold from whatever is precious.

★   ★   ★

At my parents' funeral someone had shoved a lump of clay into my hand. I stood beside a dark hole in the ground. The church service, the mourners, the prayers — they had nothing to do with my family. The undertakers had propped up three coffins — a small one in between two larger ones. The priest was young and his attempt at growing a moustache had resulted in nothing but a few sorry whiskers. His skin was poreless as if he had been dipped in wax.

Suddenly I remembered Joan Hardaway, a girl who lived on our street and went to school with me. We all knew she was a cutter, but we couldn't grasp what that really meant. All we knew was that she liked to hurt herself. Joan Hardaway was a doughy girl with a flaky scalp and yellow teeth. I saw her legs once, after PE when we changed clothes. Her thighs were covered in red spider webs. They seemed deliberate, like images drawn in the sand, illegible, but spelling out some sort of pain. I remember thinking how odd it was to create more pain in order to forget pain. It seemed illogical then.

Aware of Dr Ari's questioning eyes I realize that I haven't spoken in a while. The memory of the funeral evokes nausea, just as strongly today as it did fifteen years ago. I must stay focused; I must speak slowly and deliberately, must tell him what happened, that I threw the lump of clay and how it thumped off my sister's coffin and rolled into a flower arrangement.

I tell Dr Ari how I turned into a bystander because being in the picture seemed too painful, as if observing myself reduced the pain somehow, and vividly, I see Anthony and me, standing there, holding hands.

When they lowered the coffins into the ground, one by one, pulling away the ropes with an indifferent flick of their wrists, I started crying. I tried to pull away from him but he held on to me, squeezed my hand so hard it hurt.

'No. NO. *Wait*.' I screamed, followed by a universal gasp. Women started sobbing in the cluster of mourners, handkerchiefs pressed against their mouths, their eyes wide, embarrassment in their muffled voices.

'Stella, please, don't.' Anthony's voice was pleading. 'Stop pulling so hard. Stop pulling my — '

My sobs became louder, the tears made it impossible to see anything, but I knew everybody was looking at me, staring at the little girl who was losing it. I managed to pull my hand out of Anthony's grip and stepped forward.

I had no plans to jump in, I didn't prepare for a leap. I lost my footing when the ground caved in right at the edge, by the mat of artificial grass. I fell and landed, like a shovelful of newly dug earth, on one of the larger coffins. The scent of gardenias was overwhelming, the wreaths were sharp, making my skin itch. I rolled over, my shoulder throbbing, and looked up. Dozens of eyes stared down at me, towering, countless hands extending, waiting for my hand to reach out and grasp theirs. I sat on top of the coffin, not sure if it was my mom's or dad's, faces staring down at me. I looked past them, up into the sky. Anthony lowered himself into the hole and held me up for hands to pull me out.

Hours later everybody had gathered at our home, a house with a cold and ashy fireplace that felt unsympathetic. I sat in an armchair turned to face the front door and the first thing anyone saw when they walked in was a girl with a sullen face and a full plate in her lap. I had filled it with meatballs, potato salad, finger sandwiches, and stuffed mushrooms. Aunt Nell gave me a look, and I stacked some more sandwiches on top. I sat, plate on my lap, not bothering with a fork or napkin, and eyed the people spilling through the door. My silent guarding of the door didn't go over well; adults didn't know whether to stroke my hair or hand me a fork. No one greeted me as they entered the house but one middle-aged lady with noticeable upper-lip hair, who I had never met before, kept eyeing me.

'Hello, Sally,' she said, and offered her hand. How I wished to be a Sally somewhere, I thought, but didn't correct her, nor did I shake her hand. Her dark reddish roots made it seem as if she was bleeding from her parted hair.

'I'm so sorry for your loss,' she added.

'Thank you, Shirley,' I said. 'Thank you so much.'

She looked at me puzzled and walked off to talk to Aunt Nell.

The entire time I sat by the door, 'Shirley' kept eyeing me suspiciously. I sat for a long time and watched the stream of mourners reverse itself until finally the house was empty.

I grabbed Anthony's hand and pulled him into my dad's study. The walls were covered in black-and-white photographs of buildings, the majority of them industrial. The first one, right by the door, was the Lipstick Building, at 53rd and Third, shaped as if oval hatboxes had been stacked on top of each other. There were photographs of churches, I recognized the Riverside Church, the Bryant Park Hotel, and Grand Central Terminal, my favorite. Photographs of buildings lined the walls like family pictures, taken by my father the architect, who dealt with the aesthetics and value of buildings and lived in a world made of stone and steel, slabs and cement.

The shades had been pulled and the big cedar chest in the corner released a spicy odor, strong and fragrant. Dad kept his historical map collection in that chest. Over the years the maps' wet-rag-in-the-kitchen-sink aroma had changed to the same aromatic odor of the chest. There was also a hint of smoke in the air. I had seen Aunt Nell smoke on the front stoop and in the backyard but maybe she had started plopping herself down in my father's chair, propping up her feet, having a cigarette. I had a vision of her,

184

wearing my mother's dress, walking through the house, smoking, and making endless plans we knew nothing about.

Anthony closed the door behind us. The moist spring air played gently with the thin, parchment-like blueprints and floor plans on my father's mahogany desk. My brother looked at me, and then lowered his head. I detected shame in his face.

I looked at this face, a face that had changed dramatically over the past week, as if adulthood had come to him overnight. His facial hair so out of place, his body large and more muscular than I'd remembered. He seemed grown up, capable, and I felt small next to him.

'We don't need Aunt Nell, we can take care of ourselves. You're almost eighteen and they'll let you take care of me.'

'Stella, I can't.'

'Yes, you can. We can. Aunt Nell is nothing to us, I can hardly stand to look at her, and I wish she'd pack up and leave. The sooner the better.'

'I can't take care of you, I can't. It's not that I don't wa-wa-want to. I ju-just, I . . . ' He started to stutter, something he hadn't done in years.

Then he regained his composure, as if he decided that this childish affliction was uncalled for. His eyes were red and he paced the study, looking for words and a way out. 'I'm going to a Military Academy. I'll be leaving in two months.' His words hung between us and sucked the air out of the room. The world was motionless, even the curtains had stopped wafting in the breeze.

My throat was sore, and every time I

185

swallowed I was back in the dream where a blackbird slid down my esophagus in slow motion. Just as the dream pain of the beak ripping holes and tearing flesh lingered, so did the cruelness of his words. My heart pounded as if the blackbird was trapped in my chest, its wings expanding with every minute. I caught a glimpse of why Joan cut herself to get away from pain. If you replace one pain with another, it seems as if you're in control.

'It won't be as bad as you think,' Anthony said and I felt myself shifting, departing from my body.

An echo of heeled shoes tapping over the wooden floors came down the hallway towards the study, but then it quieted and I was no longer sure if someone was coming towards me or moving away. Either way, I felt nothing from that point on.

* * *

Dr Ari pushes a box of Kleenex my way. I'm crying, but there is no sobbing, just flowing tears running down my cheeks, my neck, in my mouth, and under my shirt. They taste like the tears I had cried the day of the funeral and I wonder if tears of joy taste any different. The memory of my parents' funeral is strong, yet I don't know why it still has such a fierce hold on me.

I keep my posture upright, trying to keep my pain inconspicuous. I'm not fooling Dr Ari, the ever-present hawk, spotting pain like prey,

186

descending, striking.

'I felt so safe in my sadness and I told myself it couldn't get much worse. My parents were dead, my brother was leaving, and Aunt Nell was picking at what was left of our family and our house, like a vulture pecking away at shiny spilled guts. I thought I'd basically reached the lowest point possible. But I was wrong. So wrong.'

I look down at my hands, expecting to see that lump of clay. But my hands are empty. We have barely peeled away the outer layer and we both know there are many more layers left to tear away, wounds to be opened deeper until white bone shines through. I am done; I am not going to volunteer any more information.

'I'm so very sorry this happened to you,' Dr Ari says.

I hear a voice. It is my own voice, betraying myself. 'Look at me. Just look at me, sitting here, trying to remember something that . . . ' I am searching for words, probing my mind, struggling to interpret the turn my life has taken. 'What now? I don't know where to go from here.' Maybe I was just a kid who lost her parents and felt alone. Maybe my childhood was tragic, but my despair had started before the funeral, way before everything, maybe even the moment I was born.

'Dr Ari, are some people born sad? I don't mean introverted and withdrawn, but depressed? Did I emerge from my mother's womb with a predisposition to . . . whatever it is . . . sadness? Is that possible?'

187

'There is a genetic vulnerability caused by neurotransmitters and biochemical agents, but there are also developmental events, like the death of your parents. Grief is a very strong childhood stressor.'

For the first time I see myself through the eyes of people at the funeral. I was what? Just eccentric? Or did I fit the bill of a disturbed, maybe even crazy girl? It's like looking in a funhouse mirror, only I'm *not* distorted. I am *that* way, a gloomy girl, sitting at the door, staring at people — that's me.

'To be honest, my glass has always been half-empty. Not only as an adult, but as a child. I don't remember any specific moment I felt happiness. I don't remember being just over the moon, elated, whatever you want to call it. After I gave birth I felt joy, I felt accomplished. The fact that I had a caesarean section in the end was irrelevant. That my body was capable of bringing forth this human being, that was joy. That's the most fitting word I can come up with. And again, what was I supposed to compare it to? Feeling happy is almost something that I can't feel, like I'm not made to pick up on it or something.' I point at the digital recorder in front of him. 'Like this recorder. It can only record audio, it can't pick up on anything else. You can't record the temperature of the room, you don't know what the weather was like at the moment when you listen to it later on. Not sure if that makes sense.'

'I beg to differ.'

'About what?' I ask.

188

'That there were no moments of happiness in your life. Maybe you don't remember every single one, but . . . ' He pauses and then his face lights up. 'When I was a child, my grandmother taught me to play *Petteia*, a board game. A simplified chess game if you will. But you win by majority, not with a certain piece or move.'

'Your grandmother teaching you a board game is happiness?'

'It was not so much the game itself but the fact that she tried to teach me some sort of lesson. I remember that you had to somehow surround your opponent's stones in order to win.'

'So she taught you some kind of war strategy, is that what you're trying to tell me?'

'I never saw it as a war strategy, just the fact that patience is always rewarded. But mostly I remember the clicking of the stones on the board. The scent of the tea, the jingling of her jewelry. Her patience while talking me through the moves, explaining the strategy. And she always allowed me to redo a move if it proved crucial. She was a kind and wise woman.'

'Do you still know how to play the game?'

'Barely. I don't think I ever really mastered it.'

'So . . . the lesson here is?'

'There are moments of joy in everybody's life. Happiness, like sadness, comes wrapped in many layers.'

'Just like memories.'

'Just like memories,' he says.

'I just have to find those moments.' I pause for a while and consider the ratio of sadness and happiness in my life. 'Sad moments are right on top, but the happy ones seem to hide.'

I turn my head towards the wall to my right. A file cabinet takes up the entire space, small drawers strategically concealing its utilitarian purpose. Smooth-sliding pullout drawers filled with obsolete paper files. Dr Ari's awards hover in symmetry, under Plexiglas, anchored with invisible wall attachments. Does he not believe in signs of weakness in his constructed world; therefore even the frames must pretend they don't need a nail to stay put?

'Anthony probably doesn't even know I'm here.'

Dr Ari raises his eyebrows, then flips over my file as if handling the folder gives him an illusion of manipulating my known past with his hands.

'Maybe that's a conversation we need to have soon.' He pulls out his pocket watch as if he doesn't trust the time-keeping abilities of the plastic clock on his desk. 'For tomorrow I want you to think of the concept of happiness.'

'Can one think of happiness?' I ask.

'A memory is a place you visit, not where you live. Happiness therefore is not a permanent state of being, but more a moment in time. Think of a moment for me?'

I shrug and remind him that our time's up.

* * *

Later that night, as I write in my journal, and I reflect on Dr Ari's story of his grandmother, I try to recall happy surroundings and details, more than the feeling of happiness. I try to think of past happy moments as having fallen into pieces and recovering them as a matter of putting them back together again.

Then an image pops into my head. The image of a building and its still beauty in stark contrast with the busy atmosphere. In that memory, my father wears a dark-blue suit and an overcoat. I wear a dress and black lacquered shoes that pinch my toes. My father has promised me a 'well-guarded secret.'

We are in Grand Central Terminal for my tenth birthday.

'When we leave the terminal,' he says, 'you'll be one of a chosen few who know about this secret.' His voice sounds conspiratorial; all that is missing is a black cloak and a magic wand.

'You're not serious, are you, Dad? You're kidding, right?'

'Estelle, I'm very serious. Do you know who Adolf Hitler is?'

'Of course I know. The dictator of Nazi Germany. I hope this isn't a history lesson.'

'No, it's not. It's your birthday after all,' he says and chuckles.

'What does Hitler have to do with this secret?'

He lowers his voice, bends down, and whispers in my ear: 'What if I told you that he sent spies to sabotage the secret?'

'And did they?'

'No. The FBI arrested them.'

'The FBI is involved?' This is so much better than anything else I could have imagined.

We reach the Main Concourse and Dad grabs

191

my hand. I look at him and then follow the direction of his eyes upwards. We are standing under some sort of astronomical mural. The background is blue, the constellations gold. It covers the ceiling of the entire Main Concourse. I'm getting dizzy looking up. I lower my head and hold on to his hand.

'What's that?' I ask.

'That, my love, is a design by a French painter. How many stars you think there are?'

I'm feeling queasy. I decide not to look back up and I just guess what I conceive to be a fairly accurate number. 'Five hundred.'

'Two thousand five hundred stars. It's supposed to be the Mediterranean sky. The larger stars are the constellations.'

'What's so special about it and why did the spies try to sabotage it?'

'Oh, no, this isn't the secret the spies tried to sabotage. We'll get to that later. I just wanted to show you this because the painter made a mistake without knowing.'

'A mistake?' I scan the mural.

'Yes, he used an old antique manuscript. Took them a long time to figure out the reason why he made the mistake. See, they ended up being backwards. Back then the cartographers displayed the zodiacs as they appeared from the outside looking in.'

'Do you have that manuscript at home?'

He laughs and says, 'Do we have the *Mona Lisa* hanging in our living room? I have a replica. I'll show it to you when we get home. Let's go.'

He tightens his grip around my hand as we

walk to the back of the terminal. We reach an old service elevator. He pushes a button and the door immediately opens as if it had been waiting for us. We get in and the elevator descends, screeching and shaking.

Of course I have ridden elevators before, but I remember them to be dimly lit and creaky cages moving snail-like and deprived of oxygen. The feel of this elevator isn't any different, yet the humming in the background seems mysterious and it might as well take me to another dimension. The fact that I am about to discover a secret is the most magical moment of my life and when it grinds to a halt, I want to beg my father *again, again, again*, but somehow that seems childish. Right before the elevator stops, my body feels weightless, as if the entire world pauses for a second.

When we get out, we are in a utilitarian part of the building. The room is huge, its ceiling higher than I expected a ceiling to be underground. One side of the room is covered with boxy metal containers with controls and the other holds old machines that look like colossal clock gears. The floor grates are large and vibrate through my shoes. I feel hot air blowing through them, and I hear giant fans underneath me.

'Here we are!' My dad is elated.

I don't seem to understand, I don't know what it is he sees, I feel like I'm letting him down, as if I'm supposed to know the significance of this room.

'M-42,' he adds.

'Right.' I don't know what else to say.

'This is a very important part of the terminal. Only a chosen few know about this secret basement. You're standing in M-42, the secret sub-level. How about that?'

I look around and I have to admit that the large gears protruding from the ground are very mysterious. 'That's what the spies tried to sabotage? Why?'

He lowers his voice as if he's trying to keep his answer a secret. 'If the spies had disabled the converters, they would have shut down the entire terminal during the second World War. It was so guarded that anybody down here without permission would've ended up in jail. Or shot.'

'Okay then.'

'Do you know what that means?'

I don't know what to say, and shrug.

'It means that you're standing in a spot that isn't on any map, any blueprint. Every building ever built has a blueprint, every building has to be designed on paper before the builders put brick on top of brick. Walls hold up the roof, floors hold up the walls, that sort of thing, and architects calculate and plan every inch of a building. You're in a room only a few people know about, yet millions pass over it every day without knowing. Pretty fascinating, isn't it?'

I ponder it for a while and I'm starting to understand his enthusiasm. 'I guess I shouldn't share this secret with anyone then, right?' I say and add a conspiring wink.

His brow furrows, but only for a moment. Then he smiles at me. 'It's our secret. One day, maybe ten or fifteen years from now, there'll be guided tours, TV specials. And then this place will no longer be a secret.' He checks his watch. 'But for now, it's our secret. What do you think?'

'It's pretty cool, actually. All those people upstairs in the terminal don't know about this, catching trains, going to work or home, unaware of this place. And the fact that we get to see it while it's still special.'

'I think so too. I knew you'd love this place,' he says and hand in hand we walk back to the elevator that will take us back upstairs to the main terminal buzzing with people, insect-like, fulfilling their destinies and a complexity of tasks, demonstrating what a wonder the world really is.

★ ★ ★

That night, as I lie awake and stare at the ceiling in my room, I try to understand what has happened, not the details or minute particulars of Mia's whereabouts, but my possible part in the direction my life has taken.

I close my eyes and travel back to my childhood, I feel the chenille bedspread under my fingers and hear the old oak tree scratch the windowpane. The only filter people have is their childhood and as my parents' ghostly apparition materializes, I concede my parents were physically there for me; they fed me, clothed me, and provided for me.

And then it hits me. My father never pulled me off a ledge, never ran into the street after me to save me from an approaching car. I don't remember receiving any physical affection from my mother but I assume that she sat with me when I was sick as a child, and I'm almost sure she made my Halloween costumes.

But once I look for more than the average proof of affection, I come up empty. It all comes down to this: I don't know how to judge my parents' love for me. Life never prompted them to take extraordinary measures, never urged them to declare the depth of their love beyond genetic affection. They cared for me. Beyond that, it was run-of-the-mill obligation. And again, my satchel holds no jewels. Just rocks.

14

'Tell me about Jack,' Dr Ari says.

We have finally arrived at the chapter named Jack, the man I married only a year after we met. Speaking of him starts to unsettle the ground. Jack, all in all, is a warm memory, yet I feel cold inside. It seemed I went from my parents' house in Bedford to Nell's house in Jersey, and then off to cheap apartments in basements. After I married Jack I was off to his apartment on William Street. It was perched on the 36th floor of the Gotham Tower Condominium Building, with its unsettling echo between the walls. It seemed like a castle and I got to live in its tower, complete with a spiral staircase. I somehow knew there'd be a price to pay to live there.

'This is a big place,' I had said and had tried, unsuccessfully, to keep my heels from clattering on the slate floor.

'You say that like it's a bad thing.' Jack took off his coat and sat his briefcase on the enameled lava countertop. The gesture was an indication of things to come; when I think of Jack now I see him either putting on a coat or taking it off, coming or going, but never really being there.

'What's the price of admission?' I asked lightheartedly, eyeing the tin ceiling promising to last a lifetime.

Jack stood by the window, enthralled by the stunning view of the city. 'Your soul,' he said

197

jokingly, his shadow disturbing the perfect sheen of the hardwood floors.

I remember how months before we had walked by protestors in front of an abortion clinic. Jack had frowned and 'Baby killer,' he had said, 'abortion makes you a baby killer.' Those were his words.

Dr Ari watches me fold my arms in front of my chest.

'Jack used to call me his princess, he was old-fashioned in many ways; flowers, gifts, opening doors, that kind of thing. But nothing was as it seemed, Jack had money problems, some investment gone awry, and he eventually took a job in Chicago. It was a temporary job but it paid well and it allowed us to get out of debt.'

After he reaches into his desk drawer, Dr Ari takes off his glasses and polishes the lenses with a cloth. Is he ready to look closer or is he just tired of smudges infesting his world?

Tapping his pen on the folder in front of him, he then opens the folder and shuffles papers around. He wants to make sure he gets it right.

'Mia was seven months old and it must've been a difficult decision for your husband to make, considering the state you were in.'

'Women raise children alone every day.'

'Tell me about how you were feeling.' Dr Ari reels me back in, not willing to let go of what's on the other end of this rope.

I look around his office, trying to focus on something that will allow my heartbeat to slow. The pounding in my temples is painful, as if there is something trapped inside of me trying to escape.

I tell him how I was tired, overwhelmed, covered in spit-up. How ever since I had Mia, I felt I didn't belong in the body of a mother. How going out just meant having to put on clothes and a fake smile for the world around me. How my dark days started with watching Jack leave in a dry-cleaned suit and a starchy shirt, smelling of shoe polish and coffee and, when the door closed behind him, how I descended into darkness. Then Jack came home and I was still alone. And I descended even deeper. How I couldn't keep up with her demands, how Jack told me, in so many words, to snap out of it. And how all those months of Jack telling me to get it together had finally paid off and by the time he went to Chicago to allow us a new start I had managed to turn myself inside out, like a dirty sock, into a better, more cheerful version of myself.

'Did you ever see a doctor?' Dr Ari's eyes are observant and concerned.

When I tell him a doctor prescribed antidepressants, he asks if I ever saw a professional, a counselor or psychiatrist, and if I ever attempted therapy.

'Therapy was the last thing I needed. Imagining the sound of my own voice going over the same old stuff made me sick just thinking about it.'

I hold myself perfectly still. I lower my eyes. I focus on the manila folder in front of Dr Ari. His hands are folded, resting on top, his manicured nails shiny and perfectly shaped. I wonder what the file holds. Police reports, medical files, photographs, newspaper articles.

'I don't want you to think that it was all doom and gloom. The fact that I created a miracle wasn't lost on me, not for a second. I loved Mia so much I thought my heart was going to explode out of my body. But when she started crying all the time, the days became endless.' The last word prompts me to shake my head.

Dr Ari's eyes have the generic expression reserved for the borderline insane. 'Did you feel like a bad mother when you couldn't stop her from crying?'

'I did what the doctors told me to do but nothing worked.'

I felt watched, observed, under a microscope. I tell Dr Ari that I saw it in their eyes. *Watch the crazy woman who can't take care of her baby.* Doctors. Jack. Nurses. People in the streets. They gave me advice, do this, do that, don't rock her so hard, rock her more, let her cry it out, hold her, everybody and everywhere, at grocery stores, at the park.

'When nothing worked, what did you tell yourself?'

'Now, at this very moment, I understand that things change. That everything passes, that the way I felt was not the way it was going to end. But back then, my world didn't reach any further than the moment I was in. I was easy pickings.'

'Did you think Mia was suffering? Did you think you had to somehow absolve her from you as a mother, from her pain? Was that a thought in your mind?'

My brain is racing for ways out and a rush of heat overtakes me. Thoughts accelerate inside my head, I want them to slow but they don't.

'There are things I can't say out loud. It's like I'm wearing an armor.'

'Can you try to write it down?' Dr Ari pushes my journal towards me. He takes a deep breath in and then breathes out, releasing his frustration. It escapes and fills the room with heaviness. 'You didn't write in your journal yesterday. Why not?'

His irritation engulfs me like a heavy cloud. I haven't delivered the goods; I haven't kept up my end of the bargain. Lately I think so hard my head hurts; every day, during our sessions, every night when I write in my journal, every waking moment, I think. Even my dreams are constant inquiries, intrusively probing for the truth.

There's a wall, and regardless of how hard I try to will myself to see what's on the other side, it never manifests itself. Instead, I get headaches — pounding, dull headaches — right behind my eyes.

'Tell me what you didn't write down.'

I raise my voice. 'It was nothing, really. A large tree obstructing the view of a building. In my dream the wind moves the branches, makes them sway, but I can barely see past them. The windows are looking at me like eyes, I'm close, so close, but then it all disappears and I'm back where I started.'

'In a dream, a tree is never just a tree.' Dr Ari tries to coax me back to the path of recollection, littered with pebbles supposed to trigger my

201

memory, so I may continue with the story he longs to hear. He retrieves my journal and studies the last entry.

Since I've arrived at Creedmoor my sleeping pattern has adjusted. The constant anxious state I was in had made it hard to settle down but the rigid schedule at Creedmoor forces some sort of tranquility upon me. I'm no longer a walking zombie, no longer unable to focus on mundane tasks.

Dr Ari explained to me that I needed to verbally state my desire to recall my dreams as I am falling asleep. I've been using a special digital alarm clock that wakes me every ninety minutes starting at three o'clock in the morning, during or immediately after the REM periods of sleep. Last night something changed. It started with dream images of a small house, only one square room. There was a river running by the side of the house. The house slightly leaning towards the river. The river was moving recklessly, its currents were powerful, almost raging. I was aware of the danger, I could almost feel the pressure the raging waters put on the walls around me. They were straining, the walls of the room were screeching and moaning. I could see water trickling through the cracks and I knew it was just a matter of time before the door would give way to the power of the flood. It was just a matter of time before the waters would gush forth and the river would pick me up and carry me away. In my dream I was searching for a way out of the house and when the alarm woke me, I was still searching.

As I nibble on my frayed nails I remember how it felt, searching frantically, heart pounding, breathing rapid and shallow. Sometimes you remember one thing, and that one thing makes you remember something else and before you know it, you remember everything.

I'm tired. Tired of reducing my memories to rubble, tired of unfolding the membranes and layers of my brain when all I do is make up stories. That's what they are. *Stories*. I'm in survival mode and my mind has muzzled the truth, instead lies I tell myself swirl all around me, suffocating the truth. *Am I a Monster?*

Instead I say, 'What I neglected to write down was that last night I remembered when I left the house to search for Mia.'

Dr Ari flips through the pages in the manila folder. He pulls out the North Dandry blueprint stapled to the property deed. A blueprint of a house, a map of its rooms, hallways, and doors. He unfolds it, and disappears behind it as if he is casually reading the Sunday morning paper. He realizes the words are upside down and he flips it over and continues to study. The waxen paper is strong; its creases resist any fold but the original one.

For a moment I'm mesmerized by the sound of the paper. I wonder if words and pictures imprinted on it alter its sound. The sound of candy wrappers holds the promise of sweetness, wrapping paper evokes Christmas mornings and birthday wishes fulfilled.

The map reminds me of my father's maps tucked away in trunks in his study, old and frequently handled. Touching them sounded like the passing of distances itself, parchment and vellum, lightweight and translucent. Made from sheep skin, its animal source outdated compared to the waxed paper floor plan Dr Ari is holding in his hands. I can almost hear the blueprint of North Dandry in his hands starting to vibrate.

Finally Dr Ari emerges from his paper fortification. He puts the blueprint on his desk. The floor plan is littered with interior walls and hallways, their orientation downward from above. Dr Ari is looking at God's view of a human attempt to create shelter from his wrath.

'Tell me about your search.'

What kind of mother would I be if I didn't look for my child?

* * *

I tried to force myself to think logically. The first thing you do when you've lost something is to go look for it. I had read articles about parents who had left infants in the backseats of cars, in strollers, and even at daycares, forgotten like an umbrella on the subway or a bag at a restaurant.

I stood on the sidewalk and looked left, then right. There was an abandoned red couch on the curb, a cardboard sign 'Take Me' propped up in the corner.

I shielded my eyes with both hands to see through the tinted windows of my car. Nothing but an empty car seat stared back at me. I hit the unlock button on the keyless remote and the trunk popped open. Mia's old rear-facing baby seat and the old empty suitcase I took to New Jersey a long time ago. I had switched prematurely to a front-facing seat because Mia seemed calmer when she was able to see me. The suitcase in the trunk was dented; the locking mechanism no longer worked. It was the same suitcase I had taken to Jersey so many years ago.

I closed the trunk with a hefty thump. The street noises were familiar, it was Sunday and from the church across the street, St. Joseph's, organ pipes sustained the tones of an unfamiliar hymn. About a hundred yards further down the street was the subway entrance. A homeless woman sat by the iron fence leading downstairs. A small dog cowered on a piece of cardboard next to her, a greasy bandana wrapped around its neck. When I approached, the dog lifted its head. The woman wore at least three or four layers of clothes. The top layer was a large black garbage bag with a hole for her head and two for her arms. Next to her sat two plastic bags bursting with clothes and blankets. Her eyes were closed but her posture was tense.

'Excuse me,' I said and watched one of her eyes open. The dog growled and got up. She put her dirty hand on the dog's back. He lowered himself back down to the ground but kept an eye on me.

'What d'ya want?' she demanded.

'Have you been sitting here long?' I asked.

She sat in silence.

'Have you seen someone leave my building with a . . . ' I hesitated. Maybe this wasn't such a good idea after all. I stepped closer and the dog

205

let out a low growl. 'A baby,' I added and realized immediately how insane that sounded.

'Got some change?' The woman pulled a banana from underneath her raincoat garbage bag.

'No, no I don't, I don't have my wallet on me, but I need to know if you saw anyone leave the building down there,' I pointed down the street, towards 517, 'kind of where that red couch is. With a baby. Did you see anyone with a baby?'

'I see a lot.' She made a sucking noise through her teeth and unpeeled the overripe fruit. Then she looked me up and down. 'A baby you say? Your baby?'

'Yes, she's seven months old, someone took her. Did you see anything?'

'Your baby's gone?' she asked and her toothless gums pinched off a piece of the banana. 'Should've kept her close.' She smacked her lips, taking another bite. 'I have a son,' she continued. 'You wanna see him? He's always with me.' She scanned the sidewalk as if to make sure there weren't any onlookers. The dog gladly took what was left of her banana.

'Your son?' I asked.

'My son.'

'I don't . . . just . . . I really just need to know if you saw anything.'

She reached under her raincoat bag, dug deep within the layers and pulled out a bundle of dirty rags. She unfolded the fabric, one corner at a time, as if the bundle contained a precious gem. When she lifted the last corner, she smiled a toothless smile. There was a large brown mass

206

nestled between the folds. I swallowed hard. A stench of decay drifted my way.

'I wish I had a home for him,' the woman said and stroked a mummified squirrel with her blackened fingertips. 'He's in bad shape. This ain't no place to keep a child. You have something I can put him in?'

She held up the bundle. An incision ran the length of the squirrel's stomach. I shuddered and turned my head. I fought to stay in control of my stomach but the battle was all but lost.

I ran less than half a block down North Dandry, towards Liberty Street. I turned into an alley to the right, the back of a deli facing Linden Street to the front, and I vomited. Then I continued to heave, unable to get the hollow cavity of the squirrel's shell out of my head.

I finally looked around: an array of fruit crates filled with wilted lettuces and shriveled cucumbers on top of dented cans of chick peas. The stench was horrific. A decaying and almost liquefied head of lettuce sat on top of a food crate filled with cadaverous tomatoes, dented cans of corn, flattened milk cartons, and a mesh bag of shriveled oranges covered in a bluish-green mold.

Walking back towards 517, I again passed the homeless woman. The dog looked up at me, but this time wagged its tail. The woman's eyes were closed, her head resting on her chest. I walked past her, down North Dandry. I opened the trunk of my car, sat the car seat on the ground, and grabbed the dented suitcase.

I kept my eyes on the woman, and even as I

207

placed the suitcase down next to her, she remained silent and motionless.

★ ★ ★

I sat on the couch in the living room for what felt like hours. It was so quiet that I was aware of my own heartbeat. I tried to occupy my mind with questions like where to look, where I had already looked, what to do next. I pushed thoughts of fear for Mia's wellbeing and life aside, as if not entertaining them made them less possible. And then it struck me, a newly formed logic, a possibility I hadn't thought of yet. I wasn't any different than the old homeless woman on the corner passing off a hollowed-out squirrel as her son.

This is crazy, all of this is *crazy*.

No one came and took Mia.

No one took her clothes and her bottles and her formula.

No one walked through walls with her diapers, no one got past the locks and bolts and bars. There was only one logical explanation for this entire scenario: there was no baby. There never had been a baby. Mia was but a figment of my imagination. How else could I explain that everything belonging to my baby was gone? Clothes, diapers, bottles. I needed proof, proof that she had really existed. I needed to convince myself that I wasn't crazy.

I got up and went to the bedroom. I took off my shirt and my bra. I stood with my back to the long dressing mirror. I remained still, preparing for a moment of truth. Certainly there would be marks on my body if I had given birth. There should be excess weight around the midsection, soft, flabby skin not quite back to its original state. There should be stretch marks, a *linea nigra*, and darkened nipples.

My sanity depended on what I was going to see in the mirror. I took in a deep breath and turned around. The woman in the mirror was lean, on the verge of being bony. Her cheekbones were pronounced, her skin seemed paper-thin. Her breasts were of normal size. There were no stretch marks, no darkened line down her belly or enlarged nipples.

I followed the contours of my stomach, hesitated at the waistband. I closed my eyes and pulled the elastic down. A horizontal surgical scar from a caesarean section, raised and pink. I traced the cord of scar tissue, the palpable bumps, the ridge of sutures, with my fingers.

It was real. I wasn't crazy after all. I couldn't believe that I'd ever doubted Mia existed and the fact that I stood in front of a mirror checking my body for signs of recent childbearing, now seemed ridiculous. But I wasn't so much surprised that I hadn't imagined Mia. I had expected a model-thin body, but I was merely skin and bones. What happened? What the hell had happened to me? When did I go from a once attractive woman to this? A few more weeks and I'd be nothing but skeletal remains.

The biggest surprise wasn't that I hadn't imagined Mia. The real surprise was that this bony and emaciated woman, this lunatic in the mirror, was in one piece.

What held her together I had no idea.

Part three

'It takes all the running you can do,
to keep in the same place. If you
want to get somewhere else, you
must run at least twice as fast
as that!'

Lewis Carroll,
Alice in Wonderland

15

Dawn has not yet given way to the morning light when an orderly escorts us to a white van. I sit in the back, Dr Ari sits to my left, behind the driver seat. His briefcase rests between us, with his right arm on top as if guarding a secret hiding between its leather skin and silk fabric lining. We depart down the serpentine driveway flanked by weeping willows. Their branches waft in the breeze like the coattails of an eerie congregation.

The orderly, who I've seen occasionally during mealtimes, wears a leather jacket over his scrubs. His name is Oliver. His fingertips are callused, and veins, like blue rivers, travel up and disappear into the sleeves of his jacket. When the time is right I will inquire about the rugged condition of his hands, but for now, I watch his fingers operating the radio. He is young and good-looking and I decide to use him as a distraction.

Dr Ari wears a suit and a trench coat. This is the first time I've seen him not shrouded in white. The radio volume is low yet I recognize Maroon 5's 'She Will Be Loved.'

French toast is churning in my stomach, but I vow to keep in control. Thirty minutes into the ride the queasiness begins to leave me, but a substantial pressure has settled between my eyes, leaving fuzzy outlines of passing cars like laser tracers in the dark.

'What happened to your hair?' Dr Ari asks.

I lean to the left but can't see myself in the rearview mirror.

'I cut it last night. Do you like it?'

I try to sound indifferent but I'm not, I actually hate what I've done to it. Wanting my outside to reflect the change I've been going through on the inside, I attempted to change something about me, something visible, something everybody would notice.

Knowing that today's trip was imminent, I wondered where to turn for support — what a juvenile notion — and remembered a specific Catholic saint. Both my parents were Catholic, and even though they weren't practicing, my birth certificate proclaims the same denomination. My brother shares his name with Saint Anthony, a Franciscan monk with tonsured hair and the patron saint of lost articles and missing persons, who cut his hair as a symbol of his renunciation of the world. I felt compelled, for a second, to shave my entire head, but then decided to shorten my hair to symbolize a new beginning. It seemed like some sort of clemency, a freeing myself from past sins. But maybe I made too much of it and it was just my way of offering St. Anthony a sacrifice to appease him, for this day seems frightening and promising at the same time. For all it's worth, I'm not bald.

'Does your hair have anything to do with our trip today?' Dr Ari seems impartial regarding my hair but asks nevertheless.

His insight into my motivation is uncanny, yet I remain elusive. 'I was ready for a change, I

214

guess. That's all.' There's this sadness again, it sits somewhere between my heart and my stomach, a feeling I've never been able to describe appropriately, more a sensation, making me crave cold water as if to calm some sort of deeply seated thirst within me. I run my fingers through my hair, starting at the right temple. It used to reach way past my shoulders; now it barely covers the scar that reminds everyone that I'm missing an ear.

I study Oliver's profile. He seems nonchalant about this trip, but I imagine him relieved at not having to administer Valium and fasten straight-jackets.

'What do you think, Oliver?' I look at him and I know he is supposed to ignore my attempts to converse with him.

'Change is good,' Oliver says and winks at me, causing Dr Ari to clear his throat.

Dr Ari doesn't mention the fact that my mangled ear is now clearly visible but I'm sure he will eventually. Impulsive as it was, I wanted the world to see that, regardless of what I've done, something was done to me.

We drive silently for a long while. Dr Ari hasn't elaborated on specific goals for the day, just told me to go with the flow, to let it happen. I hope I can bring a story back to him, lay it at his feet like a slaughtered goat, an offering to the god of lost memories.

At the same time I wonder what Dr Ari's bag of tricks holds. I keep peering at his briefcase — he seems to be guarding it rather obsessively — and I imagine surgical blades, bone saws, and rubber mallets. I picture Dr Ari stranded on an island, allowed three items of his choice. I pick for him: a lint remover, a digital recorder, and the Quran. Oliver is harder to pinpoint: a radio perhaps, a dog, and a pack of smokes?

As we approach North Dandry, I feel a stroller handle between my fingers. Other moms used to give me dirty looks as I pushed a crying infant along. Once we'd reach Drummer's Cove, Mia always calmed down, the rhythm of the drums, the noisy summer celebrations, and the dancers would always lull her to sleep.

Prospect Park appears on the left and North Dandry is to our right. When we reach 517, the van pulls over and parks at the curb. On the sidewalk, I watch a dog walker struggling with three greyhounds. The leashes are tangled, the dogs' tails tucked beneath their streamlined bodies, pointing at their deep chests.

As the dog walker asserts control over the pack, I hear a clicking sound. Dr Ari has opened his magic bag. He's holding a plastic evidence bag with a blue adhesive closure strip in his hands. He breaks the seal and hands me Mia's blanket. The experiment has begun. It's uncanny how the close proximity of the brownstone and Mia's blanket in Dr Ari's hands recreate the perfect spark that's needed to set my memory ablaze.

I force myself to look straight ahead. Scent is magic that brings forth a rush of vivid memories, time travel at its finest. Can we string memories like beads on a thread and wear them around our necks? And will greyhounds forever prompt

216

me to recall of this very experiment?

Scientific facts tumble around in my mind. Scent, the most powerful trigger of all, activates the olfactory bulb, which is connected to the brain's limbic system, therefore calling up memories almost instantaneously. When we experience a scent for the first time, we link it to an event, a person, or a moment. The smell of chlorine is forever embedded in our brain as the memory of summer days or a specific moment like panic after falling into the pool.

I close my eyes, take a deep breath, and then I let go.

There is a switch inside of me, a switch I can only describe as a powerful tilt towards another point in time. I hear the rustling and crackling of a plastic bag. I take in a mixture of baby powder, fastening tape, moisturizer, synthetic diaper, and fragrance. Mia. The odor is faint, yet produces powerful physical and emotional reactions. As much as I don't want to look at it, even want to escape the scent in the enclosed van, I surrender to its force. Whatever I have been keeping at bay unleashes like a herd of wild mustangs charging through an open gate. A memory reaches my brain as a scent, yet it's more than that. It's the all-encompassing sensation of my daughter.

Random scenes rush at me.

A newborn's face rests on my chest. Covered in blood and glop, her skull bruised, her skin a bluish tint. My brain stumbles. Her frailness surprises me, her alertness keeps me at bay.

Nighttime feedings, one after the other. The crying, its urgency yanks at me, tugs at me like a

217

rubber band stretched to its limit. Her wails tighten the rubber band, jerking at it to the point of rupture.

Madness located in my jaw. I pull the pacifier out of her mouth, replace it with a bottle before the crying starts. Like a dog's jaw I sink my teeth into the plastic and hold on with hundreds of pounds of pressure. Her pacifier handles are rimmed with the marks of my teeth.

The soft spot between the bony plates of her skull, the fontanel, holds this madness and like a wicked invitation I wonder how deep my thumb will go and how hard I have to push before the crying stops.

Short spans of sanity among the madness. Three noises capable of drowning the cries: the running shower, the vacuum, the radio. All three at once are heaven. I've established the holy trinity.

I've made a mistake. Wanting to hold her and cradle her and look into her eyes, cooing her name and smiling — all those feelings and gestures have become alien to me.

I'm committed; I change diapers, I bathe her, I feed her. But nothing comes easy. Not my love for her, not my being everything to her.

Her neediness thrashes inside of me like a creature, tearing at me from the inside out.

I'm not a good mother.

There is Jack. His face aglow, he holds her instinctively, his love is primal. His eyes adore her. A king protecting his kingdom, aware of the pressure, selfless and courageous. Our happiness depends on him. He accepts this fate. He is

rewarded by joyous crows and capers. As for me,
I'm not worthy of this crown.

The visions release me like a giant's hand returning me to the backseat of the van. Rain pounds the roof like rapid machine gun fire. When did the rain start? When did the skies darken and unleash their wrath on me? My face is wet and I'm shaking. I feel like an open wound.

I grab the handkerchief Dr Ari offers me and wipe my eyes. The rain stops as suddenly as it started. I look through the window of the parked van and see Oliver across the street at the park entrance, sitting on a bench under a gazebo, wires from his pocket reach his ears. He pets an occasional dog, and his eyes follow a group of girls strolling by. I envy him; how easy it must be to guard instead of being guarded. He takes something out of his pocket, some sort of tool, and he starts chipping away at it as if he's carving some elaborate meerschaum pipe.

Dr Ari, his digital recorder in his hand, the blanket in the other, studies my face. The close proximity of our bodies is awkward and uncomfortable.

I exit the van, give the door a determined pull and watch it slide shut on its suspended tracks.

North Dandry is tree-lined and straight as a ruler. Brownstone row houses sit in harmony like books on a shelf, all old, all narrow. Their façades range from muted yellows to reds and grays. Further down, as North Dandy turns into Fullerton, the houses switch from Gothic to Greek and Italian revival. North Dandry's brownstones blend into a cumulative front of arched windows, large chimneys, and cast-iron stair rails and fences.

The Norway maple in front of 517 rests silently in its own island of tightly packed soil surrounded by a wrought-iron fence amidst otherwise concrete landscape. I could have sworn the tree in front of North Dandry was a hemlock and not a maple.

I look at Dr Ari, waiting for him to give me instructions. Pulling a set of keys out of his coat pocket, he lowers his glasses onto the tip of his nose and fumbles for a specific key.

His voice is as composed as ever. 'The building is vacant,' he says and offers me a large gold key between his thumb and his index finger. Is his plan as easy as it is crazy; just go in and demand the building's memories? What if the building has a soul and is angry at me? Could it punish me for what's happened here?

'Unlock the door and enter the apartment. Walk through, touch anything you feel like touching.' He nods and steps aside. He lifts his right arm as if welcoming me into his home — my home. 'Go ahead.'

I take the key from him and walk up the steps to the front door of the building. I insert the key into the lock and turn it to the right. I push and the door opens.

'Entering 517 North Dandry,' Dr Ari says and turns on the recorder.

An intrusive paint odor greets me, the freshly painted hallways are harsh and white, almost blinding. My temples start pulsating the moment

220

I set foot over the threshold.

The door to my apartment is unlocked. Standing in its hallway feels familiar yet strange at the same time, as if I've travelled through time. I'm unsure of what to do next. Is there going to be a magical scent, a sound, or a taste that's supposed to answer all my questions?

I notice black powder marks on the doors and remnants of yellow police tape. Even though the police have undoubtedly gone through the apartment, the place looks tidy. No cabinet doors ajar, no drawer contents poking out. The only sign of strangers having been here are the blinds stuck halfway, leaving the place in slight disarray.

As I enter Mia's room, my heartbeat accelerates. I cannot dispute the peculiar energy of the empty crib in front of the window. The room looks as if volcanic ash has descended upon it. The crib mattress and the bumper have been removed. It seems as if the colors of the room have been adjusted since the last time I was here, everything seems brighter, and the room is bathed in light spilling through the blinds. The crib slats are covered in black powder, so are the dresser, the changing table, the closet door, and the windows. A sense of guilt weighs on me, as if I have done something that can't be undone, without knowing exactly what it is. I want to make amends, confess, but it's only a feeling, vague like a ghost, without form and body.

The Tinker Bell mobile above her crib dangles, crooked and abandoned.

The night sky projection lamp is missing its dome, a sad turtle without its shell. Someone must have removed it to examine the inside of the lamp. I step closer. Two wind-up cogs, a battery chamber. The light bulb is missing. I run my finger along the rim of the opening, remembering how much Mia loved the stars travelling across the walls and the ceiling. A sticker on the rim, partially pulled off, *Keep Out of Reach of Children.*

My hand starts trembling and I jerk back when something pecks at my finger. I stare at the crimson line and I realize I have sliced my finger on a tiny shard sticking out of the groove where the dome used to be. I rub my bloody index finger against the tip of my thumb. The blood is warm between my fingers and the sticky sensation turns a crank and, like a jack-in-the-box, the thought bobbles, then it rests, comes into focus. The melody it plays is one of thunder rumbling in my head and I witness my mind reassembling the moment the memory was created.

Blood, lots of blood.

Tears forging a soft trail down bloody cheeks.

Naked feet stumping furiously among the shards.

Bloody footprints leaving a path the length of the front crib rail.

Hands and feet covered in cuts and nicks and wounds.

My mind shuts down, unwilling to proceed. But I need to know. I need to know what happened. I grip the image as if I'm floating in the middle of an ocean clinging to a piece of driftwood.

The image returns, the random vision of a figment of my amnesiac imagination, a half-hearted truth then, the very first day I woke up in the hospital. Now I know it wasn't a vision after all.

The assembly continues; the night of the hurricane, the power outage, the smoke detector. The molten bottle parts and pacifier.

I have to go further, I have to force my mind. I am so close.

I run all four fingers of my right hand over the rim of the domeless turtle lamp. I press hard and I linger, I feel the spiky glass cut the tips of my fingers. And then I run my fingers over the spiky shards, again and again and again.

A glass dome.

Keep Out of Reach of Children.

Not a toy.

And then the memory forms, in its entirety. Seeing is believing, they say, but feeling is the ultimate truth. I wait the memory out, allow it to spiral its circular path like a balloon without its opening tied up, until it lies there, deflated, empty.

It was the day the eye of hurricane Irene had plowed through the New York Metropolitan area, drenching everything from the Carolina coast to northern New England in over twenty inches of rain within 24 hours. Mayor Bloomberg had called for the evacuation of low-lying areas in Brooklyn, Queens, Staten Island, and Manhattan.

By late evening the power in Brooklyn had gone out, intermittently at first, then my street, North Dandry, was completely without power. There wasn't a single street-lamp lit, and Brooklyn was bathed in darkness.

A battery-operated lamp in Mia's nursery was the only light source in the entire house. Its turtle-shaped dome projected a starry night onto the walls and ceiling. Mia, seven months, was finally asleep in her crib. Her small frame was settled against the bumper, arms tucked under, and butt up in the air.

It was daylight when I woke on the couch to a loud and eerie moaning. I was disoriented at first, but then realized the sound originated from the recessed exterior of the building. The wind howled and lamented, shaking the window shutters. Voices trailed my way from the living room. Suddenly I smelled burning rubber and the high-pitched smoke alarm jerked me into reality. Puzzle pieces snapped into place and the scorched smell became familiar; nothing but sterilized bottle parts and pacifiers I had left on the stove. The power must have come back on and the water boiled until it evaporated, leaving molten plastic on the bottom of the scorched pot.

The TV in the living room continued to babble, updating viewers about the state of the city's power grid. I grabbed a bottle of formula from the fridge, dropped it in the bottle warmer, and entered Mia's room, slowly making my way towards the crib.

Red. Everything is red. No. No. No.

Later, as the sun came up, shadows of Mia's eyelashes against her cheeks, I cupped her feet in my palms. And I apologized to her, again and again.

Keep Out of Reach of Children.

After my heartbeat slows, I allow myself to connect the dots. I had left the projection lamp with the glass dome next to her bed. Mia must have grabbed it, pulled it into her crib and somehow broke the dome. Mia's fingers and feet were covered in tiny nicks but after I cleaned her up she didn't look half as bad as she had while covered in blood. Her vaccination appointment was two days later. I didn't know how to explain the nicks and cuts on her hands to the doctor. That's why I missed the appointment. And consequently without a shot record, there was no daycare. And before I could make another appointment, Mia was gone.

Keep Out of Reach of Children.

I couldn't even get that right. Something I should have known, like not leaving her unattended in the tub, no, not even with a sticker telling me explicitly what to do.

I also remember not knowing half the time how I ended up on the couch or in my bed. Not being able to figure out if Mia was crying or if I was merely hearing an echo in my head. And then leaving something clearly dangerous close to her crib.

And I'm wondering what else I had neglected to do.

I leave Mia's room and go to my bedroom, where everything is covered in a layer of dust.

My clothes are still in the closet, there's an empty glass sitting on the night-stand, its yellow content dried up like honey. The scented candle fragrant with bergamot and despair hangs in the air.

I wonder if Jack's been here, if he walked through these rooms, if he tried to connect the dots as to what happened. I wonder if he opened drawers, rattled the bars on the windows. Being here feels as if I'm disturbing the past, my mere presence is upsetting the layer of microscopic particles deposited the day Mia disappeared. I want to leave it undisturbed, to maintain its crime scene status for all eternity, and I wish for supernatural powers so every thumbprint and DNA trace will expose a hint as to what happened within these walls.

I feel tired suddenly. I sit at the foot of the bed and close my eyes. Sitting here, I don't remember Mia's first words (was it something like *ba-ba* or *da-da*?), the first time she sat up (was it on the floor or in her stroller?), the first time she rolled over, held her own bottle. There were smiles, but they didn't fill me with joy. Bottles, diapers, crying, over and over, twenty times over, day by day. I was covered in dust, just like this apartment.

The kitchen still smells of stale coffee, the living room of extinguished fireplace ashes. I'm bombarded with odors more powerful than words, captivating me, odors I can't place — new carpet smell maybe, bleach, Pine-Sol — and I feel the urge to leave this place. The tangs and whiffs of unfamiliar odors go

226

topsy-turvy in my mind, and I can't think of anything but escaping the stench of guilt this house holds.

I enter the stairwell, barely able to hold on to the railing. As I walk up, I hear a familiar sound; a creak on the third step. I reach for the smooth railing, covered in numerous layers of glossy paint. The creak echoes in my head and my hand tightens even harder around the railing. I watch my knuckles emerge from under my skin like white rocks in a river bed. Suddenly I'm covered in anguish; it soaks through my clothes, opens the pores of my skin, and seeps all the way to my bones.

This time, I see nothing, not a single image. But I feel everything. I hear a voice from far away but I've no idea where the words are coming from until I recognize them as my own. And I return to the day I walked up these same steps.

'She's gone, she's gone, she's gone, gone,' I hear myself cry. 'I can't find her anywhere.'

And then floodgates open. I've returned, been magically transported through time and space, the sound of buses, garbage trucks, and children laughing shooting through me like an arrow. Pigeons cooing and a sharp slapping sound of wings.

I remember I twisted the door knob and the attic door swung open. There was light shining through a windowed door at the end of the attic leading to the rooftop. A mummified pigeon lay in the corner, its feathers devoid of vanes, merely spiky shafts attached to a skeleton.

When I felt dizzy, I closed my eyes, and then my knees hit the floor. I felt the impact, accompanied by crowing pigeons, and a feeling wrapped itself around me like a coat, skintight; I was unable to undo its buttons, the fabric had merged with my skin and there was only one way out. Don't be misled, I wasn't delusional, I didn't think I could fly. I wanted to hit the ground but darkness came before I could make good on my plan.

When I woke up, my knees were throbbing. As I made an attempt to push myself off the ground, I felt something soft beneath me. I scooped it towards my nose and inhaled. The scent had a sparkle, but not the sparkle of glitter or fireworks, not the sparkle of a Christmas day snowfall or a frosty February wind, yet it was more than the freshness of chamomile and lavender and camphor . . . but at the same time it had warmth, but not the warmth of cinnamon or brown sugar . . . the scent was a combination, a juxtaposed blend of both, it was delicate and robust all at the same time, like a worn, soft quilt from your childhood . . . yet daintier than cotton, more refined, but strong at the same time. This scent was pure and grand and it was all around me.

I opened my eyes. I was holding Mia's blanket. Silver stars stitched in the corner, next to a moon and sun, the 'Sun, Moon, and Stars' collection from Macy's.

Mia's baby blanket was staring at me as if to say *you should look harder, you should not give up so quickly. What kind of mother are you?*

228

I sense movement behind me. Dr Ari, who has followed me without my knowing steps closer, and for the first time since we started our sessions, Dr Ari feels the need to clarify, to put a name to the madness.

'You found Mia's blanket in the attic. You were not sure about what happened, you even thought that Mia didn't exist. Your postpartum depression had progressed into psychosis.'

Where is he going with this? I was a monster. I had stopped loving my baby; I was afraid of what I would do to her. I had failed her.

'You needed help, Estelle. This is nothing mothers can just get over by themselves. You needed antidepressants; you needed therapy, support, and friends. Many mothers imagine hurting their infants, even drowning them, burning them. Understand this, if you don't understand anything else: when mothers imagine hurting their children, their mind doesn't signal a wish. It's the mind's mechanism visualizing the worst outcome so you can counteract.'

I consider his explanation, but I'm torn. I try to take it all in. 'I remember a pair of scissors by her crib when I was still with Jack. I had cut off the clothes tags. Every time I saw the scissors, I imagined myself stabbing her, mutilating her body. I moved the scissors, stuffed them in the very back of the linen closet. I thought I was a monster.' The last words come out in a wail.

The more upset I've become, the calmer Dr Ari appears. It all makes sense to him, but I wish

229

it made sense to me, too.

'Postpartum psychoses require immediate treatment,' Dr Ari says, 'you lost touch with reality and you still don't know what was real and what you imagined. The statistics are very clear in that most women who experience postpartum psychosis do not harm themselves or anyone else. They don't want to kill themselves or their children. But their thoughts can become so delusional and irrational that their judgment is impaired. Suicide is rare, infanticide extremely rare. It's even rarer that they kill *and* commit suicide.'

I latch on to the word *and*. 'Commit suicide *and* kill the infant. I didn't kill myself. But I wanted to. What does that mean?'

'You wanted to kill yourself. Until you found the blanket.'

'I looked for her,' I say.

'You looked for her?'

'In every closet and under the furniture. I opened every drawer, looked behind every curtain. I went outside and looked in the Dumpster. I walked up and down the street, looked in cars. I just want you to know that I looked for her.'

'I believe you, I know you looked for her. But we're not done, we have to keep looking.'

One memory emerged and that one will be linked to the next by triggers, scents, visions, by time. My mind will arrange those puzzle pieces and form a complete picture. For the first time in a long time I have hope.

We leave the building and sit in the van. Dr

Ari pulls a golden watch from the pocket of his pants. It dangles on a gold chain and attaches to the belt loop of his trousers. The sunlight hits it and sends a blinding ray my way.

'One more thing before we continue. What you did in there, allowing the glass to cut open your fingers isn't acceptable and I don't want you to repeat this again,' Dr Ari says.

I look down at my fingertips speckled with tiny cuts and covered in dry blood. I nod.

Oliver is standing by a food truck. He holds a wrapper in one hand and a cup with a straw in the other. He puts the cup next to him on the bench and lifts his face upwards. The sun is bearing down on the van and my eyelids are heavy. The past hour is weighing heavy on me. I'm thirsty, famished.

'Estelle,' Dr Ari's voice is laden with fatigue, 'tell me what you know for sure. Tell me what you know to be the truth. Everything we have spoken about, everything you remembered today, tell me what you know with absolute certainty.'

I sit in silence for a while. The first thought that enters my mind is sadness. It's located in my stomach and feels like thirst, but no liquid has ever cured it. Even antidepressants have never limited its reach. Sadness had turned into the carnivore of my life, eating up everything in its path. It's a vortex that pulled everything else in my life downward, towards this moment. I wanted someone to find me, pick me up, hold me up against the light, brush me off with a shirt hem and consider themselves lucky having found me.

'I've been sad for a long time.'

'And after you had Mia it got worse, didn't it?' he asks.

'I love her more than anything in the world. But it was so hard.'

'Hormonal changes can be so dramatic that they push mothers from a general anxiety to a more severe disorder. Family members don't pick up on it because mothers appear to be fine for long periods of time.'

'I understand what you're telling me. But what now? How does that help me now? Or Mia? She's still gone.'

Dr Ari takes off his glasses and wipes his face with the palm of his hand. 'But you are here. And you have to do everything you possibly can to find out what happened.'

'What if I hurt her? What then?'

'Right now we are looking for her. Let's not ask questions we don't have the answers to.'

'I should have tried harder,' I say and cry again.

'Estelle, you have to be aware of this sadness from here on out. A mild depression in childhood can turn into a full-blown depression after adolescence, and you were certainly predisposed to postpartum depression. Slipping into a psychosis could have been prevented.' He clears his throat and I've a feeling he has something else to say. 'We're still in the infancy of brain research, we know there's a common mechanism, but its nature is still unknown to us.'

'Do we have to come back here again?' I ask and look over at the front door of 517.

'I doubt it. You made great progress today.' He looks at me for a long time. 'You seem to have something on your mind. Can I answer any questions for you?'

'I was just wondering, I don't understand this whole memory thing. The doctors told me I had memory loss because of my injuries and that it might take a long time for my memories to return. And some memories would never return, but the MRI didn't show any brain damage. So what is all this . . . this scent,' I point at the blanket in his hand, 'and the moment in there, on the steps, how can it just come back to me? Where were those memories? I don't understand.'

'I think it's safe to say that it's impossible to untangle the entire ball of yarn that caused your amnesia. There was trauma, there was postpartum depression, psychosis, your injuries, and whatever other condition might have played a role. In my opinion you suffer mainly from dissociative amnesia.'

'But you can't say for sure?'

'I don't think we need to define it just yet, if at all. Dissociative amnesia is nothing more than a mental interruption or breakdown of your memories. You blocked out information that is too stressful or too dramatic to deal with. That's the difference between dissociative and regular amnesia; dissociative means that your memories still exist but are deeply buried in your mind. Those memories usually resurface the moment they are triggered by something. Hence the scent trigger.' He points at the blanket in the Ziploc

233

bag. 'If your brain was damaged, the memory would have been lost forever.'

'So, in a way I'm lucky.' I remember the doctor in the hospital indicating the tiny sliver of luck I had to be alive. 'I'm lucky and this close,' I say and hold up my fingers, 'right?'

'That's the spirit.'

Dr Ari motions to Oliver. He stands up, stretches and drops the Styrofoam cup in a nearby trashcan. Oliver gets in the van and turns the ignition key. I smell the chemical reaction of his skin's melanin to the UV rays. My stomach contracts violently.

'I'm going to be sick,' I say and cover my mouth.

'Here you go,' Oliver says, suddenly at my side, shoving a paper bag in my hand.

I take deep breaths with Oliver standing next to me in the open van door.

I hear the sound of paper tearing and then a citrus scent drifts my way. I watch Oliver hold a wet wipe in front of the AC vent. Then he presses the cold wipe against my forehead.

The lemon scent seems to drown out everything around me — the waft of onions from the hot dog stand, the exhaust from the van, the musty odor from the van's AC — turning into the force of hands pressing the wipe to my forehead, allowing me to breathe. There's another scent mixing with the lemon, earthy and sweet at the same time. It's almost as sharp as pine, but not quite, more secret and not as obvious, as if the fragrance itself was clandestine, only meant for a chosen few. A scent as if it was cut straight from a hole in the ground, ripped from the earth itself.

My heart is pounding in my ears, yet suddenly the edge is a safe place to be.

16

Later, back in the parked van with the brownstone in view, Dr Ari takes a deep breath in, and rests his folded hands in his lap. 'You found Mia's blanket in the attic. Tell me what you did next.'

'I don't know why I'm so . . . so afraid.' Afraid is not even the right word. Paralyzed maybe? No, paralyzed means incapable of movement. Transfixed? Yes, transfixed meaning motionless, spellbound in a way. But by what I cannot say.

Why do I feel this way? As if I'm a wild rabbit, spellbound by the curved talons of an eagle. Something I can't quite put my finger on, a complicit state of silence, an almost Manchurian conspiracy wall I feel I'm not allowed to climb.

Like a promise I had made, a promise of silence.

'Fear is an autonomic response, don't allow it to distract you. You can't get to the bottom of it unless you let it run its course. Just accept it, but don't make it more than it is.'

He pushes Mia's blanket towards me. My hands move forward and then slightly hesitate, but I know that I have to search for all the jagged pieces of the puzzle. I grab the blanket and close my eyes. I enter the elevator, surprised that, with time, the image has turned into a perception of actually being there.

I hold the blanket as if it is a relic, a sacred

object. It still holds the aroma of Ariel and baby lotion, but more than its scent, energy travels through my fingertips, up my arms, and straight into my brain. Clutching the fabric tight, squeezing it like a wet rag, wringing it in an attempt to extract every single drop of water, and in my mind I reenter the brownstone, back to where I had found the blanket.

★ ★ ★

Blanket in hand, I went back downstairs, where I found my door still unlocked and the building silent. There was a ringing in my head and my body started tingling, I broke out in a sweat. Then it all went dark.

The first thing I became aware of was a melodious tolling of church bells. It surrounded me before I even opened my eyes. I listened for a while and realized it was St. Joseph's across the street, summoning parishioners for Sunday Mass.

The second thing I realized was that I was lying on the kitchen floor and I had pulled Mia's blanket over my shoulders. It barely covered my upper body but the solace it gave me was boundless.

The tile was cold, yet I remained still, waiting for the buzzing in my head to stop. As I picked off the few random pigeon feathers that stuck to my pants, I watched one rainbow-colored feather drift towards the wall next to the pantry, sticking to a narrow gap between the wall panel and the floor. Its downy barbs quivered in the draft, then it sucked the feather underneath the panel and it disappeared.

I sat up on the tiled floor, blanket around my shoulders, and noticed the same persistent breeze that had sucked up the feather. The draft was so strong it made me shiver. I managed to get up off the ground, holding on to the countertop, but it took immense effort to stand up on my feet. My skull was buzzing like a beehive.

The draft became stronger and colder, the closer I moved towards the panel. I had never noticed a draft around my feet before, a draft I should have been aware of by washing bottles in the island sink.

The apartment's walls, as in so many older row houses, were covered in wood paneling, partially for decorative purposes, but mostly solely decorative, not covering anything at all. There were alcoves, niches, false walls covering windows, doors leading to brick walls. There was even a door without any hardware covered in paint in the hallway. Neglecting those details probably saved money during the renovation process and I wasn't sure just how many fake panels there were throughout the apartment.

Maybe the panel the feather had disappeared underneath was one of those panels, just for show and not insulated properly.

When I tapped my knuckles against the panel's four corners, it produced a hollow sound. The skirting boards continued on both sides of the panel but were noticeably missing where the panel met the floor. Like the draft, I hadn't noticed the missing floorboard before either. No, it wasn't that I hadn't noticed before, I was *sure* the skirting boards had been uniform all around the walls. I bent down and poked my fingers under the crack. The draft became even stronger.

Moving around proved more difficult than I imagined. My vision grew blurry, my legs were wobbly, and my tongue kept clinging to the roof of my mouth. I managed to get a cup from the cupboard and I downed three cups of tap water. I had to fight to keep it down and decided to wait before attempting to eat anything.

When the pigeons outside my window started cooing, a recollection of the attic emerged, nebulous at first, then it came into stark focus. The notion of my jumping off the roof now seemed overly dramatic, silly almost, just another moment when illogical actions seemed rational and well thought out. What I knew for sure was I had to find my daughter who had been in the attic at some point and that I wasn't crazy after all.

I kept staring at the panel, the mismatched skirting boards. I kneeled down and tugged at the bottom of the panel where the draft was strongest. Nothing. I yanked the knob attached to the panel. It didn't budge. I kept tugging, gently at first, then I gave it my all, using both my hands. After initial resistance, the panel creaked and screeched and popped out of its rectangular frame. I fell back, and the panel landed flat on the kitchen floor.

I found myself staring into a compartment the size of a narrow door, its depth that of a pantry or a coat closet. The floorboards were the original hardwood boards, not porcelain tiles like the rest of the kitchen.

And there it was. The shiny rainbow-like pigeon feather. There were remnants of construction debris, wood, and drywall, countless bugs, some flattened, and sticking to the floor, some on the outer edges still plump and stout, dusty, a battlefield of dead insects.

Dust covered the floor like powdered sugar, except for a visible disturbance within the layer. And there were wood shavings and flaky particles, like coconut flakes on a cake.

There was a knob attached, not only to the outside, but also the inside of the panel. I stuck my head into the space. An icy draft descended upon me from the darkness above. A sliding door replaced by a panel? There were no visible motors or electrical wires, no ropes, no pulley mechanisms. It was definitely a remnant of an old dumbwaiter when the row houses were first built.

The discovery was equivalent to having a couple of large cups of coffee and two aspirin. I was more alert than I had been in days. Logic prevailing, short of walking through walls, this was *the* entrance point into my apartment. It was time to follow the trail and see what was at the other end.

I grabbed the opportunity like low-hanging fruit, stepped in, and looked up. The space felt like a small shower enclosure and lifting my arms was impossible without elbowing the walls around me. Once my eyes got used to the darkness, I made out a rope dangling from above. The breeze was even stronger now and there was a faint sliver of light coming from a source less than ten feet up.

17

A faint spark ignited in the back of my mind, implications obscure and vague caught fire, then fizzled. Had I not just questioned my sanity, inspected my body, climbed in the attic? I wanted to see my madness through until the very end and decided to investigate further.

I stood quietly in the kitchen, listening. I went from room to room; there was no cracking, no wailing, no flushing toilets, no water running upstairs. All I knew was David Lieberman lived in an apartment with an identical floor plan above mine, while the other two apartments next door were under construction. I had seen some of the workers but never talked to any of them, didn't even know how many there were. They wore hard hats and passed me in the hallway carrying boxes of tiles, wood, countertops and kitchen cabinets. They disposed of the rubble and debris through a bright yellow construction chute leading to a green metal container sitting outside in front of the building, but I had seen some of the workers carry boxes outside too large to fit through the chute.

I stepped outside my apartment door and listened for any sounds in the hallway. The church bells across the street earlier reiterated the fact that it was Sunday and the construction site was abandoned explaining why there was no whistling, no banging, no screeching of saws and

242

other power tools coming from across the hall. The building was eerily quiet.

The construction site was straight across from my door, its entrance covered with a heavy blue tarp. I moved its first layer. Then the second layer. I stuck my hand through and my fingertips bumped against a smooth surface. I parted the tarp's last layer and realized a door had been installed. Identical, metal and fireproof, as the one leading into my apartment. And it was locked.

I went upstairs, knocked on David Lieberman's door and waited. I knocked again. No answer. Less than a minute later I stood in my kitchen dialing his number. I heard the phone ringing through the ceiling. The answering machine kicked in and I hung up. I dialed his cell and it picked up on the first ring.

Beep. I'm sorry but the person you called has a voicemail box that has not been set up.

After I hung up the phone, I stepped back into the dumbwaiter. The end of the rope dangled from above, swinging back and forth, its end tied into a large nautical knot. I tugged gently but it didn't budge. I pulled harder. After a few tugs, I used my entire weight to test its strength. I was weak, but I was determined. I held on to the knot, locked my elbows and, inch by inch, moved, with my feet, up the wall. My slight frame and the pounds I had lost the past few weeks made up for the strength I didn't have. My hands took turns reaching up the rope, moving higher and higher until I was perched at the very top of the dumbwaiter.

I listened for a few seconds but only heard the beating of my own heart. My arm muscles twitched and I felt like a bird trapped in a chimney. A sliver of light escaped from the panel in front of me, it was not enough to illuminate the walls around me but sufficient to make out most of my surroundings.

I ignored my sore leg muscles but knew I was going to start spasming under the weight of my body eventually. I felt my way along the bottom crack of the panel, one foot pressed against the wall, the other pushing against the panel. I pulled back my right foot and kicked the panel. It popped out of its frame. I swung back to gain momentum and flung myself into the light. I allowed my muscles to rest and looked around.

My first thought was one of confusion; had I walked in circles and ended up at the same place? This was my kitchen; same flooring, same cabinets, same everything. My second thought was what wasn't there. No sponge in the kitchen sink, no coffee maker on the counter, no garbage can, no mail, no newspaper. It was the apartment of someone who either just got here or was about to leave.

There was a tool belt draped over the pantry door knob. Sitting within the dust and debris from the panel I realized I had landed on the cold tiled floor of David Lieberman's apartment.

My third thought was to snoop around.

I started pulling the kitchen drawers open, all of them empty but one. Mismatched silverware and matches, a can opener, a piece of string, and a few pencil nubs. I opened the cabinets; lonely dishes and boxes of cereals neatly lined up.

A cardboard box sat on a cheap folding table and a few more flattened cardboard boxes were stacked on the floor. Two metal folding chairs rested against a wall.

I pushed open the bathroom door. There were the usual items — shaving cream, a toothbrush, and a bar of soap on the rim of the sink — and a box of Moldex hearing protection ear plugs, still sealed, under the sink.

I opened the mirrored cabinet above the sink: aspirin, Alka Seltzer, and nasal decongestant. On the top row sat a small terracotta army of medicine containers, all filled to the brim. A couple of containers were almost empty, I recognized allergy medication by name, some pain medication.

The bedroom next to the bathroom contained a couple of large cardboard boxes marked with colorful moving company stickers which, after I gave them a shove, turned out to be empty.

Lieberman's bedroom, dark and musty, was empty but for an inflatable mattress covered with a crumpled sheet, a flattened pillow and a desk without a chair. The desk drawers opened and shut with a screech as if they hadn't been opened in a while. All were empty.

The living room was sparse, the furniture cheap and mismatched. A green threadbare throw rug, a couch with sad cushions and saggy pillows, and a coffee table with colorful magazines. They stuck out like a sore thumb, misplaced in otherwise gloomy surroundings.

The magazines were travel-related, titled *Carib-bean*, *Islands in the Sun*, another one *Afar*. *Luxury Hotels*, *Adventure Travel*, all of them neatly laid out in a row.

A flat-screen TV mounted to the wall, a dining table pushed under the kitchen counter. An office chair on a plastic mat and a frayed mouse pad completed the bleak picture.

I hit the light switch. The dining room chandelier, too bright for the small area, cast a glaring light on its surroundings. The bookshelf on the wall next to the computer held a collection of leather-bound books on military strategy. The books were in chronological order, drab, colorless, with tatty spines, old and worn as if from a library giveaway. From Genghis Khan to Napoleon, to Waterloo and World War I, which had its own row. I pulled out the first book of the top row of books and opened it to the title page. The book smelled musty and grassy, with a hint of acid. It was a leather-bound edition titled *Baron de Rais* subtitled *The Trial of Gilles de Laval, Baron de Rais*. I leafed to the introduction and then read the blurb. 'The ultimate portrait of the face of evil who has come to personify mankind's greatest fears.' I quickly shut the book and shoved it back into its spot and wiped my hands on my thighs.

The lowest shelf was full of Fodor's Travel Guides; glossy, cheerful, in alphabetical order. Amsterdam, Bermuda, The Black Forest, Cayman Islands, Florence, Italy, London, Paris, St. Thomas, Spain, Turkey. The collection looked new, with their spines intact, as if sitting on a bookstore

246

shelf, waiting to be cracked open.

I continued to look around the room. Life in 1B seemed dreary. There was a utilitarian aspect to the place; no family pictures, no knick-knacks, harsh light made the rooms uncomfortable while an annoying fan clicked away above. Its clacking seemed to urge me to move on, reminding me that I had come here for a reason.

The file cabinet had a magnetic pull on me. I opened the top drawer and it swayed towards me, stopping just short of toppling the entire cabinet. There was an array of uniform folders with plastic tabs, handwritten capital letters, all tilted to the left, in unsteady handwriting. I stared at the tabs of the manila folders. I didn't know what I was looking for, but I'd have to give it a try.

I thumbed through a few folders, clumsily and not very efficiently. There were instruction manuals for TVs, computer warranty information, and contracts from furniture and computer stores. The last folder's label was blank. I retrieved it and opened it. A collection of newspaper articles, some original, some photocopied, and some printed.

I skimmed through the articles:

Bruises that Cover Body Of Infant Are
  From Taser
Feral Child Rescued From Mobile Home
Boy Lived In Closet For Eight Years
Mom Charged After Baby Dies in Hot Car
Twins Die Of Negligence
Locked Away In Cage for Ten Years

247

Mom Of Five Hidden From Society,
Living In Squalor
Remains Of Three Infants Found In Land-
fill

A thought took shape, it rose like dough, increasing its volume, a dense mass turning into a well-risen realization, yet I punched it down, refused to allow its expansion. I couldn't allow the possible implications to take hold and so I stood rooted to the spot, heart in my throat.

This had *nothing* to do with Mia. *Nothing.*

I was oddly captivated by Lieberman's collection of horror and the level of neglect he chose to collect for whatever sick reason.

True, we saw these stories every day, hardly a summer went by without a mother forgetting her child in a hot car, infants left unsupervised in cribs while mom enters a crack house or a casino. *How could she,* we ask, but all that remains is a faint memory, if that. *I read about a mother once who . . .*

As I scan the first story, I shudder. This is beyond a mother's failing to button her children's coats, depleted school lunch accounts, and uncooked dinners. Neglect so horrific that seasoned police officers broke down on the stand. There was a mention of bite and whip marks, lesions and scabs. Scattered feces, swarms of flies, smashed skulls. Six-year-olds appearing to be years younger, in diapers, scars covering their entire bodies.

There was a medical article titled *Alarming Brain Scans and the Impact of a Mother's Love,*

248

emphasizing that children nurtured by their mothers have larger brain structures, and that developmental delays affect children for the rest of their lives. And how parents of mistreated children were also neglected by their own parents. And how, therefore, neglect is a vicious cycle. A cycle that *must be* interrupted. And *if interrupted, can be reversed.* The article closed with a list of numbers to call when one suspects abuse and to intervene, for *do we really know the extent of abuse around us, committed by our acquaintances, our neighbors?*

Was I that neighbor to him? The one that neglected her child behind a façade of wealth, passing him with a designer stroller? A colicky baby that triggered images of cigarette burns and a bloated belly from malnutrition?

Ring.

The sound of the phone startled me. The phone's caller ID displayed the name of the caller as *Seagram Construction, Inc.* When the answering machine picked up, the caller hung up.

I panicked, wondering if I had left the folders out of order. I scanned from front to back, they were at least straight and in alphabetical order. I closed the cabinet door and resisted the urge to open it back up again. I felt wary for some reason, but like a tune whose lyrics escape me, it remained elusive.

A melodic jingle made me turn, mocking the gravity of the situation. I looked out the window where I spotted an ice cream truck that had stopped in front of the building playing 'The

Mister Softee Song.' The truck remained only for a short while and the jingle carried off into the distance.

When the phone rang again, I felt my stomach twisting into a knot.

Ring.

From the corner of my eye, I caught a green object. Somewhere in my gut there was a faint hint of acknowledgment, its cheerful green apple shade — or was it lime, malachite even — seemed familiar, yet oddly out of place in a room of tans and browns.

Ring.

The green object was perched on top of the bookcase, shoved back as if someone wanted it hidden from plain view but still wanted to know that it was there.

I approached the shelf.

Ring.

The answering machine picked up.

Please leave a message after the beep.

'*Mr Lieberman, it's Frank from Seagram's Construction. I know you are out of town, but I need to do an inspection on the progress before Monday. Call me when you get this.*'

The phone went silent.

I closed my eyes, then opened them again. But there she was, like a ghost, fading in and out in her emerald glory. She sat atop the shelf. A plastic figure in a sitting position with a hidden button below her skirt that made her glow-in-the-dark wings wiggle. Tinker Bell, the tinker fairy from Peter Pan, and the centerpiece of Mia's mobile above her crib.

My heartbeat made the top of my skull pound.
She looked discarded, tossed aside. I reached out
to her. My fingertips touched her wings.

Ring.

My hand jerked backwards. I held myself still,
wishing I could will the phone to stop ringing.

Ring.

I had never looked at her this closely, had
never really paid attention to her. A green
strapless dress with a petal skirt. Blue eyes, blond
hair. Pointy ears.

Ring.

Clear wings on her back. Tinker Bell, the fairy
whose body turned fiery red when angered
because her fairy size prevented her from
holding more than one feeling at a time.

Please leave a message after the beep.

A female voice, sharp, impatient.

'*David, are you stuck in traffic or something?
You're not answering your cell and I can't leave
a message. You need to set up your voicemail.
I'll keep trying your cell.*'

I grabbed Tinker Bell and, as if someone was
chasing me, I made for the kitchen. I was neither
crazy nor delusional, I was not losing my mind.
The blanket was one thing. It could have fallen
out of the stroller, I could have dropped it by
mistake. But finding Tinker Bell in David
Lieberman's apartment was another thing. If he
had found it, had run across it in some random
fashion, in a hallway, or even on the street, by my
car, or on the steps, he would have discarded it
or left it to begin with. But Tinker Bell, in his
apartment, left deliberately on top of a shelf, was

251

proof that there was more to this man.

Am I going off the deep end again? I must focus. I must concentrate and think this through.

Tinker Bell was one thing, but was David Lieberman a kidnapper? The man who took my child?

The more I thought about it, the more sense it made. I didn't care where the truth was trying to drag me; I was willing to follow.

I entered the dumbwaiter and pulled the panel into its frame by its knob, and, to my surprise, it popped easily back into place. I wrapped the rope around my wrists, my feet securely placed against the walls.

Back in my apartment, I dialed Lieberman's cell number, and as expected, it went to voicemail. I needed to find him. If I couldn't find him, I'd have to find his sister, a woman whose name I didn't even know.

I turned on the computer and searched for David Lieberman. The results were more than three million hits, ranging from Berkeley Law School to an Endodontic dentist in Oregon, University links and a blogger of vermin-catching techniques in Australia. The usual social networking sites came up, some university faculty profiles, and hundreds of genealogy hits for names spelled remotely like Lieberman. I had a feeling finding information on David Lieberman would prove to be time-consuming and tedious.

I clicked on the image search tool and scrolled through the first ten pages, scanning the photos of the David Liebermans of the world. Nothing jumped out at me and after a while the pictures blended into a sea of eyes, noses, and smiles. I had been at this for hours and I was getting tired.

Finally, on page 23, a picture of two teenagers caught my eyes. The boy in the picture was a version of Lieberman decades ago. I clicked on the photo. It took me to the online archive of the *Millbrook Park Townsman*, a small newspaper in Dutchess County, New York.

Decades of headlines scrolled before my eyes. One entry jumped out at me: *House Fire Kills Parents, Spares Children*. No reference to the name Lieberman, yet there had to be a connection according to my search preferences. Another link caught my eye; *Gruesome Discovery Made*. I clicked on it and was directed to the full text. I began reading.

House Fire Kills Parents, Spares Children

DOVER, New York — A couple died early Friday, July 3rd, 1982, when a fire swept through their home on Sparrow Lane in Oniontown, a part of Dover, N.Y.

The victims were Abe Lieberman, 48, and his wife, Esther Lieberman, 41, according to New York Public Safety spokeswoman Irene McConnell. The couple's children, David, 17, and Anna, 13, are being treated at Dover County Hospital for smoke inhalation. Anna Lieberman was also treated for minor burns to her hands.

*According to Fire Marshal Donald Helm,
the couple was trapped in an upstairs
bedroom. 'When we arrived, there was fire
blowing out of the windows in the front,' he
says. The shed in the backyard and an old
barn were also consumed by the flames.
'The entire town is sad for the two children.
It's tragic.'*

*The fire was initially reported by a
neighbor. 'Why they didn't try to escape
into the hallway and down the stairs, we'll
never know.'*

*The children were downstairs at the time
and rescued by a team of firefighters.
Investigators from the State Fire Marshal's
Office were at the scene throughout the day,
working to pinpoint the cause. Fire
marshals and Dover firefighters searched the
rubble in the afternoon, looking for clues.*

*The minor children are in the care of the
State until relatives can be reached. The
investigation into the fire is ongoing.*

The resemblance of Lieberman as a teenager
was uncanny. He hadn't changed much; his acne
had healed and he had added some facial hair
over the years. David was the attractive one of
the two, but had the eyes of an angst-ridden
teenager not wanting to pose for a photograph.
He stood back, his body in his sister's shadow.
Anna was a rather plain girl, her frizzy hair
parted in the middle, her lips full, and her smile
open. Or maybe confrontational, I couldn't tell.

A little more browsing and a follow-up article

in the same paper came up. According to a spokesperson of the state foster care system, David aged out of the foster care system weeks after the fire. Anna stayed in the system for months until finally an aunt, Laura Dembry, came forward.

Both our stories were so eerily similar, yet a mere coincidence of events unrelated, a synchronicity that defied any possible explanation: my parents dying, an older brother leaving behind a younger sister. In both cases an aunt came and took care of the younger sibling. It took only a few more strokes to find out that Laura Dembry was a member of the Church of Appointed Dominion in Plainview, New York, a hamlet in Nassau County, not too far from the north shore of Long Island. There was no reference made as to where Anna went to live.

Details became scarce after that and the Liebermans' online story ended there: orphaned children moving on with their lives. But I knew better, I knew from experience that our own personal shadows followed us through life, and I knew that in the aftermath is where the true tragedies occur. Mine, his, everybody's. Newspaper articles weren't the end of anything. Our similar fates lingered in the air, thick and heavy, like a blanket of fog.

I randomly typed in the title of one of the books on the shelf in David's apartment, *The Trial of Gilles de Laval, Baron de Rais*, into the search engine and clicked on the introduction. '*Baron de Rais had considerable pleasure in watching the heads of children separated from* their bodies . . . sometimes he would ask, when they were dead, which of them had the most beautiful head.'

I suddenly remembered the title of the last book on David's bookshelf, as if it staked claim to the present. *The Prince of Darkness.*

A thought passed through me like lightning. What if he's gone? What if Lieberman has taken Mia and he's disappeared . . .

I thought police, I need to get help, but then I imagined how this would go. How this would unfold if I went to the police. I'd tell them about Mia, Lieberman, and his sister Anna, about my suspicions — never mind the fact that I was the perfect perpetrator, the mother who had access to the baby, a baby that, mind you, had disappeared a day ago — and who waits this long to report their own child missing anyway? Would I tell them about water I didn't have, water that miraculously happened to appear on my counter? A wallet that was missing, a wallet that had been there all along?

And the newspaper articles, they would have a field day with Lieberman's articles, for *since when is it illegal to collect newspaper articles?* Child porn, yes, you mention child porn and you have a case, but articles about child abuse and neglect? I can hear the police question me, *the man collects newspaper articles? What proof do you have? By the way, how do you know about these articles?*

Eventually I'd be unable to answer their questions. I'd become just short of even comprehending their questions, and then I'd be unable to calm down and my edgy voice would repeat the same nonsense over and over again, *Tinker Bell, Tinker Bell*, and I might as well be talking to the walls because the story was nothing but a macabre and ill-conceived soap opera, a half-baked, crackpot pipe-dream by a woman who repeated the same incoherent story over and over again.

And I would carry on with this conspiracy script and not ever make any kind of sense and then they'd put me in a cell and order a psych evaluation but — with the state of the budget and it being a Sunday — I'd have to wait until Wednesday afternoon and before I could convince anyone of my sanity, Lieberman and his sister would be god-knows-where.

★   ★   ★

These memories should be etched into my brain, be permanently ingrained in my memory. I squint and pound my temple with my fist. Every time I emerge from the past, I'm shocked. I see images: a silhouette of a man, a basket of fruit. How many times did I want to forget painful memories of my life? And now this, here I am, trying to remember them all. What a joke, and again, the joke's on me.

'Call the police.' I can't control the tremor of my raspy voice.

I watch Dr Ari pull out his cell phone and ask for Detective Wilczek. My stomach starts contracting and I exit the van. On the sidewalk, I heave and heave until only clear liquid comes up.

The stench of vomit fills my nostrils.

I watch Dr Ari through the open door, still on the phone. I watch his mouth move, occasionally his brows furrow, then his face darkens. He hangs up.

'They've been looking for Lieberman and his sister since the disappearance. Not a trace,' he says, 'both of them. Off the face of the earth.'

I hardly comprehend the words but I know what they mean. Gone. Everyone's gone. And then I ache and I realize I might have to live in this body for the rest of my life. A body that feels like it's wrapped in jagged little edges of pain.

18

After the fieldtrip to the brownstone Dr Ari suspends the sessions for the time being. It takes a couple of days for the pyrotechnics in my brain to die down. The first night I pace my room, unable to sleep. My mind plays tricks on me, one moment it goes completely blank, the next it overflows with images I can't place.

'We *must* take a break,' Dr Ari says and refuses to continue the sessions. 'Rushing this process along is not beneficial.'

I beg and plead but he remains steadfast.

'You don't understand,' he says, 'if I allow you to inflate your memories, you create a completely false and exaggerated version of the truth. You might even remember something that never occurred at all.'

The second night I sit in my room, my heart beating in my chest. I watch light spilling through my window, elongating the window squares into distorted rectangles, just eventually to surrender to the dark. I can't say that I trust myself; aren't my memories just a made-up story I get to revise once we resume our session? I run it through my mind over and over; the dumbwaiter, the newspaper articles, Lieberman. Am I so close to the truth that those visions pass under the radar, or are they so big Dr Ari could never dream I could make something like that up? I wonder where Dr Ari is going to draw the line, at what point will my story sound so ludicrous that he'll start shaking his head in disbelief.

I promised Dr Ari to trust him on this journey and so I surrender and go about my life at Creedmoor until we resume the sessions.

Four days later, as I stir my orange Jell-O into mush, Marge and I watch the anorexic women, six of them, ranging from eighteen to thirty-something, their wraith-like bodies performing eerie dietary rituals, stabbing forks into tiny pieces of sustenance, and, miraculously the tines hold on to the morsels, after the women chew elaborately, they conclude the ceremony by gulping down large cups of water. The majority of the time they merely rearrange dietary food groups into mounds of rejection, always aware of their obsession to deprive themselves of nourishment.

The orderlies fiercely patrol the borders between them and me and Marge during mealtime. There are things about Marge that puzzle me; Dr Ari is rumored to have a very limited number of cases and mainly oversees other psychiatrists on his staff. What is it about Marge that he chooses to be her psychiatrist? I know she's here because of the death of her mother but I start to question if Marge is not as innocent as she wants me to believe.

I've grown to like her and we've bonded, at least as much as this transitory sojourn allows us, and watching the women is a fun distraction until Marge develops peculiar culinary habits of her own. She stuffs large amounts of food into her mouth and swallows without chewing. Her face is expanding by the day with her sleeve hems cutting into her arms, and her waist is ballooning. She is turning into a globe, her belt cutting her in half like an equator line.

'Are you gonna eat that?' Marge points at a slice of white bread on my plate. Watching me turn my Jell-O to mush earlier must have torn her up inside.

Marge keeps eyeing the bread, not in the least bothered by the bite marks. There's no warding her off when it comes to food; she seems determined to grow beyond the walls of this institution.

'Let me have my lunch in peace,' I say, but what really bothers me is the fact that I want to ask her about her mother's death, yet at the same time I'm perplexed by my newfound aversion to secrets and lies.

'Don't get testy, I'm just asking. If you're not gonna eat it, let's switch trays.' She eyes the anorexic table and their leftovers and I anticipate dire complications in our near future. I know she is expanding her reach beyond our table to the anorexic girls. Everybody's success is guaranteed; she wants their food, they don't want food at all. A match made in heaven.

'What are you trying to do to yourself? Did you talk to someone about this?' I'm perplexed at her size; her hips expand beyond the chair and even her glasses cut into her temples. I picture the day her eyes will disappear in folds of fat and wonder how long the hospital will allow her to go on. If the anorexic women are not allowed to leave food on their plates, someone, sooner or later, ought to intervene in Marge's binging.

'Dr Ari said they'll start watching me during meals. But so what? There are ways to get food. There are always ways to get food. You think they'll give me their desserts?' Marge is eyeing the anorexic girls and they are returning the favor. I see one of the girls nod ever so slightly. A deal has been struck.

I have my own theory about why Marge has decided to be the ever-expanding woman: She's killed her mother and now wants her back. She intends to recreate her mother's body within her own skin and she won't quit until someone stops her.

I feel for Marge, yet I try to keep some distance because I don't want to get drawn into her web of obsession.

'Hello, ladies.' I hear Oliver's voice behind me and Marge's face deflates as her plan has been spoiled for now.

My heart skips a beat when Oliver puts his tray on our table and pulls up a chair. Orderlies don't eat with patients, but I welcome the distraction, he's good-looking, and smells of disinfectant, lotion, and peppermint.

'I'll be eating my meals with you from now on. I hope you don't mind?' Oliver says and he directs the question towards me.

Marge raises her eyebrows.

We all know he's here to keep Marge from killing herself with cafeteria chow. I look at his tray: two apples, an orange, crackers, and a bowl of vegetable soup, and elaborates.

'Vegan.' He bites into a cracker. 'Did I tell you

I love your hair? It's very . . . Parisian.' He shakes his head and rolls his eyes. 'I've no idea where that came from. I wouldn't even know what Parisian hair looks like.'

Oliver starts peeling the label off the orange. His hair is dark brown, his eyes a deep ocean blue. He has dark eyebrows, which slope downwards and give him a rather serious expression. He wears a playful smile like he wears his scrubs, and kindness seems to be etched into his face. His voice is deep, with a serious undertone. He's probably average any-where else, but within these walls he is a rock star. I wonder what his life is like beyond Creedmoor.

I ask what I've been longing to ask ever since he drove the van to North Dandry. 'Why are your hands so . . . beat up? Are you working construction on your days off?' I try to sound nonchalant and casual.

'I build stuff, with wood.' He chews and I patiently wait for him to elaborate. 'It's called woodturning.'

Marge is annoyed by his presence. She has gone through another change, besides the alteration of her appearance, she doesn't hold back anymore. When I met her, she was shy and timid and hardly talked to anybody.

Marge's mouth is so full and we can hardly understand her. 'Woodturning? What's that? Dressers, chests, stuff like that? Why don't you just go and buy furniture? Seems like a waste of time. Just saying . . . ' Marge eyes his orange.

'It's nothing like carpentry or building

furniture. I make bowls, lidded boxes, vessels, urns, pens — that kind of stuff. Delicate things, whatever requires attention to detail.'

'Are you gonna eat that?' Marge asks and points at Oliver's orange.

Oliver completely ignores her question. 'I'm going to eat at this table from now on. Until further notice. Just to keep an eye on everything.' He is clearly talking about Marge and her eating habits, but his words, I want them to be directed towards me.

'Show us something then,' Marge says and glances back and forth between the two of us and smiles. 'One of those wooden things.'

Out of Oliver's scrub pocket appears a rounded object, complete with a lid and a stem. An acorn, not bigger than a robin's egg.

'See, I made this from sandalwood,' he says. 'I use special tools like this one and carve the details. This is called a gouge edge. For very small details, like the acorn cap.'

The tool in his hand, the gouge edge, is a miniature chisel with a concave blade, it has a rounded and trough-like groove at the very tip. Oliver places the gouge on his tray. I pick it up. It's about the same size as a regular pair of tweezers.

Oliver holds the acorn gently by the stem. 'This is . . . ' he pauses for dramatic purposes, 'an acorn.' He holds it gently, as if it might break. 'The tool is used to carve small indents, to make it look real. I rubbed wax on the cap to make it darker.'

'Looks like a real waste of time to me.' Marge

264

gets up, balancing her tray on both hands.

Oliver mumbles something under his breath and starts peeling his orange. 'By the way,' he leans closer into me and lowers his voice, 'you'll have a visitor next week. I'm not supposed to tell you, but you never have any visitors.'

I look at him puzzled. 'A visitor?' I ask. 'For me?'

'For you.'

'Who?' I think of Jack immediately, then I abandon the thought. He had made his intentions clear, yet I can't deny that I'm holding out hope he's changed his mind. The thought of him makes my stomach feel queasy and I try to concentrate on Oliver.

'I didn't hear that part.' He pauses. 'Don't tell anyone I told you.'

I go over a list of additional possibilities — the DA, the detectives, Nell, Jack — and it prompts a kaleidoscope of faces to pop up in my mind. I'm unable to shut the images off. I try to breathe and relax but my heart rate won't slow and I wonder about Oliver's reasons for overstepping his boundaries. I try to forget about this clandestine visitor, but regardless of how hard I try, I can't.

Marge pauses next to the table with the anorexic girls. They are talking and giggling while Marge is pointing at various food items on their trays.

Oliver gets up and raises his voice. 'Ladies, no funny business, you know better than that.' He points the group towards the cafeteria exit. 'Lunch's over.'

'For you too,' he says and Marge makes her way to the dirty dish bin.

A visitor. My thoughts jumble, pull me in every direction possible. My heart beats too fast to stay seated and so I get up, grab my tray. I see the acorn and the gouge on my tray and turn to Oliver.

'Your stuff,' I say and I hand them to him.

He grabs the gouge and slides it back into his pocket.

'Keep the acorn.'

'Why?'

'I made it for you,' he says.

'You made me an acorn. What's the significance?'

'You'll see.'

'A hint maybe?'

He cocks his head to the left and says, 'You know, I think any hint would ruin it. So I'm going to let you figure it out on your own.'

'Because I'm a nutcase, right?'

He chuckles, pulling up his shoulders.

'Okay then,' I say and slide the acorn in my pocket.

I make my way to Dr Ari's office and knock on the door. I promise myself not to push him on a date to resume our sessions but I need to know about the clandestine visitor. I expect my unscheduled appearance to irritate him, but to my surprise I hear a cheerful 'Yes?' As I open the door and walk in, I make sure to remain closer to the door than to his desk. I don't know how to bring up the visitor without giving Oliver away.

Dr Ari stands by the window, a lint remover in

hand, meticulously stroking his navy-blue wool coat. I'm mesmerized how he performs such a mundane task with obsessive determination. The firm strokes of the lint brush bring up a childhood memory of Anthony cleaning a pool. A white pole with a net at the end in his hands, he skimmed debris for hours, capturing every blossom, every bug, and every unidentifiable piece of flora floating on the surface of the small pool.

I just stand there and stare at him. I don't know how to ask without him probing how I found out.

'Estelle, I was just about to send for you.' He pauses and checks his appearance in the mirror. 'Your brother Anthony asked for permission to come and see you.'

Later, in my room, I think of my brother, Anthony Paradise. I don't know what to do with this, don't know where to put all those feelings. I remember the day he had left. It was November and he wore a big coat and the air smelled sweet. We stood in front of Aunt Nell's house, waiting for the taxi to take him to the airport. The wind moved everything about, his hair, the trees, the leaves, in control over everything. We hugged and he got in the taxi. It was a day of goodbyes, feeling left behind.

I remember his olive complexion and his green eyes. Last I heard he'd gone to a Military Academy, a choice I have always been puzzled by. He graduated top of his class and there were scholarships and so many opportunities, but he chose a Military Academy instead of one of the

Ivy League schools that were so keen on recruiting him. After I moved in with Aunt Nell I asked about him constantly, but she was always short on words, and I'm no longer sure what I heard from Nell or what I made up myself.

It's hard to curb my anxiety and I want to talk to somebody, not so much about Anthony, I just don't want to be alone. But Oliver is nowhere to be found, and Marge is out hunting and gathering and expanding her frame. I realize that I have no one. No friends. I might as well say it like it is — I've never really had friends. All the relationships I've had were thin and inadequate, almost nonexistent. A faint recollection of memories shared at some point in the distant past, yet no lasting impressions, no scrapbooks, no matching jewelry or framed photographs. Not one person I can call and talk to. And even if I had a number to call, what would I say?

Hi, this is Estelle, remember me? I just wanted to catch up, so how have you been? I'm in a psychiatric institution because I seem to have misplaced my infant daughter, some people even believe I had something to do with her disappearance. I just need to sort a few things out and so your name came to mind and I just thought I'd call . . .

I can't get Anthony off my mind. His impending visit, *tomorrow, I'll let you know the time*, makes a thumping sound. It takes me a while to realize that the sound is my heart throbbing in my ears. I mention my unease to Dr Ari, I even request anxiety medication, but he denies me chemically induced peace like he

268

denies cutting me slack during our sessions. In here you deal, that's all there is to it.

For the rest of the day I concentrate on the familiar sterile and hurried efficiency of Creedmoor, an efficiency that is coupled with an energy of competence and organization.

On hard days like today, the day before Anthony is supposed to arrive, I find it almost impossible to deal with the constant intrusion. It makes me feel as if there's an eerie background music reminding us what and where we are. The ambulance sounds are not heard too often as this isn't an emergency room and patients don't arrive by ambulance, but by family members or social workers dropping them off.

Today, the sound is high-pitched and I know the ambulance is approaching and I also know that the pitch will lower once they retreat. There are the rubber soles squeaking on linoleum, the occasional loudspeaker messages that no one understands, wheels of carts and beds, even an occasional moaning. Sometimes screaming. Never silence.

Even my olfactory bulb is being bombarded. There's the scent of latex and bleach, cooking odors wafting through the hallways from the kitchen.

I try to shut out this world and I manage for the most part to focus on the scuff marks on the shiny floor and the scraped walls. Just when I think I've managed to stay in control, the sound of IV stand wheels meddle with my attempts and I wonder where one really finds silence at all. An underground mine maybe, a soundproof chamber? A monastery where monks adhere to the self-imposed vow of silence?

My thoughts go topsy-turvy and I feel as if my mind is about to explode like an overheated light bulb. Walking the halls, I keep an eye on the floor, tan with tiny specks of gray, white dots here and there if I look real close, the conversations of nurses passing me, the orderlies with their clipboards and jingling keys, the intercom with its clandestine commands, *Doctor scratch scratch, please scratch, at the lobby, scratch*, my thinking abilities keep declining and they are already far from being stellar, clogging up the few thoughts I can keep on an even keel. The world around me is like shards stuck in my brain, making me tense, even angry.

I stay in bed for the rest of the day, *upset stomach* I tell the nurse when she questions me, and at midnight, I leave my room and look down the desolate hallway. I hear nurses chat from behind the glass, far down the hallway, there's laughter, cabinets closing, a phone ringing. The scent of coffee, unbearable almost, my stomach churning.

I wonder if there's a pool in this place, somewhere in the basement, some ancient remnant of water therapy for the insane. I long for the faint scent of chlorine, so I may follow it, and immerse myself, so deep the sound waves are damped, all signals weakened so the world diminishes altogether.

I carry an empty water bottle in my hand as an excuse for leaving my room in the middle of the night. No one drinks the tap water at Creedmoor, the rusty waterline stains in toilets speak to the water quality and are a clear warning to avoid its consumption. Water coolers are on each floor and in the stairwells, and no one will question me.

The west wing is abandoned and most of the doors, rooms, and offices are locked. This part of Creedmoor is not in use, the funds for the renovation probably somewhere in the deep pockets of a wealthy donor as Creedmoor's days are numbered.

I hear footsteps, too slow for a nurse or an orderly, maybe the security guard checking whatever he checks at Creedmoor, after midnight, in the unoccupied part of the building.

I read the door signs as I pass each room and finally I find what I consider the next best thing to an Olympic-sized pool.

I enter the room to my right. I shut the heavy door behind me and remain still in the darkness until my eyes adjust. The only light spilling through the skylight is the moon. The room is chilly and I put my hands in my pockets and feel the acorn Oliver gave me, carved by a tool whose name I have forgotten.

My throat constricts as if someone has wrapped a scarf around my neck, slowly tightening it. There's no furniture; the walls and the floor are tiled, nothing but a small cell with a bed anchored to the floor. There are two wrist restraints and two ankle restraints attached to the floor anchors. There are no hard edges or corners. I feel loopy, almost high. The bed is as

271

narrow as a twin but it is sturdy, and as I sit on its edge, it does not squeak. We are in a seclusion room, its energy heavy and unyielding.

I lie down as if in a coffin. The mockery of this moment, this bed, this building, my life, the place one has to go to find silence to hear the one voice that is true, the part of us which speaks the truth if you drown out everything else. The one voice that I demand to speak up. My thoughts are removed from reality and maybe, just maybe, that's what my madness is — the blurring of the lines, not knowing where one thing begins and another ends.

Tears stream down my neck, and I wipe my eyes with the back of my hands. For one split second the moon fits perfectly into the skylight above me, fills it to the brim, its perfect contour contained in a square shape.

I open my eyes and look at the moon above. There's no sound but the ones I'm making. I want to melt into the bed below me and the moon above at the same time. I imagine Mia and wonder if someone is holding her at this very moment, or if her lifeless body rests somewhere I will never know. Maybe the less I resist the truth the more bearable it will be. My guilt is one of those things that doesn't stand up to questioning.

And then I cry. I cry knowing the walls are soundproof and, for this one moment, in this room of madness, this place of the demented, I want to find the strength to see this through. How easily I could have taken the tool today in the cafeteria, small as it was, its blade would have done the job if pointed in the right spot at the right angle. Like breathing is my need to find the truth, involuntary. Like trying to kill myself by holding my breath under water, with the feedback loops that kick in involuntarily.

And I wonder what keeps me alive. It dawns on me that self-preservation trumps a death wish every time, and part of my self-preservation is the fact that I have the fury of an animal deprived of its young on my side.

Eventually the well of tears runs dry, then I run out of tissue. When it's time to go back to my room, I stuff the tear-soaked tissue in my pockets. It feels like wet shredded newspaper, and then I hold the wooden acorn in my hand.

And I remember Oliver telling me that there was something I was to figure out myself about the acorn.

I hold it in the palm of my hand. I cup my fingers so it won't roll off and tumble to the ground. Suddenly I feel very protective of it. I inspect it, run my fingertip along its shiny brown cap and its long, recurving scales that tightly overlap. The body is egg-shaped, smooth, yet I can see tiny cracks along its base.

I ever so gently twist the acorn cap while holding on to the base. It moves and I softly lift the lid off by its stem. I flip the acorn over and onto my palm tumbles an acorn. The real thing hidden inside a wooden vessel.

I hold the cap to my nose and inhale. The scent is soft and warm, yet I detect the sharpness of an herbal undertone. Like unsalted butter. It's what I smelled, that day at the park, after I watched Oliver sitting on the bench, chipping away at something. The scent of his hands after he handed me the wipe to cool my forehead.

Truth. Maybe that's what the truth smells like. Hidden, yet present. All you have to do is not give up.

19

At four o'clock I wait on a bench by the fountain. Every time someone comes down the path, the gravel crunches and my heart skips. I wish I had made him wait for me instead because every car door sounds like a gunshot, making my heart speed up.

I want to give Anthony a picture of Mia but I have nothing of her in here, no photo albums, no foot or hand-print, her first outfit, not a single witness to her existence. The only remnants of her life are sealed away in plastic evidence bags, leak-proof, tear-and-puncture-resistant with an adhesive closure and a chain-of-custody label.

And then I hear Anthony behind me, like a feather stroking my arm: 'Stella.' His voice almost takes me down. I manage to turn around and there he is; taller than I remember him. It seems like a thief came and took him, then returned him, changed in so many ways. He is grown now; he looks haggard and gaunt, almost past his prime, even at such a young age. He's no longer the kid he was when I last saw him. I had missed him becoming a man, missed his first love, his college years, his first job. He's in his thirties and extremely thin.

He opens his arms. We embrace. He is clean-shaven and smells of cigarette smoke. The weeks at Creedmoor have conditioned me, conditioned me to infer, to allow my emotions to draw pictures and a kaleidoscope of memories with bits of mirrors creating colorful patterns rush at me. There are no Easter egg hunts, no tree houses, no family traditions on holidays. Yet vivid, with clear edges, almost a color print photograph, a Polish bakery emerges, where we used to buy Krowki, a toffee-like candy bar. And a flash of Duke, the neighbor's dog we used to play with, a Doberman mix with one ear sticking up who walked with a limp. I push the images aside.

We sit on the bench. There's a ring on his left hand, a gold band so thin it almost disappears. There are small scars across his knuckles, pale, like permanent icicles etched into his skin.

'So, how have you been getting on?' His voice is deeper than I remember.

Fifteen years later and he wants to know how I have been getting on.

'Stella.'

There, my name again.

'I'm so sorry,' he says and cradles my hand in his.

Immediately I turn into the girl I was fifteen years ago. We've been apart but, regardless of where we go and how old we are, we will always be who we were to begin with: brother and sister. I recall Nell's house, dark and gloomy, my apartment in Queens, shabby furniture and loud neighbors, all my possessions stashed away in one closet, leaking pipes — all those places I lived had never been home.

How have I been getting on, he asked. I'm torn between letting him know how lame his

276

question is and owing him an explanation. I don't know what to tell him. Words don't have the adequate power to convey the mass and weight of the two of us meeting again after so many years.

I try to keep the tears at bay which burn my throat like acid. I raise my hands, palms up. *Look around you, Anthony. How does it look? How does it look like I've been getting on?*

His eyes shift away from me. 'I'm sorry,' he says. He looks from the lawn chairs filled with patients to the large building behind us. 'I don't know what to say, Stella. This is all a big mess.' He pauses, then again, 'Big.'

I don't know if he's referring to the building or my life. Or both or neither of those things. Big clouds up in the sky, big lumps in our throats.

'I couldn't believe when I heard — '

'You've changed,' I interrupt him. I look him up and down. He is wearing slacks, a button-down shirt, and a coat. 'You're all grown now.'

He tells me about West Point and serving in the Army for the past ten years, and that he works for the FBI now.

'But it's not as glamorous as people think. Lots of overtime and not enough sleep. Nothing like on TV.'

'This place is nothing like TV either. Not half as much fun as the Cuckoo's Nest, that's for sure.'

He tells me about Abby, the woman he married two years ago. How he met her dropping off his dry cleaning.

277

'I asked her out and here we are,' he says and pulls out his cell phone.

He taps and swipes and then hands me his phone.

A picture of Anthony in a blue uniform. Identification badges, bars on the sleeves, insignia on the shoulder loops, a black beret.

I swipe the screen. Anthony in a navy suit and a pretty woman with long brown hair in a white sheath dress in front of a court house.

'That's Abby. We eloped. Her family wasn't happy about it but it's what we wanted.'

I swipe the screen again.

Anthony and Abby in a sideways embrace with the backdrop of a mountain ridge. Abby is almost Anthony's height and looks very athletic. Next to them sits a black dog.

'That's Patton. We got him from the pound. Part Shepherd, part Lab. He was hit by a car and had a broken pelvis and was about to be euthanized. They amputated his leg a week after we got him but we're not sure he knows he's got only three legs.'

I keep swiping through Patton at the dog park, Patton with a cone at the vet, Patton on the couch, sleeping on his back, three legs up in the air.

My brother got up one morning, put on a navy suit and eloped with a woman named Abby. He loves hiking. He adopted a dog with a shattered pelvis hours before he was scheduled for euthanization. He named him Patton after a general and war hero. And he has a sister who is in a mental institution, unable to remember her daughter.

'You're a lucky man,' I say.

He smiles and I realize he must have had braces as an adult. I listen to him tell me about his wife, his job, not getting enough sleep and going to dog parks. There's still an ordinary world out there, something easily forgotten in a place like Creedmoor.

'We should have stayed in touch. I don't know why we didn't.' His voice sounds strained, as if the implications of us having lost each other so many years ago weigh him down.

'We talked for a while, I remember that,' I say and turn my head as if to distract my mind, allowing me to move on. 'I moved a lot, it's just something that happened.'

Anthony takes in a deep breath, holds it for a long time.

'You've heard from Nell?' he asks. 'She must be, what . . . almost sixty by now.'

'Nell? I don't think she knows I'm here.'

Anthony looks at me, his eyes wide.

'What?' I say and shake my head. 'You've been talking to her?'

'Stella.' He cocks his head to the left like he did when we were children. Right before he said something he wasn't sure should be said out loud. 'I'm sure she knows you're here.'

'She does?'

'Do you have internet in here?' he asks.

'Yes,' I reply and catch myself scanning my surroundings as if we've decided to climb over the fence and make away. 'But it's mostly blocked. No news.'

'I don't think it's a good idea,' Anthony says.

I close the photo app and swipe my finger across the screen. When he reaches for the phone, I turn away from him.

'Don't,' he says but then lowers his hands as if there's no use.

I find the browser app and type in my name. My vision is blurred, the screen is small and so I click on the first video link.

All I see is a blank screen with an hourglass. Then an image of an airbrushed woman with too much lip gloss and hair that doesn't move fills the screen, the picture stutters for a second, then continues. I recognize her immediately but cannot remember her name. She is one of those TV legal hosts, a former defense attorney turned prosecutor, turned victim's rights advocate, turned vengeful and eternally furious television journalist.

> **Cate:** 'Welcome! This is Cate Trent from WGBK in New York. Welcome to our viewers and welcome to today's guest. In our studio we have Liza Overton, host of Current Crimes.
> Liza, welcome. I'd like to start out with a quote from your show Current Crimes from last night: 'It's not like the baby vanished, come on people, use your common sense. We have another baby killer on our hands.'
> Is this another one of your comments that is over the top? Isn't it too early to call this woman a killer? Are you trying to influence the opinion of your viewers for the sake of higher ratings?'

280

I look at Anthony. He looks away. The video continues.

Liza: 'Thanks for having me, Cate, glad to
be on your show. First of all, no one
believes the kidnapper story. Legal
experts agree that the circumstances are
suspicious, to put it mildly. There are
more questions than answers about what
happened to the infant. She wasn't
reported missing until the mother was
found severely injured in a car upstate,
roughly three hours from her home in
Brooklyn, N.Y. What mother does not
alert the authorities when her child goes
missing? Let me answer that for you: a
guilty one.'

Infant. Mother. Severely injured. Upstate.
Missing. Guilty.

Cate: 'Authorities say that little evidence
has turned up, and according to the
Police Chief, there are no indications
that they had problems with custodial
issues. The parents have been cooperative but the mother needs to answer
some questions, and there are questions
galore, I have to agree. Liza, give us
your take on the fact that the mother
didn't report the disappearance.'

Liza: 'Well, first of all, the more time goes
by, the harder it is to remain positive.

281

But the actions of the mother bother me. And no, eventually reporting the crime is not the same as screaming bloody murder when your kid's gone. But come on, Cate, let's get real. I'll break it down for you and your viewers.'

Cate: 'Go ahead, Liza, Break it down for us.'

Liza: 'Let me tell you about mounting evidence that leads to the killer, that's what this case is about. Evidence. Mom doesn't report her daughter missing. That in itself is suspicious, but there's more. Supposedly she doesn't show up for her daughter's doctor's appointment. Why not, I ask? I believe by the time the appointment came around, the deed had been done. Then there's the convenience store incident. According to my source she goes to a local convenience store and attempts to buy water — '

Cate: 'Just to let our viewers know, the tapes have been released to the public in an ongoing effort to find additional witnesses who can account for the mother's actions the days before the disappearance of her daughter. Go ahead, Liza.'

Liza: 'Thanks for explaining that, Cate. So she goes to a local convenience store to buy water. But she doesn't pay for it, leaves it sitting on the counter! No word, nothing. And mind you, the stroller was covered in a blanket! The clerk never even saw the infant. For a baby that was supposedly colicky she's asleep peacefully in her stroller? She pretended to buy water so the clerk would remember her later on, another part of her devilish plan to fool everybody around her into thinking the baby was still alive. And that's not conjecture, the clerk has spoken out publicly. And the store has CCTV, there's proof, I'm not making this up. It's all over, see for yourself. All this is in evidence, Cate.'

Cate: 'I tell you how a defense attorney will explain that. If I were the defense attorney, I'd say maybe she changed her mind. That's not a crime, right? Maybe she forgot her purse or didn't have any money on her. Covering a stroller with a blanket? Cold weather? Too many people gawking at the kid? The infant was sleeping? There are many logical reasons. Not a crime, Liza, not by a long shot.'

Liza: 'Let me play devil's advocate, Cate. Let me tell you why I have no doubt that she's the perpetrator. She disregards the appointment because the baby is already dead! And she knows that, because she killed her! And she panics, doesn't know what to do with the body. She drives around not knowing what to do or where to go and she ends up upstate New York. That's when she decides it's time to look for a place to dump this little innocent angel. Finally she has the courage to pull over and I'd bet my life on the fact that somewhere between her home and the accident site is a little grave in the woods with the remains of the child. But then, let me not go overboard here.'

Cate: 'Going overboard? In what way?'

Liza: 'I'm giving this mother too much credit. She may not have buried her. Maybe she just dumped her in a river or a lake. I'm not going out on a limb here when I say that we will never recover the body. And last but not least, she walks into the police station, waits around for a while, throws up, and then leaves without talking to anybody. Again, on CCTV. Do we really have any doubts who killed the child? I don't!'

Cate: 'There are sources, unconfirmed sources, which tell us that the mother suffers from amnesia. What do you make of the amnesia claim? And she did have pretty serious injuries, none of them considered self-inflicted, am I correct?'

Liza: 'What do I make of it? Of course she has amnesia. Wouldn't you? Don't they all? Please! I'm convinced she killed that baby. As to the injuries, as far as I know there's no proof either way, she was just banged up pretty bad from the accident. Driving in a ravine will leave some marks.'

Cate: 'But is the media to blame for the fact that people's opinions are swayed when it comes to the accused being innocent until proven guilty? Especially in a case like this, where a baby is involved, such innocence and such deep-seated hatred for mothers who hurt their own children. It's just an overall very emotionally charged case and don't we have to be vigilant not to draw unsubstantiated conclusions?'

Liza: 'I don't want to speculate on what I don't know about the case, I'd rather stick with what I do know. And I know I don't give much credence to the mother's claims of suffering from amnesia. How convenient, how useful. I don't know what happened is not going to fly when your baby is missing. At least some mothers try to elude authorities, just ask yourself how many mothers have we seen, in tears, describing some elusive abductor, a black man, a Spanish-speaking hooded man in dark clothing?

A carjacking or a masked intruder, whatever they decide to make up. Just check
the records, there's more than one case.
And in the end we find out they killed
their children! But not her, no ma'am,
she just doesn't remember. But back to
the facts of the case, it gets even better.
Supposedly, according to a source close
to the case, there are a couple of witnesses who saw her on the day the baby
disappeared.'

Cate: 'Emphasis on allegedly. That's
unconfirmed at this point, Liza, which is
my point exactly. Are you, and the
media as a whole, going too far putting
this on the air with an array of unconfirmed allegations?'

Liza: 'Let me finish first. According to my
sources, she was seen discarding a baby
seat on a heap of garbage on her street.
How do you explain that away, Mrs
Defense Attorney?'

Cate: 'I see no need to explain unconfirmed witness reports, so-called witness
reports, I might add. And I don't think
that — '

Liza: 'How about the homeless woman?
There's a witness who claims she
handed a suitcase to a homeless woman,
around the time the baby disappeared.

286

The same morning she discarded the baby seat. Really, what else do we need to know? The evidence keeps mounting against her. What was in that suitcase? And how do you locate a homeless woman? I hope they do. And where is that monster of a mom? In a cozy psychiatric ward.'

Cate: 'She's been in a horrible accident, she has the injuries to prove it. She suffers from amnesia and was committed to a psychiatric ward and we — '

Liza: 'In hiding is where she is. Because decent mothers and concerned citizens are lining up in front of the city courthouse to demand justice. How come she's not in jail? This is outrageous!'

Cate: 'I was going to say, I don't think we need to rush to judgment here. We could argue that while you are crucifying her, she is trying to figure out what happened to her precious little girl.'

Liza: 'Wait a minute, wait a minute, Cate, that's not all. A neighbor of hers has spoken out as to her odd behavior. Not wanting anyone in her house, hearing the baby cry all hours of the day and night, even leaving her baby in the car unattended. Does that sound like a caring mother to you? It will all come out at trial. I'm not sure how a defense lawyer can explain all of that away.'

Cate: 'But Liza, babies cry! And they do so all hours of the day and night. And she lived alone, her husband worked out of town. I'd be careful who I let in my house, too. Haven't we all been less than perfect as mothers? All I'm trying to say is that the media plays a huge role in the public's opinion of a defendant, and she is innocent until proven guilty.'

Liza: 'Even if you don't believe a word I just told you, be honest with yourself, the timeframe is all we need. She waited too long to report the disappearance, actually didn't report it at all until she was found and questioned. Something's just not right. That's common sense, not an assumption.'

Cate: 'But is it fair to dub the mother 'Amnesia Mom' in the press?'

Liza: 'That's what she claims, right? She claims to have amnesia and therefore it is a fair description of her, don't you think? When it comes down to it, Cate, I only say what 90% of people are thinking.'

Cate: 'I don't know about that. I hope not, I hope people use their own judgment, or

rather withhold judgment until there's
definite proof of guilt. I hope the jury is
of her peers, as the law requires.
Thanks for being on our show, Liza.
Razor-tongued, as always. We have to go
to a commercial. After the break we'll
have the local news. Be right back.'

The video halts, freezing the host's face in a grimace. There's more video links but I click on the image tab. Photos of me, one of Mia. She's swaddled in a blanket, her eyes are closed. The likeness of her takes my breath away. I swipe the screen because it hurts to look at her. There are images of news stations. I recognize North Dandry. Further down, images of women I've never seen, no makeup, staring straight in the camera. Mug shots, orange tops. Some hold up a small board with letters. Name, number, Police department. I am everywhere, in every living room, Laundromat, gym, and radio station. At every doctor's office, every car showroom.

'Amnesia Mom,' I say and fight back the tears. I've been reduced to a mother without a memory, a guilty caretaker with a missing daughter. 'I had no idea.'

'I'm so sorry, Stella. So sorry.' His eyes darken, tear up. Then they turn into slits.

'She's nothing but a ratings whore, everyone knows that.' Anthony slides the phone back in his pocket. 'I'm sorry, I told you it wasn't a good idea. They are relentless and most of what they're saying has nothing to do with the facts. People know that, Stella. Every psychologist and psychiatrist is weighing in, everybody has something to say, is suddenly an expert on the subject matter. No one is interested in the facts. Reporters have called my house for weeks.'

Pause.

'They asked me if I thought you did this.'

I want to ask 'Do you think I did this?' but I know better. 'Of course not,' he'd answer, smoothly. So smooth that I'd know he had thought about it before, rehearsed his answer.

Anthony keeps his eyes on me, then he shivers as if shaking off a thought that's making him uncomfortable. It takes me a moment to make sense of it. How is anyone supposed to know what I did when I don't even know?

'Nell told me you left and she never heard from you again . . . '

'I've never forgotten how she wore Mom's brooch and her dress to the funeral. Who does that? Who wears her dead sister's clothes on the day of her funeral?'

Anthony shakes his head. 'I remember the brooch. But it was Nell's brooch, I think, Mom had borrowed it and never returned it. I don't remember all the details, but the dress, I don't know, Stella, Nell was three inches taller than Mom and twenty pounds heavier. I don't think she would've fit in Mom's dress.'

I feel anger inside of me. 'That's what I remember. Are you telling me I made it all up?'

'I'm not saying you made it up. That's how you remember it.'

'It's what happened, Anthony. There's nothing more to it.'

'Don't be angry at me. I couldn't be responsible for you . . . I was eighteen. I was a kid. I couldn't have raised you. I love you, Stella, but I had to leave.'

'It was just so hard. I had *nothing* left. I was alone. I — '

'*We* had nothing, Stella. We had nothing. It was unfortunate, but what was I supposed to do? It happened to both of us . . . the accident, Mom, Dad, our sister. It happened to both of us, not just you. It was what it was. It wasn't going to be easy.'

'I needed you, Anthony.'

'I know you did and I should've been there. I was a kid. I wish I could do it all over again.'

I don't know what to think. Did I expect too much, or did he give too little? I don't know anything anymore. I've believed so many things for so long. Believing something else now is hard. Maybe he's right. Maybe going down all these roads, of what could have been, was a lost cause. A treacherous road. We get the life we get and that's all.

'I brought you something,' he says and reaches inside his coat and retrieves a shabby-looking book with worn edges. I immediately recall a book I used to read obsessively as a child, asking Anthony the meaning of words I didn't know. I finally realized that the words meant nothing and were just made-up for a fantasy world on a nonexistent continent. I can't remember the title nor the cover of the book, only that it was about

291

a girl pickpocketing.

'Do you remember this?'

It's not the book I long for, but a paperback, familiar, like a toy from my childhood, yet I can't make a connection. Looking at the book feels like a person you know but cannot place. I read the title, *The 365 Funniest Jokes Ever*. I turn the book over, and I flip through its pages. There are jokes, riddles, and a collection of funny stories. I see cartoons of elephants sitting on small chairs, men dressed up as women in wigs and aprons, puppies pulling diapers off babies, and the outline of a cat busting through a brick wall. Corny, funny, childlike, silly pictures.

'I bought this book for you when you were about nine. You were always so sad and I wanted to cheer you up. I knew every single joke in this book . . . every single one. Just couldn't cheer you up. Not even the funniest jokes.'

I feel as if I've let him down, back then and now.

'I read you one joke a day for an entire year. While I was rolling on the floor, laughing, you never even cracked a smile. Don't you remember?'

I just shake my head. I was nine; I should remember something. I just stare at him and my eyes fill with tears.

'Knock, knock.' Anthony's voice is soft now.

When I don't say anything, he repeats it. 'Knock, knock,' he says, looking at me with anticipation.

'Anthony . . . '

'Knock, knock.'

'Anthony, stop . . . '

'Knock, knock.'

'Anthony, it wasn't funny then, it's not funny now.'

'Just try, Stella. Just once.'

I close my eyes and try to imagine something else. But it's not working. I give up because I know he won't. 'Who's there?' I say.

'Boo.'

'Boo who?'

'Oh, boo hoo. Don't cry. It's just a joke.'

I smile. *Boo hoo, don't cry, it's just a joke.*

'It finally worked.' He pauses. 'Don't cry, Stella, everything will be all right.'

'Right,' I say but I know nothing will be all right. Anthony has a wife, a dog, a life. I love him and I don't doubt for a second that he feels the same about me. Under different circumstances we'd probably say something like *let's spend Christmas together this year* or *I'll call you next week*. But here we are, on a bench at Creedmoor. *You're not alone*, Anthony says, but it sure feels that way. *I'll be in touch, Stella, I promise*, he says. I believe him and I love him, there's not much more to it. But for now this here is my life. Mothers all over the country are outraged. I'm Amnesia Mom, a news cycle amusement. That's all I am in everybody's eyes. Guilty.

★ ★ ★

That night, as I flip through the pages of the book, like a rush of water, I remember a moment long past. Legs pulled up, I melted into the leather tufted wing chair in my father's study, reading my favorite book, *The Thief of Peace*, a fantasy novel about a town full of upstanding people turning out to be liars, and a truth-speaking thief.

I could never be sure if my dad knew I was in his study or not, he just continued to brood over contracts, building codes, or historic preservation guidelines.

There were corrupt guards and a conspiracy exposing an evil Lord set on suppressing a civil war looming over the land. The plot, even though I must have read the book a dozen times when I was young, now remains elusive. But I remember the map in the front of the book.

With almost photographic memory I recall the wood-cut-style village cabins, the river merely a black line separating the crowded settlement from the vast Lord's estate. A mountain chain behind the castle, separating the flatlands from the rolling hills of the Lord's hunting grounds. The village was surrounded by a hedge, adjacent to a pine forest. If you looked really close you could see the wolves lurking under the shrubs and twisted plants below the piney trees. The compass, instead of the four cardinal directions, was made up of the four elements.

Then my head starts spinning and my tongue feels as if it is too big for my mouth. A memory visits me, a map I bought at the newsstand. I close my eyes and hang on, stay in the moment. Images pile up like heaps of leaves.

Newspapers, magazines. Cigarettes, candy,

flowers. A soda dispenser. Chinking coins as a man with a turban dropped the change in an ashtray atop the New York Times.

* * *

The next day, during our session, I curl up on the couch in Dr Ari's office, a pillow propped under my arm. What a peculiar point we've come to. The file in front of us has no more secrets to give away, it is on me now to solve the rest of the puzzle.

'I remembered something last night,' I say.

Dr Ari sits quietly, his fingers interlaced, elbows propped up on his desk.

'Is there a map?' I ask and point at the folder in front of him.

Dr Ari opens the folder and pulls out a thick piece of paper, folded numerous times. Its edges are bent and worn like a favorite childhood book. He shoves it over the glass surface of his desk towards me and pushes the button of the digital recorder.

It's time to enter the elevator, to descend. I go down to the first floor, and feel an immense sense of calm.

I take the map off the desk and hold it. I rub it between my thumb and index finger. My fingertips feel the folds of the thick paper. An origami riddle of creases, its pleats automatically undo but are awkward to close.

I descend further.

I hear a loud popping sound ringing in my ears. It turns into a sharp pitch, and then my

295

ears ring. I've heard this sound before. A gunshot? Something inside of me shifts; I smell gasoline, metal and gunpowder.

I open my eyes and I look at Dr Ari. Everything around me starts to buzz and then the world grows muffled as if I'm under water. Dr Ari's lips move but I cannot make out any words. The world around me switches to black and white and the silent movie is complete.

Roads, traffic lights. Rain, darkness.

A dot on a map.

Dover.

20

Dover, New York. Nine thousand people on less than sixty square miles. No major highways, just two thoroughfares. Numerous hamlets and rural communities too small to be considered villages were scattered about, their inhabitants rooted within its soil like the knobbled and rugged oaks, leaning with the wind. No one lived out here unless they were born here. Or wanted to disappear.

As I drove down Route 434 towards Anna Lieberman's house, I passed miles of dense trees that changed abruptly into open fields dotted with barns. The once red boxes sagged towards the ground, stood abandoned, bleached and gray, ready to be taken over by nature.

Dover's Main Street was like so many main streets in upstate New York. The roads, lacking white center lines, wove along the hilly terrain, flanked by small wooden houses. They were worn, not so much by traffic, but by time, and concrete cracks wove their way along the surface like mucus snail trails. Some of the cracks were filled in with black tar, some left to deepen and lengthen. The narrow sidewalks, distorted by tree roots, were broken up by T-shaped power-poles with their cables draped from one pole to the next, like masts of ghostly onlookers of a parade cancelled decades ago. The houses were covered by drooping roofs and surrounded by chain-link fences keeping old, arthritic dogs at bay.

Anna Lieberman's last known address was off Route 22. Anna and David were originally from Dover, yet the farmhouse they'd grown up in, and that burned down back in 1982, was located so close to Oniontown that they might as well have been from there.

Oniontown screamed rural poverty and had a reputation of its own; three hours north of New York City, depending on city traffic, Oniontown is a Hudson Valley hamlet of Dover, not actually a town, but a collection of rundown trailers and dilapidated farms.

I turned right just off Main Street in Dover and arrived at Anna's house. The sound of an axe splitting wood echoed down the street and a garbage truck's diesel engine revved on and off. I passed 126 Waterway Circle slowly, taking in the house and the yard. Anna's backyard was fenced in by seven-feet-tall sun-bleached poles.

126 Waterway Circle, the first of six houses of a cul-de-sac, appeared unkempt but not uninhabited. The entire neighborhood was dangling lightly off the ledge of being deemed ramshackle. There was a crooked 'For Sale' sign posted in front of the house on the left.

I parked the car on the main road instead of in front of Anna's house, got out, passed the house, and continued down the warped sidewalk. I strained to read the sign in the front yard of 128 and I took out my cell phone. I had only five percent of battery life left and I wasn't going to use it on a call pretending I was interested in the house. I slid the phone back in my purse.

I turned and went up Anna's pebble walkway, a scraggly, fuzzy mess of stones and weeds cushioning my every step. The fence paint was chipped, the posts' concrete anchors gaped open, releasing the posts from their duty of keeping the fence in an upright position. Some fence sections were standing upright, some leaning, and one almost flat on the ground. The overgrown yard was covered in knee-high weeds. Whatever shrubs and bushes there were, appeared wilted, their dead leaves cracked, leaving the roots bare in the soil, exposed to the elements. The property seemed vacant, abandoned even for quite some time, if it hadn't been for an older model Chevy Caprice with mismatched hubcaps parked under the carport.

There were chairs on the front porch, and multiple wind chimes hanging from the rafters. The chimes clinked a wretched song of despair while the strings holding the metal pipes in place were about to give in to gravity. Some of the missing pipe parts had been replaced by forks, their tines bent about randomly. The drooping black roof was patched with brown shingles.

The porch slumped worse than the roof. Two crates formed a makeshift table, with two folding chairs placed on either side of them. The chairs looked as if they had been stolen from a reception; their chipped gold paint alluding to a wedding ceremony long past.

No sign of David Lieberman's truck. I took a few deep breaths but couldn't keep my hands from shaking. My purse was heavy, weighed down by the loaded gun, more a good luck charm than anything else. I had never fired a gun before and the one in Jack's closet was the first I had ever held in my hand. It was a Taurus 905, a 9mm, whatever that meant. I had spent an entire afternoon online looking up the mechanics and how to fire it, but I had a feeling that if it came down to it, handling it would leave me dumbfounded. The gun in my purse was unnerving me, adding to my tension, the facts I had gathered started to merge into a ball of yarn; secure engagement, ready to fire disengagement, drop the hammer manually by pulling the trigger while lowering the hammer with the thumb.

My knuckles rapped the paint-chipped door. It sounded hollow. The door opened and I recognized her immediately.

Like a scene from a Dutch painting the petite woman stood in the doorframe, in her hands a basket filled with vegetables: carrots with wilted leaves, white bulbous turnips turned purple. There was another green leafy vegetable I couldn't identify, maybe water spinach or Swiss chard. Anna looked wholesome holding the vegetable basket, capable of extracting life from the earth's soil. Her hands were covered in mud, her nails rimmed with dirt.

I looked up from the basket and took in her appearance.

Anna Lieberman's red hair was tied in a knot at the nape of her neck. Some strands had escaped and made her appear disheveled. I had quite a few inches on her, which caused her to look up at me. Her body was lean yet not in an athletic kind of way but rather fatigued and worn out. She wasn't at all unattractive, but seemed to have lived a hard life, past her prime.

'Yes?' she asked as she considered me. She was visibly out of breath.

'I don't mean to intrude, I . . . I don't know, I have a question.' I swallowed hard and forced my face into a smile. 'I . . . I'm sorry to disturb you. You look like you were in the middle of something. I . . . '

She smoothed a strand of hair behind her ears. She then paused as if she had decided there was no need to fix her appearance. I was just someone lost, or asking for the nearest mechanic shop or something insignificant. Her smile exposed white crooked teeth. She put the basket of vegetables on a table in the foyer. The table held a sizable stack of catalogs, the top one a glossy cover of a Greek island, judging by the white houses with blue roofs and the azure ocean in the far background.

'I was out back and I wasn't sure if I heard someone knock. How can I help you?' She looked me up and down.

Threadbare industrial carpet, frayed at the edges, extended over the threshold. She was barefoot.

'I wanted to ask you about the house. The one over there.' I took a step back and pointed at the little white house next door with the 'For Sale' sign in the yard.

She looked puzzled, as if she was unaware it was for sale, or surprised that someone wanted to buy it.

301

'I don't know much about it. Maybe you should call the number on the sign and ask to see it.' She ended the sentence as if it was a question.

'How about the neighborhood, the schools? Is it pretty safe? How about break-ins? Real Estate Agents never tell you the truth.' I added the last sentence to let her know that I valued her opinion.

'I wouldn't know about schools around here. I don't have much contact with the neighbors and I don't read the local papers.' She kept holding her soiled hands up like a surgeon ready to make the first cut. 'I need to wash my hands. Why don't you come on in for a cup of tea?'

She stepped back and I entered Anna Lieberman's house.

'Thank you so much. Buying a house is a major investment. I just want to make sure I pick the right one.'

The threadbare carpet turned out to be a square piece of leftover outdoor carpeting. The rest of the floor was covered in hardwood planks, creaking underfoot. The house was old and worn, drafty even on this mild day. There was a living room straight ahead, and another hallway to the left. The kitchen, to the right of the living room, led straight into the backyard. The house smelled of mold and musty carpets, traces of furniture polish and Lysol. There was a frayed couch with lifeless throw pillows and a crooked coffee table. Countless travel magazines with glossy covers lay strewn across the coffee table and the couch. Some cover pages were torn, others had rings from sweating glasses, leaving the pages warped. The rugs crunched like straw underneath my feet. The furniture was mismatched. It was the home of a woman who had furnished a house with hand-me-downs and donations. Everything was worn, just short of ending up in a dump or in a landfill. Yet it was as clean as one could clean an old house. The colors were muted, washed out, except for the shiny travel magazines.

Anna Lieberman led me through the hallway and straight into the kitchen where she pointed to a chair by the kitchen table. She rapidly pumped a soap dispenser while the water was trickling. The soap was unable to cut through the mud, so she washed her hands twice but still didn't seem satisfied. As she applied the third round of soap, she asked, 'Coffee or tea?'

'I don't want to impose, really,' I said. 'Whatever you're having is fine with me.' I put my hands in my lap and interlaced my fingers to keep them from shaking.

'Tea it is.' She opened a cabinet door and took out two chipped mugs. She switched on the stove and took two teabags out of a canister on the counter. She dropped the bags into the mugs and sat across from me on the other side of the kitchen table. Anna Lieberman's demeanor seemed open and friendly and I felt a sudden tinge of remorse for misleading her.

'It might seem odd wanting to buy a house in Dover, but I grew up around here. The area is kind of my home,' I said.

My inventiveness surprised me. One believable

lie after the other slipped off my lips. Why not go further?

'Actually, I'm from Poughkeepsie,' I added as I cupped the empty mug, trying to hide my shaking hands. I had seen a sign by the road and remembered the name of a town just west of Dover. 'I like the area.' My mind was racing. I didn't want the conversation to stall, but I couldn't think of anything to say. The silence stretched, became obvious.

Anna jerked ever so slightly when the kettle whistled. She poured boiling water into the mugs, the tea turned the color of cognac, and a fruity aroma drifted towards my nostrils. When the wooden knob of a drawer didn't budge, she wiggled it left and right and then fiercely yanked at it. The drawer opened and she reached for a spoon while turning towards me.

'Poughkeepsie?' she said and nodded. 'That's not far from here.' She eyed the spoon in her hand, a spoon that seemed small, almost elfin, as if made for a child. New and polished, shiny, not fitting with the rest of the house.

'About twenty miles west,' I said and tried to ignore the image that burst into my mind of yet another spoon. A spoon — wasn't it mere days ago that I had held one just like this in my hand — Mia's spoon, its rubber tip turning white when food was too hot.

When I looked at her hand again, she held a regular teaspoon that didn't resemble the one from earlier at all.

Anna returned the kettle to the stove and while she searched the cabinet for sugar, I took a closer look around the kitchen. Like everything else in the house the counters were worn and showed deep scratches and knife marks. The table and chairs were old and chipped from use. The buffet — the glass in the doors was missing — had been repainted. The paint, a buttery yellow with a green tinge to it, had been applied in a thick coat and the wood seams appeared caulked with paint. The linoleum floor tiles had risen around the edges and when I pushed the raised edges with the tip of my foot I heard a crunching sound. The fridge and the stove were ancient. The kitchen counters were cluttered with torn pages from travel magazines, flower pots and bags of soil, and small seed packages, as if I had interrupted her while she was planting, repotting, and pruning right here in the kitchen.

As she inspected her hands for cleanliness, I took in her shabby floral blouse and the skirt. The colors were faded, yet the blouse was clean and pressed.

'You have children?' she asked and ran her finger around the top of the mug.

The question caught me by surprise.

'One. I have just one. A daughter.' How peculiar it felt to speak of Mia as if she was safe at home with her father or a sitter. What was I even doing here, I asked myself, what did I expect to find? Lieberman wasn't here, his sister seemed to be some meek woman in an old rundown, drafty house tending to a garden out back. Even more peculiar was the fact that I had no idea how to even steer her in the direction of her brother and my missing child.

305

As I watched, Anna pulled the teabag from the steaming mug, never flinching as she squeezed every last bit of hot liquid out of it. She got up and stepped on the foot pedal raising the garbage can lid, dropping the teabag into the can.

A foul, irritating odor hit my nostrils. The stench was stomach-churning, sinister and heavy, permeating my every pore, yet it was sweet, with an undertone of clean in a putrid kind of way, a lemony scent maybe, but not quite as fresh, more chemical, in a potpourri kind of way. Like . . . a familiar rotten reek, conjuring images of diapers piling up in the nursery, prompting Jack to shake his head in disapproval. Diaper? Yes, diaper smell.

'Fertilizer,' Anna said. She stepped off the foot pedal, closed the lid, and placed a hand on top of it, as if trying to contain the odor. 'Smacks you right in the face, doesn't it?'

'Smells like dirty diapers,' I replied. My anxiety was catching up with me, soon perspiration would begin to soak into my clothes. It took everything I had to get a grip on myself and keep my voice from shaking.

'You wanted to know more about the area . . . ' Her voice trailed off. She paused every so often and cocked her head as if she was trying to capture a melody coming from the far distance. 'Let's see, there is a small park at the end of . . . ' I let her go on and on, and gave her a smile every time she looked up at me.

She was no longer the plain girl with the frizzy hair I had seen in the 1982 newspaper article.

Sitting across from her, the differences between the older pictures of her became obvious; her face had lengthened; the bone structure was more refined, almost angelic.

My distraction with Anna, her house, her appearance had gotten the better of me but I needed to know where her brother was, needed to know if he was capable of what I thought him capable of. I wanted to hear the story of the fire, the story about her family, her brother's story, something, really anything that would explain what he had done and where he was. Was this another one of my thoughts going astray, a thought that started out as 'I wish I could talk to his sister' and then ended with me in her kitchen drinking tea?

'You must be doing a lot of gardening,' I said. 'Just vegetables or flowers or both?' I looked at the floating teabag inside my mug and reached for the sugar.

Anna pushed the sugar bowl towards me. Her hand, free from the mud and dirt, seemed malformed, its movement suggestive of arthritic joints. The edges of the inside of her palms were pulled together by scars, affecting muscles and tendons, restricting the movement of her fingers. Changes had left brown marks within her dermis, clearly burn marks from a fire.

'I want to use the insurance money from my house in Poughkeepsie to buy a house here,' I kept on going as if in a trance, trying to erase baby spoons and foul smells from my memory. I needed to focus and concentrate. 'It's not a lot of money and I still have to buy furniture and appliances. Everything I owned . . . ' I paused to make it more dramatic, ' . . . burned up in a fire. I have nothing left.' I lowered my head for a second, partly to play the role of a victim, partly because I didn't think I looked sincere telling the tale.

I looked up to see the impact. Her eyes darkened and my words rested between us like the sugar cubes in the chipped bowl.

She stirred her tea, her hands clasping the spoon, her index finger pointing helplessly and aimlessly about.

I was good. I was surprised how good I was. I never thought that I'd be able to con my way into her house and then dupe my way into her kitchen. I wanted her to gently descend into the past and reappear with a story. The story of the 1982 fire and her brother, David Lieberman. And then we'd talk about him being a kidnapper.

'A fire? Your house burned down?' Her voice cracked and her body shifted in the chair. Her spoon dropped with a clang back into her mug. 'I'm sorry to hear that. Did anybody get hurt?' Her eyes were big, her pupils dark. She hid her hands underneath the table.

'No, it was just an electrical fire, some faulty wiring. I wasn't home when it happened.'

My next question would be *Do you live alone?* then *Do you have any family?* then I'd say *A brother? Tell me about him* then *I need to tell you something, I want you to hear me out. I have a suspicion . . .*

Suddenly she cocked her head and got up, as if she'd heard something, as if a sound,

308

undetected by me, was tearing at her. Something inside her had shifted.

I heard a gentle sound trail towards me. Almost like a baby's whimper the moment right before they wake up. I wanted to speak but the words never came to life. Instead I felt hot; perspiration started to form on my forehead. I felt feverish, like I was about to lose my mind. In a matter of seconds my body would be covered in sweat, flowing free like condensation.

I'd smelled diapers — but no, there was fertilizer, clearly she was a gardener, I was smelling odors that weren't there. No, I told myself, no, I had seen a regular spoon and *imagined* a baby spoon, *imagined* diaper smell. Now I'd imagined a baby whimper. I was hallucinating and afraid of what was going to happen next. Glimpses of figures moving about? I scanned the room for escape options. There was the back door and the front door and all I could do was get up and, with a creaky voice and shaky knees, say, 'I think I better leave.'

Anna eyed me curiously and didn't move, eyeing the untouched tea, the bag still floating in the steaming water.

'I'll try to have someone show me the house tomorrow. You've been very kind, thank you for the tea,' I said to give her some sort of explanation for my behavior. I grabbed my purse tighter.

Without a word, Anna got up and walked me to the front door.

I reached for the door knob. 'Wait!' Her voice, now sharp with more power than her petite body suggested, made me turn around and stop in my tracks. 'My name is Anna Lieberman. I didn't get your name?'

She knew nothing about me — so what did it matter? 'Estelle. Estelle Paradise.' I turned back towards the door, reaching for the knob again.

She stepped past me and stood between me and the front door. 'You're not looking for a house, Estelle Paradise. Why don't you tell me why you're really here?' Her eyes were piercing, demanding an answer.

My mind went blank, my beating heart inside my chest drowning out everything else. I tried to think of something to say, explain myself, but my mind struggled for a coherent thought. Should I just tell her the truth or keep up the façade? I decided to give her an answer that was somewhere in between.

'I'm looking for your brother David.'

'You're looking for my brother?' Her eyes flickered as if she was checking her brain for the connection of the puzzle pieces she needed to make sense of everything. I almost felt sorry for her. 'Why would you come here asking me about a house and why would you talk about fires when you're really looking for my brother?' Her voice was soft, almost gentle now. 'What is it you want from him?'

Again I decided on the middle ground. 'I'm not here to cause you any trouble, I promise you. I have questions.'

She wore a puzzled expression, one I was unable to interpret. Confusion? Fear even?

Anna repeated, 'What is it you want from him?'

310

Where to start. My baby's gone, your brother took her. I found Tinker Bell in his apartment and strange newspaper articles. 'I think your brother took my daughter.'

'My brother took your daughter?' She looked around as if to make sure no one was watching us.

I kept looking at her, undeterred. 'Tell me where he is,' I said.

'I have no idea what you're talking about.'

'Where is he?'

She was silent for a long time. 'David, David, David,' she said and my heart skipped a beat. I raised my brows, clutching my purse.

'He took my daughter. I have proof. I need — '

Anna shook her head and gestured with her hand. *Stop making things up*, she seemed to say. 'What is he to you? How do you know him?'

'We live in the same building. Do you know where he is?'

'I can't help you, you need to leave.'

'I'm not leaving until you tell me where he is.'

She put her hand on my back and started pushing me towards the front door. I pushed her hands off me and looked her straight in the eyes.

'David set the fire and killed your parents. And he took my daughter. You know I'm telling the truth. Please tell me where he is.'

'If you don't leave right now I — '

'Just answer my questions and I'll leave. Please! He can give her back . . . and I won't tell the police.'

We stood in silence for a while, then I heard

311

her voice, childlike. 'Why don't you just go to the police then and tell them?' She stepped closer. I felt her hot breath on my face. She ushered me down the hallway and out the front door. 'If you come back I'll call the police myself,' she said and slammed the front door.

I fought the urge to knock again. I walked to my car, got in, and sat without moving. The air in the car was sticky and stale and I rolled down the window. I had no idea what to do next or where to go. There was a scent of ozone in the air as though a storm was approaching.

I glanced at an open window, upstairs by the side of the house, facing my car. I watched Anna's silhouette holding something in her arms. It was small and seemed to shift back and forth. I couldn't remember seeing any bowls or litter boxes, nor did I hear a puppy whine or a dog bark. The silhouette bent over, one arm extended, grabbing something and whatever she held in her arms, it stirred. It moved away from her body and then it broke out into a wail. A wail with a familiar urgency and intensity. The crying stopped as suddenly as it had started.

My hands started shaking. Another cry sped towards me, making me gasp for air. There was a part of my brain that responded to the scream, to the familiar frequency, some sort of acoustic cue of recognition, etched deeply into my brain. *The baby spoon, the garbage smelling like soiled diapers, the whimper.* Not even close to being a figment of my imagination.

I fought the contents of my stomach and the urge to get away from the primal response to the

312

wavelength of a baby's cry. Mia's cry.

My mind burst into a riot of images and questions, none of which I could understand or answer. A tremor took over my body and I felt as if millions of flames were igniting all over my skin. My hands shook uncontrollably. I closed my eyes and allowed the adrenaline to flood my body. Spoons, and diapers, and a whimpering baby. Mia. A stone's throw away. All I had to do was wield the gun at Anna, grab Mia and run. It sounded so easy and uncomplicated, yet I couldn't move a single muscle. Completely paralyzed, I sat in the car, and the more I thought about grabbing the gun and barging into Anna's house, the more I felt discouraged and utterly terrified. I didn't remember ever being this scared in my life. And that was just the beginning. The fact that I just sat there, motionless, only made it worse. If that was even possible.

Overhead, lightning exploded in a flicker of lights. Like two sides of a coin, thunder followed and a booming sound fell from the sky. Then the skies unleashed steady droplets of rain. The drips turned into large drops, then a million spatters covered the pavement. The air was fecund with the scent of soil and earth and, within seconds, water ran down Anna's driveway and joined the runoff, disappearing into the storm drains of Waterway Circle.

The rain eased just long enough for me to see a truck pulling into Anna's driveway. The man who got out of the driver's seat was the same man who had taken my child, and he was no

313

more than one hundred feet away from me. David Lieberman opened the trunk, took out a bulky bag of what seemed like clothes, or blankets. He walked towards the house, opened the front door, and stumped his feet twice on the door mat on the front stoop. He turned and scanned the skies, then stepped over the threshold.

Suddenly I was afraid. They were two and I was one. Right now Anna is telling him about me and any second Lieberman is going to emerge from the front door and there's no telling what he's going to do to me. What were the odds that, if I were to politely ask for my child, they'd just hand her over? Zero.

I could feel the blood draining away from my gut, making my muscles twitch. I felt like an animal in a fight or flight situation. My heart beat as if it was going to crack my ribs. *Flight* I thought, *leave*. My heart wanted out of my chest and the only thing I could think of was to step on the gas and drive. Incapable, even now. Knowing she was right there, I was still incapable. I hated myself as I listened to the metronome-like flip-flop of the windshield wipers marking every inch of distance I put between my daughter and me.

21

The merciless rain had shrouded the afternoon in unnatural darkness. The sun managed to peek through a layer of gray clouds when I passed one of the barns I had seen on my way into town earlier. I slowed the car and turned into the dirt road by a tree line. The unpaved path, rendered awash with mud, seemed as if it could easily bury car tires and the standing puddles grew larger by the minute. I opened the car door and made my way towards the barn.

The inside greeted me with a scent of hay, manure, and the lingering perspiration of horses. The interior was even more dilapidated than I expected. The wood was cracked and gray, enduring the elements, bearing storms and scorching sun. One strong puff of wind, one more breeze catching the rafters just right, and it would be gone. The heavy doors swung shut behind me. I heard the pitter-patter of the raindrops surrounding me like calming white noise.

I had imagined this moment so many times, the moment I found my daughter, yet I felt empty inside. I'd thought when the time came I'd scream bloody murder, call 9-1-1. But none of that had happened. I was paralyzed with fear, incapable of doing what I needed to do. I had failed Mia yet again.

I sat on the ground. My back propped up

against a post, I pulled my knees to my chest. I remembered the first night Mia had slept between Jack and me. The full moon had spilled through the windows, casting an eerie silver-blue hue on the entire room. I had looked at Mia and she seemed to be made of ice. I was afraid of what was ahead of me, being a mother, responsible for someone's life. And with every passing day my attempts to live in a carefully constructed realm, my house of cards, had collapsed. Images popped in my head like jumpy disjointed pictures from an old reel-to-reel family movie.

The hospital, Mia being born. Me, not sleeping, being hyper-alert for days on end, being too tired to function and too tired to go to sleep. I operated on autopilot, never told Jack, never told the doctors or nurses, never told anyone. I waited for it to pass, yet that moment never came. The windstorm that had started to rage inside this little creature that I loved with all my might, but my love couldn't turn the storm into something gentler. My milk not coming in adding to the guilt I felt of not being able to provide for her. The intrusive thoughts that had begun to seep into my mind, elusive at first, then they had taken shape.

I reached inside my purse and cradled the gun in my hand. I had failed Mia and failed her again. I'm not worthy of being a mother at all. There's only one choice left: leaving her for good.

Leaning against a pole in the barn, something snuck into my mind and tore at me, this one image, this one thought, this one realization.

316

Within all this darkness, I leaned towards this feeling of primitive attachment: when Mia was born and they put her into my arms, her eyes were covered in medical ointment. They were sleek, roaming, and unable to focus. As she slept, her little fist held on to the tip of my finger, her hand too small to grab it in its entirety. Her need to attach herself to me was ancient, primal, her knowing that I was her salvation. Her thin and translucent skin had stretched over her skull, her weightless hair, her purple nails, like a message from the universe.

With the gun in my right hand, pointed at my temple, I forced myself to imagine the future and I completed the story. I saw flashes of a girl, her life, a succession of milestones — crawling, walking, running — flashes that branded themselves into my mind.

Mia dancing, twirling, reaching for a hand to keep her from falling.

Reaching for me. Bows in her hair.

Bandanas tied around her head like good-luck charms.

Chipped nail polish and crooked tiaras.

Birthday cakes.

Playground games and friends and sand-castles.

Goodnight stories.

While I sat there, feeling the icy metal of the muzzle, seconds before I'd allow a bullet to rip a hole through my brain, in that very moment, I felt as if some higher power was watching over me, sitting on the dirt floor of the barn next to me.

317

Rain ran down my back when another lightning burst was followed by thunder, shaking the barn, and sending a spark of light through the holes and gaps of the rafters and the worn-out wood. For a second, a bright flicker descended onto the ground, dirt particles floating about like magic fairy dust.

I remembered my mother's voice, soft and soothing, telling me that thunder is the sound that lightning makes, how one thing occurs and another follows. I knew it was not too late. Mia was a drop of ink in a glass of water; I was forever changed by her existence and she was right down the road. This is about more than consoling a crying baby, about more than being able to stop tears from falling. It's about growing beyond my limitations. In the past I might have been the worst mother but today I'll become the best I can possibly be.

I left the barn doors gaping open behind me, got in the car, and drove back to Dover to claim my daughter.

★ ★ ★

When I reached Waterway Circle, the wipers squeaked their way across the windshield, their slow motion allowing for a clear view of the world, but only for a second. When the rain stopped, my heart rate slowed, mimicking the pace of the wipers. Suddenly everything was clear. There was no more room for interpretation, just my heart beating in cadence with my daughter's heart in the house in front of me.

The rust-red Chevy Caprice still sat under the carport, Lieberman's truck was still parked in front of the house. I got out of the car, walked to the front door and knocked.

There was no answer.

'Anna, I need to talk to you.' I knocked again. 'Anna, please, open the door.'

I knocked again. Nothing.

I stepped away from the house to get a good look at the nursery window and saw that the shades were drawn. Suddenly I heard the front door screech and Anna stood in the doorway.

'Yes?' she asked, her right hand resting casually on the doorframe. Anna's face was relaxed, her posture loose, almost bored. She now wore a pair of jeans and a T-shirt and had her hair in a high ponytail. She also wore makeup.

'Anna, I heard her cry. I know you have my baby. I know all about — '

'I think you've got the wrong house.' She hesitated for a second, then furrowed her brows. 'Are you okay? Are you in some kind of trouble?' Anna looked over my shoulder, scanning the street. 'You're soaking wet.'

'No, no, no, no, no. Please don't play games with me. I know what I heard, and I smelled diapers, I saw the baby spoon.' I reached inside my purse and grabbed my phone. 'I'm calling the police.'

A shadow appeared next to Anna. David Lieberman, the Prince of Darkness, and together they stood on the front porch like Grant Wood's image of American Gothic. Only more sinister,

319

and without the pitchfork.

'Is there a problem?' David Lieberman spoke softly, as if not to upset me any further.

'You know who I am. Where's my daughter?'

They both stepped further out on the porch. I took a step back.

'I told her she's at the wrong house. Maybe a mix-up or something? She's insisting on a baby being here,' Anna said, her voice slow and soothing.

'A baby?' Lieberman put his arm around Anna's shoulder. 'Like my wife told you, maybe you got the wrong address?'

'Tell him, Anna, tell him I was here. And I know you have a baby upstairs, my daughter, Mia. I heard her cry. Tell him I was here earlier, tell him, Anna.'

She remained perfectly still. 'I have no idea what you're talking about. I've never seen you before in my life. You're not making any sense.'

'We sat in your kitchen, you made tea, and the cups were white, with yellow flowers, you — '

'I've never seen you in my life. This is the wrong house.'

My voice had turned into a pleading stream. 'You made tea for me, and you told me about the house next door. We talked and you told me about the fire.' I stopped just long enough to catch my breath. 'You plant vegetables in your garden. And flowers. You have my daughter. He . . . ' I pointed at David Lieberman, 'he took her from me. He climbed down into my kitchen, he took her, and I want her back.'

David Lieberman's face was blank. 'Lady,

there's no baby, there are no teacups with yellow flowers, no diapers, none of that. I don't know what to tell you, but you're freaking my wife out and I need you to leave.' His voice rang false, high-pitched, almost forced in its controlled state.

'I was here earlier. Please, Anna,' I pointed at the chime dangling off the rafters, 'all this was here earlier. The chime, the chair on the porch, the house next door for sale, everything.'

'You don't take no for an answer, do you? I'm telling you you're at the wrong house and I need you to stop screaming on my porch and leave. We don't know you.'

I stuck out my neck, trying to look past them into the house. They mistook my movement as threatening and David Lieberman stepped forward, grabbing Anna's hand. They were closing ranks.

'Don't come any closer. Get off my porch.'

I took a step back, decided to play my last trump card. 'I'm going to call the police. They'll sort it all out.' I reached into my purse and pulled out my cell phone. 'I'm not bluffing. I'm calling the police.' I pushed a random button and the phone came on just long enough to see the charge indicator blinking. Then it turned off.

'Go ahead, call the police.'

'My phone is dead,' I said, barely able to control the tremor in my voice.

Lieberman reached in his pants pocket and pulled out a cell phone. He waved it in front of me. 'You should always charge your phone. In

321

case of an emergency, you know.' Lieberman smiled.

'Is this a joke to you? Is this a game you're playing?' I took a step forward and picked up the chair on the porch. 'I will scream so loud the entire neighborhood will hear me.'

Their faces were blank, not as much as discomfort in their demeanor. Anna turned and disappeared into the house.

'Go ahead,' Lieberman said and put his hands in his pants pockets. 'For someone who goes around knocking on doors and accusing people, you're not very convincing. I'm just trying to help you,' he said and shook his head.

'Someone help me,' I screamed as loud as I could, 'they have my baby. They took my daughter from me. Help.' I lifted the chair up in the air and pointed its legs towards the window next to the front door.

Lieberman looked at me in disbelief. He stepped forward and grabbed my left wrist and shook it until the chair landed on the porch. I jerked away from him but he held on to my fingers and bent them backwards, making me wince.

'HELP! I NEED HELP!'

Lieberman pulled me towards the front door. I managed to leave bloody streaks down his forearm, when a flashing light made both of us turn around.

A police cruiser came to an abrupt stop and two uniformed officers walked towards us. One of them spoke into the radio attached to his shoulder as he hurried towards us. Lieberman let go of my wrist.

'What's going on here?' asked the older and heavier of the two officers.

'You need to search the house. They have my baby,' I said and ignored his hands gesturing me to step back further.

'I need you to calm down and follow my instructions. Please step off the porch. I need to see some identification.'

'You asked what was going on. I'm trying to tell you — '

'Identification?'

I pulled my driver's license out of my wallet and I handed it to him. He glanced back and forth between me and the picture.

'Now tell me what's going on.'

'I need you to search the house. They have my daughter. I was here earlier and now they pretend they don't know me.'

'Just explain the situation to me, don't tell me what to do.'

'My baby is in there, I need you to — '

'Please, I can't just conduct a search of a private property, it doesn't work that way.'

'How does it work then? How can I get you to search the house?'

'Who called 9-1-1?'

'One of the neighbors must have heard me scream and — '

'I did, I called.' Anna stepped back onto the porch and folded her arms in front of her body. Her voice was shaky. 'This woman knocked on our door. She's not making any sense. Please tell her to leave.'

'Sir?' The police officer looked at Lieberman.

'What's going on there?' he said and pointed at Lieberman's arm. 'Your arm's bleeding. Are you hurt?'

The second officer gestured me to follow him and led me onto the front lawn, away from the house. 'Tell me what's going on.'

'He's my neighbor,' I said, pointing at Lieberman. 'I found a figurine from my daughter's room in his apartment. He took my daughter. She's in this house.' I pointed at 126. 'I heard her cry through the window and I — '

'You were in his apartment? So you know each other?'

'No, no, no, you don't understand.' I took a deep breath in, hoping it would allow me to sound more coherent. 'Look,' I said and reached into my purse for the Tinker Bell figurine.

He stepped back and put his hand on the holster of his gun. 'Do not reach inside your purse again. Take your hand out and calm down so we can make sense of this.'

I jerked my hand back. I watched the first cop glance left to the 'For Sale' sign in the yard of the house next door. He turned towards David Lieberman. 'Is this your residence, sir?'

'That's correct. I live here with my wife.'

'Come back over here, Mrs Paradise. But keep your hands to yourself and follow my instructions.' The junior cop and I joined them on the front porch. 'You live on . . . ' He studied my driver's license again, '517 North Dandry, in New York City. This gentleman,' he pointed at David Lieberman, 'lives at 126 Waterway Circle, Dover. Hours away from your home address.'

'He's my neighbor, he lives above me. There's a dumbwaiter and I found — '

'Just answer my question. How is he your neighbor if you live hours apart?'

'He's my upstairs neighbor at 517 North Dandry. Why won't you believe anything I'm telling you?'

'Ma'am, let me assure you, I'm not making any assumptions. It's just that you're not making any sense. We received a call about a trespassing violation. You trespassed onto their property and — '

'Why don't you ask them for identification? This is David and Anna Lieberman; they are brother and sister, not husband and wife.'

'I don't need to identify myself,' Lieberman interjected. 'I can't help crazy people coming to my door. I have rights, you know.' Lieberman threw the officer an *I told you she was crazy* look.

'This back and forth is not helping. Let me just finish questioning the lady.'

We moved down the driveway. I realized that my clothes and hair were soaking wet and that, with every step, my feet made a squishing sound. I was afraid he'd ask me to hand him my purse, where he'd find the gun. If he did, I'd be handcuffed and in the back of the cruiser before I could explain anything else.

'Okay, Mrs Paradise, one thing at a time,' the first cop said and took out a small green notepad. 'You are reporting that they have your baby and that he's your neighbor. Is he the father of the baby? I'm not sure I'm following

325

you.' He closed his notebook. 'What I can tell you is that I have no legal cause to search a house. You're hours away from where you live and I can't make sense of your story.'

'Why won't you just search the house?'

'Because — '

'Because it doesn't work that way, I remember.'

'Officer,' Anna called over from the front porch, 'this is just a mix-up. I think she's got the wrong address.'

'We've been telling her that all along,' David Lieberman said and put his arm around Anna.

'I understand, sir, I'll be with you in a minute.'

When the officer turned towards me, I continued, 'Mix-up? This isn't a mix-up. He took my child. I was here earlier, not even an hour ago. She told me to leave and I heard my baby cry. I tracked him down and came here to confront him.'

'Why didn't you go to the police where you live?'

'I did, I tried, but . . . ' I was going in circles. I knew that if I continued this route, I was going to end up in a psychiatric ward in this godforsaken town.

'Ma'am, is there anyone we can call to pick you up? Your husband, a friend, anyone?'

'I don't need anyone to pick me up.'

'I'm doing you a favor here. This can go either way and I'm offering you to call someone to pick you up.'

'Let me just show you what I found — '

'I told you before not to reach into your purse.

326

Are you on any medication? Are you in treatment for any kind of mental illness? Now would be the time to tell me.'

'No, no, no. I'm . . . why are you asking me this? Why don't you ask him what kind of medication he's on? Ask him if he's crazy. He took my child. He's the one — '

'Mrs Paradise, honestly . . . ' Then his face lit up. 'Ah, now I get it.' He closed the notepad and turned a dial on the radio attached to his shoulder.

'I'm telling you the truth. If I — '

'Relax, Mrs Paradise. I know what this is,' he interrupted me. 'You're the girlfriend. You probably stood in the rain watching the house. You followed him out here and you realized he's married. He,' and he pointed at Lieberman, 'is pretending he doesn't know you. Which, by the way, is not a crime. You, on the other hand, you could be charged with disturbing the peace and trespassing. And that doesn't include the scratches on his arm, that's an assault charge. And the fact you're accusing this man of kidnapping. You are potentially in a lot of trouble.'

I had seen Lieberman earlier getting clothes from the backseat and with any luck . . . 'His car, can you check his car, just look through the window. If there's anything like baby clothes, diapers, formula, anything, then you know I'm telling the truth.'

I turned around. Everything about Lieberman was wrong. He stood in the same spot, seemingly paralyzed, yet his smile was pasted on and there were dark wet patches under each armpit.

'Please, just look through the car window, you'll see,' I said and watched Lieberman's face change from superiority to fear. His shoulders were hunched, his movements uncoordinated. He kept moving towards me, yet his body seemed to be going sideways at the same time. His face was paper white. He leaped off the porch causing the officers to put their hands on their holsters.

'My husband isn't feeling well.' Anna Lieberman pulled him back, holding on to his arm while wrapping her other arm around his waist. 'We haven't done anything wrong. I think we're done here.'

'Sir,' the cop called over to the porch, 'do you want to file charges for assault against this lady?'

'We're not filing any charges, officer. This is just a mix-up.' Anna Lieberman sounded convincing. If I didn't know any better, I would have believed her myself.

'Please check their car, you'll see — '

'That's enough.' His voice was harsh, his eyes stern. 'Either you get in your car and leave or I'm going to put these cuffs on you,' he said and pointed at his duty belt.

I wanted to drop to my knees. I felt discredited like a little child whose parents insist that there are no monsters under the bed. No one was going to help me because they believed me to be a lunatic. Again, I had failed. There was nothing else I could do. Lieberman had won. I gave the police officer a half-hearted smile and held up my car key.

'You folks are free to go about your business,' he called to the front porch. Then he turned towards me. 'I'm going to consider this issue resolved. I will escort you to 434 and we forget about all of this. Just a lot of paperwork over nothing and these good folks over there have somewhere to be. 434 will take you straight back to New York City,' he said and motioned me to get in my car.

We reached exit 434 and the officer in the passenger seat in the car alongside me waved to the right. I took the exit that would lead me back to New York City and the cruiser disappeared from my view. I wondered if they were going to follow me, make sure I'd leave town, but in my rearview mirror I saw the cruiser take off in the other direction. I had no intention of leaving Dover, none. The force of Lieberman's hand on my wrist pulling me towards the house still felt real even though it hadn't left a bruise. Something inside of me couldn't shake the fact that the police showing up might have kept me from a more sinister fate.

★   ★   ★

I had to give it to the Liebermans: discrediting me in front of the cops and getting away with it was bold. My appearance, wet and disheveled, hadn't helped, I was sure. Lieberman's face when I mentioned the baby clothes in the car to the officer, the way his features froze, was proof enough for me of his guilt. But what was I to do? Enter the house, gun in hand, and demand my

329

daughter back? There was only one thing no one would be able to discredit me on: DNA. I just needed to prove to the police that the baby in Anna's house was mine, and science was on my side.

In order to get DNA I had to return to Anna's house and that posed a serious problem — now the police had been alerted and there was no telling what David and Anna were going to do if I were to show up again. While I thought about how to proceed — a dirty diaper maybe from the garbage sitting on Anna's curb — I quickly realized I had missed my turn and passed the Dover exit altogether. I pulled over on the curb and turned off the ignition. I switched on the overhead light and unfolded the map, struggling with its size. After a few minutes I gave up.

Daylight had faded and traffic had gone from sparse to nonexistent as the autumn night turned thick with darkness, sticky almost, as if covered in ink. The moon, like a ghostly apparition in flight, on and off, appeared and disappeared behind thick clouds.

I didn't make out any movements behind me — it was more a hunch than anything — but suddenly my heartbeat went into overdrive. I reached for the gun in my purse without taking my eyes off the mirror.

A set of headlights appeared out of nowhere as if a car had approached me with the lights off and had just now turned them back on. Slowly the car pulled up behind me but no one got out. It rolled another one or two feet forward, then stopped. The car's lights went out and it was dark again. I kept staring in the rearview mirror. Finally, a car door opened.

Before my mind realized what was happening, my body reacted. My elbow hit the central locking mechanism. I hit it again, twice more, then again, until I was no longer sure if it was engaged or not. My brain messaged my body to start the car. At that very moment, the back window shattered and shards of glass rained on the backseat. Then all went quiet.

I sat paralyzed with fear. Out of the corner of my eye, I saw a shadow by the driver's window. I grabbed my purse, scooted into the passenger seat and reached for the door handle. The driver's side window shattered next and I covered my face with my arms. As I reached to open the passenger door, someone tugged at my hair through the driver's window and yanked me back in the driver's seat. My scalp pounded with pain. I turned my head and a shadowy man stood next to my car.

Fate may visit unannounced, but once it knocks, you know nothing will keep it from entering. The Prince of Darkness had come for me. And he was mad.

22

My breath comes in short spurts. I press the palms of my hands against the cold leather of the couch, next to my thighs. I try to concentrate on Dr Ari, but my eyes scamper, unable to focus. I can't contain the panic, like unfurled yarn it remains, holds no true form, yet it reaches through my entire body.

'I need to speak with the detective. They are looking for them, right? What are they doing to find them? All this here, what we're doing, doesn't matter at all. We have to find Lieberman and Anna. Mia is with them.'

'Let me reassure you that the police are doing everything in their power to locate them.' He pauses for a moment as if something is irking him. 'I don't believe we've reached the end.'

'The end?' I ask.

'We have to continue on, the end being . . . there's just too many questions unanswered,' he replies.

I feel the need to retreat for a short while, seek shelter like an animal before birthing her young. 'What does Islam say about fate, Dr Ari?'

'Muslims call fate one of the pillars of faith. I know what befalls me couldn't have missed me, and what misses me could not have befallen me.'

Dr Ari wipes his forehead with the palm of his hand as if to remove invisible pearls of sweat,

332

maybe even his way of clearing his mind. He has the tapering fingers of a scientist.

Reliving the moment when Lieberman's hand reached through the shattered window and unlocked the car door coats my entire body in a layer of sweat. I recall Lieberman's unnaturally long fingers grasping for me, like some offshoot of a bloodsucking plant. Suddenly it's all so clear. Bright as daylight, my memories reconcile, gather like oil on top of the ocean surface. Suddenly I realize he is as much afraid of the truth as I am. And that we are nowhere near the end.

★ ★ ★

Lieberman's eyes were feverish, dark and intense. The overhead light bathed us in a golden glow and the moonlight caught bits and pieces of lunacy in his eyes and reflected them towards me.

'And so we meet again,' he said.

Wanting Mia back was the only thought left inside of me. The thought of having to kill him horrified me, but I was determined. I wasn't shaking, I wasn't crying. I took my fear and hauled it into the darkness. Whatever panic took over my body, I would not allow it to reach my mind. I would contain it and use it to my advantage. This moment was as inevitable as the darkness around me.

'You worthless piece of shit.' Lieberman's voice was sharp. His comment seemed out of sorts, I didn't know where it was coming from.

He was light years away from the man who had lied to the cops earlier, beyond the man who had leaped off the porch. His eyes darted about as if spoken commands in his head were tossing him left and right.

'Next time you visit my home without an invitation, you should be more careful.' His voice had turned into a hiss.

Occupying the same space with him was electrifying. What had I ever done to him? Did he think it was his God-given right to take someone's daughter? Was I supposed to just let it be? Not knowing how to respond and watching his eyes dart about, I realized logic might not be anything familiar to him. There were moments when his face switched from normalcy to lunacy, his eyes became more piercing, started to shift about.

'Get out of the car.'

My lack of fear was mutinous as he reached for the door and opened it. I didn't move. 'Where is my daughter?'

'I told you to leave us alone. Why did you come all the way out here and harass my girlfriend?'

We had just begun, but already I was lost. Anna Lieberman was the girl in the paper, his sister. She looked just like the photo in the newspaper.

'What girlfriend? The one you called your wife earlier? You mean your sister, Anna?'

'Who are you to tell me who we are? Why'd you have to come out here? Everything was fine until you came up here.' With these words, he motioned me to get out of the car. As if by sleight of hand, a gun appeared that he waved in my face.

I got out of the car. The clouds had given way to a starry sky, and the moon was bright as if someone had flicked a switch. For the first time I could clearly see my surroundings. We were parked by the side of a cornfield, a dirt road running adjacent to it. A few gnarled trees obscured the field to the right.

I was surprised by how short Lieberman was, something I had never noticed before. He motioned for me to turn around. Without hesitation I turned my back to him. I was not afraid. He was the kind of crazy that wants to look you in the eye and see you suffer.

The colorless moon covered the world in shades of gray. I could make out the silhouettes of corn stalks. The aroma of wet soil was pungent. There was a dirt road leading between the cornfields, cutting them neatly in two halves. No car had passed us since he had pulled up behind me. The dark night seemed unforgiving, leaving no room for mistakes. A few hundred yards down that dirt road and we'd all but disappear into the darkness.

'You should've left when you had the chance.'

'I'm not leaving without my child. You should know that by now.'

'Everybody thinks you are incapable. Even the cops.'

'You know nothing about me,' I said and dug my feet into the gravel.

'Get down on the ground.'

His voice was full of anticipation but I stood unwavering.

'I'm not going anywhere.'

He grabbed my arm and twisted it behind my back, forcing me on my knees. 'You go where I tell you to go, sweetheart. And you're going down.'

'The cops are still around making sure I leave. They'll be here any minute.'

'You're just a deranged stalker, remember? No cop is looking for you, trust me.' He took a step back and pointed a gun at me. 'Stay on your knees,' he added, 'and don't try anything stupid. Put your hands on top of your head so I can see 'em.'

I did as I was told. I faced the cornfield and when I heard footsteps walking off into the distance, I turned my head. I watched him as he leaned through the broken car window, searching my purse. He stuck his hand in, then pulled out the gun. He walked to his car and, through the open window, dropped the gun on the passenger seat. He looked left and right as if to find a perfect spot to do to me whatever his crazy mind was telling him to do.

As he peered down the dirt road he was confident, so sure of himself that he was pulling the strings. The smugger he acted, the more pronounced became a strength I didn't know I had.

I darted towards the cornfield, Lieberman shouting obscenities in the background. The second I crossed the outer limits of the field and made it through the initial rows of cornstalks, I

336

knew I was in trouble. The rain had soaked the soil and after a few steps the muck sucked at my shoes and made my feet heavy. I felt as if I was stuck in one of those dreams where your legs won't obey and regardless how hard you try to get away, they just won't cooperate.

I made my way straight down a path and after about twenty feet I turned suddenly to the left, like a rabbit making a quick sharp turn to avoid a predator. I took only a couple more steps and collided, legs first, into a solid structure. I fell to the ground. My shins throbbed and my kneecaps pulsated with pain. With the moon high above, I made out a small wooden booth with a partial roof, a swinging side door, and a wooden sign with chipped paint.

Corn Maze Entrance. Please Purchase Tickets Here.

I got up and after a few stumbles caught myself and continued down the path. There was one trail leading to the left, one to the right. Before I could make up my mind in which direction to turn, I heard sucking sounds heralding Lieberman's approach. Whatever dis-advantages the wet soil had posed on me, also applied to him.

My knees were in such bad shape that running was no longer an option and I decided to hide between the stalks. I crouched down and sat in the mud. I willed my breathing to slow and I waited. Childlike, I closed my eyes, hoping that if I didn't see him, he wasn't going to see me either. My heart beat like a drum in my chest and I waited in the chilled autumn air for his approach.

The sound I heard next was unnerving. *Click.* The cocking of the gun coincided with my sucking air into my nostrils. It was over.

He came up from behind, forced my hands to my back, almost dislocating my shoulders. He held on to my arms, pulled me to my feet, and with each step the pain in my knees intensified. When we reached the cars parked by the roadside, he gave me a shove. I fell knees first on the ground. I tried to stay still but the spiky gravel digging into me made my eyes tear up. The pain produced colorful eruptions of lights tracing back and forth behind eyelids. I moaned, which made him snicker. He slid something around my wrists. Judging by the sound of it, he was attaching plastic zip ties.

When I looked up, he was standing in front of me, his outline framed by the moon. The moonlight caught something shiny in his right hand. A knife. The blade flashed some clandestine Morse code spelling deep gashes and blood soaking the already saturated soil. We locked eyes — three, maybe five seconds or more — and I found it impossible to tear away from him. He was slick with sweat.

'Who's after who now, huh? You aren't cut out for this, you should've never come after us.'

In his left hand he held his gun, the right hand kept taunting me with the knife in short deliberate surges towards my face.

'Where's my daughter?' My voice was small, puny, not at all how I intended it to be.

338

'*Where's my daughter?*' he mocked me, then lunged again, the high sheen of the blade a promise of things to come. 'It's not like you took care of her. All that crying, day and night. Was it so hard for you to take care of such a little thing? Why'd she cry all the time? You probably didn't feed her, didn't change her. Why'd you have her?'

'Mia, where is she? Where is my daughter?' I insisted.

He kept lunging towards me, taunting me with his knife. He was so close that I could smell his sweat and his anxiety. He wasn't going to shoot me, he was going to take pleasure in holding the handle of the knife while twisting it into my flesh, the warm blood feeding his frenzy. Then he'd get off twisting fabric and tightening it around my neck while watching my eyes protrude and my face turn blue. The way he was going to kill me was not important; watching me die would make his day.

'How'd you figure it all out? You didn't strike me as the quick-witted kind,' he said.

'You thought you had the perfect plan but you made mistakes.'

He was inches away from me. When he lifted his right hand, I closed my eyes. He got so close that I could smell his breath.

'All I had to do was get you out of the house. I hid your wallet, I made baby formula, I left a gallon of water for you. With sleeping pills in it. That night, I came in through the dumbwaiter. While you were asleep in your bed I stood over you with your crying baby in my arms, and you

339

didn't even wake up. I just walked out the front door with your kid and came back later through the shaft and locked the door. And the only mistake I ever made was that I didn't shut you up sooner.'

'You left her blanket in the attic. That was your first mistake.'

His eyes darted about. 'I must have dropped it when I left the building through the attic. A tiny detail I overlooked, not really important.'

'Your second mistake was that you kept the Tinker Bell charm. Like any other sick fuck, you kept something so you'd get off on what you did every time you looked at it. And you call *me* crazy?'

He laughed and made stabbing motions towards my face. 'You wanna know where the baby is? In good hands. Better hands than yours, that's for sure. Anna and I, we'll find a nice family for her.'

'She has a family.' I felt the blade pressing against my ear. His face was just an inch from mine, his lips were parted as if he was trying to kiss me. I closed my eyes. I felt his lips on my cheek, barely touching my skin. I thought rape. I thought *he's going to rape me*. I remained still, forced myself not to jerk away from him. Then his lips were on mine, his tongue forcing mine apart. I turned my head and spit on the ground, wiping my lips on my shoulder.

'Why are you doing this to me?' I screamed at him.

He didn't answer, just looked at me with his feverish eyes, pleased to have me on my knees.

340

'What did you think I was going to do? You kidnapped my child!' The last words came out in a howl.

His brow furrowed and he lightly tilted his head to the right. 'You're one sick, clueless bitch. Kidnapped is what you call it? I'm a knight who came along to save the day. I tried to tell you in so many words she was crying too much, that you didn't hold her enough. I was waiting for you to tell me how she was too much for you, how you were overwhelmed, tired, couldn't cope. But all you did was shut the door in my face.'

'I saw the book on your shelf about torturing and killing children. You want to tell me you're some savior when all you are is a lunatic stealing children. And you call me sick?'

'If you had only bothered to look closer you would have discovered the man you call a lunatic was a hero. He was destroyed by false testimony, he was not what everyone made him out to be.'

'I don't care about your books and heroes. This is the real world and in that world you climbed through a dumbwaiter in the middle of the night, stole my child and took her to your sister or whoever she is.'

'I didn't have a single moment of peace after you moved in. The baby cried all day and all night. She cried for hours, and you didn't do anything about it. You left her screaming her head off. What kind of mother are you?' I saw revulsion in his eyes and felt droplets of projective saliva on my face. 'I did you a favor by taking her.'

'If you thought I was a bad mother you

should've called CPS!' My voice had gotten louder and louder, the last words made my voice crack. I decided to plead. If he had any feelings left behind those eyes, he might listen to me. 'Please, just give her back and I won't tell anybody. Please, I'm begging, give her back.'

He smiled and for a second I wanted to believe that some sanity had returned to him. His features relaxed and he looked almost normal. I felt hope, but then he retreated back into his feverish state. His eyes widened and they were dark, as dark as the endless sky above us.

'This is a big misunderstanding. Please give me my daughter back. Please . . . ' I was sobbing now, trying to free my hands. The plastic cuffs cut into my wrists.

'What did Anna tell you? No offense, Anna's my girl and all, but she's never told it straight in her life. What did she tell you?'

When I didn't answer right away he started screaming.

'WHAT DID SHE TELL YOU?'

'Nothing. She told me nothing.'

He sucked in one deep breath as if he had just emerged from minutes under water. 'When I was a kid I had just one wish. That someone would come and take me from my parents.'

'You're getting it all wrong.'

'Shut up and listen!'

'You got it all wrong, I'm — '

'*I'm* the one getting it wrong? No, you're the one who got it all wrong. You left her in the car. I saw you leaving her in the car. I know parents like you.'

342

'You hear a baby cry and you make up this entire story.'

'I know what mothers like you are capable of.'

'Mothers like me? You know nothing about me.'

'I know the likes of you.'

The likes of me. To him I'm *one of those mothers.* An abuser. A mother who neglected her child. The demons that must be inside of him to draw that conclusion.

Lieberman started pacing back and forth, the blade gleaming in the moonlight. I watched him, hypnotized by his movements.

'Why did you take her? I don't understand — '

'I took her because you didn't want her.' He paused for a second, then smiled. 'Some mothers are like that.' And then he told his story, the story of the boy he used to be. Between moments of unintelligible ramblings and pacing in circles, he spoke of his parents, Esther and Abe Lieberman. 'My mother was just like you,' he said.

I wanted to ask questions but then I thought otherwise. I decided to allow him to peel back the layers of his madness. I listened as he painted a picture of his childhood, and his story took shape in my mind, a story of a strange part of the American land inhabited by peculiar people, a part of Appalachia far removed from romantic notions of wooded hiking trails.

He was a little boy, about eight years old, Anna, covered in freckles, about five. He spoke of how they trudged around the only neighborhood they knew; dirt paths, and dead-end roads.

His childhood was spent around a cluster of houses without electricity and running water, just a collection of trailers and shanties, surrounded by lots of garbage and not a glimmer of hope.

At times Lieberman turned and listened into the blackness, his eyes scanning the darkness as if he was making sure no one else was listening to his story of living in squalor and misery in an old farmhouse without a foreseeable exit out of a shabby hillbilly hell of a life.

Other times his voice would soften unexpectedly, especially when he spoke of his 'rescue,' his 'new family,' so full of joy that his eyes lit up like a kid telling you about a new bike. The state intervened, 'mercifully' he called it, after he showed up one too many times with bruises on his face and filthy clothes. A large lady with drawstring pants and a clipboard took him and Anna to live with a foster family.

'We had breakfast that first morning at the foster home and when they told us it was time for lunch later on, I didn't understand. Didn't we just eat? I asked. Damn, we got to eat more than once a day?

'There was running hot water and I had my own room and, what d'ya know, not all families yell at each other all day long, and not all dads slap their kids around. I didn't know there was a life without beatings, shooting stray dogs with pellet guns, and disemboweling hogs.

'That foster family, the mom worked in a travel agency. She brought home these catalogs. You could just pick a country, a hotel, and go

344

there. Like it wasn't a big deal and getting away was just a matter of picking a place. You know what our vacation was? Three months in a foster home. That's all we got. It just wasn't enough. All Anna and I ever talked about was getting away.

'But then it was all over. The worst day of my life,' Lieberman said, 'was the day they made us go back. Old Abe complied, that's what they called it. He was in compliance with the state, he fixed the place up a bit, ran some cables, scrubbed the tub and washed the sheets and before we knew it, we were back. They called it parent-child-reunification. What a crock of shit, it was fucking hell.'

He spat the word 'hell' into the night like some stale chewing tobacco. As he was continuing his story, I wiggled my hands back and forth, trying to loosen the plastic cuffs. I shifted my legs into a more comfortable position but the move caused him to swipe the knife at me.

'I prayed for them to fall asleep with a cigarette between their fingers, burning down the house. So Anna and I could live our lives.' His eyes widened and he was far away for a long time. Then his face stiffened. 'I love Anna. We started messing around in the backyard shed when she was twelve years old. And she's not my sister. Don't ever call her that again.'

He stepped closer and I turned my head, afraid of what he was going to do, his madness right on the surface. His eyes focused on me again, he started to wave the gun back and forth. 'Anna and I, we made plans. All I wanted was to make some money but where did I end up? Living in the same house with one of those spoiled rich bitches. House, husband, car, money. Ever wanted for anything? Tell me, you ever wanted for anything?'

He backed up, started to pace in circles. Then he walked towards me, gravel crunching under his boots. 'Your baby never stopped crying. Some women should not be mothers. Like you.' He screamed, his voice carrying into the cornfield, lost among the husks and stalks.

I lowered myself on the ground, sideways, with my legs half tucked under.

As if someone had snapped a leash, his eyes stilled and his words started to slur. 'You should thank me, is what y . . . y . . . you shoul . . . d d . . . Anna told me to do something, but I can't remember. I can't remember. She's gonna be so mad at me.' And then insanity owned him like the tide, wavelike washed over him, and carried him further away from reason. 'What was it, what was it . . . damn . . . ' He hit his forehead with his fist. 'I can't remember what she told me to do. So much to remember, so much . . . it's so hard to do everything right . . . ' He kept checking his watch and wiping his forehead with his forearm while holding on to the gun.

Then his face shifted and again he focused on me. 'I'm just gonna kill you.'

I felt hope leaving my body, my bones turning to dust. His voice was still there, in the background, yet no longer playing a major role.

'You have no reason to be on this earth. Just

346

taking up space and that's why you have to go.' His chest rose with primal power.

I will make him look into my eyes, I thought, and I won't whimper or cry or leave him with an image of me curled up in a fetal position in the dirt. I will not allow him to triumph over me. 'Who are you to decide who's worthy and who isn't?' I asked him. 'I'm not your mother.' I spat those words at him. 'There was nothing I could've done about her crying. She was a fussy baby. She would cry in my arms, she would cry in her crib. There was nothing, *nothing*, I could have done.'

'Nothing but fucking excuses. You sorry excuse of a mother.' He was spraying saliva, and then he paused, replacing his angry expression with a diabolic smile. 'Are you afraid? You think it's gonna hurt? You look afraid.'

I could barely sit upright.

'I can't hear you.'

'I'm not . . .'

'I can't hear you. Quiet as a mouse, huh?'

He left me no room, no place left to go. 'Where is my daughter? Tell me where she is . . . please . . . I'm her mother. Where is she?'

'Safe, bitch, she's safe without you.' He laughed. Contrived. Breathless. Diabolical.

And then the Prince of Darkness pointed his gun at me. A bright light exploded. I felt so much colder than ever before. The wind wheezed through the cornstalks and then the crisp autumn night turned to ice.

The moonlight faded and everything went dark. My last thought was that no one would

347

ever know what happened to my daughter. No one.

★ ★ ★

The next two sessions are eventless. I enter the elevator, I descend, but there's nothing left. Like a dog in hot pursuit, I'd leaped through cornfields and run my pads raw, heart beating in my muzzle, branches tearing at me. The shadows got longer, the sun was about to go down, and I had pushed myself beyond all endurance.

We sit in silence for a while. Mia is alive, somewhere. Maybe. Maybe not. The Liebermans are gone, nowhere to be found. We have come all this way, yet we still know nothing. This is it.

I look up at him and start to cry. 'What now?'

Dr Ari gets up and walks around his desk. 'We keep looking.'

'Looking for what?'

'We still don't know how you ended up in the ravine. And what happened to your ear. There are still unanswered questions.'

'Lieberman shot me. He shot me and pushed me into the ravine.'

'The car drove into the ravine, it wasn't pushed.'

I look at him puzzled.

'They can tell by the keys in the ignition. There were also tire marks. Not only did the car drive into the ravine, but it accelerated.'

'What does it matter? The police should look for them.'

'They are looking.'

348

'Then can I go?'

A long pause. 'Go? Where?'

'Home.' When I say the word I pause. North Dandry? I realize I have no home.

'You think this is over?' Dr Ari covers his forehead with his hand as if to say *you poor fool, what are you thinking?* 'Estelle, the police and the DA are not going to be satisfied with this conclusion.' He pauses, folds his hands on top of the desk. 'This is what we have: a missing baby, a mother who doesn't report the crime, even keeps it from her husband. Yes, we have a missing construction worker and his sister, I give you that, who by the way have been vagrants on and off and the police have been unable to track their every move before they lived in Dover and before Lieberman accepted the job at North Dandry. Do you know how many people just don't show up for work? Or move and don't leave a forwarding address?'

I swallow hard. 'The blanket. Tinker Bell.'

'So what? You could have found that anywhere. There's no proof. Just two people who can't be found and your word.'

'Which doesn't count at all.'

'You remembered everything else, Estelle. The smell of the blanket, the titles of books, the flowers on a teacup. But you don't remember how you ended up in that ravine?'

'Do *you* even believe me?'

'I am of no significance. The police and the DA need proof. The truth without proof is nothing in their legal world. We'll continue tomorrow.'

349

I get up and start to leave the room. At the door I turn around. 'Unless a miracle occurs, I have nothing.'

* * *

As I stab at the meatloaf and draw the prongs of my fork through the mashed potatoes, the dining room falls silent. Marge drops her spoon and then the sound of knives and forks hitting plates ceases altogether. I look up and see Marge gawking in the direction of the cafeteria entrance.

Dr Ari rushes towards our table and I detect a slight limp I've never noticed before. I rest my fork on the side of my plate. Oliver too is confused, his hand suspended in midair.

'Something's up,' he says without taking his eyes off Dr Ari. 'I've never seen him in the cafeteria.'

Dr Ari continues towards me. I push my tray towards Marge and then hope takes shape in the back of my throat. *This is it. They've found her. They've found Mia.* I picture Dr Ari sitting down, grabbing my hand, smiling at me, saying the words I've been longing to hear.

'Follow me to my office,' Dr Ari says. He doesn't sit down, he doesn't grab my hand. I lift my hand, command his silence. One more moment is all I want, one more moment of hope, of believing that they've found her but no one can misinterpret his empty facial expression as a smile.

Then I surrender and accept the end of hope.

350

Dr Ari pushes his glasses way up on the bridge of his nose. He clears his throat.

'I received a call earlier regarding a piece of evidence. The lab results have just become available now.'

'What evidence?'

'We'll talk about that in a minute. Tell me, do you remember what they found in the car with you?'

'My purse. And Jack's gun.'

'Three things. Your purse. The gun. And a piece of paper.'

I remember now. My purse. That's how they identified me. And the gun. Lieberman put it in my car, in the cornfield. 'I don't remember anything about a piece of paper.'

'It was soaked in blood. They had to send it to a lab in Florida.'

'I don't remember any paper. I'm not sure they ever asked me about it.' The air in his office is chilly and I rub my arms to keep warm.

'Tell me about the gun,' he says.

'The gun they found in my car? It was the gun from Jack's closet.'

'The same gun you took to Anna's house.'

'I guess.'

We stare at each other.

'What are you saying? What's the point of all this?' I ask, frustrated. 'Why don't you ask me what I remember, not what I don't remember?'

'I'm not asking you anything. I'm telling you

351

the gun had one bullet in the chamber when you went to Anna Lieberman's house. When you found the gun in the closet, it had one bullet in the chamber. One bullet. And when they found the gun there wasn't a single bullet in it. But your fingerprints all over it. No one else's, just yours. And you had been shot.'

'How is that significant?'

'Just a detail I want you to keep in mind. But here's the thing.'

The thing. I take a deep breath and look out the window. It's foggy and almost dark and I can't make out as much as a tree.

'We need to talk about the note.'

'I thought it was a piece of paper.'

'It was a piece of paper until the people at the Florida lab managed to take digital photographs after applying different kinds of light sources . . . anyway . . . I'm not familiar with forensic procedures but it turns out they were able to create a decipherable image of the note. I just received a copy an hour ago.'

I lower my eyes. There's a piece of paper in front of him on his desk.

'Unfortunately it took the lab this long to decipher the note. This could have been a lot easier.' He hands it to me. 'Would you read it to me?'

I extend my hand and hold the paper between my thumb and my index finger. The 8½ by 11 piece of paper is a copy of a torn handwritten note. It has a reddish tint to it. I skim over it. The letters seem oddly disjointed, I can't tell where one word ends and another one starts.

There are no more than twenty words on the page.

'Read it out loud.' Dr Ari's voice is reaching me from afar.

I recognize the handwriting as my own; rushed, hurried, yet mine.

'Read it to me,' he insists and leans back in his chair.

I read it. Silently. And I make a mistake. I don't enter the elevator, my place of calm reprieve, instead I go to Stone Harbor, the beach where I built sandcastles the summer before my parents died. Giant rocks above the tide line, yellow and blue-green, salmon pink and mother-of-pearl. The tide caresses the sand, then my toes, just to roll out again into the vast sea. Spitting waves, salty air and chapped lips. Pink and purple spiny sea urchins, tangled algae around my ankles. Barnacles and seaweed in the dead sand, so serene against the violent waves. *Little water and lots of sand or you destabilize the walls and they will buckle under the weight, just like a landslide,* my dad had told me as I scooped the fine grains into a pile. I tried, Lord knows I tried to build this sandcastle with the utmost care. I had used the perfect proportions of water and sand but it stood no chance. I make a fist. I can feel the coarse texture of the grains as I watch a tidal wave demolishing my castle.

Everyone,
I can't go on like this.
I am sorry for what I have done.
I killed my baby. I'm a monster.

I crack wide open. When I wake up I'm in a daze. Not like waking up from a deep sleep, but chemically pacified and strapped down. The nurse sitting next to me gets up and wraps a blood pressure cuff around my arm. This isn't supposed to end this way.

I'm sorry.

Part four

'How puzzling all these changes are! I'm
never sure what I'm going to be, from
one minute to another.'

Lewis Carroll,
Alice in Wonderland

23

'I want you to call the police,' I demand two days later when we resume our sessions. Dr Ari and I have been going at this for almost an hour. I've come to accept the truth. All the stories I've been telling, of Tinker Bell and blankets in attics, nothing but my brain attempting to conceal the truth. The truth is that I *am* a monster. The second I allowed myself this directness, I felt helpless terror. But there's no sense in fighting it. 'I'll plead guilty. Let's just end it now.'

'I will do no such thing at this point,' Dr Ari says and leans forward. 'Once you confess there's nothing else I can do for you. Everything will end up in discovery and used against you in court.'

'I wrote a note saying I killed my daughter. All this here, what we're doing every day, is just a farce. Call the police.'

'But her body, where is her body? What happened and how and when? There are too many questions that haven't been answered yet. I won't allow you to give up.' He raises his hands. 'This isn't helping. Let's stay focused and talk about the note for now.'

'It's not a note, it's a confession.'

'Do you remember writing it?'

'Do I remember writing it?' This is getting funnier by the minute. 'I'm done with this. I want you to call the police so I can turn myself

357

in. All this doesn't make any sense. It is what it is and you need to accept, it's over.'

'Do you remember writing it?' he repeats.

'No, I don't remember writing it but it is my handwriting. It looks rushed in a way, but I wrote it.'

'I want to show you something.'

'There's more? God help me, what's next? A map with a cross where I buried her? Maybe I carved my initials into her skin?'

Dr Ari hands me another piece of paper. 'There's something else, something I've neglected to tell you.'

There's no such thing as Dr Ari neglecting to do anything. Everything he does, he does with a purpose. I grab the piece of paper.

'It's the same note, I don't understand.'

'Flip it over,' he says.

On the back of the paper there's no writing, just random bloody smudges.

'Is this a joke?' I ask.

'Look closer.'

I squint my eyes. There's the faintest outline of printed words. I can't make them out.

'I can't make out the words, but there are some numbers. A phone number maybe? I don't get it.' I flip the note over and over again. 'I really don't get it.'

'It's a receipt from Diane's Diner, a place off 434. A receipt for two cups of coffee and two pieces of pecan pie.'

'I had coffee and pie and then jotted down a confession.' I shake my head in disbelief. 'That's quite a story.'

I try to make sense of the receipt, but it doesn't add up. I don't like pecan pie, the nuts stick to my teeth and the hint of maple is just not my thing. 'I don't even like pecan pie,' I say.

'Thanks to Google I'm a step ahead. I took the liberty to print out a photograph of the place.' Dr Ari opens the manila folder and pulls out a photograph.

Enter the elevator.

I study the photo. Diane's Diner is a brick building, one story, a neon sign, a jukebox visible through the front door. I hear a melody from deep within. Strained tunes. Refrains. It tugs at me, gently at first, then it pulls me towards the building's front door. Images rush at me, like a crowd of children, waiting to be acknowledged, one by one. Infantile, incomplete. But then they mature, fill out.

A man on the ground. Face down.

A fork scratching against a white china plate.

Pecans shaped like miniature brains.

'A song,' I say, 'I remember a song.'

I need to go back, back to when I saw the flash, when the gun went off. I remember the sound of the gunshot and how loud it was.

Deeper. Go deeper.

Loose rubble under my knees. Rasping breathing. Legs like lead, heavy. My pounding heart, throbbing pain in my legs.

Deeper.

Blue. Indigo. Or periwinkle. Persian? Royal blue? Navy blue. A tarp. A navy-blue tarp.

I sit up straight and uncross my arms.

Deeper.

I consider making the buttons disappear. Whatever I find at this diner, maybe I won't want to return to reality.

★ ★ ★

Lieberman stood in front of me, legs parted, his heels digging into the gravel. He pulled the gun out of his boot shaft and pointed it at me.

First a flash, then an explosion ripped through my eardrums. My ears went deaf for a few seconds, followed by a loud ringing tone. I closed my eyes, waiting for the darkness to spread. I waited for the pain, the burn, yet nothing happened.

Lieberman's body jolted towards me as if someone had shoved him in my direction. He fell on the ground, face first. He lay motionless, as if struck by lightning. I watched a dark spot on his back expanding into a large crimson sphere.

I stared into the direction of the sound, the same direction of the flash. A shadow emerged from behind the car. The figure took shape, like a specter gaining strength and coming into focus. A woman. Gun in hand.

'Goddamn bastard,' Anna Lieberman said. 'Never does what he's told.' She stared at his bloody back as if David meant nothing, her face is void of any emotion as if she just shot a rabid animal. After she shakes her head as if that's all it takes to get rid of his image altogether, she disappeared into the dark of the night and I was left to stare at Lieberman's body. The crimson not only covered his entire back but had pooled by the side of his body.

I didn't have the strength to get up but I managed to shift my weight away from my knees. Seconds later the Caprice's headlights moved towards me. Anna stopped next to Lieberman's lifeless body.

'Can you get up?' Anna asked and got out of her car.

I shook my head. 'I can't feel my legs.'

'Try.' She grabbed my elbow and pulled me to my feet, reaching around me, cutting the plastic zip ties. She pulled a blue tarp from the trunk. Anna shrouded her brother's body with the tarp, tucked it underneath him on the side, and then rolled him on top of it like a nurse changing the sheets of an immobile patient.

Then I followed her commands. We pulled Lieberman about fifty feet until we ended up by the booth entrance of the corn maze. We pulled him inside the structure, dropped the front panel and closed the side door.

In the car she sat only inches away from the steering wheel. She squinted her eyes as she drove through the night, southbound on 434. She made a turn into a Chevron station and parked by the side door.

Get key from management, a sign said.

'Listen closely, Estelle Paradise. We don't need anyone else to get involved, okay? Do I have your word?'

I nodded. I felt hope. For the first time in days I felt something resembling hope.

'I'll get the key.' She got out of the car and locked the doors. 'Wait right here.'

There'd be concessions, there'd be promises not to call the police. I'd assure her I'd never ever tell anyone. David Lieberman was dead and I'd promise to take these days of horrors to the grave with me. I was prepared to give her everything I owned, I'd promise her anything, I'd do anything for Mia. Anything.

Anna returned with a key. 'Go clean yourself up,' she said and handed me a plastic bag. 'There's some wipes in here. Put on the clean clothes, and don't leave your bloody clothes in the bathroom. Throw them in the Dumpster over there,' she said and nodded towards the side of the building. 'They didn't have any shoes, so clean yours best you can. Hurry up, we don't have all night.'

Getting out of the car I could barely straighten my legs and all but hobbled to the bathroom. I unlocked the door. Inside, I turned on the water and washed the filth off my hands.

I sat my muddy shoes in the sink and watched the dirt trail down the drain. I put on the gray hoodie and the white T-shirt and a few minutes later I walked out with the bag of bloody clothes in hand. I tossed them in the green Dumpster by the side of the building.

We left the gas station parking lot and less than five minutes later Anna pulled by the side of a building with large letters on a neon sign illuminated in a timed sequence. Diane's Diner. She motioned me to get out of the car.

'No funny business. Not a word, or you'll regret it.' She stood merely inches from my face, reached behind her and pulled the gun from her waistband and pushed its barrel into my stomach. 'I think we just established that I don't warn people before I shoot.'

'I knew you'd do the right thing,' I said.

'Don't be silly,' she said and pulled a rubber band out of her hair. She gathered her hair, smoothing the sides with the palms of her hands.

'Why are we here?' I asked.

'To eat,' she said and pointed at the front door of the diner.

I had hope. I still had hope.

★　★　★

Diane's Diner was all stainless steel and red and white checkered vinyl booths. There was a wall-mounted all-day breakfast menu above the counter and specials written on a chalkboard. The diner was empty but for a man in a blue uniform reading the jukebox selection.

Anna directed me to the first booth by the door.

'Diane's famous for her pecan pies.'

I put my hands on the table and realized that my fingernails were still rimmed with mud. Then the jukebox came on, a guitar, then a voice. Raspy, shaky. Johnny Cash.

The beast in me
Is caged by frail and fragile bars.

'Coffee and pecan pie?' Anna asked as if it was the most normal thing in the world. She didn't wait for my answer and called the order to the waitress behind the counter who in turn nodded and took two cups off a large stack.

'I promise,' I said, 'I won't tell anyone, I promise. Never will I — '

She looked at me puzzled, then she laughed out loud. 'I can promise you that your baby will be okay. Is a promise like that something you want?'

I nodded, feeling hot tears working their way to the surface.

'Just imagine her, in a few years, she'll have nice clothes, a room with a pink canopy bed, more toys than she'll know what to do with. A mom, a dad, maybe a brother or a sister. Someone who cares for her, loves her. All of that. Is that something you want?'

I swallowed hard.

'That's one side of the coin. Would you like to hear the other side?'

'I'll do anything.'

'I hope so,' she said and reached behind her into her waistband, retrieving the gun. She stuck it into the front pocket of her hoodie.

'Now let me paint the other picture for you. A little girl living with her daddy. And I use the word daddy loosely here. He loves her, he cares for her. He buys her pretty things. Jewelry, lipstick, dresses, whatever she wants. But she has to do something for it. Every time she wants something she has to give him something in return. The little girl loves him and she wants her daddy happy. And she does what he asks her to do. Anything.'

For a few seconds my brain refused to make the connection, but then hope ruptured. My heartbeat echoed in my ear. The pain that made my knees throb and the pain I felt on the side of my head was nothing compared to her words coming into focus.

A middle-aged waitress with wrinkled skin that seemed too large for her elfin frame put coffee and pie in front of us.

'Let's eat and then I'll explain how this is going to work.'

I crushed the pecans with my fork, stirring the pieces into the filling. I was parched. The first sip of coffee was tepid and unpleasant, some sort of bitterness lingered in the back of my throat. I downed the lukewarm coffee in three gulps, its aftertaste making me shudder.

'You're a smart girl, I think you understood what I just told you,' Anna said and mashed a piece of piecrust with her fork. She put another piece of pie in her mouth and swallowed. 'Needless to say that the plan David and I had didn't work out.'

I sat still, unable to move. 'What plan?' I wrapped my hands around the empty cup. Did the walls just shift or did I imagine that? My body felt weighed down as if my blood had been replaced by lead.

'Everything was okay until you showed up. David is,' she paused and smiled, 'was, a bit on the unstable side.'

My grip tightened around the cup. I pushed the plate with the pie away from me.

'Where was I? Oh, yeah, my brother. David and I find unwanted babies and sell them to people who want them. Unwanted basically means we take babies that are no longer wanted or who are neglected. Babies from moms who can't take care of another baby, drug users, even had one from a homeless girl, believe it or not. No agencies, no lawyers, no fees, no court papers. Nothing, just a transfer of responsibilities. Basically we match families, if you will. People pay outrageous sums for a baby. The right gender, the right age.

'Until everything went out of control. David never had sound judgment, if you ask me. All he ever talked about is this island and that beach, this hotel, and that trip. Kept bringing me those catalogs with glossy pictures, Paris here and Barbados there. Always talking about where we're going to go, what we're going to do. What a fool.

'David told me about you and from what I heard you weren't the mommy type. Letting her cry all the time. I told him a woman like you would never go for this, you got money, a house, a husband, but he didn't want to listen. I knew it was a bad idea, but he was dead set on going through with it. Said your husband was some broke douchebag trying to flip houses.'

'How much money do you want?'

'Money? Who's talking about money?' Anna laughed and then turned to the waitress behind the counter.

'May I have a refill and the check, please?' She turned back towards me. 'I'm not asking you for any money. I'm willing to offer you something, though. And if you're as good a mother as you claim to be, you'll give it willingly.'

The waitress appeared, filled up Anna's coffee

366

cup. I watched her fill my cup, then she put the check on the table.

'Whenever you're ready,' the waitress said and scooped up the pie plates.

'We're ready,' Anna said and dropped a few bills on the table.

A general drowsiness spread through my body, and I began to feel numb. Was she drugging me? I remembered the white residue in the coffee cup but the moment of alarm passed quickly. If she wanted to kill me, she could have done so more than once, there was no reason to panic. My vision jerked as if I had caught myself falling asleep.

'I'll pay you whatever you want, Anna. I promise. My husband owns property, how much? 200,000? Whatever you ask for, I . . . ' I thought I heard my words slur, but I couldn't be sure. The world around me had turned fuzzy.

'I'm sorry, she's spoken for.'

Spoken for.

It was getting harder and harder to keep it together, my eyelids were twitching and out of the corner of my eye I saw the waitress pass by our table when I had just seen her behind the counter a second earlier.

'You want to see her?' Anna said casually as she sipped the coffee.

'Yes.' My vocal cords created a sound like sandpaper. 'Please.'

I watched the waitress follow the man who had dropped a coin in the jukebox earlier to the door. Anna got up and motioned me to follow them. Zombie-like, I did as I was told, keeping my eyes focused on the back of the waitress. When the door closed behind us the lights in the diner went out.

Life unfolded in slow motion. I felt as if up was down and left was right and the world around me was becoming hazier by the second. I realized the parking lot was deserted.

I turned around and watched the waitress lock the front door. She flipped the *Open* sign to *Closed*.

There was a baby seat sitting on the table in a booth by the window. Anna motioned through the closed door and the waitress turned the seat around.

There was Mia in her red coat and boots, clothes that had disappeared out of her closet. She held a bottle in hand, feeding in short, intense bursts, pausing every once in a while, allowing the collapsed nipple to fill with air.

Electric sparks travelled through me. I stared at her through the window until our faces melted into one. I looked at my reflection, I hoped to see the face of a Joan of Arc given the gift of courage, yet my reflection in the window was that of a wild-eyed woman with matted hair and a tear-stained face.

Was hell some sort of place of endless torture and pain, of fire and brimstone? My idea of hell was far simpler, it was here, in front of this diner with my daughter behind glass. Hell was my drugged and frozen brain in panic, a mental fog of conflicting instructions. It was also heaven, electrifying. She was alive and she looked well.

'Don't leave her in there,' I cried out and

made towards the door. My leg muscles felt loose, my gait was wobbly and sloppy.

'Don't touch that door,' Anna said and pointed the gun through the window at Mia.

The diner lights faded in and out. I wondered what kind of drug she had put in my coffee and if it was lethal. And that I was going to shatter the glass with my bare hands if I had to.

As if she'd read my mind she said, 'Don't get any ideas. I'll shoot her before you even know the gun went off. Your baby will be fine, but you look a bit green in the face. Better get in the car before you pass out.'

'Can I touch her?' I was close to passing out and all I wanted was one touch to take with me.

'Don't be silly. All you gonna do is make her cry.'

'What do you want if you don't want any money?' I asked.

'I need you to make good on a promise,' she said.

I didn't allow myself to feel anything but detachment, for I knew if I pushed my mind any farther, I'd never find my way back.

'What promise?' I asked as my eyelids started to droop.

Anna didn't answer and the last sound I remembered was that of spitting gravel when Anna sent the car bolting into the darkness.

24

I felt foggy. It was like I was there, but not quite. Then the scene outside the diner popped back into my head. Anna had one hand on the steering wheel, the other in her front pocket. I could think of only one reason why I shouldn't reach over and turn the wheel towards a pole, and that was the slight possibility that Anna was going to come to her senses.

'Why'd you leave her with that woman? Please explain to me what's going on.' It was dark and I didn't recognize my surroundings. My speech was slow, but clear. 'You brought me here just so I'd look at her through glass while she's with some waitress in a diner?'

'Tell me about it. Nothing went according to plan. But you have every reason to be thankful.'

'Thankful? For what? For drugging me? For allowing me to look at my child through a window?'

'You weren't supposed to be at that diner at all, but think about it,' she paused for a second, then, 'you saw her one more time, didn't you?'

One more time. The words echoed inside my aching head, bouncing around like a rubber ball in slow motion.

'Diane will take care of the baby until her new mommy picks her up. I told you she was spoken for. And that brings me to the last part of this deal between us. Your promise.'

I didn't know what any of this meant. My thoughts were slow, like sap running down the bark of a tree. I took long and deep breaths, realizing that the drugs were wearing off quickly. What do you say when you stare crazy straight in the face? You go along with it and wait for your moment.

The car pulled sharply to the left. I recognized the silhouette of the ticket booth, we were back by the side of the cornfield. Anna stopped the car and killed the engine.

'You're going to help me bury him.' She laughed and pulled a lever under the steering wheel.

The trunk popped open with a loud thud.

'Let's get to it,' she said, and tossed a pair of stiff working gloves at me. 'Six feet long and as deep as we can dig in about an hour,' she added and thrust a shovel into the wet ground.

We started digging in unison.

After we dug a couple of feet deep and six feet long, we were exhausted. The soil was soft, yet heavy. As we rested and wiggled our fingers, I felt nothing but a strange sense of excitement. I had buried the man who took my daughter from me. Lieberman could have been a time capsule for all I cared. And Mia was still alive.

'There was only one reason why I sent him after you,' Anna said after she caught her breath, 'but he got zealous and started waving that gun before it was time. Plus he wasn't made for this business. He dropped the blanket in the attic, he almost messed up when the cops came to my house. If they'd checked the car, they'd have found clothes and formula. He always forgot to take his meds and when he did, he would lose it by the minute. You can't reason and you can't do business with someone like that.'

'But he was your brother.'

'Half-brother at best. We grew up in the same house, is all.' Anna pointed at the ground, a shallow hole long enough for a body.

She lit the way with a flashlight and I did everything she told me to do. I dragged the tarp with Lieberman's body to the hole. I rolled him in, filled it with dirt, compacted the soil by stomping on it. It took me about thirty minutes to get the ground even. When I was finished, my hands were burning and the webbing between my thumb and index finger was blistered and bloody.

'Now I need you to write something for me.' She paused for a second and pursed her lips. 'Damn him, the paper is probably in his pocket.'

'I don't think I can write anything,' I said and held my hands palms up. 'I can't even bend my fingers.'

She stuck her hand in her purse and pulled out the receipt from the diner. 'You'll manage.' Anna pointed to the trunk of her car and shone the light on it. 'Word for word. Write: *Everyone, I can't go on like this. I'm sorry for what . . .*' She paused when she realized I wasn't moving. '*. . . I have done. I killed my baby. I'm a monster.*'

I shook my head. The pen dropped to the ground. 'I'm not going to write that. You're even crazier than your brother.' My mind was moving at warp speed. All I had to figure out was her currency, something that made her tick more than selling Mia to a stranger. Everybody has their price. 'Anna, I'm begging you. I will pay you twice as much. My money is as good as anyone else's.'

'I don't need your money, I need the baby. You can't run a business without the merchandise, right?'

'I will pay you more than anyone else, I promise you. I will pay whatever you ask for.'

'I don't need *your* money. I need a solid reputation for delivering.' Anna looked at her watch, then continued. 'When they find you, which could be days or even weeks from now, they will find a woman and a confession that she has killed her baby. Having the confession means they won't be looking for the baby or me or David, for that matter. They'll assume the baby is somewhere in a shallow grave in the woods. Or a Dumpster somewhere.'

Anna put the receipt on the hood of the car. 'You said you'd do anything for her, remember?' Anna cocked her head, her smile would've seemed warm to someone who didn't know the extent of her madness. 'If you do this for me, I'll do something for you,' she said with a tempting voice as if she was a child proposing a marble exchange.

'There's nothing I want you to do for me but give me back my child.'

'You don't understand anything, do you?' Anna cocked her head. 'When they find you, you'll be dead.'

I stepped back which only caused her to raise the gun again.

'I'll be long gone and no one will come looking for us. In return I'm willing to guarantee your daughter . . . ' Anna paused and then straightened her arm with the gun, pointing it between my eyes. ' . . . a good family. A backyard to play in and private school, the whole nine yards.'

If Lieberman was the Prince of Darkness, Anna was the Prince's Darkness. 'I'm begging you. I will pay you whatever — '

'I promise you no one will break her. Children can be broken easily, you know. And what kind of mother can bear the thought of that, right? What's it gonna be? Heaven or hell, both are available. It's your choice, mommy.'

Even if I overpowered her and took the gun, would it really matter? Mia could be, for all I knew, across state lines by now, Canada even, or on her way to Mexico. Even if I got away I'd still spend the rest of my life looking for her.

'Your choice. Do we have a deal?'

I shook my head and whispered, 'Please don't do this.'

'You'll die one way or another. Do something good for her for a change.' Shaking her head, Anna continued, 'A nice home or she'll spend her childhood sitting on some sicko's lap? What's it gonna be?'

I kept myself perfectly still. *My life for hers.* My mind and my body detached from one another. I broke away from myself, floated away. *Some sicko's lap.* What one does out of love is untouchable. It looks to mend, to make things right.

I bent over and forced my swollen fingers to pick up the pen.

Anna stepped closer, she was mere inches away from me. 'A decent life for your child or a childhood in a basement.'

I willed my fingers around the pen, slid them down to the ink tip.

'White baby girls are in high demand, you know. Saudis go crazy over their skin and blond hair. Or I find her nice parents and she'll take ballet lessons and go to summer camp.'

Everyone, I wrote.

I can't go on like this, I wrote.

I am sorry for what I have done, I wrote and that part wasn't even a lie.

I killed my baby, I wrote.

I'm a monster.

★   ★   ★

The ravine was about one hundred yards ahead of me. Mia was with a woman who had served me drugged coffee and pecan pie. Tomorrow morning, people would crowd the diner for breakfast, eggs and bacon would sizzle on the grill, coffee brewing, biscuits rising. And tomorrow morning they'd find me dead in a ravine with a handwritten confession saying I had killed my daughter. A devilish yet plausible plan, I had to give it to Anna.

'There's something I want you to give to her.' I reached in my purse. Tinker Bell's eyes big and blue, as resigned as I was.

Anna put Tinker Bell in her pocket. 'This is what I want you to do,' she said. 'You step on the gas while you hold the gun. Right before you reach the ravine, you pull the trigger. Either in your mouth or your temple, I don't care. I'll keep my promise if you keep yours.'

Anna wiped the gun thoroughly with a cloth, then threw it on the passenger seat. She reached over me, and put the car in Drive, her own gun still pointed at me.

'Step on it.' I heard Anna's voice but it seemed like it took me minutes until I processed her words. A pyrotechnic onslaught of possibilities accumulated in one clear thought: kill her. Shoot her. Get help. My hand twitched for a second. Then stillness came over me. I may never be believed. I may never find Mia. The pain of the guilt I felt would never cease. All was lost anyway and Anna was right; this is *the* selfless act that will redeem me. And I did as I was told. It was that easy and that difficult.

I stepped on the gas and the car started moving. The tires dragged across the gravel, slowly accelerating. I grabbed the gun with my right hand and held it against my temple.

Fifty yards, at the most. I reached for the seatbelt, tempted to unbuckle it, to get out of the car. *Some sicko's lap*, she'd said. I had no argument left, no offer, nothing but my ability to barter my life for Mia's future.

Thirty yards. The Range Rover accelerated, moved faster, much faster.

Ten yards. My entire world was covered in a

sticky substance that reeked of metal.

One yard. I pulled the trigger. There were sparks and a loud pop. Then my ear tingled and my head snapped back. I felt as if someone had injected pepper in my veins. My body lifted off the seat and I felt weightless, like riding a Ferris wheel. It seemed like forever until my stomach dropped and the car landed. Surrounded by the sickening crunch of metal collapsing, I heard glass shattering. My body jerked in all directions. Then everything went silent.

And, like a death row inmate's last meal, I asked for one last wish. The choices were endless: time travel, a reverse button, the power to become invisible, resurrecting the dead, undoing the chaotic knots of my tangled life. I must make my selection wisely. I must be precise, cover all possibilities, and leave no room for error or interpretation.

And then my last wish took shape, primal and powerful: Mia, I wish that we'll meet again at another place and time, when my body is molded perfectly so you can curl against it.

25

When we enter the 70th Precinct on Lawrence Avenue, I recall the janitor, the urge I had felt to walk out and leave the building. I understand now that I saw the world through a lens, a lens of a brain crammed with hormones and doubts, thoughts jam-packed with contortions, deformation, distortion, and falsifications. The police would have found the dumbwaiter, would have questioned David Lieberman, everything could have been so much easier. Another notch in my belt of failings.

An orderly I have never seen before takes us downtown. As Dr Ari and I pass through the glass doors and wait by the front counter, I can see our reflections in the glass. I'm disheveled and worn; Dr Ari is pressed, lint-free, and cheerful. One impeccably dressed man, probably passing as a lawyer, and a woman with a strange haircut and a missing ear. I can feel the memory of the day I walked in here wanting to take over but I remind myself that things are different now. This time I have all the answers.

The clerk looks at us and motions us up to the counter. 'How can I help you?'

'Detective Wilczek, please.'

The clerk picks up the phone and we sit down. After a couple of minutes a detective in slacks and a light-blue shirt, his tie tucked into his waistband, walks up to us. The gun in his holster seems too small for his body. His nametag reads 'Detective Robert Wilczek.'

First the name rings a bell, and then the face. I remember him from the hospital. He was one of the detectives who questioned me. His face seems slack and disinterested, but then he makes eye contact and straightens his tie. I realize his face isn't relaxed at all but merely composed. A blue bulging vein runs across his left temple.

'I'm Detective Wilczek.'

'I remember you.' *Mrs Paradise, children don't just disappear out of locked apartments.* 'I'm here to report a crime.'

I had lost my child, then I found her, then I left her, and when I went back to get her she was gone. For a while, I couldn't remember, but now I do. And I know who took her. But not where she is now.

'I know what happened to my daughter,' I say.

He looks at me, then at Dr Ari who is determined to allow me to do the talking. He will only speak when I'm not capable of relaying the story. That's how he was when we met and he hasn't faltered since.

'We've been speaking on the phone. Dr Ari I assume?' Detective Wilczek asks and they shake hands.

'Dr Solska Ari. I'm Psychiatrist in Chief at the Creedmoor Psychiatric Clinic. Mrs Estelle Paradise has been a patient at Creedmoor for the past month.'

The detective clears his throat. 'Let's find a place to talk.' Detective Wilczek motions to the clerk behind the counter and asks her to call

Detective Riverton and meet us in Room 1.

We walk down the corridor, its blue linoleum polished to perfection. We follow the detective, like ducklings following their mother. The interrogation room consists of a table and three chairs, nothing else. The walls are made of plastic panels, the floor covered in industrial carpet.

Dr Ari and Detective Wilczek leave the room, I can hear them talking in the hallway, but I'm unable to make out any specific words.

After a minute or two Dr Ari pokes his head in. He promises to send someone from Creedmoor to pick me up once the interview is over. I'm tempted to ask him to send Oliver, but I don't want to press my luck.

Then it's just the two of us. We sit down. Detective Wilczek sits across from me, and I know this conversation is being videotaped and watched in another room, or at least recorded. Detective Wilczek's dark hair is thinning and I can see his shiny scalp through his buzz cut. His front left tooth is chipped.

I try to avoid my reflection in the mirror. I'm sure it's a two-way mirror and I'm not ready to face more than one person at a time, not even through a wall. The only one who has heard my story is Dr Ari and I feel as if I'm going to say the wrong thing. I didn't commit any crime I'm aware of. The fact that I helped bury a dead man is a mere legality that won't carry any weight, I'm sure, and not reporting the abduction is something I didn't know at the time. The laws of the land go easy on redeemed mothers, at least legally, but in my own eyes, as a mother, I am guilty of countless crimes.

Three hours later I've told them the entire story. For years I've judged myself by the way people looked at me. Have not only judged myself but considered the opinion of others the gauge by which I judged myself. I'm back at my parents' funeral, people looking at me bewildered, unsure if they should stroke my hair or ignore me altogether. Wilczek and Riverton have seen a lot, I can only imagine how many dead bodies they've come across, how many images are etched into their brains, never to be erased, how many nights they've sat in their cars, in front of their houses, wives and husbands waiting, kids asleep, unable to switch off their minds.

The rest of the night unfolds in stretches of waiting and more questions and ultimately I am escorted outside where a van is waiting to transport me back to Creedmoor 'for the time being.' Detective Wilczek tells me he will drop by and have me sign the statements 'once everything checks out.'

★ ★ ★

Back at Creedmoor I fall into a deep sleep. Wistful dreams and occasional moments of waking — yet I'm at peace with the chaos of my thoughts. I spend the following days in my room. Between meals and discussions with Dr Ari about my future, I fill up an entire composition book. I don't leave a single line blank, for its

381

completeness gives me the illusion of also being complete myself. I don't want to spend another minute wondering what I might not remember in the future. I feel as if I've been floating in open water and I've come upon an island that is able to sustain me and I don't ever want to be caught off-guard again. That's the theory anyway.

The following week I get my release papers.

'We checked out your story,' Wilczek says.

'Upon entering Anna Lieberman's residence, the officers . . . ' His muffled voice echoes in my head, as if he's speaking down a well.

I imagine his words, like a movie unfolding in front of me. Entering Anna's house, the officers walk with a mission, threadbare carpet underneath their feet. Their eyes glance over the shiny travel catalogs in the living room. They hurry down the hallway, enter the room in which I saw Anna from the street, holding my daughter.

'There were lots of baby clothes and toys,' Wilczek says and now he no longer looks me in the eyes, but reads off his notes as if he can't remember the details. 'The clothes range from newborn to school age children. There were schoolbooks too. We're still trying to sort it all out. I'd be lying if I told you we knew what that meant.'

I'm not the only one whose child they've taken, there are other mothers out there, looking. I can't even allow myself to continue the thought. My own loss is all I can handle, I'm not equipped to take on someone else's burden.

Entering the kitchen, the officers find the

382

yellow floral china I described and the baby spoon. They don't find any dirty diapers underneath the plastic pots and empty seed packages in the garbage bin.

'There were empty diaper boxes and wipe wrappers. Nothing with any DNA. The garbage had been collected that day and taken to the landfill.'

Officers found the cornfield. They dug up David Lieberman's body wrapped in a blue tarp. He died of a gunshot wound to the back. That's preliminary but quite obvious. I had buried his body. I dug a hole and buried the body of the man who abducted my child. I'm not haunted by any of this, but maybe it's the fact that the less you fight the images, the more bearable they become. The decrepit barn has not been located. Wilczek calls that fact 'rather insignificant.'

I wonder what rather insignificant means? Maybe it's just proof that crazy people get away with holes as long as they are irrelevant and inconsequential to the story itself.

The diner's had many owners over the years, this year was a seasonal operation. It closed down right after Halloween once the corn maze was shut down. It's the only one in the entire county so there's quite a bit of traffic. An elderly couple leased the diner but hired seasonal wait staff on a part-time basis and there's no paperwork, no contracts, nothing. And if that wasn't disappointing enough, it's been bleached and wiped clean.

'There's an APB out on Anna Lieberman, but

383

so far we haven't been able to locate her. State agencies are on alert and I don't see how she can get your daughter out of the country, she has no birth certificate, no passport, nothing. Sooner or later her cover will blow. The moment she seeks medical help, tries to enroll her in daycare or school, it'll arouse suspicion. Even a traffic violation or her name showing up on a lease will trigger the system. It's only a matter of time. She can hide, but only for so long.'

School, daycare. 'That could be years from now,' I say and shake my head. 'What do I do in the meantime? Where do I look?'

Hundreds of children go missing every day. Posters in store windows. On milk cartoons. Do they still do that? Some supermarkets have posters of local missing children, posters I've scanned before, appalled by the years that have passed since they've last been seen. Teenagers usually, disappeared, never to be seen again. Some thought to have run away. Running away is not a crime. Are they even looking? *Don't fight it*, I tell myself, *there's no end to this*. It's a bottomless pit, my daughter among them.

'I want to apologize to you but I know there's nothing I can say to make this better, so I'm not even going to try.'

Sorry, he said. The cheapest of all words. It's as if he's trying to cut open the snake and retrieve its victim, expecting life to go on. It doesn't work that way.

'Let us do the looking. All you have to do is be patient,' he adds.

'Right,' I say and put on my gloves.

384

Patience. It's starting to wear thin and I haven't even left Creedmoor yet. Not only is it wearing thin but it strikes me as sheer madness. The same people who didn't believe me then are telling me now to trust them and be patient?

Jack has been briefed, so I'm told by the detective, and eventually we talk on the phone. He's focused on the details and at times there are long pauses during which I imagine him taking notes, but maybe he's trying to wrap his mind around this, I must admit, rather bizarre story. He went from having a wife under suspicion to being the clueless husband and still Mia is missing. He's not very forthcoming with his feelings towards me and talks about coming back to New York soon. *Coming back* and *soon* are ambiguous enough for the both of us; I have only one goal in mind, finding Mia, Jack is probably adding a few things to the list of his own shortcomings. We are not what we are both focused on right now.

I wonder how mothers know they are better. When do we know the worst of postpartum is over and things are on their way back to normal? I imagine when they are able to laugh again, maybe just living their lives without a cloud above their head. For me, it's a bit more complicated. I can't walk into my daughter's room, pick her up and hold her close. I'm left with empty arms and getting better to me means, literally, not having to pretend to be normal. It seems as if for every minute Mia

385

remains out of my reach, I gain some sort of strength. I'm not sure what it is, but it's growing. Getting back to normal is like losing the knots in my stomach and then suddenly there is room for something else. Resolve maybe? Courage? Do I need to lose one thing to gain another for there's a limited number of items I can carry inside myself? Is that why I don't seem to have any room for Jack right now?

The day I leave Creedmoor, as it sits silently overlooking the East River, I say goodbye to Oliver. It is a clandestine ritual on my part. Not a traditional farewell — no embrace or small talk — just me touching his hand ever so slightly as I walk past him. I'm not even sure he notices. I've also realized I've lost the acorn and after an initial moment of sadness I no longer dwell on it. It has served its purpose and won't be forgotten.

I walk down the pebble walkway on the north side of Creedmoor one more time. I count five windows down and three up to find the window of my former room. I find the nest. What was once a well-built structure of tightly woven sticks and twigs is now flattened and dilapidated. The bird's nest I used to watch from my window is abandoned. No worrisome parents nearby to watch the fledglings on their clumsy flying attempts. Life goes on in so many ways.

Dr Ari sees me in his office one last time. I attempt to take it all in: the diplomas on the walls, the scent of shoe polish, the view of the smokestacks in the distance.

'I wanted to wish you good luck,' he says. 'And that I hope for a happy ending to the story.'

'There's nothing else I can do but wait for Anna to make a mistake. Luck can't be all I've got left,' I say and my eyes tear up. I blink them away.

'I'm a great believer in luck,' he says and closes my file one last time.

'Speaking of happy endings, you never told me about the woman with the egg,' I say later, as he escorts me outside, where a cab is waiting for me.

Dr Ari furrows his brow, then his eyes light up. 'I forgot I told you about that.'

'So, what was it if it wasn't the egg?'

'She's passed since and I guess it's okay if I share her story with you. It was the spoon she ate the egg with.'

'The spoon?'

'She ate off a silver spoon. The silver reacted with the sulfur in the egg, created a tarnish on the spoon. The spoon had a foul taste and reminded her of a rather violent experience in her life. The memory emerged and rather than deal with it, she shut down.'

'So that's the story of the egg woman.'

'That's it,' Dr Ari says.

'Will I ever see you again?' The thought of never seeing him again seems arduous. There's still so much more at stake with Mia being missing.

'I'd say you have no need for a man like me in your life. You are going to be okay.'

As he extends his hand, I grab it. Then I pull him into an embrace. He's stiff in my arms, but only for a second. Then he softens.

I watch him through the rearview mirror of the cab one last time, straightening his tie and removing invisible specks of cotton from his suit.

26

As the months pass and Mia remains missing, I feel fear hatching inside of me. I did as Anna told me to do in exchange for Mia's future wellbeing — I wrote the confession, I drove the car into the ravine, I shot myself — but I didn't die. What has become of Mia and did Anna renege on her promise too? Eventually Jack and I talk about the possibility of having to identify Mia's ravaged and abused body in unimaginable stages of decomposition — we agree we'll make the identification together — yet we can't quite agree on how to live our lives until then.

In the meantime, I rent a small studio apartment on 58th Street — it's affordable and Jack is surprisingly generous, and I enjoy living in walking distance to the nearby trains, on a quiet, tree-lined street.

Once his contract in Chicago ended, Jack finds a position as Assistant DA in New York City, 'entry level, no pay, and long hours.' His furnished apartment, The Tribeca Suites, allows him to remain 'in transition.' We both know what that means. We don't mention the word divorce quite yet; we allow life, according to Jack, 'to play out,' whatever that means.

Even though we both hate to admit yet another failure, we are merely sitting ducks. Marriages confronted by tragedy don't break apart because of that fact per se, but it seems as

389

if there's only so much resolve to go around and everything pales in comparison to Mia's disappearance. And so we live separately and wait for the inevitable burial of our union. I don't feel any sort of way about it, we're just another one of those the-way-it-used-to-be things that got lost along the way. We know the demise of our marriage is nearing, like a sure winter storm, its icy breath approaching the hairs on the back of our necks.

Once a week Jack and I meet at a coffee shop in a book store. There, we are encased by the contrived normalcy of people around us discussing the books they've read, trips they've taken, discussing normal things that normal people do, and I am painfully aware that we are never going to be a normal couple again.

During our time at the coffee shop Jack struggles to wrap his mind around the details of Mia's disappearance. He makes me recount every minute detail and obsesses over where he was and what he did while it all played out.

'I feel responsible,' he says, sometimes raising his voice, causing people to turn around and look at us. 'I feel it was my fault. I hired this lunatic, I took the job in Chicago, and I told you to move into the brownstone.'

My sense of guilt for not having protected my child pales in comparison to Jack's loss of potency. There's nothing he can do and he's not equipped to deal with it. And he's going on and on about what he would give if he could go back and take a different path, but he knows it's impossible. How the guilt eats at him every moment of every day, when he is going to sleep, when he wakes up, during lunch, in the shower, at the gym, watching the news, how it pops to the foreground of his mind and demands to be prioritized, an infinite punishment. How he is tired of thinking about it, how no amount of analysis is going to turn back the clock.

And during those moments, during those fleeting minutes of remorse, for a split second, I feel something for him that resembles compassion. And I hold his hand, yet I struggle to find a single word of consolation for him. Since the day he dropped me off at Creedmoor I haven't been able to cry in front of him. I don't know if I'm gaining strength or losing my soul, but it's easier that way and so I don't analyze it.

As a prosecutor Jack doesn't invest in the notion that even behind a most wicked and incomprehensible deed is a human being. His world is not so sunny, doesn't allow for any such concessions, his world has very few rainbows and frolicking puppies. He is quick to see the bad and even quicker to judge, and that's just how Jack is. And Jack judges himself. For Jack's a logical man.

While I can 'claim' — what a choice of words — while I can *claim* to have suffered from a medical condition, he was inept in his task to protect his family. This lasts for mere minutes, then Jack stiffens himself and clears his throat. Composed, he enters some sort of a twisted stage, holding the curtain for all the others to enter; Lieberman, Anna, the police. An array of guilty parties jointly responsible.

Sometimes I don't know what to say and so I just sit there and stare down my empty coffee cup. Jack's not the man he used to be. He seems to depend on me for support and on a certain level I feel annoyed by his emotions. I need him to be strong — not for me, for himself — because I was able to cope, have been coping, but I just can't add any more weight to my Jenga stack of agony.

We talk about the Utah child abduction case, a teenager who vanished on some island in the Caribbean, all parents shaken to the core, ready to break, forever searching, some up to this day, for answers.

All he wants to do is talk, talk, talk. And I let him go on and on and on, listening for what seems like days on end, sometimes tuning him out for long stretches at a time, hours even, his voice without inflection or variation, monotonous and low. Eventually his voice gets hoarse and we sit among the scent of coffee, the sound of the beans dropping into the grinder, the grinding noise eventually drowning him out completely, for just a few merciful seconds. Finally his voice turns into a raspy whisper and we both go home.

I allow months of these meetings to pass and watch layer after layer of guilt pile on top of him like shovels of soil on a coffin. I tell him to do something constructive with the monsters trapped in his head — those are his words, *monsters trapped in his head* — but Jack is Jack and that's all there is to it. I call it a legacy, *his legacy*.

'You could start a foundation in Mia's name. You could speak in front of people, to groups of parents, we could assist in searches for missing children. We could . . . Jack, there's so much you can do. I think it'd be good for you.'

'You know I'm not comfortable around people. That whole speaking thing is just nerve-racking for me. Trust me, if I could I would, but . . . once the brownstone sells I'll put up a reward. That's helpful, right?'

Then I start getting angry at him. Angry at his inability to fight the monsters. Angry at the fact that money is what he's throwing at this. Angry that he expected me to grow beyond my limitations, told me to just 'snap out of it,' yet he's unwilling to do the same.

Eventually everything about Jack strikes me as silly. Those fanged rippers, those elusive little shits he can't get under control when the real monster lived in the same house with me while he was working on foreign exchanges and equity deals. Fuck you, Jack. Fuck. You.

'I can go for days feeling normal,' he says, 'and then I think of nothing else and I feel like I'm going crazy.'

One day, at the coffee shop, I feel his judging eyes on me while I search through missing children's databases on my laptop. Like a hawk watching a sparrow, he scrutinizes me as I keep track of body parts washing up on shorelines. He frowns when I hand him a list of private detectives, and then he looks away.

Eventually the monsters have mercy on Jack. He seems to gain his strength back, his step is quicker, less restrained, the bags under his eyes have faded. He even has a slight tan as if he's spent the weekend in the sun. And I watch him, after the obligatory display of grief, mentally severing himself from the uncomfortable fact that this crisis will never come to an end. We've held on until there is nothing to hold on to anymore. And then he asks me to sign the divorce papers.

Jack will go on with his life, someplace else, with hardly a backwards glance, no call, no text, no email. He hates complicated relationships and I have no doubt that his emotions, yet again, run on steel rails. He is now a DA last time I heard, in Boston, I think, I don't remember.

And then there is the media. Any infamous reputation is directly related to the amount of details the media can dig up about your life, neighbors they can interview, and relatives that speak out on 20/20. I have none of that to offer. At the most there'll eventually be a Cold Case Files edition or a Dateline legal show. After I declined all interviews, there was nothing else to be had.

I went from the hospital to Creedmoor and even though pictures of Mia as an infant were subject to intense media coverage, photos of me are scarce to say the least. By the time I rent the studio apartment, phone calls from reporters prompt me to change my number for the first time. There are calls regarding book deals and movie opportunities. I hang up the phone and again change my number. Then it quiets down. After all, there is no trial, no 'gavel to gavel' coverage dedicated to bringing legal proceedings to the public. There is only so much media fodder and then the primary elections come up, and eventually other headlines take priority.

Anthony now works for the FBI's Joint Terrorism Task Force in Anchorage, Alaska, and heads an Evidence Response Team. The Anchorage Division also runs a 'Kidnapping and Missing Persons' office at the same Alaska office. Anthony's called me almost every week since the day we reunited in Creedmoor on a park bench. I visited him and his wife a year ago. She had just given birth to a baby boy and I could only make excuses for so long. The baby's name is William Hadley Paradise and he was two months old when I met him. I never held him, and Anthony didn't ask me to.

During one of his calls he suggests I add Mia's case to the nationwide Crime Stoppers website where people can phone in tips, anonymous if they so desire.

'Exposure is what you need. Add a reward to it and your chances increase.'

Jack offers a $20,000 reward *for tips leading to the whereabouts of Anna Lieberman and the recovery of Mia Connor.* The statistics are promising; the website has yielded hundreds of thousands of arrests, almost a million cases cleared, and over a hundred million dollars paid out in rewards. The $20,000 highlights the dark side of the operation; the number of incoming tips is enormous and while some are obviously phoned in as a joke, others take up valuable resources. The supposed 'sightings' of Anna

Lieberman are a sculptor in Santa Fe, a Siamese cat breeder in Las Vegas, and a Middle School teacher in Oklahoma. There's no attempt to enroll Mia in school, no attempt to access medical coverage, no passport application. It's as if Anna's found the perfect hiding place for her.

Anthony rarely speaks of our childhood. It's as if our foundation is shaky and he decides to remain safe. Our conversations revolve around what he calls Mia's *recovery*. I try not to think about the fact that Mia knows another woman as her mother and with every passing day I become more disillusioned that a recovery is even possible. I'll never get back what I've lost. There's this hole I feel inside of me that isn't of this world. A sadness that's stuck to me like an old faithful dog, stirring when I stir, opening its eyes when I open mine. Never far away, always loyal, steadfast. To be counted on.

What am I to do? Post fliers all over New York City? What's the point of that? A website makes more sense and so I hire a designer, but after a month I realize that for every kind word there are ten comments about my incompetence, my lack of 'mother DNA,' and those are the kind ones. Some people actually long to kill me. They don't know they'd be doing me a favor.

Regardless of how many nights I stare at the ceiling as I lay in the darkness, I always come to the same conclusion. 'I can't live like this.'

And eventually I realize I'm the only one looking. And not only am I looking but I plan on being the proverbial mother lifting a car off my trapped child. I am capable of such feat. The police continue to talk about patience and the fact that Anna can't completely fade into the background forever but I request my own copy of the documents, of all the files. I read through them, study them, and make mental notes of anything that could possibly shed light on Anna's whereabouts. And when I am through, I start all over again.

After I leave Creedmoor I call Detective Wilczek daily and he tells me finding Anna will be 'a matter of time.' A month later I call him weekly, and words like 'hiding,' 'unsuspecting,' and 'ingenuity' snake their way into our conversations.

'But we're on it. We're not giving up. We'll have to wait for her to make a mistake, and she will, they all do.'

Six months later he tells me he'll call me when something new comes up. On the one-year anniversary he refers to Anna's trail as having 'gone cold.' In a matter of months they'll refer to Mia as a 'cold case.'

Two months after the divorce is final, I return to North Dandry. I'm curious if the place still holds bondage over me. The renovations have been completed, the building has been sold. Hence the $20,000 reward Jack put up.

As I get out of the taxi, I deliberately avoid looking at the building. I pay the cab driver and I finally look up, standing perfectly still. I expect a violent reaction — blacking out, fainting, or even vomiting — yet none of that happens, just its windows' dopey eyes looking down on me. The building lies dormant and spiritless, almost

397

sad. Even the building looks as if it's moved on.

Daily I wonder how Mia looks — she is almost four — and I know she's changed and has become unrecognizable to me, and the fact that I wouldn't recognize my own child if I saw her makes me sick to my stomach.

And so I create her likeness, fill out every inch of her body, stretch her limbs, and elongate her face to fit me just right. I believe she has my fine, wavy hair, Jack's brown eyes, and my love for citrus fruits. Mia's image — the one I have created — lurks everywhere, ready to manifest itself at any given time; in the park, at a store, in the subway, on TV. Blond hair, pale skin, dark eyes. Pink lips, curved like Jack's, full like mine. I reconstruct her features and fill in the blanks as I see fit. Eventually I'll forget her scent, the feel of her hair against my cheek. Her existence will one day be erased from my mind. And it makes me angry.

★   ★   ★

The Brooklyn Frame & Photo Gallery is only a few blocks from 58th Street. The gallery specializes in custom framing for art pieces and photographs. I love the thought of conserving moments in time. I show our customers catalogs with samples of matting. I dust the frames that cover the wall behind the counter. I proclaim the advantages of classic frames over antique or contemporary looks, I speak on naturally treated hardwoods, finished corner artisan hardwoods, welded aluminum and steel, unique Plexiglas frames, finished corner gold-leafed frames and our large selection of modern and decorative moldings.

Five years have passed and framing other people's memories consoles me on many levels; I'm a bystander, yet I partake in the joy of others since I doubt I will ever again find joy for myself. It is a strange way to live, yet I can function within this limited level of participation, a level having been familiar to me all my life.

On a bad day I want to tell them to preserve their memories because they might be taken from them before they even imagine a future, before they clip a pink bow in the blond hair of a girl with dark eyes and pale skin.

The look on the customers' faces who pick up their framed photographs, those moments are like the parents of my future; they create the person I want to be one day. Other days, when I hear a crying baby or walk into a restroom where a mother just changed her baby, the smell of baby powder renders me helpless.

The NYPD stopped searching for Mia years ago. They know she is — or was, at one point — with Anna Lieberman. She could be anywhere and nowhere. Mia could be with Anna still, or sold to the highest bidder. Or maybe they live somewhere, in another country or another state. Maybe they went down to Mexico. Maybe Canada.

The other day, on my way to work, I passed a little girl, smiling and skipping along beside her mother in a school uniform. Suddenly fear rose inside me. I actually took a step after the little girl before I forced myself to cut off my thoughts. Don't be stupid, I told myself, that's not Mia. Except . . . my panic rears up again and again, panic that she might live somewhere close, yet I would never know.

For years I'd seen babies in strollers and toddlers in buggies and thought: 'That's what Mia would look like now.' Those fleeting images of her, images that cause me to stop, bend over, and collect my breath, find me in the most unpredictable places, in the most random forms. A strand of hair, a little finger pointing at something. A wailing baby, a crying toddler, a bawling kid in the park. I see Mia everywhere. Little girls who look like her cross the street beside me, they hold their mothers' hands, they enter school buildings, and they hang off monkey bars in parks. Mia's likeness holds another woman's hand and it tears me up inside.

★   ★   ★

My therapist, Dr Langston, who I see twice a week in the afternoons, has a skeleton model in the corner of her office. The day we meet for the first time, I remark that she's not an orthopedic doctor and that the skeleton seems misplaced to me.

'Bones are all we really know about humans. Pretty much everything else is just conjecture. Miracle recoveries, new diseases, the brain, we are basically clueless,' she says and squints at the skeleton. 'I call him *Musterion*, it means *sacred secret* in Greek. A reminder that we know

400

nothing about the human condition.'

Her large office window faces the west and during our sessions the room floods with golden light. It makes me smile every time I walk in. I've been keeping a secret from her and today I finally decide to come clean.

'There was this woman and a little girl, on Delaware and 49th, the girl wore a black down jacket. Her ponytail had come loose under her hat, it sat crooked and the woman made no attempt to straighten it. One of her pink gloves dangled on a string attached to her coat, her other hand hung on to the woman's hand who I assumed to be her mother.

'I remember the woman's stride, wide and bouncy, had caught my eyes. But what alerted me was the red hair she pushed nervously under the hood of her duffel coat. The gesture seemed suspicious, hasty, meant to deceive. I trailed them but after a few minutes I felt heavy and stiff, unable to keep up. They finally slowed down and boarded the B11 bus.'

I remember I sat behind them, catching my breath. The bus windows were fogged with the heat and breaths of the dozens of people on the bus. There was a man in a blue uniform, two teenage girls with purple hair and nose rings, a few shift workers with empty eyes and lunch boxes on their laps. The rest were old people in orthopedic shoes and drawstring pants on their way back to their senior living facility. The little girl's head rested on the woman's shoulder, then her forearm, eventually her lap.

'Did you think it was your daughter and the

woman who kidnapped her?'

'There was a general resemblance to Anna Lieberman, as I remember her, but the woman was taller, older, maybe even the girl's grandmother.'

I tell Dr Langston that when the bus reached Sunset Park, the woman gently stroked the girl's cheek. She made eye contact with the girl and placed her hand in front of her right eye and pulled away as if pulling on a string. The girl responded by raising her index finger. Sign language, I thought, and realized what had compelled me to follow them in the first place was the fact that they seemed disconnected from one another. The woman gently slipped the pink glove over her hand and smiled at the girl. The girl bared her miniature teeth back at her. I watched them as they leisurely strolled off to the subway.

'Did you continue to follow them?'

'No, I didn't, but I wondered what I would do if it was her. The pills I take make me tired and I'm out of shape and what if I had to run after someone?'

Dr Langston looks at me puzzled. 'You're not thinking about stopping your meds, are you?'

'No, I'm not. But on my way home the other day I stopped to buy a pair of running shoes. And I've been running ever since.'

Seated on the edge of her seat Dr Langston listens to every word I say.

'I feel I have to do something more. I check online, I follow the news, I . . . maybe . . . maybe I will recognize someone, or make out a voice

I've heard before. There's still the waitress that the police never found. And I know Anna is still out there. I just can't sit still anymore.'

'You run to find clues as to where your daughter is?' Her eyebrows raise and form half-moons of apprehension over her eyes.

'I know it's not very logical and that's why . . . that's why I've been thinking about becoming a crime analyst,' I say.

Dr Langston forgets to blink, then she clears her throat. 'A crime analyst?'

'Yes. I'm thinking about it.' It had never crossed my mind to become one, but there it was, floating in the air. From hasty comment to a possibility to do something, then a resolve of some sort.

'Maybe we should talk about this before you — '

'I don't think you understand,' I interrupt her. 'I've been calling the detective for years, the one who worked the case. They never had a single lead, the case has gone cold. Nothing. How do you not have a single lead?'

'From what I understand — '

'It drives me crazy that she's somewhere, right now as we sit here, she's doing *something*. Right now, as we speak, she is living somewhere, wearing a dress, with her hair in a ponytail, speaking, playing. I refuse to believe that she's lost. It's not like a stranger grabbed her off the street; we know Anna took her. I understand that all the other leads, the diner, the waitress at the diner, turned up nothing. I get that. I may not be able to find my daughter, but Anna, Anna I can

403

find. A needle in a haystack maybe, but hell, there's a haystack and there's a needle in it. All I've to do is take each single blade of hay and remove it. And I'll be left with the needle.'

'I just want to make sure that you don't — '

'Become obsessed? You worry that I'll become obsessed with finding my daughter? Listen, Dr Langston, this is not a healthy life, I know that. But I'm not concerned and neither should you be.'

'As your therapist your mental health *is* my primary concern.'

'Then tell me what to do, tell me what would you do? Sit around and wait? One more summer, one more Christmas? Another five years?'

Dr Langston remains silent as a broad bar of sunlight bathes her in an angelic light.

I laugh, loud, from the gut. Crisp, with a hint of evil.

She presses down the button of her ceramic pencil. The porcelain shell looks expensive, a Mother's Day present maybe — I've seen photos of her children on her desk — a token of appreciation from people who love her. She aligns the pen with the yellow notepad paper.

When she doesn't answer I nod with unwavering intensity.

'I'm not managing my grief well, am I?'

'Managing is the important part.'

I've read the terminology. Mia is considered a 'long term missing' child. All subject matter experts from a wide array of disciplines have considered all possible strategies. Nothing else can be done. This is the end of the line, I'm the only one standing.

'Sometimes I get up in the morning and I feel that today is the day. Today is the day when the phone rings and there's a lead. A picture. A trace of something.'

I don't tell her that just last week, on a whim, I went to Dover and stood in front of Anna's former house. I don't mention the fact that I went back to the cornfield and that I poked the earth with a stick where I buried Lieberman. That I had coffee at the diner which now sees a pretty steady influx of customers.

I've done my homework. Dr Langston is merely a companion on my journey, a spectator of my grief, if you will. Her main mission is to bear witness to my pain. According to her manual she is to emphasize the importance of ongoing support for individuals like me. She is to tell me that I must attend to my own physical and emotional needs. She is to help me prepare for the long term and the fact that my life must go on.

Dr Langston listens and honors the few stories I have of Mia. There isn't much to tell, really, she was born, afflicted with a colic when she was only a few weeks old, a colic that never passed and then she was gone. No anecdotes of learning to crawl or her first steps. It was all struggle for both of us all the time. When I run out of stories to tell, and we go in circles for a few sessions, she hands me an address of a support group in a church basement.

'Did you ever give the support group I told

you about a chance?' she asks me the following week.

'Not yet,' I say and I have no intention of going at all. The thought of listening to other people's pain is not my idea of finding Mia.

'It can be quite therapeutic and might help you make sense of your new world.'

A world without my child doesn't make sense at all, I tell her. Please attend a meeting, she says, and even though I don't see the point, I don't want to ever again look back on anything with regret. Give it a chance she says, and so I do. I go to a meeting that very same day. I give chances, it's the only thing I have to give these days.

Only a handful of cars dot the church parking lot as I pass spindly trees amidst concrete islands and weeds poking through the asphalt. I count eight cars.

I scan the flier taped to the door. *Healing Hearts*, it says. *Weekly meetings. Grief Support After The Loss Of A Child*. The group meets at six. At five there's an AA meeting on the schedule. Tai Chi for seniors starts promptly at eight.

Grief is universal, the flier says. Join a group of people who have experienced a loss, who tell their stories knowing they will be respected and held in confidence.

I enter the titanic room with intermittent columns holding up the ceiling. It is stuffy and reeks of mold, Freon, and stale coffee.

I make my way to the back where the fluorescent lights shine a merciless blaze on a group of people. I count seven. A man with a folder on his lap. Two couples. One middle-aged woman and one fairly young woman.

I take one of the vacant chairs.

'Hi, my name is Eric,' the guy with the folder says and counts heads, then notes the number of people attending on a notepad.

'I'm a licensed grief counselor and the facilitator of this group. Most of us know each other but we have a new face here tonight.'

Eric makes eye contact with me and strokes his beard.

'Just so we're on the same sheet of music, let me go over the principles again. Everyone here has experienced the loss of a child. We're here to talk about that experience with people who are likely to understand. There'll be words of wisdom, words of support and sometimes . . . ' Eric pauses and glances at a couple holding hands, 'sometimes our words cause even more pain. Be patient with each other and remember, we're not a social network, we're not a therapy group. Everything we say is confidential. Always.'

I look around while I listen to Eric. A couple with identical T-shirts, the word Hope, the 'o' being a butterfly. The woman's pudgy fingers rest in the man's hand, as if he is keeping her from darting for the door. Or off a bridge, I'm not sure. The man introduces himself as Dwight, his wife as Kathryn, 'but she goes by Katy,' he adds. 'We lost our daughter to cancer a year ago.'

The middle-aged woman in an outfit that I didn't know still existed — pink stretch pants and a pink shirt with embroidered flowers — is on the verge of tears.

'I'm Regina,' she says and dabs her eyes with a cloth handkerchief. 'My son suffers from a mental disease. I haven't seen him in five years.'

The other couple, 'Kristy and Dave,' wear sweatpants and flannel shirts. And crosses around their necks. 'Our son went on a motorcycle trip two years ago. He never returned.'

And then it's my turn to introduce myself.

I practiced at home, went over my words dozens of times, expecting the inescapable and obligatory introduction of my loss and I faltered every time. I haven't lost anyone. At least not yet. Mia is alive but I don't know where. I feel out of place, even more than I imagined when this moment played out in my mind.

'My name's Estelle,' I say and take in a deep breath. I'm not sure what to say. My loss is unique, I'm in some elusive limbo state, not quite circle of life, yet all-encompassing.

'Hi, Estelle,' Eric says. 'Welcome to Healing Hearts. Who have you lost?'

I remain silent. The young, very large woman to my left takes pity on me.

'I'm Mary,' she says. 'The first time can be difficult. This is only my second time here and last week I told the group about my sister Lilly. One day, in third grade, she didn't come home after school.'

Mary pauses and I scrutinize her profile, want to see exactly what grief looks like on such a young face. Mary can't be older than nineteen or so and must be close to five hundred pounds, her thighs are swollen beyond the metal chair's seat.

She wears stretch pants and a large black T-shirt. There's a velvety, light-brown ring around her neck, indicating an advanced state of diabetes. I wonder if she knows. Her fingers are stubby knobs, her nails are bitten to the quick. Her face seems almost unaware of her loss, her porcelain skin is plumb and subtle, her eyes bright, surrounded by long lashes. Nothing about her speaks of pain but her shaky voice. I don't notice any tears but Mary wipes her eyes with the back of her hand nonetheless. Maybe people run out of tears eventually, I think.

'May Christ hold her forever,' Kristy chimes in, and crosses herself. 'God's love is eternal.'

Mary stares at her, and after a brief pause, says, 'Amen.'

Fuck, I think, for fuck's sake, have these people lost their minds?

'Left my car lights on,' I say and leave.

★ ★ ★

When Dr Langston asks me about the group I tell her it's not for me.

'Different priorities, is all.'

'I know it's not easy to speak in public about Mia. Each parent's expression of pain is unique,' Dr Langston says.

'I'd rather talk about finding her.'

'I'm worried about you, Estelle.'

'Why?' I can feel myself getting angry. Dr Langston watches my emotions intently and she knows she's hit the mark. Challenge is part of the manual.

'We've talked about this before.'

'Are you telling me to stop looking?'

'No, I'm not. I want you to dedicate a part of each day to finding Mia. And the rest of the day I want you to dedicate to you. And maybe allow yourself to consider the other possibility.'

She's been trying to get me to say it for weeks now. She will never hear those words from me.

'She might not come back.' Dr Langston's voice trembles ever so slightly.

'You know what?'

'What?' She scoots to the front of her chair and listens intently.

'I think I left my car lights on,' I say.

27

The air is sharp. Liquid ice stings my nostrils and seeps into my lungs. The first ten minutes of running in the cold sucks, but then I get warm and cozy. My legs loosen up, my breath settles into a steady rhythm and I go into autopilot.

Three miles later the cold air has dried out my airways and, after another mile, my lungs start to burn and a hacking cough forces me to stop every few minutes. The cold pavement crawls through the bottom of my running shoes up into my legs. Three layers of clothes, a thermal cap and tights are no match for New York's arctic air.

I finally give up and surrender to the cough. I spot a Starbucks down the street and decide to stop running for the day. I cut across Flatbush towards Prospect Avenue and pause in front of an electronics store. Hot air blows up a shaft and through a crate, warming my feet. There's numerous flat screens mounted on the walls of the store, all of them tuned to CNN. Silent pictures move across the screens when another coughing fit rips through me. I cup my hands around the coffee cup and the news ticker on the bottom of the screen catches my attention.

Breaking News.

My breath mingles with the steaming coffee and I jerk back as the hot liquid scalds my lips. I watch the headlines pass by.

Fundamentalist church raid underway.

Compound under investigation of child abuse.
84 children taken into custody.

I watch dozens of children in a neat line hold hands as they enter white buses parked by the side of the road.

Behind them a group of women emerge from a building, shielding their eyes from the cameras. Some of them step off the porch as if to follow the children being carted off, others remain on the porch, crying, holding on to each other. Their pastel-colored dresses are buttoned up to the neck, reaching all the way to the ground. Their every step kicks up the dress seams, offering a glimpse of stocking-covered legs and dusty orthopedic shoes. Their hair is pinned into tall waves high above their foreheads, their faces are scrubbed clean. Red-rimmed eyes and blotchy cheeks complete the picture of utter despair.

Another news flash creeps over the screen.

Children to remain in state custody while authorities investigate allegations of abuse.

One of the women's braids has loosened and her red hair is reaching all the way to her lower back. She screams at the men escorting the children into the bus while the other women stand in silence, wiping their tears. A state trooper is motioning the woman to get back on the porch. The woman's red hair floods around her as she raises a hand towards him as if to curse his very existence. Then the camera zooms in on her. Her lavender dress and her poufy strawberry hair can't distract me from her hand. Deformed, covered in burn marks.

412

My intestines turn into a corkscrew, then my body surrenders. A flash, followed by a star falling towards the dark ground, illuminated, shining bright. A recollection, then a memory. Anna, the teenager, the aunt. *Laura Dembry*, member of *The Church of Appointed Dominion*.

My mind stills and the world around me turns fuzzy.

The haystack. I've found the haystack.

★   ★   ★

'Detective, this is Estelle. Estelle Paradise.' I have trouble catching my breath.

There's a long silence on the other end of the line.

'Mrs Paradise.'

'I'm calling you because I need your help.' I have trouble talking and breathing at the same time.

A pause. Then, 'I'm no longer working with the same department. I've been reassigned. I can give you a number to call if you — '

'Are you watching the news?' I interrupt him when I finally catch my breath.

'The news?'

'Police raided a compound in Texas. They took all the children.'

'I'm not watching, but I'm aware.'

'I called the precinct. They won't help me.'

'I'm sorry, I don't understand.'

'Can we meet somewhere?'

A long silence. 'Mrs Paradise, I don't — '

'In one hour. The Starbucks on Prospect

Avenue. By the park entrance.'

'There's nothing I can do for you. Like I said, I'm no longer — '

'In one hour. I'll be waiting.'

'Hold on a minute, I still don't understand . . . what's the raid got to do with anything?'

'It's about Anna. I found her,' I say and hang up the phone.

★ ★ ★

One hour later the words pour out of me. The raid in Texas. The children. Anna Lieberman, the woman with red hair, is one of the mothers from the Dominion Compound in Denton, the same church her aunt belonged to. And maybe, just maybe, one of the children I watched on live TV boarding the buses, is Mia. And no one at the precinct is willing to hear me out *because any information on the minor children recovered from the compound will not be discussed until DNA analysis has been completed.* And then they hung up the phone.

'How can you be sure the woman is Anna Lieberman?' Wilczek's voice is intense, almost sharp.

'I think I'd recognize the woman who took my daughter. I also understand this is an ongoing investigation, but I need to know where the children are.'

'They won't release any information until the investigation is complete. It's not really out of the ordinary that they don't want to talk to you about the case.'

414

'No one else is even hearing me out. All I need is a DNA sample.'

'I don't think I'm the right man for it, I don't have access to the Denton compound case. Besides, I don't know how I can help.' He raises his hands, palms up. There's a change in his demeanor suddenly, like a cloud's shadow overhead. 'I can't do anything that's against the law.'

'I'm not asking you to do anything illegal,' I say but I don't really know the legalities, and I don't really care, which is just about the same thing to me.

'You don't understand, I've had a lot going on lately, there were some problems at work, and I don't need to get caught up in something . . . ' His large thumb presses down on the domed plastic lid. 'Look . . . ' he says and hesitates ever so slightly, 'not that it makes any difference to you, but I'm going through a divorce. New York state maintenance is not exactly cheap. And I have a son. I can't risk my job right now.'

I ignore his comment. I have no interest in his problems. I swallow, tell myself this doesn't mean no. It means nothing. There's a way, there's *always* a way. 'One girl, Wilczek.' I study the dark circles under his eyes and his wrinkled shirt. His eyes are empty dark holes, lifeless. But I don't care about any of this. 'There's one girl with my DNA. That girl, five years old, is my daughter. And I need to find her.' I imagine nurses with cotton swabs swiping the cheeks of children with large and frightened eyes. 'I know

415

there are lengthy backlogs in every crime lab in the state and it could take months to get it all sorted out, but — '

'Do you have any idea what kind of circus you're dealing with? There are hundreds of DNA tests to be done. Figuring out who belongs to who will take months. And let's not even take into consideration that they probably gave wrong names and ages. Everybody is someone's mommy, every man's someone's uncle or daddy. It's like untangling hundreds of fucking miles of Christmas lights.'

'But if she's one of them, we'll find her.' He cringes when I said *we*.

'Yes, I don't doubt that but you'll have to wait. The DNA testing will take some time.'

There's too much frozen anger inside of me and I've been waiting for too long. 'Hear me out, okay?' I fold my hands as if I'm about to pray. Did he grimace or did I imagine that?

'Five minutes,' he says and leans back.

'All I need to know is where the children are.'

'It's been five years. What if you don't recognize her? What are you going to do? Line them up, swab their cheeks? Demand a hair sample? This is madness.'

'Let me worry about that.' I'm not sure myself. Am I going to recognize her? A part of me is convinced that I will. Maybe it's madness but I have no choice.

'It's illegal on my part,' Wilczek says, furrowing his brow.

'No one is going to care once they find out one of the girls is Mia.'

'It's illegal and not admissible in court. And I could lose my job.'

'There won't be any trials. The same people who crucified me when Mia disappeared owe me. You are one of them.'

He swirls what's left in the bottom of the cup and then downs it. 'I can't promise anything.'

★   ★   ★

That night, I awake from a restless sleep. I have kicked off the covers and now I'm cold. I must have forgotten to close the blinds for the light of the moon spills into my room, its unforgiving brilliance restraining my breathing like a giant cat sitting on my chest. Reality seeps in slowly. When the pressure becomes unbearable, I sit up.

At night, when my mind drops its guard, the extent of what my reality is becomes too much. My thoughts turn daunting, unscalable. I close my eyes, allow fright to wash over me. I lie still as the panicky wave pounds me, crashes against me, shaking and weakening my foundation like waves eroding the base of a cliff.

I remain silent, patient. My fists are knotted, pushed against my stomach where the fear originates. I give in, offer myself like a token, and I feel the pain subside. It pearls off me like water off an oily surface, unable to hold on. Fear is no longer permanent, it passes and so will the doubts. This might be my last chance.

★   ★   ★

417

I go to work. I've learned to operate while I'm burning from the inside out and sitting at home waiting for the phone to ring is more than I can bear. Around noon I hear a faint chime above the gallery door, its announcement so timid I almost miss it. Detective Wilczek is wearing a suit, a coat on top, and his eyes are wearier than I remember them. He has something to tell me, but I can't read him just yet. He nods and we both stare at each other.

'Do you think you could take a break?' His demeanor lacks urgency. 'Maybe we could go for a walk.'

I turn towards the framing room behind me. It's filled with sounds of hammering nails and the glue wafting towards me is making my temples pound. I grab my coat from the hanger and lead the way.

New York in January is like living in a freezer. We stick our hands in our coat pockets as we pass naked winter trees lining the street. Temperatures are in the low twenties, spring is still months away and warmth is so far removed from people's minds that it almost sounds like a fairytale no one can believe in.

We turn to the right, towards a park. The cast-iron fence near the entrance is covered in ice. Our breaths mingle as we walk.

'Anna's gone,' he says. He allows it to sink in and waits patiently.

'When?' I ask, and my heartbeat accelerates rapidly.

'This morning. After the children were removed, most of the mothers were allowed to

418

return to the compound. Her aunt told me she left the day of the raid. Took all her belongings and a car, a blue Pontiac. Aunt wasn't forthcoming with the plates.'

'Where are the children?' I ask.

'In state custody.'

'Are they all in one place or split up?'

Wilczek cocks his head and his eyes narrow. 'I have a feeling you are about to do something really stupid.'

'Do you know where they are or don't you?'

'I'm not sure, they usually end up in foster care or shelters, depending on their ages.'

'Can you find out?'

'Even if I could I wouldn't tell you. Don't you get it? All you have to do is wait.'

I don't have the patience to wait, don't even have the patience to respond to this waiting business.

'What if Anna takes her again? Are you going to believe me then?'

Wilczek inhales sharply. 'What are you saying?'

'I'm saying the fact I didn't die in the ravine messed up her plans. No one wants a baby the entire state of New York is looking for. She didn't keep Mia all this time just to leave her behind now.'

'*If* Mia is one of the children . . . *if.*'

'*If* she takes her again it'll be too late. And where will I look then? How likely is it that I find her again?' I've raised my voice and stare back at a couple who are eyeing us, wondering if we're having an insignificant lovers' quarrel.

'Tell me where the children are and leave the rest to me.'

'That's a frightening thought. You can't possibly expect me to do that.'

'You can't possibly expect me not to ask.' I won't give up, he must know this. 'How long do you think until she finds out where she is? She'll try to abduct her again. She's smart, she's been under the radar for five years and never got caught.'

I do the math in my head. Days, we have merely days to act. And I have no clue how to convince him to help me.

As we walk on we pass a little girl with sleek hair dancing on her head. She's skipping up and down the sidewalk while her mother rocks a stroller back and forth.

I take in a deep breath, then I slow down my steps, peek at the kid in the stroller. Wrapped up in a pink blanket, hat and mittens, is a toddler with a round face and rosy cheeks.

'What a beautiful baby,' I say. 'She looks so happy.'

As mom goes on and on about how Emma, that's her name, cries a lot and is difficult overall, 'drama queen' she calls her, but calms down when she's being rocked, I just nod when appropriate and manage an occasional smile.

'You have kids?' Mom asks me.

I stare at her for a second. 'No,' I say and I feel the word vibrate in my throat, as if my body recognizes the lie I just told. It's complicated, not the sort of thing you discuss on the street in passing.

Mom looks back and forth between me and Wilczek. I assume she's torn between 'are you

420

trying,' 'maybe one day' or some other friendly token of sympathy for a still childless couple.

I nod and manage a 'stay warm now' comment, and Wilczek and I silently continue our walk.

'Do I have kids? That's a hard question to answer, isn't it?' Wilczek's eyes narrow. Then he looks away. He knows what's coming but he can't get away.

'You said you had a son?'

'Yes,' hesitantly, his eyes move around as if he wants to make sure no one is watching us.

'You see him a lot?'

'Every Sunday.'

'How old is he?'

'Two.'

'What does he like?'

'The usual, you know, cars, trucks, that sort of thing. Ice cream. Cookies.'

'Let me think . . . two years old you say.' I point to my temple as if I try to remember something. 'He turns the pages of a book, he can open drawers and cabinets, he feeds himself with a spoon, is easily frustrated, and shy around strangers. Very affectionate, lots of hugs and kisses?'

Wilczek stares straight ahead.

'He can walk up and down the stairs as long as he holds on to your hand, right?'

I step in front of him and stare straight at him.

'Do you know how I know this? Kids' social and emotional development? Physical milestones of toddlers?'

I step forward ever so slightly and put my

421

hand on top of his coat where his heart is. Do I feel a slight tremor underneath his coat? I have to improvise and I have to be good. I grab his other hand with mine.

'I read it in a book.' I hold his cold hand in mine until it warms up. He's trying to pull back but I squeeze even harder. When I finally allow him to pull his hand away he steps back and hides it in his coat pocket.

He turns and walks away, but his steps are no longer defiant. I've won.

★   ★   ★

After I leave work that day I clean my apartment. I start on one end and obsessively wipe down every surface, vacuum every corner, spray Lysol in every nook and cranny. I am reminded of the police questions that I left unanswered as to why I bleached North Dandry. There was the stale air and the filth, the dust, and the remnants of my shortcomings. There was also the urge to right some sort of wrong, and my clouded mind believed — just like the police — that I had cleaned up a crime scene — but now I consider the fact that it was an attempt of a deranged woman to bring Mia back to a proper home. A home with clean kitchen counters, shiny bathrooms, and a lit fireplace. When I grant my thoughts this directness I realize I wanted to have just one chore left; to hold Mia in my arms.

The phone rings. I pull the yellow latex gloves off my hands and toss them into the kitchen sink. The oven cleaner fumes linger in the air, making my temples pound. I watch the gloves float on the surface of the murky water. Then they sink. Their cheerful, sunny color swallowed up by the depth of the ceramic farmhouse sink. My pruney fingers struggle to hold on to the pen as I scribble down the address.

★ ★ ★

St. Pancras' Path is an unassuming three-story building covered in beige siding with a screened-off porch. A side door leads onto a spacious playground with a slide, three swings, a sandbox, and a see-saw, all equally spaced behind a cast-iron fence. There's an alcove above the front door with a stained-glass window, depicting Saint Pancras the patron saint of children, a man in usual saint garb, baring his hands outward in a welcoming gesture.

I've been sitting in my car for hours. I hardly slept last night and it's catching up with me. My back is stiff and the urge to get out and stretch my legs is getting harder and harder to ignore. The Ritz crackers and diet soda are getting old. It's been raining on and off and the possibility of the children spilling out the side door to go to the playground is waning.

I can feel the fear in my chest waiting to take over. It wants to propel me to an even darker place but I don't allow it. I take a deep breath in, I close my eyes and imagine sweet air and birds in the sky and my body begins to relax. I conjure up a scene that's been hatching inside of me since I recognized Anna Lieberman on TV.

Seeing Mia again, for the first time.

It's a weekday, a comfortable forty degrees, and Prospect Park is deserted except for a few joggers with headphones in their ears, closed off in their own worlds. And a handful of people walking their dogs.

Trees and benches are all around us, squirrels, and a scent of wet soil. There's a playground by the park entrance and a small lake to the right. A lake with ducks a short walk from the park entrance.

I imagine a small Ziploc bag filled with stale, cubed bread that I prepared earlier that day. I sit on a nearby bench and a car stops behind me in the parking lot. The crunch of gravel echoes in my ears. Then the ding-ding-ding of an open car door.

Out of the corner of my eye I see a child in a purple puffa jacket, jeans, and black boots running towards the playground. Her knitted hat is rainbow-colored with earflaps and a large pompon on top. It bobs as she runs.

A social worker, let's call her Elena Cruz, a kind, tired and overworked middle-aged woman, is trailing her.

In my vision the playground is surrounded by a fence; the only way in or out is through a small gate. Mia runs straight for the gate and before I'm able to take her all in, she's swinging off a monkey bar.

Mia's body is stretched as her little hands hold on to the bars. The metal is cold and she's not wearing gloves, but she doesn't mind. Her midriff is exposed as she dangles back and forth, trying to gain some momentum by swinging her legs.

The social worker sees me, smiles and nods at me encouragingly. I get up off the bench and make my way to the monkey bars. Mia's head is stretched backwards, her legs and feet are kicking.

She is beautiful. Not in a way a mother thinks her child is beautiful, but in a saintly way. Curls spill from under the earflaps, her eyes are large and brown and remind me of Jack's. Her eyelashes are sparse yet long and her little miniature teeth, placed perfectly in a row, smile at me.

'Hi,' she says, her voice strong and confident. 'Look what I can do.' She swings her legs harder and harder.

'Guess what I have here.' I pull out the bread bag and hold it up by its corner and I swing it back and forth.

She looks at me, her eyes questioning, pondering the significance of the bag with its odd contents.

'Bread. Wanna go feed the ducks?'

Her eyes widen and I can see her excitement. Her curiosity is taking over, she jumps off the monkey bars and scans the surroundings. 'Ducks? There's ducks?'

'Yeah, there's ducks. Right around the corner.'

She looks at the social worker, and when Elena nods, she jumps off the monkey bars and grabs my hand. Holding the hand of my daughter is otherworldly. I feel chipped paint flakes between our skin and I gently wipe the

425

paint chips off her palm. Feeling the warmth of her skin is almost undoing me and I try to keep from shaking. I blow in my cupped hands pretending I'm cold, all the while I feel like burning from the inside out.

'Have you ever fed ducks before?'

She shakes her head and I hand her the Ziploc bag with the cubed bread.

'First time for everything. Ready to go?'

We walk towards the lake, her hand in mine, the bag dangling off her other hand. I long for someone to take a picture, to capture this very moment — with her hand in mine — as we walk to the lake. In the sunshine the lake's surface looks like a perfect looking glass.

As we stand at the lake shore and throw in the bread, the ducks zoom in on the cubes, then slightly speed up. Their necks are elongated and their green feathers glimmer in the sun as their heads dip into the water. As soon as their beaks emerge again, they are off searching for the next piece of bread to devour. They search for another cube of sustenance, zoom in and peck at it all over again.

We watch the ducks trail away from us, rippling the water, disrupting the lake's smooth surface.

'I'm Mia,' she says and sounds grown up, her voice still high-pitched, yet mature. She wipes her nose with the back of her hand.

'Mia,' I repeat her name. 'That's a beautiful name.'

In the distance, we hear the quacking of the ducks.

★ ★ ★

The sound of a car door jerks me out of my imagined scene and back into reality. A shadow slides into the passenger seat.

'How long have you been here?' Wilczek seems even more disheveled than yesterday, his eyes are bloodshot and he smells of cigarette smoke.

'I didn't know you smoked,' I say to make this moment seem more mundane. I'm surprised, to say the least. I never expected him to show, can't even grasp what his role is going to be. I'm not quite sure what I'm doing here myself, I just want to catch a glimpse of my daughter. I don't dare hope for more. 'And you look like you've been up for days,' I add and look at my wristwatch. It's not as cold as it was earlier but I shiver nevertheless.

He ignores my comment and checks his cell phone. 'So . . . what's been going on?'

'Just people coming and going,' I say lightheartedly. 'So far there was a UPS delivery and the morning paper.' After a moment of silence I ask, 'Do you think Anna knows where Mia is?'

'She won't find out unless someone, theoretically, tells her aunt, I guess.'

Theoretically. Someone tells her aunt. I think about the implications of his statement. I study his profile and fight the urge to hug him. He's come through for me in a big way. Telling Anna's aunt, knowing that word will get back to Anna about the children's whereabouts is a possibly dangerous situation but I get it. He's a cop and

427

he wants to solve this case. He wants to put handcuffs on Anna, make her pay for what she did, unravel the ball of yarn of evidence found in her house; pictures, toys, children's clothes. Justice is what he's after. I just want my daughter.

'So what's the overall plan?' Wilczek asks.

'I don't have a plan per se at this very moment,' I say and wonder what got to him in the end; his son, my pleading eyes, or the woman with the stroller.

Wilczek puts his hand on top of mine. 'I'm going to go talk to them. You stay here and don't move, okay?'

His hand on mine feels awkward and part of me wants to move away — the touch seems almost intimate — the other wants his hand to remain.

Wilczek gets out of the car and I watch him walk up to the building in his wrinkled coat. He presses the buzzer and I hear a prim female voice through the intercom.

The rain has stopped and the sun is breaking through the seemingly insurmountable layer of clouds. I step out of the car fearing my legs will end up cramping on me if I sit still any longer. I appease my stiff knee joints by walking up to the cast-iron fence of the shelter playground. The playground is covered in wood chips and an occasional candy wrapper sparkles in the sunlight. A lonely woolen cap soaked by the rain, sits abandoned on a red bench by the backdoor of the building.

I stand by the fence next to an oak tree. The

428

roots have warped the concrete and I step further towards the property. The trunk's girth hides me perfectly and while I stare at the backdoor, I see movement through its glass window.

Then everything slows down and speeds up at the same time. The front door closes and faintly I hear footsteps on the concrete coming towards me. When I turn, I see Wilczek running towards his car. Simultaneously the backdoor opens and children spill into the playground. Wilczek gets in his car and slams the door shut, as if he's on a mission, has seen something I don't know about. I scan the area but nothing seems out of sorts.

Child after child make their way down the steps, towards the playground. I watch them intently and when my cell vibrates in my jacket pocket I completely ignore it. The children have taken over the playground equipment; girls' legs swing like pendulums in unison to gain momentum on the swings while the rest of the kids climb up a ladder to go down the slide. A young woman in a bright red wool coat sits on the bench, shielding her eyes with her hands from the sun.

Then I see what Wilczek saw. The blue Pontiac sits on the opposite side of the road facing north. The driver's door opens and a woman in jeans and a black parka emerges, pushing a mass of red hair under her parka hood. As the woman crosses the street she scans the sidewalk, then the playground.

My heart no longer reacts to fateful moments. Maybe I have become accustomed to being tested, maybe I'm so shocked my brain can't conceive the relevance of this moment. Anna and I make eye contact. Before I can move, Anna runs across the street, disappears into the Pontiac. She takes off northbound.

As I stand paralyzed under the oak, I watch Wilczek trailing the blue Pontiac. He stares straight ahead while his hands are glued to the steering wheel. He lifts one finger and ever so slightly points towards Anna in the car in front of him when I appear in his field of vision. I nod at him.

When both cars have disappeared around the corner, I step out of the shadow of the oak tree and towards the front door of the shelter.

★ ★ ★

'Excuse me.' A woman's voice. The same woman who minutes earlier sat on the bench supervising the children in the playground. Her hands awkwardly clasp her coat in the front as if she didn't find the time to zip it. She smells of coffee.

'You are one of the officers? I saw you with the detective earlier, outside, in the car. He told us to be on the lookout for a woman and gave us her description.'

I nod in agreement and pull up my shoulders. My nerves are catching up with me. I try not to shake but I do. I am close, *so close*. 'There was an emergency and my colleague had to take off.'

'I'm Dr Wallace, staff child psychologist.' She hesitates, then points towards the gate. 'You're so cold you're shaking. Please come inside and warm up.'

She unlatches the playground gate and I enter the yard. I just now realize that the children have left the playground. It lies deserted, void of laughter and scuffling boots. A couple of mittens are covered in wood chips on the walkway. The gate closes by itself behind me with a *clang*. When we get to the backdoor her fingers run over an electronic lock display.

'I see you're prepared,' I say and hide my hands in my coat pockets.

'We take in battered women with children sometimes,' Dr Wallace explains and after the electronic buzzer sounds she turns the door handle.

I no longer care about Anna and what happens to her. Her fate is her business, I'm here for my daughter. The fact that Anna did show up is proof enough that Mia is in this building. The world around me, the psychiatrist, the door in front of me, everything seems to be shifting, folding in on itself. I decide to surrender myself completely, something Dr Ari has taught me. I no longer need to imagine an elevator, I am able to conjure up my mantra at a moment's notice; allow the universe to unfold. Fate. *What befalls me couldn't have missed me, and what misses me could not have befallen me,* Dr Ari's voice echoes in my head.

We stand in a long narrow hallway with shiny linoleum floors. There's a faint odor of soap and something sharp and lemony. A cube shelving unit holds coats, bags, and gloves. To the left of us is a large tiled room with miniature sinks and shiny faucets with oversized knobs. A large poster says *Hush, Rush, Flush*.

As we pass by the bathroom Dr Wallace turns around. 'I didn't get your name,' she says and hangs her coat on a hook next to the shelf.

I tell her a fake name and thank her for allowing me to wait inside.

'We were just about to do our afternoon group activities,' she says and points at the reception seating area. 'You can wait here if you want.'

I nod and take my seat on the couch. Dr Wallace enters a room across from me. A large round table sits in the middle of the room surrounded by colorful chairs with a hook for an apron. There's a stack of paper in the middle of the table and a lazy Susan-style revolving tray with an array of paint tubs filled in bright primary colors.

Dr Wallace claps her hands and from the far side of the room a group of children storm the table and squabble over the chairs.

I count twelve children, seven boys and five girls. I wonder how far I can go, how far I'll be able to intrude without causing suspicion.

Three of the girls have long blond hair and wear identical clothes. They favor each other yet differ in height. Their demeanor is guarded, focused on each other instead of the world around them. They sit next to each other and seem to wait for a clue from the middle girl, the tallest of the three. When she ties the apron around her waist and reaches for the paper, the other two follow suit.

The two other girls, one with a brown ponytail and fringe covering her eyes, are more subdued, almost aloof. The girl with the ponytail keeps swiping her fringe to one side. The other girl's hair looks like she's had an unfortunate encounter with a pair of scissors.

I walk down the hallway, look at a set of photographs hanging by the door. The photos of people shaking hands at a ribbon-cutting ceremony and a plaque with donor names hardly register.

I watch the children finger painting and when Dr Wallace looks up, I check my wristwatch. The children dip their fingers in the paint tubs and I scan their faces, quickly. I don't know what I expected, some sort of powerful reaction yet I feel no connection, no pull, no recognition. My hands continue to shake as I scan their faces, over and over. There weren't any birthmarks on her, no scraped knee scar that would help me identify her. I imagine Mia's baby face elongating, straightening the dip between her nose and her brows. On the inside I can feel the rotation of the earth, the slow turning on its axis. I want to grab each girl in this room and press her against me for my blood, my heart, my soul, will surely react. I feel tears on my cheeks and I wipe them away. I must remain strong now, I'm closer, but not there yet.

I discount the three blond girls with their cornflower eyes. Mia's eyes were brown, like Jack's. Her hair used to be blond but children's hair darkens over the years.

Two high-pitched voices erupt and two of the

boys argue over a tub of paint. One of the boys, his apron has become loose, guides the boy back to his chair by firmly placing a hand on his back. The boy starts crying and the girl with the ponytail says something to him. I wonder if I'd get away with taking a seat in the far corner of the room when I hear Dr Wallace tell the children that I'm a police officer. I never confirmed I was. *There was an emergency,* I'd told her. *My colleague had to take off.*

The children turn and stare at me. The crying boy is inconsolable and when he realizes that everybody's attention has drifted away from him, he dips his entire hand in the tub of red finger paint. He is immediately annoyed by his sticky hands and tries to get the paint off by violently shaking his fingers. Then he turns to his left and wipes his hands on the shirt of the boy sitting next to him.

The three blond girls start screaming and attempt to save their pictures from paint spatters by snatching them off the table.

Dr Wallace's 'everybody listen up' goes unnoticed. Now the other boys also dip their hands into the paint tubs. The doctor's face is visibly tense and she pulls the entire turntable towards her in order to claim the paint. The children are now amused and smear paint over each other's shirts. Someone is laughing uncontrollably, then numerous loud bursts erupt that turn into giggles.

Dr Wallace is frantically screwing the lids back on the tubs. 'Everybody listen. We are going to wipe our hands and settle down.' She looks at

434

and gestures me into the room. 'Give me a hand, will you?' she says and stuffs a handful of wet wipes into my hands. 'I'll handle the boys,' she adds and directs them to individual chairs along the wall.

I hand the girl with the ponytail and the fringe a wet wipe. She looks at me, puzzled and doesn't move. I gently wipe the red paint globs on her fingertips. She wiggles her hands out of mine and checks the stickiness of whatever is left by rubbing her hands together.

Her eyes fill with tears. Her painting on the table is covered in paint splashes, torn at the edges. The picture is of a stick figure in a yellow dress with large green dots for the eyes.

'That's my mommy,' she says and points at the scribbles, 'but now it's all ruined,' she adds, her lips pouting. She wipes her eyes with the back of her hand, swiping her bangs to the side.

'Maybe we can fix it,' I say. I want to save this picture for her, want to make everything all right. I want to tell her that we can cut out mommy and glue her to a clean sheet of paper. That sometimes you can start over and nothing is ruined after all. I stare at the stick figure's crown of red hair, a color that adds an odd sense of clarity to my perception.

When she makes eye contact with me, her eyes swallow my words. Those are Jack's eyes, one raised eyebrow, scrutinizing the world.

A spark suddenly births a memory, long forgotten underneath countless folds of days, months, and years; the blood that haunted me in the days after waking up in the hospital. The

435

memory of little hands covered in a layer of sticky crimson, a trail of bloody feet disturbing the surface of a white sheet. The dome lamp, the shards, the moment I had learned to tuck away for so many years. My ultimate betrayal as a mother when it so clearly stated *Keep Out of Reach of Children*. In a twisted impossible way the memory of the blood merges with a sense of sheer euphoria. I'm here, Mia. I've found you. I would never give up on you. Going on without you was never an option.

I fold a wet wipe and encase her hand. Her thumb emerges, clean and shiny. The very tip is covered in round white bumps as if ice is trapped under her skin.

My stomach drops and my entire body starts vibrating. I gently take both of her wrists in my hands. I flip over her hands and wipe one finger at a time with a broad sweep. Countless white lines emerge, covering her fingertips like icicles, remnants of a night long time ago, a turtle lamp and a mother who was fallible. I hold on to her hands, want to erase everything that's not right, and I hope her trust won't evaporate.

'All clean,' she says and hides her hands behind her back. 'What about my picture?'

I don't cry, something almost unachievable, yet I succeed. I don't want to scare her, don't want her first memory of me to be one of tears.

'The picture,' I say and manage a crooked smile, 'how about we draw a new one?'

★ ★ ★

436

Wilczek appears some time later. Maybe an hour, maybe longer. His eyes are vacant but his tightly clasped jaws speak volumes.

'She knew I was after her. She tried to get away, but in the end she couldn't,' he says and punches keys on his phone. His hands are shaking. Finally he gives up. 'I called for backup but she had wrapped her car around a pole on Woodside Avenue before backup even showed up. Anna's dead.'

Anna's dead. A mere echo of what's important.

'Do you remember the lamp? The broken dome lamp from North Dandry?' I don't wait for his answer, I can hardly catch my breath. 'Mia cut her hands on the shards and she has scars on her hands and she looks like Jack,' I say and wonder if I will ever stop shaking.

'God,' he says. Just God. Nothing else. His jawline relaxes yet his emotions seem confined within a narrow range. Then something breaks through in his eyes. They widen and look moist. He's no longer the mere curator of his feelings. 'God,' he says again, over and over. He lights a cigarette and inhales deeply.

His phone rings. Before I can say anything else, he takes the call and walks away, leaving behind a trail of cigarette smoke.

'Wait,' I call after him.

He turns around, shutting off his phone.

'Tell me everything,' I say and step closer. Everything that moves stands still. I feel the bizarre need to know the state of the body of the woman who took my child and kept her from me

437

all these years. In a twisted impossible way I *must* know exactly how her life ended.

'I trailed her and by the time we get to the first light she knows she's being followed. She starts panicking. She's looking left and right, weaving through traffic, then just steps on the — '

'No, not that. Describe *her* to me.'

'She didn't take the time to strap herself in. The pole cut her car in half, the front of her car was basically nonexistent. Her knees were touching her chest, they were mangled. Her forehead had a long horizontal gash.'

'I wanted to talk to her.'

I don't know what I would have asked her. Why didn't you just give her back? Why did you keep her? Did you take good care of her? Does she know she was taken?

The questions humming around in my head are vast in numbers, yet Anna's death has robbed me of any answers, any conclusion, any closure. Therefore any further thought about her is of little consequence. This moment is bittersweet if there ever was one; I'm leaving without Mia yet again, but this time I know she's alive, and soon I'll hold her in my arms. Taking her by force is not an option for I don't want to inflict any more trauma on her.

'I guess I can't have it all,' I say, my mind already occupied. There's someone else who owes me something.

28

The very next morning I enter the glass temple of the Donner Broadcasting building, a symbol of its economic power, defining the city of New York as much as the identity of the company itself.

As I sit on the black leather couch with shiny steel legs, I gaze through the horizontal stripes that interrupt the etched glass doors. I tell her assistant that Amnesia Mom is wanting to speak to her.

Before the assistant can even announce me, I enter the office of Liza Overton, host of *Current Crimes*, the woman who dubbed me *Amnesia Mom*. Her cell phone clutched between shoulder and ear, she points at a chair in front of her desk. Her facial expression is that of a blank sheet of paper. It's been five years and it takes her a few seconds — I patiently watch her scanning my face — but then she recognizes me. Her jugular on her neck begins to protrude.

'We have to talk,' I say and lean back in the leather chair and cross my legs. 'I need your help.'

'My help?' Now her face moves. Her eyes get smaller, her lips thinner. 'What's this all about?'

'You have a way of swaying the public, right?'

'I'd like to think so.'

'How about the police?'

'I'm not sure I understand. If you want a

public apology from the police you're in the wrong place.'

'I am not looking for an apology from anybody. Certainly not from you or the police. You have made my life hell, you have crucified me in the eyes of the public. You know that. And for that you owe me.'

'I owe you?' her hand jerks towards the phone, but then she pulls back.

'There's two things I need from you. One, I want you to do a follow-up show tonight. Two, with that show I want you to put pressure on the cops to initiate an investigation. Call the Police Chief live on the air if you want.'

She throws her head back and laughs. Deeply, from the gut.

'Seriously?'

'I've found my daughter. And I need you to get the police to do a DNA test. So I can get her back.'

'You've found her? Where?'

'First things first. Is that a yes?'

'What's in it for me?'

'Imagine the ratings.'

Liza Overton pushes a button on the phone, and tells her assistant to hold all calls.

I tell her about the raid, the children and adults, hundreds altogether, whose DNA tests will take months. After all, a crooked brow and tiny cuts on fingertips don't prove anything. It's true, I don't need apologies from anybody. I need a DNA test. Nothing more and nothing less. Tonight.

★ ★ ★

That same day, as I watch the evening news, I dial Jack's number. At some point in time Jack became increasingly hostile towards me as if my existence was a sheer reminder of his shortcomings. He picks up the phone immediately. He fears the worst, I'm sure.

'Are you at home?' I ask.

'What the hell? What's going on?' His voice is sharp yet I detect trepidation behind his harsh words. We haven't spoken in years and there's only one reason for me to call.

'I need you to turn the channel to *Current Crimes*.'

'What's going on, Estelle? What the hell is going on?'

'Just do it,' I say. I don't know why I make him wait to hear the news. It would be easy to just say *I've found her, she's alive, she's safe*. My cruelty claws at me — after all he's Mia's father — but then I step beside myself. It all comes back to me, the weeks after the police started looking for Anna Lieberman. I spent every single day explaining myself; why I bleached the house — I wanted to give my daughter a proper home — why I put locks on the doors — Jack left me there by myself, I was afraid — why I gave the suitcase away — a son in the form of a hollowed squirrel needed a home. I spent countless hours answering questions about the search history on my computer and why I looked up how to fire a gun. I waited months for the police to recover guns and match the bullets, months for them to

441

check into David and Anna Lieberman's background, precious time that wasn't spent looking for them. And now, *even now*, after I found Mia — *I found her* — the police cites a conflicting investigation and unlikely coincidences. Their refusal — their sheer apathy — to hurry along a DNA test is just another stab into a wound that has never healed.

The evening news host fades out and *Current Crimes* fades in.

I hear '*Breaking News Tonight*' and the voice of Liza Overton. Her makeup is immaculate, her hair stiff as always. I hear her high-pitched voice over my TV and simultaneously over the phone with Jack.

I wait.

'*Five years ago an infant disappeared from a brownstone in Brooklyn. The mother was the primary suspect in the case, and referred to as Amnesia Mom in the media. In a strange twist of events the child was believed to have been abducted and has never been located, exonerating the mother after many months of putting all the pieces together. Fast forward, five years later, the child is still missing. And here's the kicker. A cold case at this point, there's reason to believe that the mother has found her daughter but authorities are less than cooperative to solve the case. Yes, you heard correctly. The mother has found the child after five years. Don't go anywhere, when we return after the break, we'll get you caught up with the latest developments in the case of Amnesia Mom.*'

Seconds later, I hear something over the

phone that sounds like a wail and I assume Jack knows Mia is alive. I wish I could see his face when they say who found her. I hang up the phone and stare at the TV.

Current Crimes fades out, a commercial fades in. I switch to CNN and wait.

★ ★ ★

Jack's flight from Boston to New York is delayed. He tells me not to wait for him and he'll meet me at the New York State Office of Children and Family Services.

Between the media coverage and Wilczek putting pressure on the police, it took all of three days. A social services agent, a rather large man with a shabby briefcase, oversees our first meeting. There's no park, no playground, and no ducks. He calls it 'the exchange' and after he has me sign some paperwork, he tries unsuccessfully to snap his briefcase shut.

'You've been briefed?' he asks and for the first time makes eye contact.

'Yes,' I say and think about that little something called 'anticipated relationship quality,' a term encasing everything that's expected when children are reunited with parents after a long time.

'We don't know if she was abused or even adequately taken care of. She's come to know someone else as her mother, other people as her family. She has no idea who you are.'

Makes two of us, I think, but don't say it out loud. My biggest fears are that she won't want to

443

be with me. That she'll hate me when she finds out the truth. And she will never love me.

After an evaluation, the judge will grant custody. The final transfer won't occur until a judge agrees. The legal term is 'safeguard for the child's welfare.'

He turns and opens a heavy metal door. For a second the social worker looks like he wants to shake my hand.

I walk through the door and wait for Mia and it finally sinks in. No more tracking body parts and children in landfills. No checking online databases, no more jerking when the phone rings. I've read somewhere that the pain from the loss or death of a child never heals, not until you are reunited, whenever that may be. I'm one of the lucky ones and today is the day.

This moment is so otherworldly that my body remains completely still, as if its magic cannot be contained within my flesh and bones.

What will I say, I wonder, when I get to hold her? Will I speak at all? Will she pull away? The moment is here, finally, *mere seconds* away. *Seconds.* As long as it took to tie her shoe, unfold her diaper, brush her wispy hair when she was a baby.

I sit and fold my hands in my lap. Compared to all those years I spent without her I *must* make this moment count, I *must* make up for all that was lost.

When I hear the door open I look up.

I don't think in minutes or seconds any longer. I will allow this moment to unfold as if I'm a photographer who wants to get it right, wants to capture a moment that will last forever. I look up and there she is.

And then my heart explodes.

KIDNAPPING COLD CASE SOLVED: MIA CONNOR REUNITES WITH PARENTS

Brooklyn, NY — Mia Connor, separated from her family when she was kidnapped five years ago, was reunited with her parents, Estelle Paradise and Jack Connor, today.

Her mother, Estelle Paradise, was a suspect when she was unable to account for her whereabouts in the days after the disappearance of 7-month-old Mia from her crib in Brooklyn.

After the disappearance Ms Paradise spent months in a psychiatric institution. During her stay it came to light, solely through her testimony and therapy to recover her memories, that David Lieberman, a man who lived in the same building, and his sister, Anna Lieberman, were responsible for the kidnapping. The case never picked up speed in the weeks and months after the abduction and went officially cold a couple of years after.

The conclusion of the case was based on

Ms Paradise recognizing one of the suspects during an unrelated case. She has declined numerous book and movie deals over the years and yet, Liza Overton, host of Current Crimes and one of her harshest critics after the abduction, went on TV and broke the story that Estelle Paradise had found her daughter. When all news outlets were flooded with the news, police expedited the DNA test. Mother and daughter were reunited days after the story broke.

Accusations of police negligence and a possibly botched investigation, given the fact that no other avenues were pursued in the days after the abduction, have come to light but at this point no lawsuit has been filed.

'We are happy to report that the family has been reunited,' said Joanna Walls, spokesperson for NYPD. 'This is nothing short of a miracle and we couldn't be happier for the family.'

My mother was a woman rarely seen without her camera. I remember her propped up in bed, among an array of pillows, her camera resting beside her. In her hand a book, a study in light, or angle, or perspective — one of those.

In that memory I climb into my mother's bed and angrily shove a worn and yellowed copy of *Alice In Wonderland* at her.

Mom.

She smiles at my accusatory tone and, thinking I want her to read to me, she speaks without looking up. Not now, she says, and wraps one arm around me. How about you read to me?

I finished it. Did you remember to buy me the other book?

I forgot. I'm sorry.

Do you remember the title?

Through The Looking Glass, right? Same author?

I don't answer, my punishment for her forgetfulness.

What's a looking glass? I ask.

Kind of like a mirror, she says, it allows you to see yourself the way other people see you.

Isn't that a mirror?

She doesn't answer and continues flipping the pages of her book. How I hate her books, and her camera and her way of being preoccupied

448

with everything but me. What good is a book without words anyway, I wonder, and what good is she anyway, she never talks to me.

She closes the book, puts her arm around me, and then strokes my hair with her hand. That's how we sit, for a long time. Sometimes I fall asleep, but she's always there when I wake up. Holding me still.

We do hope that you have enjoyed reading this large print book.

Did you know that all of our titles are available for purchase?

We publish a wide range of high quality large print books including:
Romances, Mysteries, Classics
General Fiction
Non Fiction and Westerns

Special interest titles available in large print are:
The Little Oxford Dictionary
Music Book
Song Book
Hymn Book
Service Book

Also available from us courtesy of Oxford University Press:
Young Readers' Dictionary
(large print edition)
Young Readers' Thesaurus
(large print edition)

For further information or a free brochure, please contact us at:
Ulverscroft Large Print Books Ltd.,
The Green, Bradgate Road, Anstey,
Leicester, LE7 7FU, England.
Tel: (00 44) 0116 236 4325
Fax: (00 44) 0116 234 0205

THE FINAL SILENCE

Stuart Neville

Rea Carlisle inherits a house from an uncle she never knew. When she forces open a locked room, she finds a leather-bound book. Tucked in its pages are fingernails, locks of hair, and a list of victims. Horrified, Rea wants to go straight to the police, but her father intervenes — he's worked too hard to have his brother's twisted legacy ruin his promising political career. So Rea turns to the only person she can think of: disgraced police inspector Jack Lennon. But Lennon has his own troubles, and they only get worse when a brutal murder places him in the crosshairs of DCI Serena Flanagan. Hounded by a police force that doesn't trust him, it's up to Lennon to unravel the secrets of the dead man's journal, and a conspiracy that's stayed buried for decades.

THE BITTER SEASON

Tami Hoag

After moving to the Cold Case unit, Detective Nikki Liska misses the rush of pulling an all-nighter and the sense of urgency when hunting a murderer on the loose — her current homicide case dates back twenty-five years, and there is little hope of finding the killer. Most of all, she misses her old partner, Detective Sam Kovac . . . Sam is having an even harder time adjusting to Nikki's absence, saddled with a green new partner younger than pieces of his own wardrobe. But he is distracted from his troubles by an especially brutal double homicide: a middle-aged husband and wife hacked to death in their home with a samurai sword. One woman might link these mysteries — but she is being watched. Can Liska and Kovac find her before it is too late?

PAINKILLER

N. J. Fountain

I cannot go on like this . . . I feel such a burden to you. You are young and can start again. You deserve that chance. By the time you read this I will be dead. Do not grieve for me, for I am now without pain . . . Monica Wood has been living with chronic pain since an accident five years ago; her days are passed in a haze of pain and memory loss due to her medication. Monica's husband Dominic is her carer, but he must go out to work since she no longer can. On one of her good days she finds a suicide note; a note she doesn't remember writing — and she begins to question everything. Who *did* write the note? And if someone tried to kill her once, what's to say they won't try again?

AFTER ANNA

Alex Lake

A girl is missing. Five years old, taken from outside her school. She has vanished, traceless. The police are at a loss; her parents are beyond grief. Their daughter is lost forever, perhaps dead, perhaps enslaved. But the biggest mystery is yet to come: one week after she was abducted, their daughter is returned. She has no memory of where she has been. And this, for her mother, is just the beginning of the nightmare . . .